I0670597

MARIAH'S DREAM

GRACE BRIDGES

Copyright © 2015

Artwork, Cover Design, Map, Interior Design, and Typesetting
by Grace Bridges
Map texture by Flickr user Calliope
Used with thanks under a Creative Commons 2.0 licence

Edited by Chila Woychik and Jill Domschot
With valuable input from Fred Warren and Jan-Lazo-Davis
Proofed by Liberty Speidel and Barbara Hartzler
Author photo by Michelle Pendergrass

All rights reserved

Published by Splashdown Books, New Zealand

http://www.splashdownbooks.com

Dedicated to all those who have stories inside them, like me;

all who forget sometimes who they are, like Faith;

and all who want to start over, like Mariah.

contents

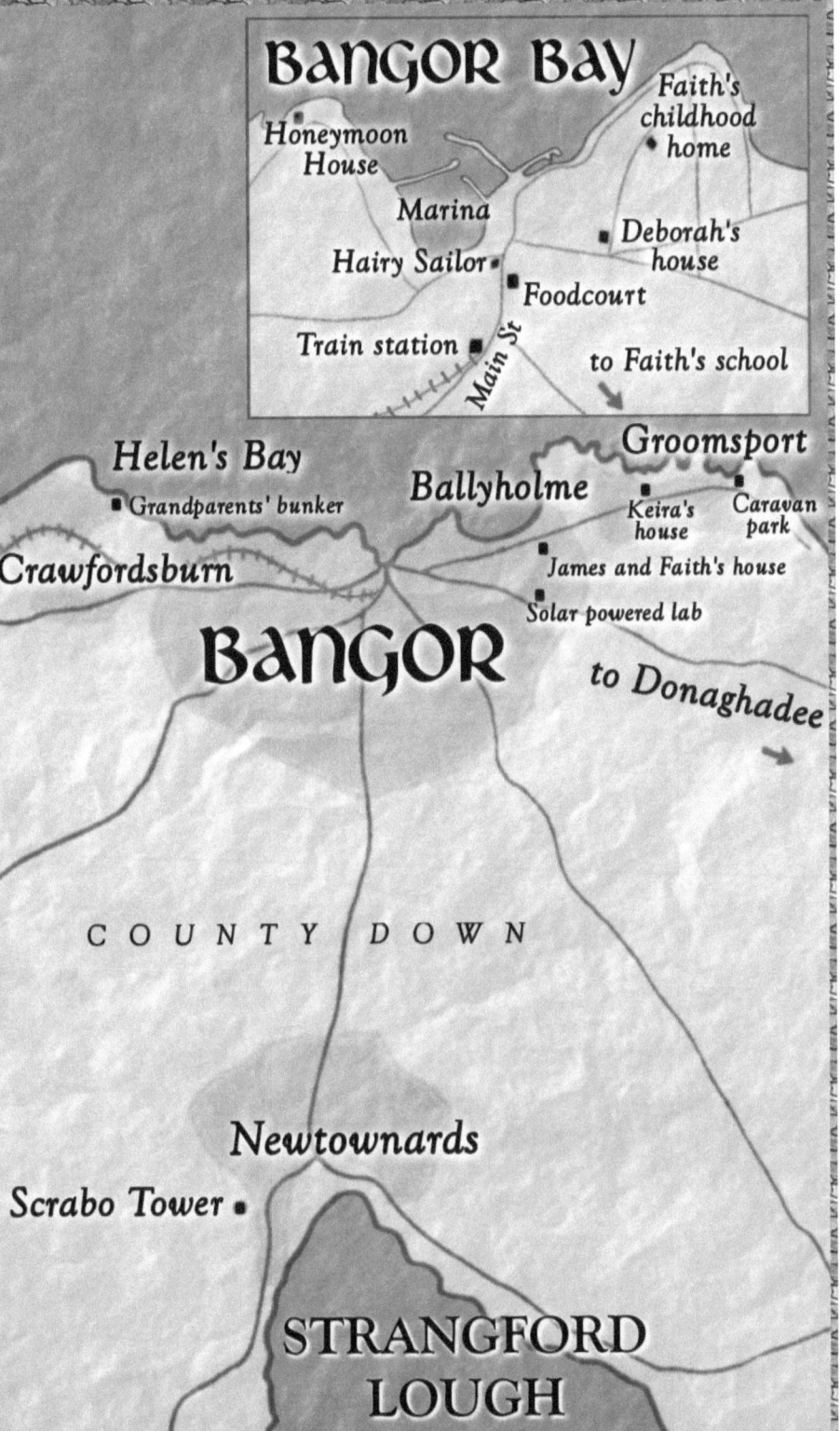

BANGOR BAY

Honeymoon
House

Faith's
childhood
home

Marina

Hairy Sailor

Deborah's
house

Foodcourt

Train station

Main St

to Faith's school

Helen's Bay

Groomsport

Grandparents' bunker

Ballyholme

Keira's
house

Caravan
park

Crawfordsburn

James and Faith's house

Solar powered lab

BANGOR

to Donaghadee

COUNTY DOWN

Newtownards

Scrabo Tower

STRANGFORD
LOUGH

1

mariah

Belfast lay grumbling under a late-afternoon shower, soft rain. Gentle daylight seeped from thick clouds and fell upon the old red-brick buildings and the potholed streets. An occasional figure on a bike dodged the obstacles, hurrying to vanish in the web of alleys bowelling the City. It was an hour when no able-bodied adult wanted to be seen shirking. The elderly stood on front steps, calling after street-wild grandwains who would one day inherit the same drudgery as their work-weary parents.

The rain fell on urban valleys of dead earth, leached of all nutrients and seeded only with impotent spores that no longer carried the potential for life. It fell on a few hardy weeds that clung on in scattered corners, impervious to the viral terminator gene. It fell on back gardens that once brought forth fruit, and now no more, their trees standing naked to scratch the sky in frustration, their once-verdant beds now a thick useless muck. It fell on broken rooftiles of homes all in tight rows, trickling downwards to dampen and rot.

The rain fell into the River Lagan and the mighty Lough of Belfast that spread its mouth wide beyond the City, towards the fortress of Carrickfergus on the left hand and the idyll of Bangor, feted of yore, on the right. It fell on the hills of County Antrim and County Down, clearly visible through the slight precipitation, where a few old trees still kept their green tips.

As dusk descended, the rain also fell on the tin roof of an abandoned lean-to in the yard of an equally abandoned, burned-out shell of a house that backed onto one of the old Peace Walls, built in the last century to stop Protestants and Catholics from shooting one another. There had been much talk of removing the walls, but certain factions still harboured a desire to silence the descendants of their ancestors' enemies—even now. So the bricks and wire remained.

Rocks clattered over the walls each night and lay on either side when day broke, but the roof of the lean-to was stout enough to momentarily repel these small attacks. Inside the shelter, a lone dog awoke from his slumber with each new onslaught.

With each falling rock the dog would raise his head from his paws and peer into the wet darkness. Satisfied that nothing beyond the usual was amiss, he rested again until the next assault. At some point, the rock-throwers desisted, and the dog allowed himself to sleep with just one ear cocked up.

At first light, he rose, stretched first forelegs then hind, and ventured forth into the day. He trotted through the ruined house and along the street, keeping to the walls' fresh morning gleam, sniffing at corners and leaving his own calling card here and there. He nosed a fresh pile of garbage, but it held nothing edible.

The dog was on the large side of medium, a sensible mix of several unidentifiable breeds. His nose stretched long and his ears folded over to form soft triangles on each side of his face. He was brown with dapple-grey patches and deep golden eyes that carried a wistful regard, if anyone was paying attention—most of the time, they weren't.

He was alone and did not run with a pack; now he stood tall on all fours and inhaled the clammy air. Dogs were coming. He glanced back once in the direction of the lean-to, but he had left nothing there. If a pack was on the way, he would vacate the area and search out a new place to lay his head and hunt for food.

Baying. They had found his hidey-hole, were onto his scent. If they were desperate enough, they would tear him to shreds and use his bones for toothpicks. And everyone was desperate. He stretched his neck and eased into a full gallop on spindly legs.

Human figures stood several blocks ahead. He slowed and tongued the air to taste their scent. Something was wrong; these were the kind with weapons and machines embedded in their flesh.

The dog slunk into a recessed doorway, tail between his legs. Howls echoed up the road from where he had come. The run had exhausted him more than it would have if he had eaten lately, so his eyes drooped shut; he forced them open again. The pack would catch up to him soon—their claws clattered close behind. He would try to sneak past the cyborgs just at the right moment, when the other dogs encountered them.

"Hey!" yelled a cyborg. "Those mangy curs again..." She raised a metal finger. Four times it flashed and shot into the pack. Two fell.

The dog in the doorway was about to run, bullets or no, when the door behind him opened. He leapt around, ready for fight or flight, but it was only a young human, tousled-blonde and barefoot, fisting her eyes in a dirty face. She lowered her hands and they stared at each other.

The howls eventually grew to a din. The child reached for the dog's ear and pulled him gently inside; he did not resist. More shots outside, then the howls died away to nothing. The girl opened the door and she and the dog looked out.

The cyborgs were gone, but the dog decided he might stay here a while. He settled down on his elbows, the girl beside him.

My name is Mariah. I hate my name—it means bitterness—but it's what people call me. Often I asked my father why he chose it for me. "Dunno, I guess I like how it sounds," he would say. That might explain why my brother was called Darian.

This journal is just in case anyone's left to read it when I'm gone—whenever that is. I write slowly, carefully, then pause, my pencil hanging over the blank book. This is a tale of everything, and of the end. I'm not going to spare you. I had friends, but now I am almost completely alone.

If you are still alive to read this, then you deserve to know what has been lost. Because it's gone…

There were once more than seven billion humans. You read that right. And they belonged to thousands of cultures, each with their own language. They lived in all the wide and scattered places, and sometimes they lived together in cities.

I lived in such a city—still do, in fact, but it's very different now. Its name hardly matters any more. Belfast. There were hundreds of thousands of people in Belfast when my story begins.

My home. I love it. In my mind it's as it used to be, bursting with life, a million lilting conversations filling its every nook. Its worn red-brick downtown and the wild beauty of the coastlines. The lush greenery that was ours before we lost it.

Things changed when the government sold out to the corporations, not so long ago, when I was a child. It was all about profit. They abused us. Raised the price of food and restricted the availability of viable seeds. Drove us to poverty and slavery.

We had vegetable gardens, once, but they died out. My friend Naomi told me it was all the fault of the terminator gene which stops plants from reproducing themselves. Soon there were barely any plants at all, no compost to nourish the earth. Our soil became sterile.

We worked hard for our food, such little as they gave us. The land was government-owned. Company-owned. So was the food supply. They commandeered the entire workforce, supposedly for the development of fast-grow fertilisers and best use of resources.

My job was programming and data entry in a food records office. My friends looked up to me because I worked with computers, but it was all pretty meaningless. For a long time they doled out food at midday, a meal enough to survive on.

When I was twenty-three, the portions began shrinking…

Mariah frowned at the slop in her tray, then addressed the boy with the ladle. "Hey, Jonesy! Bit skint today?"

She held it towards him to ask for more. Just a kid, and the canteen was his first job—he'd been here since he was seven, and he was usually jolly enough. But now…he had a face on like his ma died.

"Hey," she said again. "You okay?"

His response was too quiet. She leaned in, hand cupped to her ear.

"Not allowed to give any more."

Mariah made like a fish.

"Boss says. Same for me too." His lip trembled and Mariah smiled and mouthed an okay. It wasn't his fault.

"Ge'rra move on," came the call from farther back in the line. Mariah gripped her mostly-empty puke-inducing blue plastic tray with pale knuckles and walked away, slumped.

A hush fell over the workers as they collected their ration and sat to eat between the bare concrete walls. Today's main meal—the only meal for most—would not, could not satisfy. Some new tax or fee, no doubt. Mariah burned inside, even while she scooped up every drip of the watery porridge.

The door opened to admit a middle-aged Senate medic wearing a ragged white coat and toting an ominous black briefcase. A pair of Senate guards flanked the exit behind him, hands on their holstered weapons. Groans went around the room. The medic sighed, just as reluctant to administer his services as the workers were to receive them. He cleared his throat and read from the crumpled note in his hand. "Compulsory vaccinations for a new strain of Ebola. Virus discovery dated 5th of June." He squinted. "Or 6th. Can't make it out. Never mind. Right, line up, will you?"

"That must be the one my gran is all but dying from right this very minute," said the woman seated nearest to Mariah. "It might get her yet."

A teenager shook his head as he extricated long limbs from the opposite bench. "The Senate is just experimenting on us. It's all a fraud."

Unwillingly, the queue of workers snaked towards the medic and his needle. He worked silently, whipping off each used tip almost as soon as it was out of the recipient's arm, ready with the next in seconds.

Mariah's fingers sweated. She was not fond of jabs. She crossed her arms and shuffled along with the rest, glancing at the guards. There was no escaping this, even if she believed it was harmful. And who really knew for sure, anyway? Her gaze returned to the floor.

The doctor seized her wrist and unclenched her elbow. "Relax, willya? It'll be easier for the both of us that way."

She glowered at him. The needle went in, burning.

"Is it airborne?"

"Hmm?" The doctor pushed on the plunger for what seemed like a very long time but could only have been a few seconds. "No, not airborne. Thank goodness we don't have that to deal with again. There you go, all done." Finally the pressure released, he let go of her arm and it fell away from the needle with a tearing sensation.

Already he reached for the next in line. She was alone with her pain, the previous patient having escaped the hall already. Mariah licked her thumb and pressed down on the puncture as she slipped out between the guards, hoping like hell there wouldn't be any side effects from the shot this time.

A distant buzzer sounded. Just a few more digits and this report on Antrim Farm B would be complete. *Antrim*...Mariah grew wistful. Far as anyone knew, that was where her brother had been taken: the best of the able-bodied, though the few who came back said it was a hard existence even if the food was better.

"Oi!" A tousled red head popped up behind her computer screen wearing an enormous grin. "Whatcher still goin' fer?"

"Liam! Don't creep up on me like that. You know I like to finish a report before I go. I'd only have to redo it in the morning."

"I was just wonderin'..."

"Spit it out, ya great git."

"If'n ye'd like me to accompany ye home."

"You mean ride alongside?" Mariah was unsure where Liam lived, but perhaps some of the route might be shared.

He nodded earnestly, a wee bit too fast, so that his forelock flew up and down above intensely hopeful eyes.

She stifled a laugh. "Actually I'm to meet Naomi at Cultra beach. Another time?"

"All right. But I ain't letting ye forget."

"Enjoy yer evening, then." Mariah returned to her work, only to notice some seconds later that Liam was still there, chewing his lip. She stopped typing. "What's eating you then?"

"Not here." He tilted his head ever so slightly towards the door.

"Hang on just a tick then." She tapped the final numbers into the system, checked that everything was complete, then clicked to store it in the data archive where government agents would ostensibly use it to assess which farms had the best production rates, and assist those in need of improvement. At least, that had been the plan back when she'd helped set up the programming and the network to make it possible.

Outside, she turned to Liam, hands on hips. "Well?"

"I was delivering a message to the manager today. She wasn't there at the time, so I set it on her desk—and my eye caught another letter sitting there. One of those window envelopes, you know? Well, someone hadn't folded the paper quite right inside, and the first line of the message was clear in the window."

"What was it?"

"It said, 'Transfer of Mariah F.' I cudden' see the rest of the name, but it has to be you. We don't have any other Mariah here."

"Liam, who...who was the letter from?"

"That's the strangest part. There was no real return address on the envelope, it only said 'Non-Public Unit' and then a number."

Mariah sagged.

"It's bad, is it? I never heard of it before," said Liam.

"You're not in programming."

"No, just data entry, how come?"

"I don't know much about it, but word gets out among the code monkeys, you know. These non-public labs...they're so secret, no one is allowed to go home when they work there. Liam, people *disappear* when they get transferred to those places." She'd built a circle of friends that was strong, if small, and she would do anything to prevent herself being taken away from them. Even with them around her, the aloneness loomed over her far more than she liked.

He reached over, gripped her shoulder awkwardly. "Is there anything we can do?"

"I could run away...go into hiding...try to live off the land and not let them find me...Oh, what's the use? They'd get me eventually."

Liam grinned. "Not immediately, and you don't have to run, either."

"Huh?"

"I stole the letter, of course. Then tore it up and dumped it in the long drop. It's under a pile of shite by now."

"And you didn't even read it."

"Not my business. I just wanted it gone."

Mariah allowed herself a smile. "Thanks, I guess. They'll send another when they realise it didn't get through, but you've bought me some time, for sure."

"You're welcome, hey. See you on the morrow." Liam swung onto his bike and sailed away.

Mind abuzz, Mariah unlocked her bike and mapped the route to Cultra in her head. She knew it well, of course, had ridden there many times to meet her friend. It was a significant distance for both of them, but the quiet beach provided soul solace. The question was whether she should use the long route for a quieter ride or cut through town and save herself ten minutes.

The shortcut won out. She left the industrial district and rattled down into the central part of Belfast, its red-brick buildings aglow in the evening light that hid for this gilded moment their true dilapidated state. The more modern buildings, once pretty with glass façades, stood as shattered skeletons of their former selves. Traffic was heavy, like she'd expected, but since everyone was restricted to bikes now, things were relatively sane. Shuttered shops spoke of shortages and the loss of private enterprise. Garbage lay rotting on the ground, thrown out of upper windows by the people who lived there. Mariah lifted her gaze to the building opposite Clarence Street and caught sight of the ratty-haired woman who leaned there in a second-storey window as she was wont to do.

Mariah trundled round a corner into Howard Street. There was shouting to one side, from the direction of City Hall. She approached with care, senses bristling, ready to swerve into a side road if need be. Howard Street was still empty—and then it was full.

The crowd poured out of Linenhall Street and kept on coming. They pressed against City Hall, more and more of them until there was no way round, and they pushed along the road towards her. She skidded to a halt, computing an alternate route though labyrinthine alleys. She could finally make out what they were shouting about.

"Down with rations!"

"One, two, three, four, give us food and give us more!"

Mariah turned the front wheel of her bike for a clean getaway but one of the protestors spotted her, a tall woman with long brown hair.

The woman yelled at her. "Hey! Join us, why doncha? The more the merrier, and we can change something!"

"Do you really think that'll make a difference?"

The shouting grew louder, the crowd moved closer. Mariah stared the woman in the eye for a moment, then stood into her pedals and raced away with cries of "Traitor!" trailing behind her—then, as if in afterthought, "Yer ma's a munter!"

Mariah quashed the sudden desire to tell the eedjit her ma was dead. She rounded a corner and sped along, one short block, then two, then three.

Sirens wailed. Every police truck in Belfast might be converging on City Hall. The street in front of her was deserted: everyone was either protesting or hiding. Flashing lights approached. She flung herself off the road and ducked into a deep doorway, hoping no one would notice her bike with its wheel still spinning. A colonnade of vans screeched past.

Mariah emerged then, certain no more were coming. She mounted up and moved on. In the distance the protestors' chanting turned to screams. And...gunshots. "Lord ha' mercy," she whispered, pedalling herself farther away—more alone than ever, a solitary moving shadow in a petrified, quickly darkening cityscape.

***

It was almost night now, the sea and sky a deep blue-black. The old trees rustled softly, their roots somehow so far underground that they were able to cling to life despite the dead topsoil. Mariah dug her fingers into the cool, dry sand and its chill rose into her bones, though summer was close. A few stars winked into view above, more visible now than they had been in the age of universal electricity.

Mariah kicked at the sand. "It's no good. We canna go on like this. Isn't there some change coming? Some way to increase food production?"

"They say food is short, but perhaps it's no' as short as all that," Naomi said. "Do you remember back when you and I were in school together? When they gave a dinner enough to fill you, and a pint of milk."

"Milk! Dinna make me drool."

"Okay, so there's a shortage, but not like the rationing suggests. They're panicking."

"You're not hungry, are you?"

"No. When you work in the growth industry, there are plenty of failed experiments to eat."

"Is there enough to smuggle some out?" A particularly loud rumble emanated from Mariah's midsection and she became painfully aware of her friend's higher job status.

"You poor thing, you're starving. I'll see what I can do, but the security is pretty tight."

"It's not just me. Everyone I know is hungry. Even you."

"One meal a day is below the starvation line any way you look at it."

"We've got to do something." Mariah stopped pacing and dropped onto the sand. "Do you remember the time I found that wild blackberry bush on the coast by Bangor?"

"Yeah, you stripped it bare and carried the fruit to all your friends."

"What if we could find places where the soil is still good? And grow food there?"

"It's possible. We'd have to farm worms and compost everything we could."

"There's gotta be people that would help."

"You know it would have to be kept a secret."

"What?"

"Mariah, I work for the food industry. The thing with the terminator gene getting out—that was deliberate. They don't want hunger to go away. It keeps people working."

"We won't work long if we suffer malnutrition."

"No, and things will come to a head. Secret food will only prolong the status quo."

"That may be true, but people are hungry now. I have to do something. Are you with me?"

"Well, duh!" Naomi stretched over and mussed Mariah's hair, then grew serious. "Now listen. I think I can get some bio-fertiliser to start us off—it's based on mould. Highly effective."

"Fantastic. We need to scout out a place to start, and figure out who's going to help."

"Certainly Liam will. That boy's keen on you like a beacon in the night."

Mariah shoved Naomi's shoulder, glad the falling darkness hid her reddening cheeks. "Is not!"

"Is too, and you know it."

Sigh. "It's just...it's the wrong time. The world is such a hard place, and we never know when one of us will be snatched away." Liam was a good friend. The best, even. But if Mariah really let herself love him...only then maybe to lose him...she couldn't.

Naomi was a silent presence beside her in the dark while the waves inched ever nearer to their toes half-buried in the cool sand. The horizon dimmed; the water and sky finally became one with the full coming of night.

Summer's early dawn had passed, but the day was still fresh and new. Castlereagh was a nice enough suburb—at least, it must have been nice in its past. Now, like everywhere else, its houses fell into disrepair for lack of maintenance, as residents were forced to work longer hours for less food and had nothing to trade for building materials in any case. Hedges and trees had died, dried out, and been carried off for firewood; the only green came from weeds of largely non-edible varieties that struggled in sheltered corners.

Mariah flung the tip of her trowel once more at the pale, sodden earth, breaking up a little more of the inhospitable backyard plot. She shovelled it into her cracked flowerpot. Just a little more, and she'd have enough loose soil to combine with dead weeds she'd gathered, plus a little organic household waste, and she might someday be able to coax her precious seeds into new life. Her treasure was nothing more than a tiny strawberry Liam had found who knew where. It wasn't a given that the seeds on it would even germinate. But she had to try.

The back door creaked open and she grinned a greeting at her Da, who stumped down the three steps and extended a cup to her, steaming in the morning air.

"What's this, then? I thought we were all out of tea."

"We were, so I thought, but I was hunting in the kitchen and found this old package."

She sipped gratefully at the weak brew. To think that tea had become such a luxury—her mother had downed easily ten cups a day before the shortages.

11

"Mixing up a batch of compost, are we?" Da nodded at the terracotta container.

"For them seeds." She shook the dregs off the trowel and sighed. "So little. Even if they all grow, what difference is a handful of strawberry plants going to make?"

"Aye, if you look at them in isolation. But they could be the start of something. Lead you anywhere."

Nod. She wanted to believe it. The workday awaited her...but not quite yet. She pasted on a smile for her Da and savoured the tea, such as it was.

⁂⁂⁂

Mariah paced softly down the dark city street, dodging the scope of the security cameras. She'd left her bike two blocks away. Every window held a possible betrayer, any shadow might be a Senate soldier waiting to nab her for breaking curfew. She took fright at a figure in a doorway, but he ignored her. Only a resident having a quiet smoke. She passed on by and entered the alley in the next block.

"Pssst!" The whisper came from a cluster of rubbish cans behind what used to be a really good Chinese restaurant.

Mariah froze and cocked her head, but nothing else came, so she took another step. This was definitely the place they'd agreed on.

"*Pssst!*" More desperate this time.

"Password?" she hissed back at the invisible attention-seeker.

"Oh, uh..." Rustling. "This year, a harvest."

"Right y'are. Now, come out where I can see ye."

Liam's familiar red mop popped up from his crouch, but he wasn't alone. A darker head rose beside him.

Mariah jumped back. "You brought company."

"Aye. Peter's all right. He's with us."

"If you're sure he can be trusted."

"Hey, I'm right here—" Peter was about to say more, but Mariah stopped him.

"I'm not about to jeopardise this effort before it's even gotten started." She tapped her foot as if waiting for evidence of Peter's trustworthiness. Liam's word should be enough for her, but at this stage, she couldn't be too careful or they might nab her before she could do a single solitary thing.

"Well, uh…" Peter scratched his head. "My Da was a farmer out in Antrim county. Until the soil died, that is. I miss growing things summat fierce."

She inspected him suspiciously for another moment. His dark-eyed gaze grew distant, wistful even.

Ah, what the hell. She shook his hand. "Think you can tell the difference between live soil and dead?"

His eyes brightened. "Reckon so."

"Well, when you can, go scouting around the back country. We need to find places where things will still grow."

"I'll go with you," said Liam to Peter. "I have the same day off as you."

"Hold yer whisht," Mariah whispered. There it was again—the lightest of scuffles from the direction of the street. "Someone could be listening."

There was no time to lose. But she still needed to tell them one thing. "We're meeting tomorrow night in the old Bangor mall. Where the foodcourt used to be. Tell your friends, the ones you trust."

"So far out of town?" asked Liam.

"We need our centre of operations to be close to open country. More chance of finding good land there."

"Okay. Then we'd better get out of here for now. See you on the morrow."

"You go first," Liam said.

Mariah edged back towards the open street. Two soldiers loitered at the intersection she needed to pass, and snatches of their conversation drifted to where she waited. She'd have to take a large loop to avoid them and still get back to her bike. When their backs were turned for a moment, she ducked out and hurried away without a backwards glance.

Cold daylight forced its way into the shutter cracks on glassless bunkhouse windows. Darian blinked, stretched a little, but touched the wall on one side and pushed on it. The thin boards creaked when he released the pressure. If it was already light…then he'd slept in again, and his workmates had decided to leave him to his fate. He groaned and swung upright between rows of empty bunks. Outside, he hurried to splash water on his face from a bucket on the ground by the door—making sure it was the right bucket first.

The large porridge pot rested on a rough table not far away in the dusty yard between huts; it had already been scraped empty. He reached in for one tiny morsel that clung to the ladle.

So much for breakfast.

Sure, it was his own fault for sleeping late. No one had woken him, though; no doubt so they could eat his share. He didn't blame them. Darian only hoped that the rumours would be true one day, and they'd let everyone go home.

Six years of this. He jogged along the muddy track that led to the growing fields. His assigned area was on its ploughing-under cycle where supplies of chemical fertilisers and cow and chicken manure were hoed into the earth to make it more fruitful before planting. Darian often wondered about the cows and chickens, and about the milk and eggs. In any case, none of this showed up in their rations.

Well before he arrived at the field, the smell told him today was a chemical day. Hello, sore throat, nose and eyes. His mind seized on a distracting idea: he hoped there'd be something different for lunch today than the same oats they grew, the same oats they always ate.

Darian reached the field gate in the high, impenetrable fence, and attempted to slink in unseen.

"Oi, you!"

Lucky for him, the closest supervisor was Andi, a somewhat gentler representative of the World Senate, and one he hoped might someday return his regard when they were on more equal terms. For now, he had slacked on his job, and she had her own job to do. She dictated the standard consequences. "Half an hour late equals two hours overtime. Sorry."

Darian grimaced. His back anticipated the pain already. Also, he would miss the evening meal. Without a word, he hefted a bucket of foul-smelling goop and slung a long hoe over his shoulder. It was going to be a long, long day.

Brown soil surrounded them for a hectare bounded by the tall black fence. Figures with buckets and hoes were scattered across the expanse, most hard at work, some returning to the vat at the entrance to refill their supply of chemicals. The high hills of Antrim soared up some distance beyond the

14

barricade. As ever, the hardy hawthorns provided just a hint of green scattered across the slopes. Lifeless, blackened alder and ash trunks pierced the earth from below, a bed of rusty nails for the iron sky to press against.

The fast-food kitchens stood rusting behind their counters; layers of bird poop darkened the peaked glass roof. From the corner window, there was a straight line of sight down Quay Street under a grey late afternoon sky to a sliver of grey harbour. Just a few boats in it these days—although people lived in them, Mariah doubted they were seaworthy. Blossoming gardens on the waterfront, families walking the pier, and just around the corner, more blackberry bushes than anybody could hope for...all alongside tidy homes with their own vegetable patches. But now the pretty homes had faded, the earth they sat on damp as ever but refusing to bring forth food.

"This used to be such a beautiful place." She turned away from the view of the dilapidated outdoors and paced back to where Naomi sat at one of the tables bolted to the floor. "Where are they all?"

"You didn't tell them a time. It's early yet." Naomi patted the next seat. "Set yourself here and tell me your evil plan."

"Evil? Right. Peter and Liam have been hunting for places where stuff still grows. When we find a spot to start with, we'll cultivate what edible plants are there already and bring in more from wherever people have saved seeds."

"We'll have to grow seeds separately at first until we're sure they're not infected with the terminator gene. Then we can keep our plants reproducing."

Such a gargantuan task. "Are there even any seeds left that won't terminate?" Mariah thought of her as-yet dormant wild strawberry seeds. Then again, she was no gardener.

"Well..." Naomi's face grew even more serious. "We have some at work. Maybe I could sneak some out, just one or two of each kind. It might go unnoticed."

"You'd be in big trouble if you got caught."

Both laughed, but stopped abruptly as a grey head became visible in the stalled escalator well. The old lady heaved herself up the last of the too-tall metal steps and moved slowly towards them. Her face was aged, her eyes bright, even though she leaned heavily on two walking sticks.

"Are you the ones as want to grow food?"

"Depends who's asking. Are ye for us?"

"Oh, this year a harvest and all that. Certainly."

Mariah narrowed her eyes. "Who told you we'd be here?"

"Well, er, my neighbour's grandson. He got it from someone at his work."

Okay. That might be anyone.

"I'm Deborah." She slid into the third chair and inspected the large room. "Years since I were in here last. Why, they even sold me a bag of hot chips just over there."

Mariah exchanged a worried glance with Naomi and moistened her lips. "You even know what this is about?"

"Food is what it's about. Now listen. I have a house not too far from here. I've been careful with my garden and the neighbours let me take care of theirs too, so we have some decent soil."

"That's almost too grand to be true," Naomi said.

Metallic footsteps clattered again in the escalator. It was the two boys. Worn and clabbered with mud, they joined the little group and straddled chairs at the next table, draping themselves on the seat backs.

"We found a couple of nooks out in the country where things are growing," said Liam, "but of course we'll need to try cultivating it to see if it really is good land."

Mariah smiled. "We have an expert right here. Guys, meet Naomi—she's a horticultural biologist."

The fellows sized her up, then Deborah cracked her stick on the floor. "Listen. We can't meet here again. Will ye come to my house? 45 Cliff Road."

More feet tramped up the escalator, and they weren't trying to be quiet. Mariah shot to her feet. "Quick! The fire exit." They scrambled for the stairwell entrance and almost fell down it in their hurry. Mariah eased the door shut and found herself next to Deborah, so she seized her arm and all but carried her with Peter's help on the other side.

At the bottom, Deborah pulled free and dusted herself off, waving her walking sticks. "I can walk jest fine, thank ye. These are for showin' 'em I'm harmless."

Officers shouted in the food court above, but the door remained closed. The stairs spat them out in a back alley littered with abandoned bins-for-hire. Mariah dodged them and checked the street. "Clear. They're all inside."

"We'd better split up," said Naomi.

"You girls go along the seafront. We'll go up into the town." Before anyone could agree, Peter zipped around the corner and out of sight. Liam shrugged and followed.

Mariah turned to Deborah. "Come with us."

"No, lassie. I live on the cliff. I'll just be on my way home. D'ye think I came up the Lagan in a bubble? You go on now, it'll be fine." She hunched over her walking sticks again. Her eyes twinkled and Mariah suspected she was more than able to talk herself out of any trouble that might arise, even if the police did stop her. She'd be safer when the others left. Although…her unannounced arrival preceding the police did smell slightly rotten. Mariah hoped Deborah was trustworthy, but now was not the time to ponder. She grabbed Naomi's wrist to get her moving and they dodged to the shelter of a nearby doorway.

"Oi." It was Deborah, in a loud stage-whisper from the alley corner. "My house, tomorrow, all right?"

Thumbs-up. Mariah prayed it wasn't a mistake. The two girls made a mad dash for the street corner by the harbour and vanished towards the rocky shore where the blackberries once bloomed.

2

fΛlth

JUNE 2004

Hungry. Faith was hungry. A terrific roar emanated from her stomach. What she wouldn't give for some Irish stew right now. Somehow she was always hungry, no matter what she did, although there was really no reason for it. "You're ten, you're a growing kid," her parents would say, and laugh.

As for herself, she nursed a burning passion to store as much food as possible, and never to waste any, not ever for any reason.

She wandered the narrow rows of her garden, plucking out a weed here, flicking off a bug there. She turned the tap and watched the water spray from her irrigation system. When she shut it off, there was a silence filled with pleasant dripping. *That's right.* She had come searching for something to munch on.

Her ma and da had given her care of the garden in front of the house in Bangor. So as her appetite remained enormous, she made it her business to grow a green thumb. There was much to learn, whether about composting and fertilising, thinning and pruning, or cultivating from cuttings. Faith's afternoons and weekends were spent in weeding, watering, digging and staking, her evenings in front of her computer, researching online for the most effective methods. On her way home from school each day she would search out new routes to gather cuttings and shoots to add to the variety in her patch.

Lettuces, cabbage and spinach grew against the front hedge. Just behind them were the strawberries, pretty when they blossomed or fruited, the first thing anyone would see when they walked by on the street. Then came the cucumbers, beans, courgettes, capsicums and aubergines. Along the front wall of the house stood the varieties of tomatoes all carefully staked, and around the side an old apple tree with pumpkin vines clambering a compost heap beyond. Faith had taken care that everything grew to its full potential. When she became hungry between meals, which was often, she needed only to raid the garden itself or the preserves she and her mother made from its bounty—jars of tomatoes, apples, pickled greens, jellied strawberries.

Her gaze roved across the neatness of the proud stalks and swaying leaves, offset nicely by the cream-coloured house. Although it was visibly aged with peeling paint and the crack in the kitchen window, it only added to the charm of the place.

She plucked a few each of the yellow and red cherry tomatoes and bit down on them one by one, savouring the sweetness and the subtle differences between them. She parted leaves and spied a last cucumber that had been hiding from her; it was an early variety and the rest were all pickling already. This one she'd missed. She gently separated it from the vine and ran her fingers along its glossy length. It wasn't huge, but it'd fill a wee space, as her grandma always said. She took a bite and almost dribbled juice. *You only get this kind of flavour when you grow it yourself.*

Soon it was gone, but her stomach wanted more. She moved to the strawberries. It was too soon for them, really, but she lifted the leaves and found some smaller ones had already turned red. These wouldn't grow any more anyway, she told herself. She plucked a big handful and settled carefully on a bare patch with her back to the hedge that served for a fence.

She had eaten about half and was beginning to feel just a bit full at last when the sound of whooping boys stopped her mid-chew. She knew who it was. Frozen in place, she hoped she was unseen. She hoped they would ride past.

A quick glance through the leaves revealed the pack outlined clearly against the houses opposite, all identical to her own. They slowed. Faith curled up on the ground, strawberries forgotten. *Just leave me alone!*

Bikes clattered to the ground right on the other side of the hedge. She flinched. There were dragging sounds and hushed laughter. She stared at the bedroom window, willing her Da to wake from his nap. No such luck. He would wake soon enough, but it would be too late.

Unless…

Faith gathered all her courage and wobbled to her feet, lurching up behind the hedge to come face to face with a phalanx of waterblasters and pellet airguns. Maybe she imagined it, but they drew back slightly at her appearing.

That illusion melted when the ringleader, Ewan, leaned into her face. "Well, if it isn't the garden gnome herself!" They called her that in school, taunted her with singing. She didn't care about that.

"You want food?" she blurted. "I'll give you food. You can have whatever you need. Just—*please*—don't waste it."

"Hear that, lads? She doesn't want us to waste it." He raised the waterblaster. "In fact, that's exactly what we came here to do."

Switches flipped throughout the gang and the buzz of pressure buildup filled Faith's ears. She spread her arms, a useless protection between her garden—*her garden!*—and destruction. Surely they wouldn't shoot her in cold blood…surely…

The blast caught her in the stomach. She landed, sodden, in the strawberries, and screamed, blinded with water, while the rushing liquid razed all around her. Airgun pellets zipped into the ground, several stinging her skin and some even pinging off the house. *Da! Wake up!*

She dared not open her eyes for fear of getting shot and truly blinded. Vegetable flesh splattered across the exposed parts of her skin. The plants were history. She trembled at the intensity and physicality of the attack; perhaps she could get back into the shelter of the hedge.

She rolled blindly over cabbages towards her tormentors, groped for the hedge and found it, then tucked herself tightly in. Lettuces were beneath her, but even this destruction committed by her own taut self barely registered now, although her subconscious screamed at her. *Never waste food. Never!*

The boys' laughter and taunts swelled between volleys. Then someone grew reckless. Pellets struck higher—they hit glass, and left more than a mark.

The door opened. Da roared and fired his pistol into the air. The onslaught stopped and there was a scramble in the street as the evildoers made haste to get away.

Faith opened her eyes. The first thing she saw was her father running towards her. The second thing was the garden. Plants were uprooted, earth turned to sloppy mud, ripening vegetables shot full of holes by the plastic pellets that lay scattered everywhere. If there was anything left, it would be a miracle.

Her body ached, but her soul hurt more. She tried to speak but only garbled sounds came out. Da reached her then and wrapped her in his arms.

Everything is gone. All of it—wasted.

She buried her face in Da's shoulder and wailed.

3

mariah

june 2079

The dog hovered at the edge of the backyard with the little girl. He still refused to approach the older members of the family, and he was wary of the closed-in space. A wall to the next yard had been broken down and removed, doubling the previous yard size, but it was still tiny. The only exit was through the house, so he remained close to the back door, watching the other children at play.

The boy and girl were of similar age and might have been twins or a year apart perhaps. Their hair was brown, like the dog's, and they wore layers of well-worn clothing that had truly seen better days. They giggled and chased each other around and around the expanse of damp dust between the walls. Their grandmother appeared in the doorway, hands on hips. "Why don't you go play with the others, Alice, ya wee rapscallion?"

Alice only peered up at her darkly from under thunderous eyebrows. She clung tighter to the dog's shoulders.

"Flea-ridden beast," said the gran, and sighed. "But he does seem to make you happy."

The door of the other house opened and the dog shot his attention there in case quick movement would prove necessary. But no, it was another grandmother, and another three children who tumbled out around her. They greeted the other boy and girl and all launched anew into their game of chase. The second gran hobbled across to join the first, and they settled into two rickety folding chairs against the crumbling exterior of the house.

The sun was well on its way down and when it cleared the patchy clouds from time to time, it cast shadows of the two-storey block and its chimney-pots across the yards and walls. The grans chatted, and the dog kept half an ear trained on their tone in case it should turn threatening.

"Even less food for the workers now, I suppose you've heard."

"It's a crying shame. Not enough for themselves, let alone for their wee ones."

"We've lived a long time, so we can manage on less now." She indicated her own stick-like limbs. "But the children..." Her eyes roved over the playful gang before her, still full of energy for now.

"The black market's slowing down too. No one has any more valuables to trade."

"Aye, our Jasmine's after trading away her wedding ring. And her so set on keepin' it."

The other gran raised an appraising eyebrow. "An' how long will that keep her wee-uns in porridge?"

"Not more'n a week, in fact."

There was silence for a moment whilst a pair of housemartins wheeled far above the laughing children.

"Wish we hadn't voted for that villain Prendergast."

"Aye, as if using food for currency would help."

"To think we'd live to see the day."

"Wonder what became of him."

The other leaned in conspiratorially. "There's some as say he hid away in a computer."

"Pull the other one!"

"No, no. I'd not believe it if 'twernt our Aileen who told me. She says there really is such a thing as...now, what did she call it again...virtual reality.

24

A better world, but not real. And the Senate promised him that as his reward for the changes he made here."

"He believed them? So he really was just a feckin' eedjit."

"Aye. Thought he was the dog's bollix, that one."

The famished children had tired quickly and sat in a circle flicking one pebble at another in place of the marbles their ancestors had owned. Alice sat on the step with the dog, digging her fingers into the soft fur of his neck. Moving shadows and the draught from the open front door betrayed the return of one of the parents.

Heavy steps approached. "Is that mutt still here? I asked you to get rid of it." The father's tone was not as unkind as his words.

His mother-in-law turned her face from him. "I ain't feeding it, never you mind."

"That's as may be, but the longer it's here, the softer you'll get. I know it, so I do."

The second gran mumbled an excuse and re-entered the other house. The father settled into her vacated chair with a groan.

"How was work then?"

"Oh, same as usual—big pile of shite. And the feed is ridiculous. Two bites of porridge they gave us. Two bites for a day's wage! I canna live on that meself, let alone care for the rest of ye." His speech was measured, but the man was too twitchy for the dog's liking.

"It's a disgrace, is what it is."

"I suppose we can start trading the furniture, if anyone wants it. It's getting older but it's still in decent shape for some newly commissioned Senate soldier with oats to spare." He spat on the ground, then narrowed his eyes. "There's something else as might help, too."

"Is that so?" The gran was sceptical.

The father got up, went into the house, and rummaged loudly in the kitchen drawer. The clatter ceased and he reappeared in the doorway, face set, the glint of sharpened metal in his hand.

The old lady's hand shot to her mouth. "Alice, send doggy inside to daddy."

Alice only held tighter to her companion. Her gran had to pry her hands loose and push the dog into the hallway while holding onto the child, who began to scream.

25

The man opened the bathroom door and guided the dog's head inside the windowless, malodorous space. Cracked porcelain had leaked effluvium onto the floor. Without an alternative exit, the dog stopped, uncertain, all his senses on alert. The man pushed on his rear. He gave a low growl, and his hackles rose. The man pushed again and the dog spun around, baring his teeth. The man advanced, forcing the dog to move backwards by blocking his way.

The front door opened, bringing mother and a gust of fresh air. Man and dog gaped at her for a second—then the dog zipped out through the gap and away into the Belfast street.

The man flung the knife to the floor. "Feckin' bollix!"

In the lunchroom, Mariah cleaned up the wee bit of slop Jonesy was allowed to give her. She finished, licked the tray without shame, and relaxed for a moment, watching the dust motes float through the ray of sunlight that entered the lone window. In her expert opinion based on this evidence, it was lovely outside. Not that it made much difference to her, stuck in here all day, except that she might not get wet on her way home later, if the weather held up.

Someone clattered a tray onto a table and Mariah flinched. Since Liam had told her of the transfer letter, she'd been nothing but a bundle of nerves. So far there was no sign that a replacement message had arrived, but it wouldn't be long now. She'd have to consider her course of action—whether she would really try to make a run for it, leave everything behind in the effort to survive.

A humming sound stilled the chatter of hungry workers and they turned their attention to the rarely-used projector above their heads. A message from the local Senate representatives—perhaps they were going to try explaining the reduction in rations.

A talking head in a suit appeared on the concrete wall, much larger than life. When he spoke, Mariah trembled involuntarily at the strange accent. He wasn't local at all. He announced a special global news bulletin. Global…he must be American. From the World Senate itself.

"The Senate regrets to inform the people of the world that there has been a disturbance here in America resulting in substantial loss of life. It is believed that a group called the Guild is behind the incitement of widespread rebellions which continued for several weeks but have now been successfully suppressed."

Murmurs hissed around the room. *Angry* murmurs.

"The Guild was an illegal faction aiming to remove control of food from the Senate. This kind of mutiny puts everyone in danger of starvation—" *Yeah, right,* thought Mariah, "—therefore with regret we had to use force to dispel it."

The man blinked down at his papers, gulped, and went on. Poor guy. He was just a slave like everyone else. "Be assured that we are making the best use of our resources to distribute food fairly. Attempting to procure it yourself is clear provocation to insubordination which can undermine the very foundations of this society. The Senate thanks you for your continued compliance."

Mariah slid down in her seat when the image vanished; the muttering grew louder. *Don't be silly,* she told herself. *No one knows what I have planned.* She forced herself to keep a calm appearance, even though horror washed over her. The Senate had ordered the killing of who knows how many people, just because they tried to get their own food.

The Guild, huh? She hoped some of them had survived.

***

Deborah's house was not hard to find. The area used to be one of the better ones in Bangor, just one street back up the hill from the foreshore, but like most places it, too, was worse for wear since the current Troubles had begun. Houses sagged, paint peeled, windows warped. But in the gaps between the buildings, the sea shone just like always: deep, mysterious and dangerously blue, carrying the scent of freedom. If only fish hadn't become so scarce...

Mariah dragged her attention away from the elusive glitter of the briny horizon and scrutinised the faded pink front of number 45, Cliff Road. She had made excuses and escaped early from work, so she was here several hours before she was expected. Time to do some research.

Research, in this case, meant hiding behind the twiggy hedge of the uninhabited ruin opposite, and watching carefully. Not that there was anything much to watch. Mariah wasn't sure what she was after. Something smelled fishy and she wanted to dispel her doubts and accept the offer of help. On the other hand, if she spotted any strangers coming or going in the next hours, that would be a red flag.

There was no red flag. Only an interminable afternoon, but at least she was enjoying the sun.

A bike approached from the direction of the city. Naomi. She gave her a few minutes to enter the house, then emerged from hiding, wheeled her bike across the street, and followed the stepping-stone path between barely-alive apple trees and patches of moderately growing weeds.

She tapped twice, softly, and waited.

The curtain in the front room stirred, and a shadow beyond it. Locks clicked from above and below and centre. The door opened to reveal Deborah. "In you come," she said. "Naomi is already here."

She must have really put on the speed to get here so fast. Or maybe it was her day off. Mariah followed Deborah into the front room and grinned at Naomi before sitting down.

"Could ye face a wee drap o' tae?"

"Yes, please." Mariah answered before she thought. Deborah's supply would be precious. "Actually, no, I'm okay."

Deborah frowned down at her. "You like tae, you're getting tae," she said, and bustled off to the kitchen. The sitting room was your typical grandmotherly setup, floral wallpaper, lace curtains, overstuffed chairs and embroidered pillows, little china knick-knacks, and a vague smell of mothballs. Of course all of it was rather the worse for wear, but that didn't prevent it from being homey and comfortable.

There was a muffled knock at the door and Mariah startled. "It'll be the boys," Naomi said. "I let Peter know earlier—went past his work on my way here and he was going to get Liam. And you, too, I thought."

Mariah avoided Naomi's curious glance. Deborah whooshed in, set a steaming cup and saucer on the side table by Mariah, another by Naomi, and fluttered on past to the door. Again the locks snapped open and the sea breeze crept in. When everything was bolted again, nervous male laughter floated into the room.

"Hullo then," said Peter, with a glance for Naomi, then he settled by

Mariah and gazed at her just a little longer than was comfortable. Liam stood awkwardly, there being only one chair left, then slid down to lean against the doorpost.

Deborah flapped around some more, and when everyone had their cup of tea, there was a silence while they sipped it. At length Deborah placed her half-emptied cup atop her saucer and cleared her throat.

Whatever she was going to say drowned in the blat of a motorcycle engine that pulled up close enough to make the front window rattle—then it stopped.

Mariah quivered once and stood, ready to run. The people in the room could have been statues for all they moved, except for Deborah: she frowned, shot to her feet, and headed for the front door, careful to shut off the sitting room behind her. The locks snicked.

"Why's she opening it?" groaned Peter.

Deborah's voice remonstrated with whoever it was. An answer came, too muffled to hear, then the door slammed and locked again. In the next instant the motor started up again and Deborah herself burst back into the sitting room, smiling.

"All right, what's going on?" Mariah growled through gritted teeth.

"Just my son."

"How does he come by a motor?"

"He's…he's a soldier."

"Fer feck's sake!" muttered Liam. "What the bloody 'ell are you playin' at?"

"I'm sorry! He works second shift and usually comes home on his break, brings his ol' ma some of that there Army food. I've told him it'd be better if he stayed at the barracks now till he finishes up."

"You're sure we can trust you?" Mariah said.

"I hate the Senate as much as any of you. Please, believe me." Tears welled up in the old woman's eyes. "I didn't want 'im to sign up, sure I didn't. They might make a cyborg out of him—pretty slim chance, I know, but too much of a chance for his ma."

They might have made one out of him anyway, Mariah thought. Even civilians weren't exempt from being chosen for cyborg duty.

Naomi walked over and laid an arm around Deborah's shoulders. "It's all right."

Naomi was too trusting. Mariah scowled, but caught a scathing glance from her friend and suddenly had the sensation of being in the wrong place altogether, as if someone had pasted a paper cutout of her into a completely random scene.

"I do have to tell you one thing, though," said Deborah sternly, a crease in her brow. Everyone froze. "The inside toilet don't work, even though it looks grand and all. I have a long drop outside for that."

The mood in the room lightened. Mariah almost giggled. Deborah muttered something else under her breath, but then they all froze again: another vehicle, larger this time.

"Police!" hissed Liam. "Where can we hide?"

"The basement." Deborah pointed. They all tumbled out into the hallway. She hauled open a door at kitty-corner to the back door, and motioned them inside. Mariah, second last to enter, found herself groping down a flight of dark steps. Deborah squeezed herself in and shut the door, cutting off all light except for a tiny crack.

Mariah, right behind Deborah on the stairs, hissed at her. "There'll be hell to pay if your son sent the cops after us."

"I swear, he didn't even know you were here with me."

"Are you sure he didn't see all our bikes out front?"

The vehicle drove up and down the street, then idled somewhere close by. Loud banging from upstairs nearly shocked Mariah out of her skin. Her imagination painted vivid pictures of the police surrounding the house and taking them all away to who knows where.

But banging was all that happened. Finally the engine's hum faded away and didn't return. Deborah opened the door and Mariah blinked in the hint of fading daylight.

They all poured out into the hallway. Mariah laid a hand on the doorpost. "Shame it's so visible, or it'd be a brilliant hideout."

Naomi's voice echoed from farther below. "You guys have to see this!"

"Do you have a light?" asked Peter. Deborah, frightened into silence for the moment, scurried off to the kitchen and returned with a few candle stubs and a matchbox. She lit them one by one and passed them out.

"Thanks," said Mariah, and stepped back into the blackness, venturing deeper this time. The stairs twisted partway down and she squinted at where she was walking. Then the space opened out in front of her and Naomi's dark shape groped along a wall. She turned when the candlelight flickered on old bricks.

"Wow," said Liam, "this would be a great place to meet."

"If the door were hidden," sighed Mariah. There was no point hiding underground with the door in plain sight.

Peter blew out his candle and headed upstairs. "I have an idea about that. I saw a wardrobe in the room opposite…"

In a minute they were standing around the heavy old wooden closet. Liam pulled the doors open.

"My poor husband's things," said Deborah.

Peter swallowed. "May we take them out?"

Deborah nodded.

The boys busied themselves piling the well-worn plaid shirts and patched pants on the room's sagging iron bed. Some of the shirt buttons had been replaced with roughly carved bits of wood.

They inched the wardrobe away from the wall. "For this to work, we'll need to take the back off," said Peter.

"Do you have a claw hammer?" asked Liam.

Deborah nodded again, and brought it to them quickly. She cringed at the creaks as the nails were pried away, but Peter smiled at her. "Look, the back is still one whole piece. You'll be able to put it back on."

It took all four of the young people to shuffle the wardrobe out into the hall. Liam and Peter worked on undoing the hinges to the basement door, which they then flipped over and re-hung to open inwards. Finally, they shimmied the wardrobe tightly against the doorway.

"Bit of camouflage, anyway." Naomi said.

"I'll think of a good story to tell my son."

***

Twenty skinny huts like a miniature Nazi operation. Around them, the fields, each fenced off from the others. Darian had only seen the one he worked in, but if it was anything to go by, then the entire farm was suffering an unstoppable loss of output. If this soil died, would they let him go home? What a terrible thing to have to wish for.

Darian slunk into the empty bunkhouse. It was penumbral and quiet and he ran a finger down the rough-hewn door as he shut it. Over at the far end, his bed beckoned. Had been calling all day, in fact. He'd twisted something in his back during the morning hours, agony piling onto his fatigue. Now at day's end the others were eating, but he was just—too—*tired*. He wasn't sure if that had ever happened before and wondered if there was something wrong with him. Malnourished? That was heresy, here in the lap of the Senate, with the much-vaunted three-square-meals policy of the workcamps. Right now, all he wanted to do was sleep. Maybe he'd be a bit better in the morning.

He eased down to sit on the bunk. The mattress was not particularly soft, nor particularly flat, which might not help his back much. Still, rest was better than work, and there was no third option. After twisting his fists into his lumbar, he teetered around and lay down full length. He had to jiggle his position this way and that to ensure that neither his head nor his feet came in contact with the walls, because they boxed him in. He supposed he was a bit OCD about that.

Rest. This is what he had daydreamed about all day long, through all the pain and wishful thinking. He just wanted to go home for a while. Da would cook him up a stew if he could scrounge some edible weeds, Mariah would tell technical tales of her workplace doings, and Jemima, his collie, would give him a fantastic greeting. If she were still alive, of course. There was no way of knowing—even though he was less than thirty miles away.

He had daydreamed of rest and now he would just as likely dream of work while he slumbered. Murphy's law, he supposed. Although…rest wasn't all he'd pondered today.

Andi had picked on him for faffing about. Mentioning an injury would have done no good, so he had tried to keep pace with the others. This endeavour had a rather patchy success rate with the result that Andi had dogged his steps for much of the day. He reckoned she was trying not to be mean about it. Just her job and all. In fact, he was glad of her persistence, since Encian Jack, the field's other supervisor, left him alone. Encian's haranguing would not have been so bearable as hers.

The door creaked, shocking him out of his almost-sleep. Adrenaline rushed through his arms and legs. He took a deep breath or two. Just someone finished with dinner early—he almost smelled the meal on them. He shut his eyes again.

The redolent scent of cooked potato wafted again. His stomach thundered, but exhaustion won out. He wouldn't go chasing his dinner now that he was horizontal.

"Ye'll be needing to sit up for a moment there."

The gentle voice stunned him fully awake and he swung upright, cracking his head on the bunk above. "Ow!" The new wave of pain abated and Darian opened his eyes.

Andi Sumner, camp supervisor, held out a bowl of tater stew.

It was dusk again when Mariah crept around to Deborah's back door for the first time. Nearer the basement, less visible from the road—it made sense to divert their comings and goings to this side of the house. There was a narrow, cracked concrete path that ran from the front yard to the back, though there wasn't much back yard to speak of. Mariah tapped on the glass, then inspected the few square feet of dead dirt between the door and the back fence. The cliff edge fell away steeply here, so that the next house was a good deal farther down. If she stood on tiptoes, the sea came into view just where it faded into the twilight sky. It exerted a pull on her tonight, a yearning she might have followed more often if the world were a different kind of place.

The door jerked open and Deborah yanked her in before shutting it again in an instant, silently.

"Evening," said Mariah.

Deborah held a finger to her mouth and pointed at the wardrobe. Soft glimmer and muted conversation floated up the stairway while Mariah groped her way down. She stepped into the room, Deborah close behind, and gasped. There were at least twelve people present—everyone had been spreading the word, though they had to be careful. She smiled as she spotted a colleague she'd told just today. Candles cast flickering shadows on the old red and brown bricks that encompassed the awkward crowd.

Chatter died down. All eyes were on Mariah. She gulped hard, sliding down the nearest wall to sit on the floor. The crowd followed her lead and sat also, scattered across the uneven concrete of the basement floor. Deborah had gotten a small stool and settled herself on it.

"Before we start, I must have your word that you will all keep this place and this group secret from the authorities. Take great care inviting new members. Do not betray the cause." There was an uncomfortable silence. Mariah decided to lay it out plain. "Swear it."

"I swear," said Peter, and one by one the others followed his example.

A young girl waved her hand. "What exactly is our goal? I mean, I know it's about growing food, and I want to help, but what are we going to do?"

"We're going to find hidden places where the land will still produce. We'll cultivate them and reintroduce healthy clippings to dead soil. We'll farm worms and use biofertiliser when we can get it—" here Mariah glanced at Naomi—"and harvest the food for our own use as well as distributing it to those we know can't work and get at least some food that way."

Peter spoke up. "We've found one place that should work for starters and possibly a second. They're in the back country near here, where no one ever goes. I'll make a work plan to include those of you who are able, so it can be cared for every day."

Mariah closed her eyes for a moment and straightened her slump. "We'll call ourselves the Guild, to honour those in America who pursued the same goals and died for this great cause."

A middle-aged man fished in his pocket and held up an object that swung on a string. "I carved this out of wood. I have reason to believe it's the Guild symbol." He passed it to his neighbour, and on it went around the room. Mariah nodded at him and he went on. "Once, years ago, the police came through my neighbourhood. They wanted to know if anyone had seen an insignia like this, because it was suspected to be involved in illegal food schemes. They had one with them that they showed me. I had no idea what it was, but when the announcement came last week about the Guild, I put two and two together and carved this one from memory. It's a bit different, I think, so the police shouldn't be suspicious."

The carved piece reached Mariah and she turned it over in her hands. At first she assumed it was the shape of a flower, eight small petals and two larger ones at the bottom. On closer inspection she realised it was a stylised handshake: the small petals were the fingers gripping each other and the large ones were the wrists.

"This is beautiful, uh…"

"Murry, that's me."

"Murry. Thanks for showing us that. Perhaps you'd like to help the others make their own if they want to wear one?" She handed it back to him, but he stopped her with an upraised palm.

"I can do better than that." Murry reached into his pocket again and pulled out a handful of the pendants already on strings. "I thought I'd better come prepared."

Mariah clutched hers, watching while the others received theirs enthusiastically. She lifted the string loop and slipped it over her head, the charm now safely hidden under her shirt. Close to her heart.

4

ꝼαιth

Faith adjusted the angle of the heatlamp one more time and grinned. It was a poor representation of the sun, but it would serve her purpose. The garden model perched below it, on a shelf attached to a display board that explained how the system worked: a plot-by-plot solution that combined hydroponic racks with steep raised beds, their diagonal sides serving as extended planting areas. It had been quite a feat to get the plants to grow in this miniaturised version, but careful selection and trimming had done it. She misted water over the live plants one more time with a spray bottle—the irrigation wasn't functional on the model—and ran her eye down the texts and pictures she'd created to back up her plan: a way to grow more food than ever before. *More food. Always more food.*

She was particularly proud of the fact that the system was constructed out of waste materials and things that existed already. There would be no need to manufacture anything new. Plumbing supplies, plastic sheeting, shredded paper and farm manure formed the building blocks of the future's food supply as she envisioned it. Half of each plot would have raised beds and the other half stacked hydroponics, to be switched around each year and give the soil a rest.

A shadow fell across the doorway and was gone. Faith straightened and noticed the hall was empty. Late afternoon light drizzled down from the high windows, across the carved school crest at the apex, the quilted banners sewn by the Home Economics class, and the heavy velvet curtains tied back on either side of the platform. Rows of colourful displays on tables filled the entire space and even the stage area. Everyone else had set up and gone home already. She would too. She hoped the judges would recognise the usefulness of her ideas when the science fair opened for real in the morning. Finally she stapled the official entry form to the corner of her display.

She flipped off the light as she left the hall and thought she heard cursing. "Sorry, is anyone there?" she called.

No response. Ah well. She shut the door, making sure it was locked from the outside, and skipped down the front steps. Her trusty old 50cc scooter waited there. She straddled it and hit the ignition, letting it warm up.

When she raised her head, there sat Ewan's motorcycle parked two rows away, the only other vehicle here. She frowned. He wouldn't, would he? He'd always hated her for no good reason other than that she worked hard and succeeded. He'd gotten in so much trouble for destroying her garden years ago that he never dared attempt the like again. She was sure he must have grown out of that kind of behaviour, so she put the mystery of his bike out of her head and zoomed off.

The sun dipped low as she passed by the Ballyholme promenade; she sniffed deeply of the salt air and only just remembered not to close her eyes while she was driving. She pulled up by the bus stop atop the sea wall to take in the view of the wide beach, the moored boats at one end, the fields rising slightly at the other. A brown dog cavorted alone in the foaming shallows, and she wondered where his people were. Probably somewhere among the scattered beachwalkers, though none were close by. Faith stared at the dog, almost with a sense of déjà vu, as if she knew him very well indeed.

But she didn't, not really. She shook her head and resumed her journey towards home.

The next morning dawned bright and cheery. The dew had been heavy, leaving gigantic water drops to glisten in the sun from every direction as they weighed down each leaf and blade of grass. Faith took her time in the shower, enjoying the luxury of a little approved lateness afforded by science fair day. She wandered into the kitchen, towelling her hair, and noticed the clock. Oh, crap. She'd taken too long. She snatched a banana and crammed it down her throat as she grabbed her bag and coat. Soon she zipped into the school driveway and up to the two-wheeler parking by the hall.

She walked into the lobby just in time to encounter two louts in neon orange "Organiser" badges carrying her display out of the hall. "Hey!" she shouted, pointing. "What do you think you're doing?"

The boys dropped her display in an out-of-the-way corner and turned to face her. She couldn't be sure, but she suspected they were Ewan's lackeys. They had no right…

"Cool yer jets, luv. No entry form. Can't be judged without one."

"But…" She spluttered. "I put it on there myself, last night."

One of the fellers pointed again at the display board. "Nothing there."

She peered at the place where she'd attached it and gulped. He was right. Someone had done more than just rip it off, though—even the staple was gone, leaving only two tiny holes. "What about the electronic records of my entry? Did you look up my name?" She pointed to the place she'd pasted her name under the display title…*no*. It was gone too, and none too gently. She fingered the ripped backing. "Okay, the exhibit name, then?"

"Teacher did, I reckon. And I reckon he didn't find it."

He? Then it wasn't her own teacher, Mrs. Smythe, who had checked. She would have known how to find the entry. Faith had to find her and sort this out.

She knelt quickly by the model garden. Two of the hydroponics layers had collapsed onto the others at one corner, squashing the tiny plants. Well, she'd fix it with tape if she had to, but first…

"Faith Diamond! What in heaven's name are you up to?" It was Mrs. Smythe, with a teen girl in tow. Faith thought it might be her daughter, the one who went to a different school, but she was too distraught to pay attention.

"Wow, am I glad to see you. These guys said there was no record of my entry in the computer. I'm sure you can find it, right?"

Mrs. Smythe laid a hand on Faith's arm. "That's just it. I saw them dragging it out and I've been searching. There's nothing."

Numbness crept up Faith's legs and she wobbled. "Can you re-enter me?"

"Fraid not, luv," said one of the thugs. "Entry deadline was last week. You know that."

Aye, she knew that, and she'd entered. She was vaguely aware of the bright sunshine still pouring down on the day, but now it carried an ominous taint.

The boys moved off and Faith showed Mrs. Smythe and her daughter the evidence of tampering. By this time she was near tears—it reminded her all too much of that other defeat she'd had at Ewan's hands. She was sure now that he was behind this, since his bike had been here last night—but there was no way to prove it and an accusation would only make her look silly. *All that work, wasted…*

"That's really too bad," said the girl, and knelt down beside her while she vainly tried to prop up her model. "I'm Sarah, by the way. Will you show me how this works?"

Faith smiled. "Glad to. See here, the trays are watered from a central source, and the sloped beds give more surface area…"

5

mariah

July 2079

The dog padded along a flaking alley wall in the densest part of Belfast, fossicking in occasional piles of garbage and keeping his eyes peeled for smaller scavengers. Already tonight he'd dined on two bony mice, but it was not enough, never could be. Square buildings rose overhead on each side. Their windows were cracked and dark, the inhabitants righteously asleep. A scrabbling sound came from some distance ahead, maybe a rat. The dog's mouth watered at the thought and he trotted silently towards it, finally rounding a lopsided bin—and almost into the arms of two cyborgs sitting on stairs to a boarded-up door.

"Whoa there," one said in a surprisingly normal-sounding voice.

"It's just a dog."

"Yeah, he must be hungry."

"No kidding. Here, boy." The man stretched out a metal hand, then regarded it in the glint of a row of small lights that shone from his forehead.

"I suppose all this is a bit off-putting."

The other cyborg, a woman, rummaged in a pocket of her cargo pants. "Hold on there…yes!" She pulled out a hunk of bread and stood slowly. After setting it carefully on the ground some distance from the stairs, she retreated and sat again.

"Are ye mad? That food was for you."

"I had enough."

The other only shook his head. The dog sat on his haunches for the longest time, smelling the metal in their bodies, but also smelling the human sweat and blood and tears as well as the tantalising aroma of the bread that lay on the ground between them. The cyborgs did not move.

A howl in the distance; the dog turned in that direction, ears perked up high. The packs were far away this night, none of his concern. He huffed out a small sigh and stepped towards the bread. He picked it up, eyed the guards who were still as inoffensive as a child, and finally backed off just a little before settling down to eat.

The bread was hard, but it didn't matter. He held it in his paws on the ground and gnawed on it with strong teeth, all the while keeping a close watch on the cyborgs.

The woman grunted her pleasure that he ate, then turned to her companion. "Quiet tonight."

"Aye, thank Jaysus. I dinna like having to chase people down." His gaze took on a haunted veil.

"You're right about that. How many d'you reckon you've kilt?"

A pause. "Me, personally?"

"No, yer great-aunt Hilda. Of course you personally, ya git."

"I dinna like to count, but…I do anyway." He hung his head. "At least fifty. Though I don't rightly know how many we did fer in the riot of '77."

"True enough."

"An' yerself?"

"Meself what?"

"How many?"

A long pause. "Couple hundred over these five years. I must be heartless. Children, too, when their parents were caught shirking or stealing, them's the rules, same if a Senate employee tries to do a runner, line 'em all up and shoot 'em."

"Me, I try to let the wee-uns make a run for it."

"Yer a good man, Shane."

"No, no I ain't, and that's the truth."

"Pshaw. At least yer tryin' to stay human. Me, I gave up when they implanted me." She flipped open the top of her finger to reveal a gun barrel. "I'm just a killin' machine."

"Oh, Fiona, that's not true."

"Aye, we all do what we have to."

He clutched a crucifix that hung from his neck, and it made a clatter on his metal fingers. "I wish we'd had another choice."

"It was this or die, was it not?"

"I amn't sure this was the better of the two." Shane sighed.

Fiona reached her hand of flesh to Shane's real one and clutched it; the movement was so sudden that the dog cocked his head to the side with a growl.

Shane lifted her hand and stared at it in wonderment, then studied her face, which was hard to do because of the wraparound shades that hid her eyes and threw the eerie lights of a heads-up display onto one side of the interior.

She reached up with her other hand and metal clicked on plastic. "I canna take them off. You know they're plugged into the...the socket there."

"It doesn't matter," said Shane, and ran the back of his finger down her cheek, then kissed it. She responded by leaning in to taste his lip.

The dog, having swallowed the last of the bread, watched this strange behaviour for a while, concluding that not all cyborgs had to be completely inhuman. But just then, some implant in Shane's forehead touched some part of Fiona's shades, and there was a flash of light.

Both reeled away, groaning.

Shane leapt to his feet and roared. "Feckin' implants! Feckin' Senate! We kill for you and you can't even let us love! That's it, I quit."

Fiona grabbed at his arm. "But...you can't."

"Oh, really? Watch me." He turned around and stomped off down the alley, turning to wait after a few paces. "Are ye not comin' wi' me?"

Fiona hadn't moved. "Like I said, Shane. Maybe they really did cut out my heart."

Then she raised her finger and shot him in the nose. He teetered and fell heavily, dead before he landed on the cobbles with a metallic crunch.

The dog scrambled to run. He hightailed it back the way he had come, Fiona's sobs the only sound in the silent, inhuman night.

Mariah hid her bike in a ditch away from the road, covering it with dead branches. She edged through a stand of hardy evergreens for several minutes until she reached a small clearing protected by a dip.

It had been a full week since she'd first visited here. Now at last she had time to come again—to ensure the earth stayed damp, to identify and remove any unwanted plants, and to check the progress of the incipient crops. This one was all hers since the team had found several other places to work with.

She pushed through the last branches and stopped short. The clearing was making a strong attempt at new growth; the pumpkin and courgette vines spread across the ground and even into the edges of the forest, and there was some fresh green shooting up though the tilled soil. But the rhubarb plant—for which Mariah had held such high hopes—had wilted fully away. She ran to its now-shapeless hulk and almost wept. Should have checked on it sooner...

The evening light was fading above the treetops. Quiet shadows filled the forest along with the restive evening movements of its smaller dwellers. Somehow they managed to survive in this dearth of green things—of course the gardens like this one would attract them. Indeed, there were significant nibble marks in much of the new growth, rendering it largely inedible. Mariah didn't begrudge them. Mice and squirrels were just trying to survive like anyone else, but it would be nice if they didn't outright kill the plants they were feeding from.

It would be fully dark soon, so she knelt to take care of the weeding while the plants were still visible. She grimaced as she surveyed the mess the animals had made, and then as she tore out the dandelions—they would obstruct the other plants, but they were grand food in themselves and she ate some of the leaves and flowers whilst she worked. The remainder she stuffed in her pocket for later.

She worked steadily until the scraggly rows of spinach, green beans and turnips were clear of weeds. She sat back on the edge of the clearing and surveyed her domain, a shadowy verdance in the dimness. It was so little. Surely, though, it would make a difference for those who ate from it.

Then she stiffened. That was a footstep, a crunching in the pine needles from the direction of the road. She leapt up and bounded across the rows to the black shadows on the other side of the clearing, then drew back into the murky woods until she was fairly certain of remaining unseen if someone should stumble into the garden.

The footsteps grew closer and a figure must surely come into view any second now, but the person stopped just out of view. Mariah held her breath. The slightest rustle drew her attention to the path where she'd entered herself. She had just enough time to hope that her bike was hidden well enough, or at least that the night would keep it from discovery, when the visitor stepped out into the open.

"Mariah?"

"Naomi, is that you?" Mariah emerged from her hiding place and dusted herself off. "You scared the bejeebers out of me."

Naomi laughed softly. "Sorry about that. I hoped you'd be here."

"What's up then, that you need me?"

"I've just come from Groomsport village. Met a family there who's had nothing to eat for a week. Their da's died, and the ma just gave birth. She's got two others under five, too."

Mariah regarded the rows of plants. "D'ya reckon some of this would be ready to take to them?"

Naomi brought out a candle and lit it, cupped the flame with her palm. She crouched down and inspected the plants, wax dripping over her fingers and into the fragile earth. "Yeah, we should be able to take a good bunch of spinach and some turnip greens. Maybe some leaves from the pumpkin plant, if we're careful to avoid the buds."

"I have a heap o' dandelions in my pocket from weeding. They can have those too." Mariah felt in her pocket and her stomach rumbled in protest. But she'd eaten once today already, even if it was just what passed for "lunch". Her thoughts drifted to that poor starving mother and her children. A whole week…she was hungry often enough, but usually only until the next time she went to work.

Naomi held out a cloth bag. Mariah dumped the dandelions in, and by candlelight the two girls set about pinching off the biggest spinach leaves, a few from the pumpkin vine, with parts of the turnip tops, leaving the roots to carry on growing underground.

The bag was nearly full when Naomi straightened. "This is a good start. We don't want to deplete the harvest."

Mariah finished by emptying her water bottles in a wide zig-zag over the valiantly struggling patch, then she turned and led the way back out towards her bike and the long road to Groomsport.

"You're sure this is the place?" Mariah squinted at the hovel, at least half a mile east from the far edge of Groomsport proper. Moonlight peeping through shredded clouds illuminated several shells of mobile homes scattered around the vicinity. Some were clearly inhabited despite, in a few cases, the lack of a roof or wall. Their target's home was not one of these but a ramshackle hut built of broken pieces of flotsam and wrapped with ratty tarpaulins. The valley lay open to the sea, glistering night waves crashing on the pebbly beach not far away.

Naomi nodded. "Yeah. They've been here since their da died and they canna pay for a real house." She stooped to the opening that might serve as a window, and called out. "Hello?"

There was a scuffle inside, and a baby cried out weakly. A door opened—if it could be said to be a door, since it was only a board leaned against a large hole. Skinny hands shoved it to one side, and a sharply angled face peered out, worried at first, then melting into relief.

"Thank goodness it's you. I thought you were pulling my leg when you said you'd get food."

Naomi held out the cloth bag. "It's not much, but it should help fill you tonight."

The woman snatched it and held it in the doorway for a moment. "Does it have to be cooked?"

"It'll taste better if you cook it. You can eat it raw too, just be sure to chew it well so every shred can be digested. Either way, you'll need to destring the pumpkin leaves so it's not like eating thorns."

The woman's face went blank. Obviously she'd never eaten pumpkin leaves before. Mariah caught movement below—two little pale faces stared up at Naomi.

"Come in and share it with us," said their mother. "I know it cudden' have come cheaply."

"Oh, we couldn't," said Mariah.

"I insist."

Naomi gave the smallest of shrugs and moved to step inside. Mariah followed. The place was tiny, stinky, and blacker than the night outside except for the fire that struggled beneath a smoke-hole in the roof. The baby cried again; the mother caressed its hollow cheek. "I'll have some milk for you after this, m'love."

Mariah sat herself down on the damp dirt floor as best she could. The children settled opposite, their haunted eyes unsmiling in the firelight's flicker.

Naomi accepted the bag from the mother and reached in. She withdrew a large pumpkin leaf and set about demonstrating how to remove the stringy bits on the underside that carried the majority of the tiny prickles. Mariah took another and slowly stripped it of thorns to give to one of the children. Hopefully the mother wouldn't notice in the dark that her guests were not eating. She passed the bag to the children and smiled to herself as they seized large handfuls of easy-to-eat spinach. Finally, the mother took the bag almost reverently, admonished her children to chew each bite fifty times, and stuffed several dandelion leaves into her mouth. They would take a while to chew to a pulp, but would remove hunger for a time. The children counted on their fingers and giggled.

Mariah watched the family eat. Her own stomach was empty, but her insides were strangely warm. *This* was what they'd begun the Guild's work to do.

❧❧❧❧❧

Weeks passed. The dozen members of the Guild became two dozen, and they crept about the countryside in the dimness of evening, caring for little gardens that produced good quantities thanks to the bio-mould Naomi provided. Soil quality improved from the weeds they left to die. Harvests increased. Soon the turnips and potatoes were ready, followed by other vegetables that took longer to ripen. Bags and baskets were passed through

47

half-open doors in the dead of night, families cried their gratitude, and there was enough for the Guildspeople themselves to make an occasional meal together. The mood around town lifted as hunger lessened a little. People whispered of the mysterious benefactors who left food on doorsteps.

Mariah leaned against the rough wall and observed the crowd in the basement. It wasn't much they could do. But it was something, it was being felt, and it raised the power of hope.

Naomi touched her shoulder and beckoned. "Come upstairs. I have something to show you."

"Sure." Mariah took the proffered hand and hauled herself upright, then followed her friend up and out of the wardrobe, up the main flight and into Deborah's unused back bedroom. A decrepit iron-framed bed sagged in the corner, its stuffing hanging out of a rip and disintegrating into dust. The room was cast in the reflected gold of evening light and even a few sparkles from the petulant sea. Mariah drank in the sight of the water for a moment.

Naomi sat on the drooping mattress and lifted the flap on her canvas backpack, then hesitated. "You won't tell anyone about this yet? The time will come, but it's not now."

Mariah watched intently as Naomi reached inside the bag and brought out an object covered with a scrappy but clean plastic bag. A strangely familiar smell wafted into her nose and activated her tastebuds. Naomi removed the covering and revealed the impossible: a slice of red fruit that filled both her hands and, for all the world, looked like it had been cut from a giant strawberry.

Mariah looked up at Naomi's face and down again to the fruit. "Is—is that real?"

"Yeah. Grew in my bedroom overnight."

"Overnight?"

"There were seven of them. Seven strawberries. All this big. Since last night."

Mariah reached out a finger, stroked the knobbly red skin. "Your fertiliser. You made one that works faster. Bloody hell. How did you do it?"

"I've been staying after hours, combining loads of different viruses and things with the basic fertiliser."

"Ohhh. Your boss doesn't know." The seriousness of the situation became clear.

"Here, let's eat this. I don't want to waste it." Naomi held it up and gave a small smile.

"But the others downstairs—"

"They've got plenty for now. I'll tell them about this soon enough." Naomi split the piece in half with her thumbs and handed one over. "I'm sorry it's a bit rubbery. I didn't water it enough."

"Pshaw. Don't worry." Mariah turned it over in her hands. It was heavier than she expected, but was every bit like an ordinary strawberry except for the size. A memory came to mind. "You brought me strawberries once before."

"Much smaller." They both grinned, and raised the fruit as if it were a toast.

It was all Mariah could do to keep herself from oohing and aahing at the taste. True, it was a bit dry, a bit bland, like Naomi had said, but it was real. At least, she hoped it was real and this wasn't just some convoluted dream.

She raised her eyes to the window and blinked at the sunshine sparkling on the sea. Swallowed and took another guilty bite. She turned to Naomi again and was about to speak when the light changed and she was drawn to the ocean again—now suddenly dark with the threat of an ominous black cloud that had swept in over them.

A frisson of foreboding ran through her and she gulped, the strawberry like ash in her mouth. If food crops grew overnight...if they gave such huge harvests...

It would change everything.

⚜

The Guild gathered again a couple of nights later. Mariah braced herself for the uproar Naomi's announcement would cause. They'd been spreading the word among the others that they should bring a sealed container, but without giving further clues as to what it was for. Mariah crouched in her customary corner, clutching an old, cracked plant pot that was anything but sealed and not particularly clean either. Ah well, hopefully it would do.

Naomi duly explained that this was a new type of fertiliser, and dished out a wee bit of foamy stuff into everyone's containers. She made a face at Mariah's plant pot, but dribbled a dram into it anyway.

49

The others continued to line up and Mariah returned to the corner, peering into the bottom of her makeshift container. The foam swelled up and fizzed even now.

But there was more…in the crack, where the dirt had accumulated, something green sprouted. She was sure it hadn't been there before. It wavered and grew a smidge more before her very eyes. She blinked and refocused. It grew even more.

Naomi gave out some of the substance to one more person and shut her container. Mariah was about to call out to her, but she happened to glance down at the flowerpot again. Green leaves shot up its inside walls, moving with a life all their own. "Look," she called out. "It's doing it already!"

People gathered round and she handed off the freakily multiplying dandelion—the leaves were now big enough to recognise—and she smiled at Naomi while the others passed it around. "Must have been some seed in the cracks."

The plant pot returned to her hands and she stared, both aghast and delighted while a stem appeared. Then a bud. Then it opened, a fully blooming golden flower.

"Oh, Naomi," she whispered, "what have you done?"

***

Before she left Deborah's basement, Mariah had fished out a computer chip holder that now contained a properly sealed bit of scummy fertiliser for her garden at home. She also still had the flowerpot, and in it the foam rose up and threatened to spill. She ran out to her bike, threw herself aboard and launched down the street with the flowerpot in one hand. Someone had eaten the dandelion and most of its leaves, but it was already growing again.

It wasn't like she could just throw this stuff around willy-nilly. Yes, they had all agreed to spread it, but it made most sense to do so in places where food was already growing. She struggled to remember who had been growing gardens along her route home. She took a guess and shuddered to a halt, then dumped some of the foam over a dilapidated fence. And the neighbour's for good measure.

The ride home took her twice as long as usual, with the stops every few houses where there might be some kind of chance that it could provide food.

Dandelions were universal, of course—you could eat the whole plant, and even where the soil had been too dead to let them grow, she was sure there were plenty of dandelion seeds about that would activate now and provide a lovely surprise for people all along the streets she passed through.

She rolled down past the haunts of C. S. Lewis, through Crawfordsburn with its old half-timbered public house and all its fine homes, whose residents also hungered and were in dire need of this thing she gave them under cover of darkness. Continuing on, she skipped the speedy but desolate highway, taking instead the route through the intricate urban tangle of homes and peering over walls to discover where something very hardy might still be growing. She did her best to avoid coming to a dead end at a Peace Wall and only had to turn around twice in the maze.

She passed through the poorest areas of town, where the tightly-packed houses became more and more decrepit with age and abuse, with missing bricks, broken windows, and plastic bags precariously affixed over holes in the roof. Surely the concrete yards here would prevent any kind of growth—but no, weeds still clung to cracks, so she let them have the treatment too.

Finally she reached her own home. It was late and no candlelight showed. Her father would be long asleep by now. Silently she leaned her bike against the house, and moved to where she had buried a couple of dried-up but self-sprouting potatoes. She tipped the flowerpot and poured goop onto the earth. She tipped some more. She upended the flowerpot, set it back some distance away, then plucked several dandelion heads and a clutch of leaves that had grown in it while she pedalled. But there would be fertiliser on them. She had forgotten to ask Naomi whether that was a bad thing to eat or not, so she figured she had better wash them before she ate them.

Better yet, she would wash them and leave them for someone else to eat in the morning. She had had a couple of meals today, of sorts. Although…there would be absolutely *tons* of new dandelions grown outside by morning.

She shut the door quietly and ran the greens under the kitchen tap, then considered that tomorrow everything would be different.

Then she ate every last scrap of her dandelions. Tough and bitter though they were, she was grateful for them, for she would not have to sleep hungry like so often. She fell exhausted into bed in her little cubby at the top of the stairs. A soft nose pushed into her hand and she fondled Jemima's ears. With the collie beside her, she lay awake a long time, half-imagining she could hear the plants growing outside her window.

The deep blackness of a candleless night enveloped the bunkhouse and its mostly sleeping inhabitants. Darian lay awake, thoughts churning in his head—mostly about Andi. She was as kind to him as anyone could possibly be under the circumstances, where she was supposed to be his slave-driver. He still dreamed of going home, but increasingly the dream included taking Andi home to meet his father and sister.

Wide awake, he huffed out a breath and swung upright. Sometimes there was no point in trying. He drew the door open, wincing at the creak, but aside from a stirring in one of the beds, no one made a sound. Darian exited into the starless night and slapped his elbows against the evening chill. He paced a little this way and that, then set off between the two rows of huts. Not much of a walk, but it was all he had.

His worn-out sandshoes pinged in the dusty gravel, the only sound in this whole night. Oh, perhaps a branch rustled far off in the hills, but the lack of wind now echoed the same calm that enveloped his way of life in this place. It wasn't so bad. For a prison, that is.

He reached the end of the housing and turned around to come back. He'd walk until his mind, too, reflected calm. Step. Step. Step.

He paused. A footfall not his own. "Who's there?" he whispered, eyes wide and sucking in the empty black of the night.

A shadow separated itself from a building and approached. Even though his eyes were completely adjusted to the dark, Darian could make out no detail until she was right upon him. "Andi!"

"Cudden' sleep? Me neither." No trace of the workday boss in her tone.

He didn't know what to say. "Walking helps."

"Then let's walk." She headed off, a blob of slightly blacker black.

Darian hurried to catch up, then realised she was leading him away from the houses and towards the fields. He'd never been this way at night. "You're not going to get in trouble for sneaking out with me?"

"Naww." Doubt in her voice. "Who's to know, anyway?"

We hope.

They passed between the high fences of field after field. Darian had not come this far since the day of his arrival. His nocturnal walks had so far taken him only around the dormitories where he was theoretically free to wander. But this time, eventually they reached the main gate of the camp. He remembered coming in here, six or seven years ago now, bright-eyed at the expectation of working for real food in decent quantities again. He had soon been disembarrassed of that notion.

They came near the gate. Darian placed his palms on it and peered through the cracks between its metal panels. Outside…was nothing. Just as black as anything else tonight. Perhaps that was the vague outline of the quiet road winding away between the hills. Nothing else.

He turned around and sank down with his back against it. Often he was able to forget, but this made it plainly clear that he was not allowed to go home. Movement and a slight rattle at his side told him Andi now sat on the ground beside him.

Darian tilted his head backwards to lean on the gate and surveyed the unlit clouds. "I wish I could go home."

"Me too."

Silence flooded in for another moment, and he turned to where her face must be. "Wait. You mean you can't leave either?"

A movement flung a strand of her hair across his nose. Golden-brown hair, he remembered. "No. I was drafted just like anyone. But I'm too skinny for the physical work, so they made me into a monster."

"They did *not.* You're the kindest, gentlest person on these fields." He thought she turned her head away. "You seriously can't just walk out of here?"

"No."

"Then…then we're the same."

A petite hand explored him for a minute before finding his fingers and resting there. "Yes, we are."

The shock of her touch raised his heartrate sky-high. So she *did* like him. He wrestled with his passion, but failed miserably. Except he wasn't miserable. All of the pent-up longing and yearning now found a way out. He grabbed at the air where he imagined she would be. *Contact.* He found his hands running up her back, her shoulders, her face, while she gripped his upper arms.

Nose to nose, he paused. His own breath bounced back into his face and the scent of her sent fireworks through his being. "Do you want this?"

This time, he felt her nod and she eased into the kiss. It was long, and dizzying, and went straight to his head, just as it should. When at long last they pulled back to breathe a little, she seized his hand and hugged it to herself. He buried his face in her hair and inhaled.

Some time later, a sound roused him from his bliss. His fingers were deep in her tresses, his face in her neck, but something wasn't right. He withdrew and sat up.

"What is it?" Andi scrambled upright, still clutching his hand.

"Company!" he hissed, and pulled away, searching for some place to hide. It was impossible. The track was wide and straight between the fences, and led only to this gate. There was no way to remain undiscovered. Unless...*escape?* He clawed at the face of the gate; the only handhold was a lock?—handle?—something set into the door at about waist height. If he leapt just right...He backed off for a run-up. Stride—stride—jump-kick —carry it forward. His toe caught on the protrusion just like he wanted, and he used the momentum to lift himself up higher. He slammed into the metal and his raised hands just snagged the very top of the barrier. He jiggled to get a better grip and reached a hand down for Andi.

Light from distant hand-held torches now played across them, so he caught sight of her terrified face as she strained to reach his fingers. "Come on, you can make it!"

Her short stature played against her. She vaulted again and again, once brushing his fingertips but unable to get a grip. She stepped back and raised her head to him. "You go on. I'll be all right, I'll tell them I nearly caught you."

Leave? When he'd only just found her? No way.

Darian shimmied around, teetered, let himself drop to the ground. He landed on hands and knees. "Quick, get me in a headlock. Now!"

She did so, faster than he dreamed possible, and squeezed his neck like she meant business. Her training kicked in, he supposed, but she didn't *really* have to throttle him...He gasped and struggled in her iron grip.

The lights approached, almost blinding after the hours of empty night, and Darian tried to see which guards had come.

Andi answered that for him, at least in part. "Encian Jack, thank goodness you're here. He'd have got away from me."

He made a convincing attempt to escape her hold, only letting her regain control at the last moment. He glared at Encian.

Encian strode up and cuffed him in the side of the head. "Come on, back to bed with you. This's worth overtime for a month, you know."

He knew.

∗ ∗ ∗

Mariah woke with a start. Something was wrong…no, something was changing…something had happened. Shreds of a surreal dreamworld clung to her fuzzy brain a little longer, until she became fully aware.

The fertiliser! She shot out of her warm chrysalis and rushed to the window. The entire back garden was an efflorescent mess of leaves: the lighter ones topped with dandelion blossoms, and the darker ones that slunk along the ground, those were the potatoes.

She hurried to dress and crashed out through the front door, then moved carefully through the waving greenery and peered down to see where a potato might be. Then she tripped and fell face first into the dirt. At least it hadn't rained the past couple of days. She rolled herself into a sitting position and reached under the leaves to find what she had stubbed her toe on.

A rough surface met her fingers. Scaly yet solid, rounded with large knobbles. She pulled leaves away. A giant potato lay half-buried in the sod and half-exposed to the elements. It must be two feet long, though its shape was more like several rugby balls joined together.

Surely it couldn't be the only one. She groped around and found another, then a third. Too much for just her and Da to eat. She unearthed one and carried it to her bike, then balanced it on the back carrier and strapped it there with string wrapped several times around a piece of sacking to hide it. The second one she dragged up the steps and propped against the kitchen cupboard. The last? She'd need to deal with it later, make sure it was distributed.

On second thought, she scribbled a note. Through the gap in the dried-up hedge, she tucked it in the crack of the neighbour's door. The grandfather who was too old to work would come and take care of the extra food. In times like these nothing would be wasted. Not ever.

Mariah turned to the corner where she'd left the dirty flowerpot last night. It was gone. Gone from view, at least—several square feet of space were covered by a growing mound of scum, with weeds running rampant around its edges. This stuff was going to be hard to get rid of. Back inside the house, she searched out a proper lidded container so she could transport a small quantity.

She set off on her bike, slowed by the extra weight of the giant spud. As she turned onto a main road, her mind worked to remember the addresses of the needy who lived near her route: those who were old, or sick, or families with many young children. She took a left, coasted for a block, made a right and pulled into a front garden before drawing out a knife to carve off a family-sized hunk of potato. "Here goes, then."

The inhabitants of the house had already spied her, and the door flew open as she raised her hand to knock. The old housewife eyed Mariah with suspicion. "What do ye want?"

"Uh…to give you this." Mariah thrust the chunk of spud at the lady, who did not reach to accept it.

"This be some new government trick to make us ill."

"No! No, it's not, I grew it in my own garden."

There was movement in the dark hallway and a hunched man loomed into view. His eyes gleamed and grew wide at the sight of the food. He shoved past his wife to seize it with both hands. "We'll not be saying no to food, luv."

Mariah backed away.

The woman scowled at her husband, then sighed, and finally shrugged. Her gnarled finger raised high. "If'n we're harmed by that there tater…I will find you and I will…"

Her last word was lost as the husband slammed the door. Mariah blinked and continued on her way.

It was later than usual when Mariah dragged herself through Deborah's front gate that evening. Her container of goop had expanded again while she worked, and she'd whispered news of it to those of her colleagues she trusted. Perhaps some of them would come here tonight to carry the fertiliser home. Along the way she'd stopped again and again to pour from her own reserves into the pathetic gardens that people had tried to coax into life. Well, they'd be very living before long.

She pushed her bike around to the back of the house and slipped in the unlocked door, then cracked open the wardrobe. A stuffy aroma rose up to meet her along with a rumble of chatter. Must be a crowd all right.

The two doors safely shut behind her, Mariah groped her way down into the basement proper and blinked in the dim candlelight. The room was filled beyond capacity. She searched for familiar faces and spied Deborah grimacing in a corner. *Poor old dear, this probably isn't what she thought she was agreeing to.*

Then again, none of them would have expected *this*. She gulped. Just then, Peter, Liam and Naomi pushed through the crowd towards her. Naomi wore a thunderous frown.

"They came here to get fertiliser," said Peter. Everyone carried a container. But they weren't small ones like she and her friends had used. They were buckets and basins.

"They want me to fill up all of those," Naomi said. "I tried to tell them just a little bit will be plenty, that those bowls will be full in a matter of hours from a dab of fertiliser, but they're not happy. They want more and they want it now, and I don't have it."

Mariah shook her head. Some in the room wore grim expressions and others gesticulated angrily. It wouldn't be pretty if they got out of control. "Explain it to them again," she said. "Maybe it'll sink in this time."

Mariah clapped for hush. "Friends, we welcome you to this meeting of the Guild. We'll start distributing fertiliser in a moment—"

A short, skinny little woman shoved her bucket in Mariah's face. "And where'll ye be gettin' enough to fill all these?"

Others echoed her sentiment.

Mariah patted the air with both hands. "Listen, I've seen this thing in action. If we fill those buckets, the foam will grow and spill out all the way home. Now we don't want that, do we?"

A subdued muttering. Perhaps they were listening to her, so she went on. "Believe me when I say a wee bit in your bucket will expand to fill it by morning." She sighed. "In fact, it never stops growing."

Peter and Liam stood ready with their containers of slime. Mariah pointed at them and Naomi. "Make four lines, everyone! This could take a while, please be patient."

She took her place beside them and dosed a dribble of fertiliser into the short woman's bucket.

"You're sure about the growing?"

Mariah nodded. "Absolutely."

"If you say so, then." She shuffled off towards the stairs, and another bucket was shoved in front of Mariah.

"Thanks," said Naomi, off to her left.

"For what?"

"Making them listen."

"Oh."

"I'm just thankful it worked."

"True enough." Mariah poured and poured, then waited a little for her scum to grow back, then poured and poured again.

There would be no more going back.

Near the end of the week, Mariah made her regular trip to her assigned Guild garden. Since starting to use the fertiliser, it produced far more food than she could carry away in one trip, so she prepared herself mentally for several rides back and forth to the homes of the people who needed this. There would be a lot of dead plants to weed out, too—they'd soon discovered the fertiliser killed its host after a few days of rabid growth. Mariah sighed at the waste, then set to, dragging the dead material into the woods. When she finished, her back ached, but the garden was respectable, with plenty of plants erupting from the earth to replace those that were lost.

She loaded up her new, taller back basket with a giant turnip and the side panniers with enormous spinach leaves that had to be rolled up to fit in. Curious, she tore off a strip and tasted it, then grimaced. The leaves had grown too large to be palatable. But she guessed they were still nutritious. She stuffed a misshapen carrot into each pannier to balance the weight, then tied her sack over the top. Not that she really needed to hide any more. Sights like this were becoming more commonplace, although she still wouldn't like the authorities to spot her cargo.

Swinging into her seat, she pondered who would need this food the most. Then it came to her. The grandparents caring for wee ones in that bunker near Helen's Bay…where she'd taken the handful of treasured strawberries Naomi had once brought her before any of this had started. Surely they would be glad of the help.

She pushed off and pedalled hard, grunting at the extra weight. Guilt washed over her that she hadn't considered those poor people before now. *My stupid brain, forgetting the most important thing.* Sure, it was farther off the beaten track than most people lived. But she had even been to Helen's Bay on her last rest day, with Naomi, and didn't bring food. She should have remembered.

The road was long and her burdens heavy. Across dead hills and fields, then city fringes, and through the silent suburbs she whooshed, certain these walls also held hungry individuals even though satiety was spreading like a slow fire through the city—but she would stay with her goal.

Finally she rattled down the beach access road and dismounted. A chill blew in off the waves; the sea was choppy this afternoon, and a spatter of rain pelted her. Dark clouds made it seem later than it really was. She slung the two pannier bags over her shoulders by their straps; she'd have to return for the turnip. A trudge along the sand brought her to the same mysterious wooded pathway up the promontory where she'd visited before.

A child's screeching echoed ahead. Mariah smiled. There was good strength in that voice. She approached the bunker's opening—a leftover from a long-ago war, it provided a barely adequate shelter for these souls. "Hello?"

Several children ran up but stopped short. They were thin, possessed of good colour but some were streaked with tears.

Then an old man loomed up behind them in the dim interior. He balanced the screaming toddler on his hip. "It's you, come to taunt us with your gifts. Well, you're too late."

"Too late?"

He scowled. "My wife was poorly and suffered the most from the hunger. Two days ago I wandered far and wide to find something for her to eat, and someone gave me some of this miracle fertiliser. We used it and had plenty of bitter wild greens by the next day, but my Aggie was too far gone. If

59

we'd had the food sooner…"

No—

One of the little girls clung to a bigger sister and stared up at Mariah with huge, sad eyes. "Granny went to heaven today."

"I—uh…" Mariah reached for one of her bags and opened the flap. "I'm so sorry. Can I give you these carrots?"

"Begone!" The grandfather stepped forward, and the child he carried glared at Mariah. She stepped back and stumbled on the rough track, landing hard on her rear and the palms of her hands. The spinach and carrot fell out of the bag, but she wasn't about to collect them up. Surely the food would be eaten.

Under the condemning stares of the remaining family, she got her feet under her and jogged away back down the path to the beach.

⧉⧉⧉⧉⧉

Mariah's hands hurt. She'd rinsed them in the sea while the weather eased, but now she doubted the wounds were still clean. The physical pain brought more guilt, more horror at what her forgetfulness had caused.

Petrichor rose up in the wake of the rain, but she was unable to enjoy its heady fragrance, amplified by the enormous quantity of newly-grown and recently expired greenery that exploded, tangled, from every corner bearing a trace of dirt. In some places, vines crawled over fences and up house walls, covered leaky roofs, shaded cracked windows and jammed rickety doors. Huge wet leaves reflected sparkles of white light from the cloudy sky, and front gardens fairly heaved with produce.

Now everyone had plenty of veggies growing, whether outdoors or in containers inside. Mariah had even taken to going door to door in one of the poorest streets, but only succeeded in giving away the giant carrot. "That'll add some nice flavour to my stew," said the droopy lady who took it off her hands.

She exited the wildly overgrown front yard, taking care not to trip over any of the thick tendrils that wove their mat across it, and wilted down beside her bike. She'd noticed the absences at work. People no longer needed that little bit of slop any more. The Guild, so newly-formed, was no longer needed in the newfound ubiquity of growing things—yet this had been their

60

aspiration from the start.

I've gotta talk to Naomi. Everything was upside down. Mariah heaved her protesting body aboard the saddle once more and set off for Finaghy.

It took her the best part of an hour to cross town. This time she stayed away from the centre city, suddenly unwilling to see what chaos the fertiliser might have caused there. So she pedalled through the suburban streets, one yard's jungle at times barely distinct from the next, the homes drowning in organic matter both living and dead and many inhabitants gleefully harvesting the crops with the coming of night. They smiled and waved at her, a thing unheard of until only recently—but she set her face ahead, grim in her quest. The faces of Aggie's widower and the crying children floated ever before her mind's eye.

She found her way to Naomi's street and pulled up outside the tiny house. Clutching the remaining bitter spinach in her one hand and the turnip in the other, she knocked with difficulty.

A curtain twitched at the little window beside the door, then the locks clicked and Naomi's father looked out. "Mariah! Thank goodness you've come."

"Why, what's going on?"

He pointed through the doorway at the end of the kitchen. "Naomi's in her room."

There was something he wasn't telling her. And he sagged like someone had died. Her thoughts whipped back to Aggie. *No…*

Naomi's elderly mother watched Mariah from the settee that also served for a bed. The only bedroom—Naomi's—adjoined this room, and Mariah paused, her hand on the doorframe.

Naomi sat on the narrow bed and stared blankly out the window. On the desk, a broken glass globe hunkered in a larger plastic pot of soil, lifeless strawberry leaves cascading from the ephemeral creeper. A folded piece of printed paper lay beside it. At Mariah's gentle throat-clearing, Naomi rubbed her eyes and smiled. "I'm glad to see you," she said.

Mariah forgot about her earlier consternation at there being too much food. *What a silly problem, anyway.* "Tell me what's up."

"I got a letter yesterday from the World Senate in America. They—they found out it was me and they ordered me to go. To America. They want me to explain myself to them."

Mariah grabbed the letter and read its terse lines. The bottom fell out of her world. Aggie's death might pursue her forever, but she wouldn't tell Naomi. Not now.

6

ꜰᴀɪᴛʜ

2009

Faith sat in her room at sunset, too engrossed in her work to get up and switch on the light. The flickering screen before her held the culmination of her life's work.

It was perfect. She bubbled inside—it was all she could do to keep from dancing. Sure, it needed some finesse on the programming side, but she hoped this version was enough to win some funding.

Sarah had been cheering her on in the years since they met; every spare moment was spent on the work, yet Faith made an effort to go to Sarah's house and deliberately do nothing in particular from time to time. The two had become familiar over the years even if Faith stopped short of claiming they were good friends. The relationship was far too uneven for that. Faith felt she was expected to listen more, tolerate more, give more than her counterpart ever gave back. Maybe it was just a personality thing.

Sigh. *I'm too intense for my own good.*

She closed her eyes for a long moment and leaned back in her chair, hands clasped behind her head. She squinted at the flat ceiling, featureless except for the solid blue lampshade affixed in the exact centre.

As she straightened, stretching her back, her gaze crept over the familiar objects in the room, still bold and bright in the final glow of the day. Blocks of plain colours characterised the square furniture—a boxy black-framed bed, cubic green dresser, and tall blue bookcase. The red desk faced the western window, beyond which the sun rapidly approached the horizon.

"Her" piece of sea, the sliver visible from here, commenced its regular evening glow between the hills and promontories to the west of Bangor, where the Lough of Belfast narrowed down towards its city. Faith peered at the familiar sight, just like last night's sunset, and the one before, and every one she had ever watched from her lifelong home.

She smiled. It was a daily gift just for her. Even if it rained during the day, by sundown it had always cleared up. Bangor was a beautiful place to live.

Faith returned her attention to the contents of her computer and scanned the details of her proposal one more time. It was the same land use system she'd come up with years before for growing food—half raised beds and half stacked hydroponics, switching around each year. Now she'd added one final ingredient: solar panels to power the irrigation pumps so that the whole thing was self-contained and self-watering, provided the tank stayed full. And with the amount of rain wont to fall on Ireland, it was a given. If the system was to be used in drier countries, the tanks would have to be topped up regularly, but that was another issue altogether. Perhaps she'd tackle that later.

She was applying for a government grant which she planned to use for hiring a programmer. The entire system could feasibly be reduced by someone with the proper skills to a user-friendly phone app, where a farmer could enter land measurements and desired crops, then be instructed how to go about planting them in the most efficient manner possible. That was what she wanted: abundant harvests aided at the grassroots level.

Suddenly she found herself clutching her stomach and laughing until she cried. With some hard work and distribution, this system might actually make a difference to world hunger. *That* was what she lived for.

She raised her head, checked her application one more time, and hovered over the *Send* button. The sun plunged behind the hills and tinted the nearby ocean with vermilion. A grin crept over her face.

Click.

The buzz of many voices echoed around the industrial exhibition centre, currently home to a weekend agricultural trade fair. The giant ventilation pipes above and the foil ceiling took nothing away from the style and polish of what went on below. Faith had her very own booth—an idea that took some getting used to, until she tired of mooching around looking at her own displays and sallied forth to introduce herself to some of the suits who wandered the aisles. Sarah read her book whilst swinging one foot from the bar stool in the back corner, strangely detached. It must be a really good book, Faith thought, and turned back to her passing audience.

"The funding grant allowed me to build a user interface, which can be used on nearly any device someone might have," she explained to the current client, who'd said he was the vice-president of a startup farming supply franchise. If his distribution network took on her product, it could go nationwide very quickly. She tapped the screen which brought up a crisp 3D diagram of a sample planting pattern, and tried to keep the tremors out of her voice. "See here, it tells the farmer exactly how to follow the technique."

"Impressive," said the young man. "How old did you say you were?"

"I didn't say. I'm seventeen." Faith chuckled.

"Well, you can certainly be proud of this accomplishment. I think it would be a good fit for our range. My boss will be here any minute—he's the one we have to convince." He waggled his eyebrows conspiratorially then took out his phone and turned away to make a call.

Faith slipped back to where Sarah watched. "What do you think?"

"Sounds like a done deal." Sarah said and returned to her book.

Faith smiled. "I hope you're right."

The vice-president peered at his watch, then along the aisle, and smiled. "Here he is now."

Faith followed his gaze to a suited entourage approaching at speed. Recognised the face of the large man on point. Her guts turned to jelly. *Ewan.*

He sneered at Faith and scowled at his second-in-command. "Roger, what the hell are you playing at? We don't do business with *children*." His voice lowered and he mumbled out of the side of his mouth for her benefit alone. "Especially not this child."

"But—but, Ewan—"

"Shut up, Roger. This youngster'll never come to anything." Ewan strode off, dragging Roger by the jacket sleeve.

"Ye canna treat a woman like that," Roger said.

"I'll do as I wish." Ewan's voice carried all the way from the end of the aisle. "And you'll keep your opinion to yourself if you want to hold onto your job."

Faith clenched her fists and squeezed her eyes shut over the sudden tears, hoping irrationally that this was a nightmare and she was still in her bed at home. Seconds later, Sarah's hands gripped her shoulders. "Flamin' eedjit. He's got no right to speak so."

"You don't understand. That's the same Ewan as kept me from entering the school science fair that time."

"And isn't that the same bully as ripped up your garden when you were wee?"

"Aye, that he is."

"How is this even possible? Wasn't he in your class?"

"Only because he had to repeat three times. After the third fail, he quit school. I guess he's twenty now. Old enough to start a business." Faith let out a sob. "Come on, let's pack up. I want to go home."

"But the fair isn't over yet. You might get a really good customer if we stay."

"I—I can't! Look at me." Faith was sure she looked a wreck, all red-eyed and blotchy.

"Nothing some paper towels and a wee bit o' cold water won't fix. I'll be right back, don't you worry about a thing."

Sarah walked away, but Faith thought she might leave anyway. Sneak off now before her friend returned. It was cowardly, yes, but she couldn't risk facing her nemesis again. She blinked and caught sight of Roger approaching. She scrambled to her feet. If Ewan was with him…

But he wasn't. Roger smiled weakly. "Look, I'm really sorry. I haven't been working with him for very long and I've never seen him behave that way before. I had no idea he had such a nasty streak. I think I'm going to give him my notice. If he wants to be a bully, he can be by himself."

Faith didn't have it in her to smile, but if one person got away from Ewan, perhaps today's humiliation might have a redeeming factor. She shook his hand in a daze and watched him walk away.

Moments later, Sarah ran up with a fistful of paper towels and a cup of ice water from the dispenser. "Was that Roger? What did he want?"

"Oh, he reckons he's going to leave Ewan's company." A smidgen of a smile twitched Faith's lips up at one end. Sarah's laugh carried around the cavernous hall, turning smug-faced heads that craned around from other aluminium-and-plastic booths like long-necked giraffes.

7

MARIAH

AUGUST 2079

Something was amiss in the city. The dog sniffed the air, redolent with decaying greenery. He hid in a brand-new jungle that had freshly appeared on a previously bare patch of earth known as the Mountpottinger Road Green. Now all of a sudden it was green instead of brown, lush instead of muddy. A giant potato rested between his paws and he worked at it with his teeth, freeing small pieces to swallow. He took his time; he was replete for the first time in his memory.

The raw vegetable was all but indigestible for his canine innards, but he had not found any cooked slops today. Even rotting potatoes would have been better, because of the decomposition that broke down cell walls to make the food's content accessible to him, but strangely, there were none in this patch. Someone must be taking care of it. So to answer his hunger, today he ate the potato fresh and his stomach still grew comfortably full.

He ate at his leisure, ignoring the gritty texture. When his stomach finally protested the excess, his eyelids grew heavy and he laid his head down to rest beneath the dancing leaves. In his mind their shadows ebbed and flowed like a tide of threatening figures—cyborgs, a pack of dogs, the family father who'd tried to corner him.

He twitched in his sleep and the neural images shifted to his mother, and himself a pup again, scrambling for her teats in the jumble of his siblings. An instant later his memory failed him and the vision ended. He woke with a start to see a real figure standing nearby. Before he could move, the aged human stumbled into his hiding place.

"Fer feck's sake! Is that one of me taters?"

The dog got his feet under him and his wits about him. The old man was unarmed, but called down curses and flailed his hands. The dog vanished into the bushes and slipped out into the street, heading north in the falling dusk.

After a short distance he turned into Madrid Street and loped along between the terraced houses. The white brickwork around their windows had fallen into disrepair, but the tiny walled front gardens now overflowed with life. At a corner he kept left, staying on the Catholic side—the district called Short Strand was riddled with enclave walls so he soon had to turn left again, finding himself blocked into a maze of dead ends and walls topped with barbed wire.

Fading republican murals decorated the gable ends of house rows, while on the other side, a few tattered Union flags still flew from somewhat more austerely-styled Protestant houses.

Yet another wall across a road prevented further progress. He would have to turn around and go back the way he came. People were appearing in the streets now, having been released from their day's travail, so he kept well away from them.

As the houses filled with voices, so the kitchens filled with good smells. The dog sat imbibing the scents while the sky grew dark and the humans rediscovered what it meant to fill their stomachs. He found his way into a backyard by a gate that someone had left open, and snuck into a shed to shelter overnight.

A short time later, he was awoken by the back door opening. An aroma of cooked food. When the door closed again and the candlelight inside was blown out, he ventured near the stoop and found a quantity of vegetable stew had been tipped on the ground. Carefully, he tasted it, then wolfed down the lot in a few fast gulps. He licked his muzzle to clean off every last drop and returned to his place in the shed, where he turned around three times and went to sleep.

❦

Mariah huddled by Naomi in the shelter of a head-high rock protruding from the coast beyond Ballyholme. They'd ventured along the seaside path despite inclement weather, as they'd done often before and, Mariah hoped, would continue to do in future. It was surprisingly easy to find this piece of wilderness: just go to the end of the beach and keep going. The path snaked around between the promontory's empty fields and the jagged black rocks of the water's edge. Then they'd found this enormous standing stone to hide behind for a slight break from the drizzle. The wind was brisk and sunlight sparkled on the waves just below them, but Mariah sank under the leaden weight of loss.

She'd tried to convince her friend to hide, to stay here in relative safety, but Naomi thought she had a chance at convincing the Senate to authorise global use of the fertiliser. It was a chance she couldn't resist, even at the risk of whatever might befall her in America.

They had tried to be perky—Naomi tried to tell Mariah to be strong, but in the end it was clear to both: they might never meet again.

Mariah linked her elbow into her friend's and crumpled into silent sobs. Naomi leaned into her and held tight, their tears mingling over clenched fingers. The breeze picked up and the clouds began to darken and spit.

Mariah opened her eyes just in time to see what looked like a wall of water in front of them. There was no time to cry out; in the next moment, the rogue breaker crashed over the two and retreated just as quickly, leaving them soaked and breathless on the turf. Still clutching each other, their gazes met and they gaped for a second before bursting out laughing.

The guffaws rang out loud and long. Finally, Mariah had to slip out of Naomi's grip and wrap her arms around an aching belly. She lay back in the sodden grass, squelching.

"Well," she said, "that might be the funniest thing that ever happened to me." For the moment, she'd ignore the fact that it might be the saddest day of her life, too. Rain fell now in earnest, hissing endlessly into the grey sea.

Work. There wasn't much point any more, was there? Mariah shovelled her first spoonful of porridge, the only real reason to show up at the "office". She got a bit more from Jonesy these days due to gaps in the workforce where people had decided to go it alone and grow all their own food.

Naomi had been gone a number of days now—four or five, Mariah speculated, but she found it hard to keep track. She'd heard the buzz of the airplane arriving early that morning, and soon after as it left carrying her one true friend. However, physical distance couldn't keep Naomi out of her head—Naomi, and panic about her own impending transfer that surely grew nearer each day.

The news projector above the eatery flickered and went live, throwing the Senate logo of leaves and stars against the concrete brickwork. Mariah froze, spoon halfway to her mouth. Surely this was what the world waited for. Surely the Senate had seen sense and would decree the full distribution of Naomi's fertiliser. *And she'll come safe home—*

A newsman stuttered his introduction onscreen, keeping his head bent towards his papers. "The—the World Senate greets you and wishes you a good workday."

Yeah, right. *Get on with it.* Mariah almost growled at the disembodied head.

"The Senate wishes to inform the peoples of the world that the Irish scientist, Naomi Wallace, has been convicted of crimes against the government and executed…"

Numbness swept over Mariah. The food in her mouth turned to stone and she spat it in her tray, barely able to take in the ongoing barrage of words.

"…the substance she invented is now declared completely illegal…"

Mariah stared at the table that swam before her eyes. She shoved herself away, nearly knocking over the bench she sat on, and fled the hall with a hand over her mouth.

She ran along the outside alley and stumbled towards the row of outhouses shared by several workplaces. In the dimness of the hut, she slammed and bolted its door before collapsing against it, heaving and shaking. The contents of her stomach threatened to explode and she clamped both hands harder over her mouth. But the fight was already lost. She turned to the hole over the stinking pit and retched, wailing and choking between expulsions of acidic vomit.

Naomi was gone…just like that. Cries tore out of her throat, ripped shreds from her soul, and fell unheard into the open sewer.

Dazed, she came to herself and realised no daylight was visible in the cracks between the planks. How long…no matter. It was dark. *What will I do now*—just go home and try to keep living?

A fragment from the newscast played over in her mind. *The substance is illegal*…the fertiliser. It was well known that the Guild was responsible for its spread. It would be easy to find out that she stood at the head of the Guild. Mariah ran a finger over her palm, dented in the shape of a flower where she'd gripped the Guild symbol. She tucked Murry's carving back inside her shirt.

She exited the hut, wrinkled her nose at the smell of piss on her clothes, and slipped into the shadows to find where she'd parked her bike that morning—just that morning, when Naomi was alive and there was hope that the authorities might be reasonable.

Nowhere was safe any more.

❦❦❦❦❦

Mariah whooshed down the backstreets on her bike. Her mind ablaze, unknowing, almost unseeing, it was all she could do to stay upright. She couldn't go home. Couldn't stay out here. They'd find her.

A cloud sailed away from the moon, and light spilled onto the streetscape. Here, the houses reminded her all too much of Naomi's home in Finaghy: small, one-bedroom homes built in rows right against the roadside. All was silent and neglected, a ghost town in the white glow. Mariah braked and tried to cover her face with her hand. Anyone could see her. Every shadow threatened the end of her life—she fled from the thought even though living on without Naomi was impossible to conceive of.

Deborah's house. It was her only option.

She turned right at the next intersection and stood into her pedals to conquer the uphill approach. Around the bend of the road, a light flickered, registering seconds later in Mariah's mind. She dove behind a hedge, with no choice but to leave the bike hurriedly leaned on the outer side of the bushes.

She curled into a fetal position and went still.

The vehicle drove slowly by. Mariah was sure its lights penetrated the leaves and would give her away. For a long time the only sound was her own breathing—hard and fast at first, then easing back to normal. Animal instinct released her and she sat up blinking.

She swung back onto the bike and leaned into the slope. Speed was of the essence. She escaped the city dwellings and turned onto the highway: a gamble, for it would be hard to hide if another car came along, but she'd get there faster.

After leaving the highway, it wasn't much farther to Deborah's—just ten minutes' hard riding or so, through the centre of Bangor town and up the hill. The familiar pink house loomed up before she expected it. Round the back, dump the bike, slip in the door. She pushed it shut and leaned up against it for a moment. All was silent in the dark hallway, so she opened the wardrobe and entered the sightless stairway to the basement. Round the corner, a shimmer of light reflected on the wall along with the murmurs of several people in agitated discussion. She reached for the edge of the curtain they'd installed just a week ago.

Gasps hissed round the room, followed by a collective sigh of relief. "Mariah! We thought they'd got you." It was Liam, his normally happy face creased with worry.

She grabbed hold of him and he let her bury her face in his shoulder.

Peter finally caught her eye. Her breath caught at the intensity in his stare. Liam supported her as she took a step and fell into Peter's arms.

"It's okay," he said, and cradled the back of her head.

"No it's not. It can never be okay again."

"Sorry—"

"Oh, forget it." He hadn't meant it like that.

A hand touched her shoulder. Deborah, trembling. "What are we going to do?"

"Why are you asking *me?*" Mariah said. Everyone looked at her, expectant, somehow, wanting her to say what would come next. She didn't know anything—she'd lost what little grip she had on life, had less than nothing to contribute.

"I think you should stay here," said a small voice from the back of the room. It was Jontie. "The three of you. You're our leaders. Now that the

74

Guild is illegal, they'll be after you first—and it isn't hard to find out you're in charge."

Agreement around the room. "Yes, you need to stay out of sight," someone said.

"We can bring you whatever you need."

"Don't let yourselves get caught."

Peter and Liam came to stand on either side of Mariah. "Live under the ground?" she mumbled.

"Maybe it's for the best," said Peter.

"You can't be serious."

No answer.

"I want you to be safe," said Deborah. "You're welcome here for as long as you need it."

The room's occupants burst into action. Groups assembled to run various errands—fetching food and bedding, informing the families that their Guild leaders were safe but wouldn't be coming home for a while.

Mariah sank down against the wall, and the buzz slowly subsided. When she opened her eyes much later, the lights were dimmer and piles of supplies were stacked by the doorway curtain. A shadow moved in between. She recognised the silhouette of Peter's shock of hair.

"So ye've returned to us at last. Here, get yourself a mat and some blankets." He pointed over his shoulder. "Get some proper sleep too."

Mariah didn't know if she could ever sleep again. But perhaps she could sink into some semblance of nothingness and escape her torturous thoughts for a while. She tried to move, but her body refused to obey.

Through her torpor she saw Peter moving near her. He spread some quilts and flicked back the top layer like a proper bed. She almost fell into it, and he leaned over to pull the covers up around her neck. "Rest well," he said.

Mariah lost count of the days spent living underground with no daylight to tell her the passing of time. She inferred it might have been three or four days, but she couldn't be sure. Not that it mattered now—she was absent from work, making her a wanted runaway. To say nothing of the rest.

She tossed and turned in her blankets until it became pointless to try sleeping any more, so she sat up. One sole long-burning taper showed the shapeless forms of Liam and Peter across the room; their soft breathing reached her ears. Quietly, so as not to disturb her companions, she slipped to her feet and arranged the blankets in a lump on her mat. Let them believe she was still sleeping.

She pulled aside the curtain and was immediately assailed by the stink of the nightsoil bucket they'd placed in the stairway. It took her back to the first wave of grief in the outhouse at work, and she clapped a hand over a sudden sob, eased by and groped up towards the world of the living. She cracked the door in the back of the wardrobe, but there was still no light to be seen. Great, just her luck, she'd come out in the middle of the night. Oh well, perhaps it was safer so. She opened the front of the wardrobe and stepped carefully into the hall and then out into the brisk air.

The fresh breeze revitalised her. Between the black shadows of mostly skeletal trees, the sky lightened ever so slightly, and that might just be the faintest glimmer of dawn on the edge of the water.

That was it. She had to get down to the shore. Her bike was still right where she'd dropped it when she arrived here, its tyres still good and firm to a squeeze between finger and thumb. She set it upright and wheeled it slowly to the street, then hesitated at the gate.

The Guild needed her—their work was far from done, even if she wanted to be anywhere but here. But to get out for a little while after all this time in the dark was a pressing personal need for the sake of her sanity. She pushed off down the street.

It was not far to the start of Ballyholme Bay. Down the final hill, she reached the coastal road and turned right to pass by the tattered remains of the marina, where fine boats once moored. A few lay half-sunken between the pontoons, sad relics of days gone by. The light was now just enough to make out the opposite end of the bay, the low, craggy paths she'd walked with Naomi. Mariah sighed.

Past the boathouse, she pulled in and proceeded down the ramp to the sand. The bike she abandoned against the concreted retaining wall. Sunrise now approached, but the beach was deserted, as it should be and as she wished it to be. Gentle waves reached for her feet and danced away again, bubbling with more exuberance than Mariah could stand.

She stumped along the sand, strewn with smelly decomposing seaweed. No matter how hard she tried, she found herself staring again and again at the rocky promontory that had been her favourite place in the world before losing the friend who appreciated it as much as she did. It became clearer in the growing daylight, though the sun had yet to make an appearance through the iron-faced clouds.

A sound behind her sent a paralysing shiver through her body. They'd found her? She forced herself to turn around.

"Peter! Don't give me such a fright. What the hell are you doing out here, anyway?" She had an idea what he would say, but it was a fair question in their situation.

"Following you, of course. What are *you* doing out here?" His breath came in short gasps, like he'd been running after her.

"I'm going crazy in that hole. Aren't you?"

"Aye, sure. I understand. But we'd best be getting back now, so we had."

She nodded. "I was about to turn back anyway."

The two strode off to the west, silent, each keeping their own counsel. At the end of the beach, Mariah retrieved the bike and pushed it alongside Peter while they ascended to Cliff Road once more. The glow beyond the clouds grew brighter and slowly painted the streets and houses in stark grimness.

It was fully day by the time they ducked into Deborah's garden. But the street was still deserted. "Funny," whispered Mariah, "folks'd oughta be on the way to work by now."

Peter only nodded, and opened the series of doors for her to precede him into the airless cellar. She sighed and stepped through. Below, she once again sidestepped the poop bucket and pulled back the curtain.

"Flamin' daredevils!" Liam roared. "What do youse think ye're doin?"

Mariah grinned. "Sorry. I couldn't handle staying down here any longer."

"D'ye reckon it's any easier for me? And it's certainly not fair of you two contrary lovebirds to sneak off and leave me sleeping, to wake and think ye've been snatched away!"

Lovebirds? "No, no, it's not like that—"

"*She* snuck off. I followed to make sure she was safe," Peter said.

Liam shrugged. "Not much difference, is there?"

"Look, I'm sorry. I'll tell ye next time I have to breathe." Mariah said. "*Both* of ye."

Movement on the stairs cut short the discussion and all three whirled towards Deborah entering with a tea tray.

"Oh, you shouldn't have." Mariah closed her eyes for a moment and inhaled the delectable scent. "That stuff is like gold."

"I figure you need a treat sometimes. Heard you fighting. For sure, it can't be any fun being stuck down here."

"Well, thank you," said Liam, "I won't say no."

They shared out the tea, rich brown and bitter. Mariah took a sip and let out an involuntary "Ahh!" She thanked Deborah.

"Least I can do, to ease your time. No new plans yet, then?"

The other three looked at each other.

"We'd better wait it out a little longer," said Liam.

A few hours of deadly boredom later, they had another visitor—this time it was Jontie. She set down a bag with food. "Here, have something to eat. But you should know—you can all come out now."

"Come out?"

"Well…um—the thing is, nobody's working any more. Not anywhere—the farms, the factories, the offices."

A full rebellion. Mariah's mind raced. That meant the Guild wouldn't be in any worse trouble than anyone else. They could come out, but the entire country was surely now in the Senate's bad books.

Mariah shook a little, remembering the rebellion in America not so long ago. How the Senate had so ruthlessly quashed it.

Oh, my Ireland. We're in for it now.

∗ ∗ ∗

Darian dragged himself bedward from the field, starved and exhausted. It was his second week of overtime hours and no suppers and he didn't know if he would make it through the month. Andi had tried to sneak him some of her food, but he forbade it when he discovered it was her own meal she wanted to give him. So he hungered, and travailed, and slept badly in fear of waking too late for precious breakfast.

Today the clouds had shone bright white, had illuminated the black metal fences and nearly-naked hills in sharp outlines and heavy shadows where the lone trees stood scattered. Almost as if a great floodlight had been turned upon the planet. Now the dense starless night had fallen again. Darian had shovelled manure into the failing farmland for twelve hours on two bowls of porridge, and he was supposed to be grateful. "My arse," he muttered loudly.

He approached the dorms and stopped short at the sight of people dancing and singing and generally making merry, though there couldn't possibly be a beer in sight. Could there? He moved closer, step by careful step, tried to decipher the uproar. It was no use—these people weren't coherent.

The camp guards and supervisors stood warily around the edge. Some of them chattered excitedly to each other and cast worried glances at their charges. Andi wasn't with them.

When he reached his own building, his roommates gathered round and one or two slapped him on the back. They'd happily steal his breakfast, he remembered. He'd keep on his toes.

"We get to go home," one crony blared, and slung an arm round Darian's shoulder like a drunk.

He blinked. "Home?"

"Everybody quit work. Just like that. There's nothing the Senate can do."

He wasn't inclined to trust his colleagues, yet the widespread party atmosphere lent at least some credence to their claims. Someone launched into a raucous song, and nearly the whole camp joined in. Darian slunk back into the bunkhouse and eased the door shut.

"It might be true," said a voice behind him.

"Don't sneak up on me like that! Me poor heart." It hammered illogically, sapping what little strength remained to him. He groped his way to his bunk and sagged down on the edge.

Andi's laugh tinkled in his ear. She must be sitting right...*there*. His searching fingers encountered her lower back and he let them rest. "What's going on, do you know?"

Her hand alighted on his lap. "Someone's engineered a miracle fertiliser. There's going to be enough food for everyone and more besides."

"So this led everyone to quit work?"

"Well…" She exhaled. "Seems the whole populace is growing plenty in their own streets and backyards. They dinna need the ration any more, and that was their only reason for working."

The bedlam outside attested to the spread of that belief. Then, relative silence, and someone shouted a call to action. There were cheers and whoops and, to Darian's ear, it sounded like the crowd was moving away. "Are they just…leaving?"

"We're all locked in just as much as you."

Darian recalled the gate and its toehold. "Given enough time, they'll figure a way out."

"Shall we join them?"

"Of course…But I was thinkin'…" He gulped. He was sure his face was red, but at least it wouldn't be visible. "I was thinkin' not just yet."

"Like maybe on the morrow?"

"Yeah. Like maybe that."

The three fugitives, reluctant to walk about openly just yet, remained in the basement that day. Over the course of the hours, various Guildspeople came to report of goings-on outside. Dancing in the streets, huge communal meals—and word of a large gathering that evening in Ormeau Park by the river, near the centre of Belfast city.

At this news, Mariah's curiosity overcame any desire for safety. If the authorities were to clamp down now, their roles as Guildspeople would fade into the antics of the whole city. She stood up from her mat. "Guess we should probably go to that."

"If you say so." Liam was still a little grumpy from the escapade that morning.

Peter shrugged. "I suppose it doesn't matter now one way or the other."

Said and done. Mariah headed for the stairs, picking up the bucket on the way. They could at least shite outside like normal people now. She emptied it down the long drop outside the back door and shook her head at her own thoughts, the value she placed on such a simple thing.

In Deborah's front room, the old lady sat with curtains wide open, watching the street. "People have been running and skipping past like you wouldn't believe," she said.

"We're going to go to that gathering in the park," said Mariah.

"All that way? Well, you're young enough. I'll stay here and hold the fort. See you later on, perhaps—although, you might want to go home to your families."

Peter grinned. "Very good point. But I daresay we'll be back soon. The Guild surely still has work to do."

"Aye, that's true. Go on then, and take care o' yerselves." Deborah waved them away with a flap of the hand. They exited by the front door for once, but had to duck round the back to get their bikes. Mariah found herself gaping at a group of teenage girls who whooped and skipped as they progressed along the road that led first to Bangor, then to Belfast.

There was an impromptu ceili on Bangor's waterfront where Main Street met Queen's Parade and Quay Street on the edge of the harbour, in an open space that used to be a carpark. Rows and circles of people danced back and forth on cracked tarmac to the skirl of a tinny fiddle and deep bodhran played by a lively senior couple. More than one stolen kiss occurred as the dancers paired and split in the weave of the traditional steps, now a round of eight, now twos or fours, now facing lines making an archway with their arms for each twosome to skip under in turn.

The heat of the day was past, and just as well. Mariah and her cohorts cycled into town by the inland route, passing the several miles of familiar, fruitless Senate fields that lay between Bangor and Belfast. On the fringes of the city suburbs they passed several neighbourhood feasts in front gardens, politely declining invitations to join in with the revellers who dipped themselves generous portions from steaming tureens of Naomi's miraculous vegetables.

An ever-growing stream of people joined them as they approached the central city area. Singing rang out from all directions and Mariah decided the general mood was most akin to drunkenness. Drunk on happy. But she feared the happiness had a wobbly foundation.

The ride at this leisurely pace took hours, but she was glad to be outdoors again at last. The city had come alive since last she saw it: instead of the accustomed grim hopelessness and blanket of grey despair, people wore smiles and tended wildly lush gardens along every street, on the roundabouts and berms, and even in gutters where the dirt had gathered over years of neglect.

Finally, near the fall of dusk, they reached the edge of the park. They entered through the open wrought-iron gates and under a stand of old ash trees that stubbornly sucked life from far beneath the dead layers of earth. The grass was long gone, of course, and they made their way across bare brown dirt to the back of the throng gathered in the main northern expanse of the park.

It was almost impossible to find a way in among the dense crowd.

"Hold my bike?" Mariah didn't wait for an answer, but ducked into gaps and forced her way forward. She had never experienced so many people in one place before, and wrestled with a sense of imprisonment.

After some time she reached the edge of a staging area where someone had set up an amplifier and microphone—though where such a thing could have come from, Mariah had no idea. She'd believed only the authorities had access to technology—and she didn't like where that idea led her.

Someone was speaking through the device, someone she didn't know, but she strained past the noise of the crowd, and made out part of what he was saying. Something about Naomi's sacrifice being worth it, because now the world was changing and would become free…

Anger rose up her throat and she hollered at him. "Load o' bollix, ya sweet-talkin' gobshite!" She didn't think anyone heard, but then people started pointing at her.

"That's the leader of the Guild!"

"Mariah, speak to us," someone called out.

She found herself torn away from the crowd, and carried bodily to the speaker. His face filled with awe when he learned who she was, and he spoke to the crowd. "And now, let's hear from the first Guildswoman!"

In a moment she found the microphone pushed into her hand, and she was lifted to the shoulders of those who dragged her there. Some in the crowd chanted, "The first Guildswoman! The first Guildswoman!" until they realised they were stopping her from saying anything.

Finally, they fell silent, and she breathed a lungful of air. She had no idea what to tell them; only that this wasn't right. Then she began, and the words came from deep within her.

"People of Belfast! You say this day is your revolution, your arrival of freedom, your return to fair and just living. Maybe it seems that way right now, but how long will it last?"

Mariah's voice reverberated unnaturally across the park. She stared out over the masses, adjusting her grip on the microphone. The cheering faded slightly.

"You think everything is fixed just because your stomachs are full for the first time in memory. Well, it's not! We have lost Naomi, who solved the food shortage..." Her voice broke a little. "...and who was a great friend to many of us. Your foolish actions today have certainly angered the Senate. Did you not see what happened in America when there was an uprising? Did you not hear that every second person *died* for noncompliance?"

She drew another ragged breath to finish. "The Guild is not impressed with this behaviour. Aye, I dreamed of changing the world, but not by force. Not by quitting without permission. But by deliberate planning, forging a peace with the Senate in a way that would see things improve on a proper foundation. We could have stayed at our jobs while we set things in place, could have let things continue as normal for a little while longer until the authorities were more ready for change. Why didn't we—*you*—think about the consequences of these actions? Troubles are coming, like no troubles this old land has ever seen before, and you brought it on your own heads. May God have mercy on us all."

In the shocked hush that followed, Mariah dropped the microphone. The amplified thwack of its landing caused the crowd to wince, so she took the chance to slide down from the shoulders of her would-be admirers.

She forced her way back to Peter and Liam. "Get me out of here!"

8

faith

september—november 2010

Faith reclined in the padded coffee-shop chair and stirred her mocha. The Hairy Sailor Café had only been open for a few months, but it had quickly become her favourite Bangor drinking hole—its quirky mix of dark varnished wood, leather couches and colourful art, combined with the harbour views from the upper level, made for the perfect ambience in her opinion. Her head hurt a little today, although there was nothing to stress about. She stretched her arms and watched the lazy play of moored yachts. The metallic twang of the rigging that slapped against swaying masts just reached her ears through the glass, and she closed her eyes, wondering what exotic places these boats had seen.

The scrape of wood on wood called her back to the here and now. Sarah collapsed into the small table's other chair. "Hullo, sorry I'm late."

"No matter. I like waiting here."

A waitress approached and Sarah ordered a tea—black with mint—before leaning back and letting out a long breath as she regarded her friend. "How's things going then?"

"Tolerable, thanks."

"Did that deal with Roger's franchise go through for your LandCare app?"

"Sure did." Faith hardly believed it herself. "It's taken him a year to get set up since he got out from under Ewan, but he made good on his intention and is stocking my software in all his branches."

"That's what, four different distribution deals you have now? Lucky thing. Must be a decent living."

Faith screwed up her face. "Oh, come on. Not that huge. Enough to help Mum and Dad out with some household costs, and a wee bit for continuing research and tools."

"Like that?" Sarah indicated the portable computer on the table.

"Oh, it doesn't have the processing power I need for my formulas. It's just for out and about." Faith sipped her drink and noticed Sarah was still staring at the computer. "Be my guest."

While Sarah inspected the little machine, Faith returned to staring out the window. Clouds scudded by, giving a dappled effect to the marina and the curves of the bay on each side. She let her mind wander to the footpaths that went on from there: to the west, a route that grew progressively wilder for an hour or two until emerging at Helen's Bay; and to the east, the urbanised coast road that led in a wide circle around her own house to nearby Ballyholme.

The sound of the computer being set on the table brought Faith's attention back to her friend who, to her horror, appeared tired and haggard, and she hadn't even noticed before now. *Unobservant git.* "So how are you doing?"

Sarah looked up under a creased brow. "Well, not so great. In fact, that's why I was late. For one thing, I think I'm getting that bad strain of flu that's going around this season. But that really is the least of my problems…"

Faith settled back, prepared to listen intently. But while Sarah continued to talk, Faith apprehended with consternation that she could not follow the words. The headache became a stabbing throb. Something was very wrong here. *The flu?* No, that would be silly. She tried to say something, to break the foggy spell that had fallen on her, but she couldn't even squeak.

A blackness rolled slowly in from the edges of her vision. Sarah's face vanished from sight last of all, then there was only darkness and silence, paralysis and bitter cold. *Nothing*. Not even a wisp of a thought crossed her blank mind. It was empty of everything. *That was a thought*. So it was. But there was still nothing else. *Waiting*.

Slowly she became aware of a chair's pressure from below. She was sitting. She tried to open her eyes, but realised they were already open. But she couldn't see. She blinked. Some of the black haze dissipated and a face came into view. A worried face, a terrified face, but not a face she recognised. That terror struck into her own heart, though she knew not why.

She moved stiff lips. "Wha—"

"No, don't try to talk," said the scared stranger.

She blinked again and the room became clearer, though still dark around the fringes.

"It's okay, we've called an ambulance."

I don't need an ambulance. I'm fine.

No I'm not. I've caught a deadly plague.

I…who's I?

That's what's wrong.

She didn't know who she was, any more than she knew the person seated opposite.

But that wasn't right. A person should know who she is.

I lost it. Lost who I was.

Everything was gone. It used to be there; that much was certain.

She flexed her jaw, locked eyes with the stranger, and finally forced words out, the first necessity that came to mind. "Who are you?"

Shock registered on the other's face. "You really don't know. I'm Sarah."

Sarah…The name should be familiar.

"And me? Who is this?" She indicated herself.

Sarah gaped. "No way. You can't have forgotten who you are."

A pleading glance convinced her otherwise.

"You're Faith."

Faith. Nope, not ringing any bells.

There was a commotion behind her…*Faith*…and she gripped the armrests of her chair and turned. Several people emerged from a stairwell and approached at a run. They carried bags and cases.

She sought Sarah, but she was backing away, pointing and yammering. The new people surrounded Faith, grasped her wrists, supported her back, touched metal to her chest. One shone a light in her eyes.

"What are you doing?" She struggled in their grip. Sarah was nowhere.

Someone rested a hand on her shoulder, and she clutched it. Oh, how she needed that touch. "Don't worry. We'll take care of you," said its perpetrator, a short woman with brown hair.

"Who are you?" said Faith. At that moment it was the most pressing question she could ever remember.

The woman smiled. "I'm Emily. Come on, let's go downstairs."

They guided her to the stairs and helped her descend, holding her by the arms from all around. Voices floated down from behind.

"What happened?"

"She just sort of went blank." Sarah's voice. Good, so she was still near.

"This is the first time, then."

"Yes. I'm sure of it. We've been friends for years."

We have? Faith still knew nothing but her name.

As they proceeded down the stairs, lights came on. The sensation was so strong that Faith tilted her head back to check whether a bulb had been activated above her head. But no. It was only in her head. She knew who she was again.

Faith Diamond, wannabe hunger eradicator, had just lost her mind.

There was no more time to think about it. They bundled her outside to the waiting ambulance and opened a door.

She resisted their pushes. "I—I'm fine. I don't want to go to hospital."

The pressure from many hands eased off. "Come now," said Emily, "we don't know what just happened. You should get yourself checked over at least."

Faith scrunched her eyebrows. Maybe they were right. She looked back up to the window she'd sat at, and vaguely recalled that she'd been up there thinking. The masts and rigging tinkled louder out here.

She considered her life, all the aspects of herself she'd forgotten in those terrifying minutes, and that were not yet fully hers again. "How long was I out?"

"Almost an hour." Sarah said behind her.

Faith shook her head slowly. It was as if everything she was, everything that made up this person she was supposed to be, had been sucked out of her head and lay arrayed before her. She could survey it now, since the lightbulb moment on the stairs, touch it if she wanted, but it was no longer a part of her. Suddenly she was very tired.

Emily took her hand. "Let's get in."

This time she didn't argue. She let them sit her on a trolley, where she lay down so they could attach a safety belt across the waist. The vehicle grumbled to life. She was so sleepy…she just wanted to go home.

Presently the engine cut out and they were hauling the trolley into the waning daylight. "It's okay, I can walk," she protested.

Emily patted her hand. "But you don't have to. Just relax."

Faith wanted to insist on getting up, but found her hands and feet were strapped down. She searched Emily's expression and found nothing there. A sob escaped from her, stronger than she could hope to control. She writhed and moaned while they pushed the trolley inside the building, through busy hallways and into a large room, where they pulled curtains around her and left. Emily was last to go, with a smile and a wave.

"Wait, don't go." Perhaps Faith mumbled through the shudders, but in any case, Emily didn't return. It was then that Faith realised Sarah hadn't come with them. "I have to pee," she said to the empty room.

She tugged at her restraints, but it was useless. She hated the helplessness, even if things were a little vague right now. And this wasn't even necessary. She could have just gone home to bed if Sarah hadn't freaked out and called for help. Though, she had to admit it must be a pretty scary thing to happen.

Faith was still wriggling uselessly when a nurse entered. "I just need to put in a cannula to start the processing. Let's get some fluids in you."

Needle? "No way! I hate needles. I'm fine. Just let me get up, please?" Memories of jabs floated through the haze in her head, more vaccinations than she would ever consider necessary, but that couldn't be real. Right?

The nurse pulled a taut smile and shook her head slightly. "This won't take a second." She seized Faith's wrist, tightened the strap holding it down, and prodded the back of her hand with gentle fingertips.

The sting sent jolts through Faith's nerves and she swore.

The nurse's smile vanished. "There you go." She set a syringe in the cannula and drew off a vial of blood, then attached a saline drip.

"Sorry," growled Faith, "it's just yer job. But all this—it's really not necessary."

"We'll let the doctor be the judge of that." The nurse patted Faith's cheek and swished away.

Faith stewed angrily for at least half an hour before the doctor came in. He was young and darkly bearded. He bent over and frowned at the patient notes. "That's strange, nobody's filled out your details. What happened to you? Why are you here?"

How peculiar. She herself had forgotten who she was, and nobody here knew either. Faith was sorely tempted to tell him it was all a huge mistake and would he please let her go. But then she might never find out what was wrong with her—or if it might happen again. "I—I lost all my memory. For about an hour. I didn't know anything. I'm remembering now, but I'm still a bit scattered."

He looked up sharply. "Then why did they restrain you? This makes no sense at all."

"I was...uh...quite upset."

"Well, let's get those off you. I'm sure they don't help your peace of mind." He reached for the straps and soon she was loose. She went to pull out the cannula but he prevented her. "Leave that in, please."

The needle's sting had dulled to a throb, so she acquiesced with a grumble and sat up on the edge of the trolley. "What are you going to do?"

"I'll order some neurological tests—electrical brain measurement, magnetic scans and so on. Might take most of the evening, but it's good to check everything out."

It didn't sound pleasant. Faith bit her lip, but she was too curious about her affliction to run away now. Then she noticed her handbag on a caddy nearby. Emily must have brought it in. It was good to see something familiar, and to be able to recognise it. She seized it and pawed at the latch for a moment—the new computer! Had she lost it? Finally she got it open and found her tablet in its case inside. Her heart slowed some, then she withdrew a business card from the front pocket and gave it to the doctor.

"I'll let your parents know, too. You shouldn't be by yourself."

Her parents...she'd barely thought of them. She'd forgotten them in the blackness, then failed to gather them in since. All this kerfuffle and despair had distracted her from thinking about herself and the things she needed to remember and make her own again.

She nodded grimly to the doctor as he left and grit her teeth for the undesirable hours ahead. First, a long bathroom break—the pain of waiting was almost unbearable. Somewhat relieved, she returned to sit on her trolley. She was still sleepy, but too agitated to rest when she knew tests were coming.

Soon enough, an orderly came to take her away. In the first test, an assistant spent a long time attaching wires to her head with goop and gunk, then running a machine that inscribed lines like a seismograph. When the wires were finally removed, the goop and gunk remained stuck all over her scalp and in her hair.

After that, she had to wait for some time in a corridor and then had to lie on yet another bench that slid inside a cylindrical machine. It was altogether too tight for her liking, but she clenched her eyes shut and endured it—even though the contraption grew louder by the minute and made more frightening noises than anything she'd ever had this close to her head. After almost an hour inside it, the orderly took her back to the original room. She shook even after everything was quiet.

After a very long time, she relaxed a little and drew a fresh breath, just in time to see her parents rushing in, almost stumbling over each other in their eagerness. But they didn't speak.

"I must look a fright, hey? It's the stuff they put in my hair."

Nobody laughed or even smiled. There followed the most awkward of silences, in which Faith tried to get her parents talking and they refused to comply. Finally she gave up and lay back to rest.

It was late when the doctor returned, test results in hand. Faith shot out of her light doze and sat up. "Well, what have you got?"

The bearded doctor frowned again. "Nothing. No abnormalities anywhere in any of the tests. It's inexplicable." He addressed her parents. "Keep an eye on her. Don't let her go out alone."

Faith seethed. She was too old to have to be supervised everywhere she went. But she'd deal with that in her own way. Soon enough, the restriction would be forgotten. "Let's go," she said, hopping down from the trolley. Her parents moved to support her, but she waved them away. "Where are you parked?"

Dad indicated towards the rear of the building, so they set off through the halls. The farther they went, Faith's parents gradually moved closer until they gripped her quite tightly by the shoulders. She decided it wasn't worth fighting over. Maybe it helped them feel better.

They emerged from the hospital into a chill night. A beggar squatted by the door, rattling his cup of coins while they walked by. Faith fished out some change for him. They located the car, loaded themselves in and drove home in silence. This was too weird. "What is up with you guys?"

Her parents looked at each other and shrugged. It was like this was beyond their ability to cope, so she didn't press the matter.

Once home, she rushed to the phone to call Sarah. "Hey—it's me."

"Hi."

"I'm fine. The tests all came up clear, it's all a great mystery."

"Sure."

"I'm home now. Are you okay?"

"Yeah."

"Don't give me that. You don't sound okay."

"Homework," said Sarah, and hung up.

Faith stared at the phone in her hand for a moment. Everyone had gone weird on exactly the same day as herself.

She retreated to her room and sat at the desk, reading over some printouts to do with her LandCare formulas. Suddenly it all seemed so empty, so far away, as if she hadn't spent her whole life working on this. She remembered the beggar at the hospital. Her system worked fine on farms, but poverty was still rampant in cities. Something had to be done…something that went beyond the scientific and reached into people's souls.

If everyone understood about sharing, surely hunger could be eradicated like she dreamed.

Faith flipped open a calendar to check the date for an upcoming new version of her software, then crinkled her brow and paged back a couple of times. Wow. It had been two whole months since that nasty memory loss episode in the café. And that was definitely the worst.

Oh, it had returned at least once more in the intervening time, but she had been alone and couldn't be certain. Sometimes she would wake late, disoriented, and with a little of the panic that had accompanied her entry to the hospital. She had to wonder if the same complaint had struck again. Still, it was better to be at home and recover her wits in familiar surroundings. She wasn't going to tell anyone about such instances if she could help it. Being dragged through hospital processing that did absolutely nothing counted as the single most horrendous experience of her young life.

She finished the planning for the new release and sent the information to the programmer and distributors, then stared out at the picture-perfect sunset. Exactly the same as always—never ever any different. She stood and turned slowly, taking in the white-painted room, the bright boxy furniture, the idyllic view, and the picture on the wall. It showed the main street of Bangor, empty but for one figure viewed from the back. Faith had always liked to imagine it was herself. Now she could make out the location of the Hairy Sailor Café just before the masts of the marina jutted into view. This time when she stared at the picture, there was a heavy sense of foreboding in the dark, cinereous clouds, as if something terrible had happened and she was the only one left. The deserted streetscape showed dilapidation and dirt: curtains sagged, garbage blew in eddies, and she almost heard the clatter of broken windows rattling in the wind.

Faith lifted the framed painting from its hook and gripped it on both sides. The darkness in it threatened to swallow her. "Gah!" She flung it down and the glass shattered, tearing the paper, but not yet beyond recognition. Bending to finish the job, she seized a shard and slashed across the now-morbid scene, heedless of the blood that flowed from her fingers.

She'd never seen Bangor's main street that empty.

Soon she'd bundled up the whole sorry mess and snuck it out to the rubbish tin at the back door. Back at her desk, pressing a paper towel to her cut hands, she stared at the place where the picture had been and remembered what else was missing—Sarah.

Her friend had been conspicuously absent since the café incident and cut the conversation short whenever Faith called. They'd crossed paths in town a couple of times, but Sarah had always been anxious and pleaded great hurry.

It was time to do something about it. When the bleeding stopped, Faith snuck downstairs again and pulled her scooter from its place behind the house. She had only a transitory worry about what might happen if she had an incident while driving. It wasn't far—and she was determined to get to the bottom of this.

She flicked on the headlamp in the gathering dusk and zipped out the front gate without her parents stopping her. They'd been oddly distant in the last two months also, barely talking to her except to fret about her going out alone. But as she'd predicted, restrictions had relaxed over time. She doubted they'd even care about this little excursion.

Soon enough she pulled up to Sarah's house, a dwelling not much unlike her own: two storeys, tidy white-framed windows topped by concrete rooftiles, and a garden out front. Except the Smythes' house was painted green, not yellow, and their garden was just a lawn, impeccably mowed. Her heart fluttered a little at the boldness of her presumption, but she hated being ignored. She marched up to the door, hesitated the merest moment, and rapped firmly.

Mrs. Smythe opened, wide-eyed at first, then she smiled. "Faith! What a surprise. Lovely to see you." The two hugged awkwardly. The transition from teacher to friend was not an easy one, even though Faith had finished school some years before.

"Sarah's in her room, why don't you go on through?" Mrs. Smythe said.

Faith grinned, bolstered by the warm welcome, and bounded up two steps at a time. The bedroom door stood a few inches open. She knocked anyway. It creaked a little on its hinges. She rested her palm on the handle, about to push it wider.

The door was snatched out of her hand. Sarah's wild gaze took her in.

"Well, aren't you going to say hi?" Faith propelled her friend back into the room and perched on the edge of the bed. A framed painting of some dark conifer trees hung on the forest-green wall and she stared at it, willing Sarah to be all right, whatever that meant.

Sarah dug all her fingers into her scalp and finally found words. "I thought you weren't supposed to go out alone."

"Go on wi' ye. I'm fine."

"Are you sure?"

Faith hesitated, and Sarah let out a frustrated sigh. "See? If you don't know yourself, what am I supposed to think?"

"Why have you been avoiding me?" Faith tried to keep the accusation out of her tone, but was not entirely successful. The betrayal hurt too deep.

"I guess it's been pretty obvious."

"No kidding."

Sarah sank down, not beside Faith on the bed, but on the floor at the opposite side of the room. She buried her face in her hands for several seconds before looking up again.

"Faith, I'm sorry, and this is as hard for me as it is for you. I was hoping you'd understand, but you've come wanting an answer, so you're going to get one."

The sense of foreboding from the painting swept over Faith again. She gulped.

Sarah wouldn't look directly at her. "When you lost your memory…it was the scariest thing that ever happened to me."

"You don't think it was worse for me?"

A strange expression flitted across Sarah's face and was gone. "I never want to see that again."

"Well, duh. Neither do I."

"You're not getting it. That day, you didn't know who I was. You kept asking."

"I couldn't help it!"

"That's exactly it. That was ghastly." Sarah shuddered. "Can you guarantee that won't happen again?"

Silence.

The two stared past each other until Sarah spoke again. "There you go. That's why."

"Can't you…I dunno, get used to it or something?"

Sarah's face darkened even more. "I told you, I never want to see that again. You do understand, don't you?" Her voice took on a pleading tone at the end.

The revelation doused Faith like a bucket of ice water. "You never want to see *me* again."

9

mariah

september 2079

The river ran dark. In the gloaming, the dog loped south alongside it, away from the entrapping walls of Short Strand. The water had stopped him, made him turn at right angles from his original trajectory. This area had little to show for the recent explosion of plant growth, because the riverbank had always been brick-bound with its bare promenade and large buildings on either side. Metal railings still stood to prevent unwary humans from falling into the current, although now their paint flaked and the substance had well begun to rust.

The dog came to the iron spans of the Albert Bridge and had to go over it, because the promenade ended. The wide roadway lay strangely empty of traffic, whether on foot or bicycle. He ran on: past a red-brick factory with a zigzaggy roofline, several other industrial buildings including some repurposed houses, and a large fenced-in concrete yard that once held cars. It was a bleak part of town, without so much as a bricked-in garden or tree circle where the new growth could take root. He passed several small roads full of tiny terraced houses just as bare as the main street, but at the far end of each cul-de-sac the greenery burst forth from the embankment. He paused, a paw in the air, then ran down the last street to force himself through a hole in the fence and across the open area that lay towards the Lagan. He scented the flowing water ahead of him again, but he tumbled first out onto another road.

It was then that he smelled humans—very many people, more and more as he approached the river and moved downwind of them. The dog crept by the park wall, cringing at the strong odours of the great unwashed who filled the area on the other side, mostly silent as a woman's voice spoke loudly to them. A haze of body heat radiated from the park along with the mutterings. There was scattered cheering, and more silence, and he apprehended the rising tension. He had to get out of here.

The grumbling, lilting susurrus swelled as the dog passed an open place in the wall. The edge of the crowd broke and scattered towards him—he upped his pace to get away. The road rejoined the river for real and he flitted from shadow to shadow as laughing knots of people wended their way towards home.

He reached the next bridge over the Lagan and crossed quickly into a neighbourhood of yet more tightly terraced homes. Here, more people arrived but most of them remained in the street, talking and laughing. Soon enough the smells of food wafted from many kitchens. The dog ducked into a mews and settled behind a rusting vehicle carcass to wait.

The wait was not in vain. A back door opened and a replete young man carried the dregs of the family meal to the back wall, and tipped it on an odorous heap where a monster pumpkin vine presided over the days-old compost. But this time the dog did not want the potato stew. He was patient just a little longer, until the boy had vanished indoors and slammed the door; then the scratchings of rodents began.

The dog sat still and watched whilst the rats stuffed themselves so full that their little bellies became visibly round. Then, when they were food-numbed and slow on their feet, he pounced, taking them in a leisurely row and lining up a half dozen of the largest before he left off hunting and settled down to eat. He crunched through their skulls and ribs, briefly tasted their undigested dinners, and chewed on their stringy tails until nothing was left.

With Liam and Peter waiting somewhere ahead, Mariah ducked her head and hustled through the crowd. Silence remained. Then a partygoer's shout broke the atmosphere. "We're free, everyone!" Cheers followed and restored the mood.

After a long, convoluted push, Mariah made it to the edge of the crowd and burst out onto the road by the river, where there were only scattered bunches of people.

Liam and Peter awkwardly balanced the extra bike between them. Mariah grabbed it with a word of thanks, and breathed deeply, now that there was room to do so, but it didn't stop the seething. "How can they be so reckless? Thicker'n shite and not even half so useful. Surely they know the danger they're putting the whole country in by refusing to work."

"We don't work either, these days," Liam reminded them. "And I reckon you're a right one to be talking about reckless, when it was you that just shoved in there and told 'em what's what."

Despair clawed at Mariah. They were far too entangled at all levels to escape serious consequences. She bit her lip as the three pushed their bikes to the next corner.

"What shall we do now?" asked Peter. "It's late, and it's a long way back to Deborah's."

"Let's go home. We can go back to Bangor tomorrow and see what needs doing." Mariah turned in the street, seeking orientation.

"We'll escort you home," said Liam.

"Aye, we insist," said Peter.

She acquiesced and directed them to a road out of the city centre that would lead to her nearby suburb of Castlereagh. As they approached familiar haunts, she recalled last leaving here four days ago. No, three. She'd headed to work, none the wiser, and Naomi had still been alive…

Peter must have seen the tears running down her face even though it was dark, for he steered closer and reached out a hand to her shoulder. Liam stiffened at her other side. Too bad. She needed the support; attempted a smile and accepted the gesture at face value—it was all she could do in view of the horrendous now.

They reached Mariah's family home in about a quarter hour and paused outside the gate before she went in. She reached for the latch, and turned back. "I'll come back to Deborah's tomorrow morning. Watch yerselves in the meantime."

The two nodded, then rode away side by side, a cool distance between them. Mariah pushed on the gate and it creaked, just like always. She shut it carefully behind her and crossed the tiny garden to the house. Tiny it might be, but vegetation now grew rampant there, like every other garden along the way. She leaned her bike against the housefront, fished out her key, but before she could jam it in the lock, the door was yanked open.

"Child! Ye've come back to us." Her father's gaunt frame filled the doorway, accompanied by her brother's sheepdog Jemima. He gripped a little kerosene lamp in one hand and stretched the other to her. "Or is it dreamin' I am?"

Mariah ignored the hand and stepped close to embrace him. "Yer not dreamin', Da."

He turned slightly and called into the recesses of the house. "Darian, yer sister's home."

A shadow loomed in the hallway and came nearer, the brother she barely knew. "Wha—how?"

"Workcamp's dissolved. Everyone gone home, including the supervisors." He gave a wry grin and reddened. "Actually, one of them's my girlfriend proper as of last night. Guess I have you to thank for that."

"Let me look at you." Mariah came near and grasped him by the shoulders, thin but solid. His wavy brown hair hung unevenly over prominent eyebrows. The light from the lamp cast deep shadows around his eyes, but she suspected they'd still be there in daylight as well. Workcamp was never gentle on the young lives it swallowed—mostly never to return. Jemima capered about from one member of the family to another, pushing her nose into a hand here, a knee there.

Her Da bustled into the kitchen, leaving the hall swamped in darkness. "Must add another carrot to the stew…"

She groped her way after him, followed by her brother. Da, true to his word, seized a carrot and set to chopping it in a frenzy. It was larger than a standard carrot, but not giant like some of the ones she'd grown in her patch.

When the pieces were safely in the boiling pan atop the pot-belly stove, Da joined them at the table. He placed his hand on hers. "I'm so sorry about

Naomi."

Mariah dipped her head. There was nothing to say. She doubted Darian had even met Naomi all those years ago, before they took him away.

But he sat up. "*That* Naomi? She was your friend?"

She nodded. "We were close, yes. We founded the Guild together."

"What will ye do now?" asked Da.

She swallowed. There had been no space to consider that. "I went to that rally in the park tonight. In town. It was like the whole world was there. They made me speak."

Her father and brother stared transfixed, so she elaborated. "I told them this is all wrong. Forcing the issue by refusing to work—that's only going to make the Senate madder than they already are."

Darian gaped and Da nodded slightly. Mariah allowed herself a dry chuckle. "I bet I'm not particularly popular now."

Da got up to see to the stew and pronounced it ready. He filled two bowls and set them before his progeny, then went back to get his own and another for the dog. As they were about to dig in, he grasped them both by the wrists. "I'm a thousand times grateful for my children, and doubly so that I may feed them both well this night."

Mariah swallowed her tears and forced herself to smile at his sweetness. Naomi's parents would never eat with their daughter again.

But this family was incomplete too, she reminded herself—their mother, lost these many years to a mysterious fever that would never have been fatal in the days of accessible doctoring. She shut off the topic in a corner of her mind. "So, a girlfriend, eh? When do we get to meet her?"

Darian's eyes gleamed with a faraway gaze. "We just got to town today. Andi's gone to her folks of course, but I'll go and bring her tomorrow or so."

The stew was warm and hearty if somewhat flavourless, like all of the fertilised produce. Mariah supposed it was a result of the enormous fruits, but at least everyone had enough to eat. *Which might cause the Senate to kill us all.*

They ate in a pleasant enough silence, though Mariah felt the weight of the whole land upon her and her alone. By the time she scraped her bowl, her eyes were drooping, and she excused herself to her own bed.

She climbed the stairs and brushed through the curtain that served as a door on her little cubby. Her fingers lingered on its familiar heavy cloth, then on the bedcover her mother had knitted out of holey jumpers. She'd rarely slept anywhere else in her life; it was strange to return after being elsewhere for a time.

There was no energy left to consider getting undressed, so she fell into bed fully clothed. Thoughts chased around in her mind so that she expected to toss and turn half the night.

It was not so. She woke to the sun high in the sky, well slept for the first time she could remember. She stretched like a cat and swung herself upright.

The events of yesterday crashed over her, but it was more like a distant wave. She wouldn't let this new day be dampened. But she did need to get back to Bangor and organise what the Guild was going to do next, now that things were changing so drastically.

She trotted downstairs and after Jemima greeted her enthusiastically in the hallway, found her father and brother who were drinking tea in the kitchen. She accepted a cup with some fried potato and attacked the meal with gusto.

"You look like you're in a hurry," remarked Darian.

Mariah nodded. "Have to go sort out some Guild stuff. But don't worry. I'll be back."

Da frowned. "What's to sort?"

"Well, I don't even know if we need to continue at all, seeing as there seems to be plenty of food around. Gotta ask the others and decide a way forward." She set down her empty mug and stood.

"Go then," said Da, "but hurry back when you can."

"I will." She hugged them both long and deep, so long that Darian fidgeted, then she waved at them one more time from the gate and set her face towards Bangor.

<hr>

Mariah had been cycling for about a quarter hour and was almost out of the Belfast suburbs when a child came up and walked beside her.

She did a double take: it was young Jonesy, from work. He didn't speak at first. She looked at him out of the corners of her eyes, then he smiled at her. She smiled back. "Hello."

"Hiya."

This was awkward. "Uh…how are you?"

"Can't complain. Got food."

"Aye, that helps."

He fell in beside her, and she slowed so he could keep pace. They went on in silence for a few moments before he spoke again. "Reckon you were right."

"Huh?"

"Last night. In the park."

"Oh." Memories rushed in like a patchy signal, flickering images of her anger and the unreal accolades of the crowd. "I'm sorry I was so hard on them. They just wanted to celebrate."

The boy shook his head. "It's not sensible to turn things upside down all at once. Even I can see that."

"Why you? Why do you agree with me when you might be the only one?" Mariah swivelled to face him once more, only to discover he'd run off down a side street. He waved back to her once and continued on his fleet-footed way.

Strange. But maybe he wasn't the only one. Interesting that people were still thinking about what she'd said, anyway. She allowed her synapses to drift again.

On the north side of Sydenham where she would join the railway track, a group of people had gathered in front of the embankment. Some called and waved as she came closer. Most had bikes. Her heart thudded. If they were waiting for her, then they might not have the best intentions, considering the general unpopularity of what she had said the night before.

She forced herself to keep walking calmly, without flinching, although she wished her Guildmates were there. In the next moment she chided her own silly desires; even if Peter and Liam were with her, they would be outnumbered by this gang.

"I'm going to Bangor. Do you want to come?" It was the first thing that came into her head to say.

There were nods in reply, and slowly the whole group fell in behind her, Jonesy among them. Perhaps he'd told them she was near. These were friends.

She released the breath she'd been holding and headed out along the footpath that accompanied the old track for some way, it being a fairly direct route to Bangor. When the path veered away towards the airport, they switched to the railway trackbed itself and continued on. It was overgrown, but straight and level. The entourage variously pedalled carefully in the gravel or picked their way from sleeper to sleeper. A vaguely familiar mongrel mutt tagged along behind, and Mariah snorted. Come one, come all, indeed.

They passed the ghostly, dilapidated city stations one by one and came to Cultra. From the high track Mariah surveyed the stretch of golden sand below and remembered the times she'd spent here with Naomi.

The railway led through narrow canyons cut into the suburban terrain, and came to the terminus at the top of Main Street in Bangor. They climbed out of the station pit at the end of the line, helping each other up to platform level with all the bikes. Mariah led the way towards Cliff Road and Deborah's house. The sun had vanished and a cold wind spat occasional wet droplets at them under low, scudding clouds.

Finally, she stopped outside the gate of the flaking pink house and dropped her wheels in the street. There was a clatter as others did the same. "Wait here a moment," she instructed her followers, and walked up to the door. No need to be secretive any more, right? Everything was different now.

The door opened and Deborah peeked out, eyes widening when she caught sight of the crowd in the street. "Where'd you get all them?"

Mariah shrugged. "They just kind of came along."

"Well, I don't know as they'll fit. There's quite a few bods downstairs already. But we can try."

Mariah shuddered at the idea of entering that airless hole again. "How about the hallway? Or the front room? We don't need to hide."

"Aye, I suppose so."

She beckoned to the folks in the street to come in, and sank down against the old-worldy wallpaper in the hallway while others filed past and seated themselves around her. The Guildspeople crept from the wardrobe when they heard the racket, and took up positions also. When the wide hall was packed, with the doorways to each room occupied, and the stairs full too, the remaining people clustered at the open back and front doors. This allowed the draught to sweep straight through the house, but with so much body heat, the fresh air was a blessing.

She searched the faces and soon found Peter hunched in upon himself by the back door. Liam was nowhere to be seen. Jonesy crept to her side and reached for her hand; she gripped his small fingers, unsure what he needed.

There was none of the usual chatter—Mariah felt a little vindicated if it meant they had taken her seriously last night. Still, she was in the dark as to what was actually going on, so she leaned over to one of the women who had walked the rails with her just a bit ago. "What do you people want from me?"

The woman raised her head, red-eyed and surprised. A quick glance around told Mariah that her attempted whisper had fallen loudly into the silence. A loud sniff drew her attention to Deborah, who was flicking tears from her eyes.

Mariah scanned the room and this time picked up what she had missed before: the despair on the faces of young and old, hanging heavy in the air above them. Jonesy leaned closer to her side. The wind gusted through from the seaward side, and rattled the house; she scrambled to a squat in a sudden panic. "What's going on?"

Across the hall, Deborah's mouth fell open. "You don't know...how did you manage not to hear...well, never mind that..." She muttered a little to herself, closed her eyes and took a breath.

"It was broadcast to workplaces this morning," explained the woman next to Mariah. "And the word spread from there. I'm sorry, I thought you would have been told..." She clutched at Mariah's arm and squeezed tears out of tightly-shut eyes.

Cold fear gripped Mariah. "Someone tell me right now!"

"The Senate messed with the fertiliser," said Peter, barely audible under the growing gale. "They made it into a biological weapon."

"What? But—but how—?"

"You remember the scare years ago when Ebola mutated and became airborne," said the woman.

Jonesy swallowed hard. "An' they've been giving us shots for this, that an' the other virus ever since."

"They spliced that airborne Ebola with Naomi's fertiliser," said Peter.

Mariah waited, frozen in place, for someone to explain what exactly that meant.

It was Deborah who finally dropped two words into the deadly silence. "It multiplies."

Visions of the brown scum overflowing in mugs and buckets filled Mariah's mind. If that were now deadly...*and* airborne...

"Tell me what it's done," she ordered.

The woman dug her fingers into Mariah's arm. "It's wiping out the Americans. They say the Senate is gone, along with all of New York, and it's moving fast into the next states."

"Then we really are free," Mariah muttered to herself. *But at what cost…* To the room she said, "Is that what you want? To organise our own government again?" It would be a tall order. Yet if people were looking to the Guild for leadership, it made sense to take on the task.

People stared at her curiously, so she stammered on. "Isn't that the next step—since the Senate will never bother us again?"

"Some of them escaped in a small plane," said Peter, without lifting his head. "They arrived here this morning."

Deborah fisted her eyes. "Word is, one of them has fallen ill with this new Ebola."

Peter finally looked up. "Liam went to find out if it's true."

"Ahem." The sound of throat-clearing from the front door preceded a shuffle in the people gathered there. They moved back and made room as Liam entered. White light poured in around him from the thick, bright clouds, creating for a moment a sort of halo of rays around his darkened shape.

He nodded almost imperceptibly at Mariah, then took a breath and shut his eyes for a moment. "I just got here—not sure what you've been told—but I found the Americans all right. They're still with their plane at City Airport." He frowned. "It is as we heard. One of them is sick and probably won't last the day. Others are already showing symptoms. They thought they got away, you see, because they were still well when they left New York."

"Is no one helping them?" Mariah asked.

"I talked with one from a distance on the tarmac. He stayed inside the plane and all the rest were still in there too; he told me to stay away. There's no hope for any of them now, he said. After he spoke to me he sealed himself in with the others."

"But are we safe?" asked someone near the back door.

Liam rubbed his temples and sat himself cross-legged in a tiny space left on the floor. "None of them came out at any time. It hasn't even touched our soil, so to speak. But he did say it's deadlier and works faster than the original Ebola… just a day or two of incubation before it gets into the final stages. He also had some good news. You know how they claimed to have killed

Naomi…"

Claimed?

"The man who spoke to me thinks that may not be true. The old men of the Senate were known to like pretty girls, so it's unlikely they would destroy one who fell into their hands. He thought she was probably in a holding jail when the plague began to spread."

Mariah shivered. She hoped beyond hope that the old men hadn't had a chance to fulfil their fantasies with her friend. On the other hand, Naomi would have even less chance against disease if she was locked up.

Liam was still holding his head.

"Are you all right?"

"Yeah, just tired. It's been a crazy few days." His regard lingered on her for just a moment.

She broke the gaze and found everyone looking at her again. "So what do we do now?"

"I guess everyone was hoping you'd have an idea about that," Deborah said into the heavy silence.

The almost palpable negativity became too much for Mariah. "Forget Ebola! Liam has ascertained that it's sealed away from us. We need to find a way to go on, now that the government is gone and we're not going to starve."

Peter frowned. "I heard that the Senate delegates were trying to restart their own little local regime."

"Someone always tries to profit…But if we work together, they won't have a chance." Mariah stood up, tears in her eyes. "You are witness to the birth of a new Ireland. Let's make it a good one!"

With that, Liam rushed outside.

***

Mariah dismissed the gathering, but they left reluctantly and many insisted on asking her questions for which she had no answers. She wanted to check on Liam, so she shooed the last of them out and stepped into the fresh air herself with a chipped mug of water.

She found him sitting against the house wall, and handed him the drink before settling beside him. "Are you all right?"

Liam slurped some water before answering. "Sure. Just stressed, you know. Not every day you speak with a dead man." His speech was slurred.

Mariah giggled. "You need to swallow properly before you try talking."

The giant deformed plants in the yard hid them from the street. Mariah tilted her face to the apple tree, greener than it had ever been before. She turned to quiz him further and found him gazing intently at her.

In the next moment he placed his hands on both sides of her head and pulled her face gently towards his. Surprised at first, she flapped her arms ineffectually and then decided this wasn't so bad. She grabbed at his shoulders and his tousled red mop and clung on even as tears leaked from her eyes onto his cheeks.

At length, unwillingly, she released him and they sat a long while, forehead to forehead and hand in hand. When she drew back it was to wipe her eyes. "I must look like crap."

Liam only smiled and continued to grip her other hand. "It's days like this I imagine I can see the future," he said, gesturing in front of them as if the vegetables contained a magic pathway. "A future where no one is hungry and no one has to work."

"We can't eat if we don't work. No food will grow."

A strange expression crossed Liam's face. "Like slaves. No one has to work like slaves any more. Think of it, Mariah! You and me and all Ireland and someday, our children…" His eyes fell shut and his mouth hung open.

"You need to get in your bed." Mariah attempted to stand, but he gripped her arm.

His eyes gleamed. "Will you get in with me?"

She tapped him gently on the brow with the palm of her hand. "Not when you're doolally in the head like this. Now get a move on."

This time she managed to get to her own feet, and pulled him up with an effort, as he was terribly unsteady. A blotch of colour caught her eye on the ground where he had been sitting: red.

She faced him, horror coursing through her. "Liam! Are—are you bleeding?"

Her quivering finger pointed out the tell-tale spill. He turned, said something that sounded like "Urghh", then promptly got his feet tangled and fell face-first into the vegetation. More red adorned the seat of his grubby jeans; Mariah could barely bring herself to look at it. Then, under the apple tree, he convulsed and vomited—red again.

He's dying. I kissed him. A haze descended on her brain as she stared at the stinking, bloody mess. She clapped a hand over her mouth to keep from spewing, and ran into the house.

From that moment she entered a sort of blood-drenched haze; in the face of the constant nightmare of now, her mind switched into animal instinct and blocked out most of what followed. Time took on a strange teint as if all of it was happening at once. Only brief apertures of actual consciousness existed for her, but even those were like staring through a dim tunnel. The worst had come.

⸎⸎⸎⸎⸎

Deborah and Peter stand by the back door, talking. They turn towards me at my frantic entry. My words make no sense in my head but I spit them out anyway, Liam is bleeding dying dying bleeding out there, help him help, let it not be true. Peter charges past me and Deborah begins to wail, the plague is in my house, the plague is in my house first. Peter supports Liam and half-drags him to the bathroom, I hear water, water, gushing, splashing, red, red everywhere. I touch my mouth again where I kissed him, where I loved him, do I love him—would I want him, he wanted me but he is sick, no one ever wanted me like that, it can't be real, just his sick mind. It is all too horrible, too disgusting beyond words, too unfair when we were about to start afresh. *I close my eyes.*

A sound rouses me. It is dark outside, it is someone coughing, I look up at Deborah covering her mouth. In a moment Peter is at my side with water, Mariah, I thought you fell ill too but you're not bleeding, I think it's just shock, come on now, snap out of it, we need you. Deborah is still coughing, trying to contain it, but just as Peter and I turn towards her from our place on the floor, a drop of red slips between her fingers and makes for her carpet. Terror mars her ancient face watching the slow-motion sliver of blood floating down. Oh gawd oh gawd screams the old lady and rushes to the kitchen, to do what I cannot say. Peter stares into my eyes. Where is Liam? He drops his gaze at the question and points towards the back bedroom door, holding on is Liam, at least for now. Peter's voice is slow and sad, *he cups*

109

my face in his right hand.

Someone is crying in the front doorway; it is a child, one of those who was with his parents when they followed me along the tracks and gathered here. He is maybe all of four years old, he is smeared in blood and completely distraught. I am alone, I go to him and nearly keel over at the smell, he has been sitting with dead bodies, poor, poor baby, I hold him and let him smother his sobs in my shoulder. By now Peter has heard and he follows me into the bathroom where we get the wee fellow clean. But no sooner have we wrapped him in a fresh towel than he soils it with blood. He wails even louder at the sight of it. Peter clutches the boy to his body, his face towards me is desperate even as he makes soothing sounds. He wraps him in more towels and lays him on the settee in the front room where he falls into a fitful sleep. I do not know where Deborah is. *My eyes are so heavy…*

I leap to my feet. Peter is talking quietly with someone at the door, but turns at my movement. It is a grim day, I cannot say which, but I have a vague memory of Peter spooning soup into my mouth although I did not taste it, I swallowed. The shadow at the door is gone and Peter floats towards me. It's bad he says, already too many victims to count, it is ruining our land. I must go to my family I say, his expression softens, of course you must and I should too but who will take care of these here? Deborah staggers out of her room, not to worry laddie, I'll take care of them, you just come back when you can. But…but she coughed blood, says my disbelieving glance to Peter. She is better, it was only the once, let us get going. To Jonesy, *you go home too, all right?*

I find my bike and swing aboard, finding myself wobbly in this constant haze of horror, but I do not have the luxury of time to walk all the way to the other end of Belfast. Blood is in the streets where people have been taken as they walked, dread lies heavy upon the beleaguered city, I hear crying and it breaks my heart but I pass by again and again, firm in my resolve. Finally I am home and Da and Darian cry out in joy to see me. Our hugs are long as if it has been more than just a day or two. Jemima is more subdued than usual and whines as she lays her head in my lap. Like last time Da cooks us a good vegetable stew and we sit around the table far into the night. *It is good to be here.*

In the morning Da coughs a little but insists it is nothing. We sit together all that day and the next, enjoying one another's company as much as we can considering how afraid we all are, but the cough does not go away. Darian catches it too and soon the two of them are hacking up blood. I help them to their beds and hover around for most of the night until I fall exhausted into my own cubbyhole. I dream of falling into an endless black pit where there is no end to the terror. I awake screaming and jerk upright. There is a smell, a bad one, and I rush to my father's side, alas, his bed is full of blood and his soul long departed. Darian stretches a hand towards me, mumbling, but there is little left to hope for. I kneel and grip his weakening fingers. "Tell Andi..." he wheezes, then his expression changes. "You. Please, survive. You have to. For me." His eyes close. Does he mistake me for his lover? Jemima nuzzles him, but he wakes no more and his dog is bleeding badly too. She climbs up beside him and lays her head on his chest; it will be her final rest. I curl up in a corner of the kitchen and let the keening *tear out of my throat.*

When I come to myself it is dark again but I can never sleep. I await the day and clutch my knees, shivering and moaning each time the weight of the disaster crashes down on me. I think I carried the infection to my father and brother, yet if that is so, it is beyond strange that I still live. Surely I should have succumbed long ago but there is not a hint, not a sign of anything amiss in me except for grief. The first and faintest pearlescent dawnlight creeps over the eastern ridge and I promise Da and Darian I will return to bury them. Astride my metal steed once more I force myself to turn *towards Bangor in the near-darkness.*

Liam is gone. The news sinks in slowly alongside all the other tragedies. I wonder if anyone ever told his family he was sick, or if they are even still alive...Deborah is trying to be valiant but can barely get up and the house is a total mess of slick blood and puke. I try to help but there is little I can do, no one has recovered as far as anyone knows. The next day Peter comes back and when questioned about his family, can only shake his head as the tears run freely. I run to him and hold him *for a long time.*

One morning we wake and everyone is gone. I do not even know when we lost Deborah, there is such a fog over these past days, Peter tells me it has been most of a week since it started but I only remember snatches, like small windows opened onto the carnage from some hidden place. We knock on doors along the street but no one answers, they have all been taken, are we the only ones left in all the city? Desperate to find life, we assign ourselves suburbs and streets and spend days—weeks?—wandering among empty homes, calling and searching for anyone who might have survived as we did.

Surely we cannot be all alone.

Mariah turned into yet another deserted urban street. It was all so very normal, the terraced houses lined up wall-to-wall, no greenery visible here as the front doors exited straight onto the road, the birds chirping from the rooftops. But no human was there to give greeting. Several times a cat had followed her, only to fall back when she got too far from its familiar territory.

She had long discovered it was impossible to knock every door in the city, so instead she made a point of calling out loudly as she went down the streets. If anyone was alive, she hoped they would be able to respond.

Much as she didn't want to, she constantly churned the past weeks over in her mind. Most of the worst of it was lost to a sort of melancholic trance, some vault in her brain where she buried the horrors, never to be seen again. Yet some images would remain with her the rest of her life—the little boy crying at the fateful stains, her father dead before she got to him that morning, watching her brother's life seep out. She couldn't remember eating except for her father's stew and the time Peter had fed her in her stupor, and running a hand over her belly, she deemed it maybe a bit more hollow than before.

So much time had passed and Mariah and Peter were still healthy. They had to conclude they must be immune for some reason, although she wasn't ready to accept any of this—let alone that only two had survived. Hence the search through the city. A signal fire would have been another option, but they worried it might get out of control.

"Hello?" she called. "Anyone here?"

She passed several more houses and repeated her call. Just before the end of the block, she heard a whimper of a cry like a child's but a little lower-pitched. Mariah stopped and turned slowly, but could not make out a direction. "Hello? Where are you?"

Another whimper. It came from in front of her, so she approached the house, a weathered brick front like all the others in the street. She almost stumbled into its recessed entryway. In that dark corner between the steps and the house curled a dark-haired woman.

Mariah bent over her. "He—hello?"

The woman jerked her head up. Wonderment crossed her face. "Are you real?"

"Real as can be. Have you had any symptoms?"

"Not a one. My man and three kids though, they're all in there, plus all the extra boarders." She stabbed a thumb back towards the house.

"You poor thing. Will you come with me? There's one other still living that we know of."

The woman crossed her arms and turned her face away. "I just want to die."

"Come on. We'll find a way to go on." Mariah's voice quavered. "What's your name?"

"Aileen."

"I'm Mariah. Now come, we'll get some food into you."

Aileen's features darkened. "You're *that* Mariah? The Guildswoman?"

"I was called that, once."

"Get off my property. Now. It's you and your kind that brought this upon us."

Mariah scooted back, scraping her palms in the dirt. "I'm sorry—I'm so sorry. We never wanted this. Only to feed the hungry…"

"Piss off." The bundle of anger that was Aileen coiled even tighter in her corner.

Mariah managed to gain her feet. "If you get lonely, we're at 45 Cliff Road in Bangor."

Aileen glared up at her. "I'll die first."

❧❦❧

The German stood alone. No one else in his village had survived. He was—had been—a family man, surrounded by his alpine clan even in these times of enslavement. There were still cows in these secluded mountains, and

113

grass in the high meadows, so they had been subsisting by dint of meat and dairy until the plague came and struck down first the overseers of the official food-processing plants, then the section managers, and finally the workers and their children.

He buried his wife and sons and stood a long time over their graves in the gathering dusk, with the sunset striking the mountain opposite into burning gold. It would be their only memorial.

The cows still let him milk them so he did not hunger. But this was no life, without human contact. With the coming of the snow, he decided to leave the mountains, to leave Bavaria and even Germany if that's what it took.

The local overseer had the only motor vehicle in the district. The survivor had driven a car of his own many years ago before it had been outlawed for the common people, so he inspected this one and, after several attempts, got it running. He loaded it with what foodstuffs would not spoil. Said goodbye to the only place he'd ever known and rumbled down the twisted road into the valley.

Death was everywhere. He passed decaying bodies in every settlement. No place had remained untouched; he turned his heading to the west and drove across unfamiliar lowlands.

He crossed into the state of Baden-Württemberg and found things no better there. Soon he learned to predict the proximity of a city by the fetor of the air. Soon after that, he had the bright idea of using the stink to avoid passing right through cities of corpses, navigating by his nose. Of course, there were no other vehicles to be found in the countryside, so he had to venture into a town later in the day when the fuel gauge sank low. After a search in an industrial part of the municipality, he siphoned the petrol from two different abandoned vehicles.

The darkness tightened around him while he continued to wrestle the steering wheel in a generally westerly direction; finally, when the night was black and his eyelids drooped, he stopped at a flat place on the country road and attempted sleep in the van's back seat, in the midst of the silent, dark woods and the silenced land.

When dawn's crisp viridian-filtered light awoke him from his restless tossing, he drank the last of the milk he had brought. He started the van, glanced with concern at the quarter tank remaining, and set off once more.

The gauge sat on empty and he topped a rise where the landscape opened up before him, a broad valley that held an enormous city still too far off to pong. Perhaps this was Frankfurt am Main. He eased into the downhill slope and let gravity turn his wheels for as long as he could until they slowed of their own accord. Then he gently applied the accelerator again on the flat.

Finally the motor sputtered and died. The German estimated another fifteen or twenty kilometres to the city's edge, much too far to push. He sat a while, rested his head on the steering wheel, then disembarked—with a whack to his head for his own denseness—and set out walking. He would seek another vehicle in the city and continue on his solitary way.

10

faith

OCTOBER 2013

Faith huddled inside her coat and strode along the city street, her sensible heels tapping out a deep staccato on the pavement. Streetlights gave off haloed glows and reflected a thousand times over in puddles and drop-spattered windows. The autumn rain fell in a slow and steady Belfast patter that muted both noise and visibility. She pulled her hood tighter, and frowned—but not because of the weather. That was normal.

There'd been another row as she left the house tonight. "I told you I want you to stop going there," her father had insisted.

"Can't you find something…*safer* to occupy yourself with?" her mother chimed in.

"But they're just people," Faith said softly, "people just like anyone else. Being homeless doesn't make them murderous."

"Maybe not, but it does often make them criminal."

"Only because they're hungry!"

"Honey, if you think that's really all it is, you should take off those pink shades now and then."

Faith sighed loudly and a passer-by shot her an odd look. Of course there were those who stole to support an addiction, but they were fairly easy to spot. She sought out lonely souls to befriend, to ward off her own loneliness if she admitted it to herself.

Oh, she lacked for nothing, the sales from the LandCare software ensured that, but she'd never gotten close to anyone since Sarah—if she even counted at all.

Faith passed under the venerable brick doorway of the Mercy Shelter and paused to shake off some of the wet. She hung her coat in the back room and entered the small but well-equipped kitchen, where a healthy hubbub indicated dinner preparation had already begun. One or two of the older, matronly types greeted her before returning to their own gaggle. Faith didn't mind that. She was the anomaly here. She seized a knife and set to work on a pile of onions. When she finished, the tears ran down her face. She moved on to carrots, potatoes, and celery in turn, then took a shift at stirring one of the pots where everything boiled together. The shelter's version of Irish stew was a forgiving recipe, accepting all donated ingredients without discrimination. Tonight, several caterer-sized tins of baked beans also found their way into the mix after all the fresh vegetables were good and soft.

The enormous tureens were transferred to the servery hatch one by one using a stout trolley, and Faith stationed herself behind one with a ladle and a stack of bowls. She peered out into the dining room, now filling with the motley colours and low chatter of their regular clientele. The plaster walls, with their corniche flourishes in the upper corners, were dark with age and the older ladies had been calling for a new coat of paint, but she found them charming in an old-world kind of way.

Somewhere a bell rang, and the public approached the servery in neat rows. Faith tried to smile at each person she served, but lost track at some point in the proceedings. Time passed in a blur until finally all the hungry guests were fed and she carried her own bowl to a table. Its other occupant saluted her, blue eyes sparkling, fingerless gloves raised from his long grey beard.

"Hullo, John."

"Hullo yerself. Been workin' hard?"

She nodded and slurped some of the stew. "And how are you keeping?"

"Can't complain."

"And who'd listen if ye did? That's what my granddad always said—Conor McCarthy, as Irish as they come."

John grinned. "Now there's a man I'd like to meet."

"You'll have to be good, John, and follow him to heaven."

"Oh." John fell silent and let her finish her meal. She sat back and closed her eyes for a moment. John leaned on his elbows. "What's got you down?"

"My folks don't like me coming here."

"Is that all? Why, you're old enough to make your own decisions."

"I know, I know. I should have moved out of home years ago." Faith jammed her fingers into her hair. She wasn't about to explain the memory loss as a reason to stay in a safe environment. "No, you're right, that's not all. The Mercy Shelter is running a volunteer trip. To Germany. Apparently homelessness and hunger are a real big problem over there and our bosses thought they'd like to send a group to help."

John eyed her. "You want to go? Sounds like a good thing to do."

"It's just—how can I justify spending money on myself when I could donate it for food here?" There, she'd said it. Surely a beneficiary of local donations would have a proper perspective on it, tell her to stay here and feed everyone.

"We're all right here," said John. "We get plenty of donations. Did we ever run out of food yet? No."

"But we often run out of beds. I hate turning people away at night."

"And there's a new shelter opening soon across town. Lassie, ye canna cure all the world's ills by yerself, but you *can* make more of yourself."

His words rang in her ears as she balanced in the aisle of a swaying bus on her way home later that night. Making more of herself was a noble goal. A chill ran down her back as she considered the possibility of losing her memory while away from home, but then she paused to count time on her fingers. Three years...a full three years since the first memory loss, and she'd never had another that bad. *That you know of*, she reminded herself, but her confidence ballooned—right beside her fear.

Germany. *I can do this.*

11

mariah

The Zhuang walked alone in the raw light of day. She had fled the family farm, from the haemorrhaged bodies of her sisters and aunts in the kitchen and greenhouse, past the fallen menfolk in the field and the slaves the government had sent them to attempt an increase in their output of food. She had reached the road beyond the ancestral lands, passed the cliffs where she used to freeclimb, passed the eerie silence of the village where she once went to school, indeed had passed out of any familiar place, and kept walking, because she knew nothing else to do.

Her kinfolk had come to France these many years ago from the old country of China, or Zhonghua as they called it among themselves. Born here, she had been seven years old when the Senate took its grim control; she had not left the farm since then, and barely remembered the times before. Now…there was nothing left at all, no one living even in the nearby settlement.

She walked the country road, heedless of direction, mind blasted by grief and horror. Her young body was lithe and strong despite the moderate starvation she'd endured. She walked a long way before thoughts of food flitted through her head.

Dandelions sprouted at the side of the road; she squatted there and ripped them out and ate the entire plant from flower to root. Fingers filthy, she grubbed for hidden roots in the frigid dirt, but they were all gone.

A roaring rumble approached her from the east.

She glanced that way and boggled at the thundering monster blowing up a trail of dust in its wake. So fast she could not hope to escape it, but she had to try. She turned her back on it and pumped her legs to desperate speed.

The white truck drew level with her and slowed to match her pace. Finally it stopped and she outran its position. Metallic noises echoed from the roadside ditches, followed by rapid footsteps.

A man jogged up from behind and stopped her with both hands on her shoulders. She stared numbly into his face, not knowing what to say.

"Madl," began the other. "Was tuste hier alleine?"

She screwed up her face at him, said just one word. "Quoi?"

The man replied in halting French. "I am Bastian, I came from Germany. Everyone is dead. I am looking for a safe land. Come with me." He gestured to the truck.

Whole countries dead? She struggled to understand the scope of the disaster. Let herself be helped into the cab. Held on tight and shrieked as the German commanded it to leap forwards.

When she believed she might not die of the fright, she yelled at him over the sound of the engine. "I am Zhu. I am fourteen."

The city sagged in chthonic silence as the dog loped, confused, through its stilled byways. A life on the streets had accustomed him to keeping a sharp ear out for all sounds, whether human or cyborg or dog or rat. Now there was nothing except occasional wingbeats overhead and the soughing of unrestrained plant growth. There was no sound; the stink, on the other hand, was colossal. He found bloody corpses everywhere, most with viscera hanging loose, chewed by smaller creatures now lying dead in their own blood nearby—dogs and cats and rats. Hunger and desperation he understood all too well, but when he fathomed that their gorging on the meat of fallen humans had cost them their own lives, he stayed well away.

Once he heard movement up ahead, a scuffle that must be more than rodents. He approached with caution, hoping against hope that a human might have survived.

Sure enough, a figure sat almost motionless against a house wall. Her head turned when the dog nosed into view, and there was a scrape of metal against stone. It was the cyborg, Fiona. Her flesh hand twitched as if trying to reach for him. Her metal arm and legs lay immobilised, useless.

"Here…boy." Her voice was scarcely more than a whisper. Blood leaked from her eyes, nose and ears. She forced a rattling breath.

The death in her fist could no longer touch him. He snuck closer and nuzzled her hand, but she was unable to lift it.

"No power anywhere to charge my batteries," she mumbled, as if that would explain the Ebola. "I guess I'll be in hell before the night is out."

The dog settled close by, loathing the scent of approaching death, but the woman needed his comfort. He listened attentively while she confessed her hundreds of murders in as much detail as she could muster, and her blood pooled on the concrete beneath her. She finished with Shane. "I could have loved him, you know, if things were different."

Finally, she ran out of stories, and ran out of voice. A corner of her mouth quirked upwards ever so slightly while she stared at the dog.

After a little while, the dog realised there was no longer a soul behind the stare, no breath in those nano-enhanced lungs that had allowed her to resist so long. Slowly, he backed off and vacated the area. Her flesh parts would now melt into decay although her augmentations might last here forever.

Instead of meat, the dog ate vegetables as was his habit, but he couldn't get the stink out of his sensitive nose. He ran through the west side, here one day, there the next, searching for he knew not what. People? A place without the dead? Finally he returned to the river waterfront and crossed over, heading north. The air was clearer here and he raised his head as he trotted, sniffing happily, his curious tail poised tip-upwards like a recumbent question mark.

This was an industrial area with only sparse vegetation. The dog had eaten that day, so he was unconcerned about food for now—he was just glad to breathe untainted air. He came to the enormity of the Harland and Wolff shipyard, and glanced skywards at Samson and Goliath, its gigantic yellow cranes.

He sat a while at the seawall by the Titanic drydock where the great iron ship had been manhandled into being by thousands of engineers, riveters, and child workers who fetched and carried. It was almost as if their cacophonous labour, the groaning of the gantries and girders, the clink of hammers on rivets, still echoed down the years along with the resonant cheers of the hundred thousand who turned out for her launch, shouting their pride in the world's greatest oceangoing accomplishment—and then the terrible shame at the disaster inflicted upon their dearest project.

For four years the city had poured herself, heart and soul, into the Titanic—before gleefully sending her off to Southampton to begin her task of ferrying the rich and the ragged across the Atlantic. Her loss had been a great blow to the shipyard and indeed to all Belfast. No matter the many other ships built here that no one had ever heard of—well over a hundred of them—only the catastrophe was remembered.

The descendants of the shipbuilders and the cheering crowd had come to terms with these failings, had even found ways to profit. Yet they were all gone now, seeping slowly back into the earth whence they came, losing daily what semblance of humanity remained on their bones in whatever parts of the city they had gone to die. Here was only silence and blessed pure air.

Night fell, and the dog found shelter from the dew in a vaulted shipyard building, where once mustachioed and waistcoated designers had toiled with their slide rules and formulas over nautical blueprints on long sections of linen held up by long tables.

When morning's grey light poked its fingers through the dirty glass, the dog went out again to the seawall. There, he sat so still for so long that a careless seagull landed nearby, encumbered with a rare fish larger than its head.

Two twitches of his whiskers later, the dog had snapped the gull's neck in his teeth and relished a meal of fish and fowl while he watched the restless water in the wide mouth of the Lagan.

The African cast his appropriated line into the sea, a dead sardine provided the bait. He was hoping for something larger to eat.

His dinghy rocked in the winter waves, the long oars tucked inside the stern, the outboard motor saved for situations of extreme need. There were a few hours left before he would have to return or risk being dragged far out to sea on the powerful ebbing tide, or stranded on the mudflat until water rose again in the next nine-hour cycle.

He ascertained that his rod and line were in order, then sat back with a sigh. Ahead of him, the flat coast of Basse-Normandie faded into one of its mooded mists, excepting only the dark, angular shape that was the medieval fortress of Mont St. Michel. It jutted out far beyond the flatlands, an imposing, tangled pyramid of roofs and steps and alleys. The abbey on the rock was almost a thousand years old and had seen centuries of clerics and tourists who approached the summit by its winding roads; now it would see no more.

The African had explored it, now that there was no one to tell him it was off limits, and had taken up residence in one of its towering chambers high above the violent tides. He liked to watch the water come and go—a sign of something still alive in the world.

He focused on his rod and willed a fish to bite. Therefore, he was not surprised when, some time later, there was a mad jerking on the line. With painstaking slowness he reeled it in. When it got close to the boat, it fought all the harder, but the fisherman couldn't ease his aching muscles.

Finally, he brought it in, a frantic, flapping grey mullet of forty centimetres. Perhaps two kilograms of meat if he took care with the cleaning. He took up a knife and stabbed its point at a practised angle into the fish's brain; it twitched once more and was still.

He glanced up at the bay drenched in late-afternoon sun, realised the battle with the fish had cost him too much time. The tide had turned, was now on its way out, and he did not want to spend the night on the ocean alone. A stranding on the sand might be a little better, but then he'd have the galloping return of the fourteen-metre tide to deal with—and that in the black of night.

No, he had better use some of the precious *essence* to get himself to safety. He checked the lever was in neutral, pulled out the choke, turned the throttle to the start position, and gripped the starter cord. He pulled it out until it resisted him, then wrapped it around the palm of his hand and gave it a short, sharp tug.

On the third attempt it started. The mechanical grousing echoed over the water, vanishing into the salt marshes that spread wide around the mouth of the river Couesnon.

Once activated, the motor sped his way back to the ramp at the foot of the fortress, at the place where the causeway joined the rock of ages. Metal hull bit muddy bottom; he flipped the motor off and raised it out of the water before leaping over the side, gripping the painter. He tugged the boat through shallow water and across the wet sand until he reached the vertical slot in the wall where it was safe to tie it up to the ring and bar that allowed it to rise with the tide.

Mullet in hand, he rounded the corner of the wall to make his way to the top of the outcropping.

"Stop right there and hand over the fish," said a voice. The African almost dropped his treasure, but recovered and found himself staring into the face of a desperate babtou.

The white man waved a long knife that wobbled in the air and did not give the impression of actually being dangerous. Icy wind tongued both their faces for a long, silent moment. The African took the time to slip the fish into his belt, then pulled out his own small knife, flipping it artlessly from his left hand to his right.

"Hey, I don't want trouble, I just want food," said the babtou.

The African grunted and walked through the archway into the fortress. "Come share it then."

❧❦❧❦❧

Mariah awoke with a start and a whimper to pitch blackness. She turned her head towards a soft scuffle in time to see Peter's match flare and light a candle, which he set in a stand. The basement went from dark to dim and she remembered: they'd elected to sleep down here last night because upstairs was bloody and smelly and the dead still lay in the rooms. She wrinkled her nose—this might have been the best option at the time, but it was not free of the stink.

"It's all right." Peter approached and touched her shoulder. "We'll be okay."

Mariah gulped. "Can—can we clean up the house? Please?"

Peter nodded and stood to his feet. She followed him up the stairs, a hand over nose and mouth. Upstairs, she ran to the kitchen and pulled dish-towels from a drawer. She handed one to Peter and tied the other across her face, bandanna-style, for some barrier to the smell. He did the same, then they climbed wordlessly to the top storey.

Carnage defiled the rooms and halls where the dying had staggered about in their final panic. Flies buzzed around, and Mariah refused to think about their offspring. Bodies lay askew in doorways, half in and out of rooms, hanging out of beds and chairs. So many had come to the Guild for hope in their final hours, only to end up perishing in the very house that birthed it.

Mariah steeled herself and gripped the arms of the nearest corpse. Glancing down briefly, she recognised the blood-smeared face of Jontie, who had worked so hard against hunger. Eyes and mouth hung open in a grotesque expression of surprise. Mariah ground her teeth as Peter took up the feet and moved off.

He led them out the front door and gate, paused, and turned to the right. A few houses down, he entered a high-growing garden and there they set down their burden.

"Is this it, then?" Mariah grimaced at Jontie's resting place among the weeds.

"Don't tell me you want to bury them all."

It was hopeless. There were too many, in every house in every street. She sagged. "I guess not."

They returned again and again, emptying Deborah's house of the dead one by one. The old lady herself was one of the last to go, and when they laid her beside the others, Mariah plucked a stray daisy and tucked it under her cold, age-spotted hand.

"Are there any more?" Peter asked as they returned.

"Yes, in the back room, but that's the last, I think." Mariah resisted the urge to wipe her sweaty face. She didn't want her hands anywhere near her right now.

She strode into the house and down to the last door, but stopped short with her hand on the lintel, and whispered so softly that only she heard it.

"Liam."

He lay curled on the floor with a relatively peaceful face; someone had closed his eyes. For that she was grateful. She ducked her head as tears fell. *He loved me.*

"What is it?" Peter joined her in the doorway and swore, slamming the wooden post.

Mariah wept freely as they carried him down the cracked road between gardens of overhanging crops that lined up to salute his passing. They set him down beside Deborah, and Peter gripped Mariah's shoulders as they regarded their lined-up friends beneath the swaying greenery. He pulled her gently. "Let's go."

Back at the house, the smell and flies were only slightly better. "It's the blood that attracts them. We'll have to scrub everything."

Peter acquiesced, and they found soap and buckets. But the ancient carpeting was beyond help, so they decided to simply cut out the bloodied parts and clean the boards underneath. Soon a pile of stinking carpet grew outside the front door, and when they had all of it, Peter carried it away to some unknown place.

The smell now somewhat improved, Mariah finally noticed the sun was well on its way down. Maybe that was enough for one day. She still wanted to scrub the walls and wood floors, but tomorrow was soon enough. They had the rest of their lives, after all.

After they washed up in the bathroom, with its water fed from a clean roof tank, Peter cut up part of an oversized courgette—after all that, the fertiliser still worked—and they ate it raw in the basement, still the only fully clean room in the house. Mariah found the strength to smile at Peter. "Thank you."

"For what?"

"For helping to give this day some purpose."

"All our days have purpose. We just need to find a way to go on."

They slept one last time in their oubliette—this time with only minimal olfactory unpleasantness—and arose to attempt full disinfection of all the rooms in the house. The mattresses were all ruined; so were those in the houses they investigated along the street. Then Peter remembered a house that had been empty, down past Main Street, and they took a walk.

The stink of death wafted everywhere along with swarms of flies. Some bodies even lay in the street. Mariah forced herself not to look—there wasn't anything more she could do. Now and then the wind from the sea would caress their faces with fresh air, which she sucked in with relief.

The empty house showed blue sky through its collapsed roof where the makeshift tarpaulin flapped in the wind. It yielded several clean beds, so they set themselves to the arduous task of carrying a couple of heavy mattresses back up to Cliff Road. The old ones they tossed over a wall down the street.

Mariah snagged several scrubbing brushes of varying age from the empty house, too, and after the beds were in order, she and Peter set to work to remove every trace of sickness from their dwelling. In time, everything smelled of soap, and she declared the two upstairs bedrooms fit for use. They investigated Deborah's linen cupboard and found clean sheets. Plenty to be had in any other house in the city, too.

They dragged two freshly-scoured wooden chairs to the back step of the house and sat by the open back door a while in the evening, watching the sea change colour between the roofs of the dwellings on the seafront road. The buzz of flies reached their ears now and then.

"I guess we could knock those houses down now and no one would care," said Peter.

Mariah snorted. "You and what dozer?"

"Better yet, we could move into one."

"After we just got this place tidy? Not on your Nelly." Mariah considered the sliver of darkening water. Sea views were pretty low on her list of priorities right now.

Her ponderings were interrupted by loud knocking at the front of the house. She and Peter exchanged astonished glances and leapt to their feet. They dashed up the hallway to the front door and yanked it open.

There stood Aileen. "I got the right place, I see."

Peter was quick to insist that the ladies take the upstairs bedrooms while he would occupy the back one downstairs, where Liam had died. The bed had no mattress now, but its old spring base would do for tonight before they fetched a new one from the empty house on the morrow.

Aileen shrugged away her change of mind; she was little inclined to talking, which Mariah took to be both a sign of grief and a sign that she was no less bitter about the Guild than before. She couldn't blame her. *I don't much like the idea of the Guild myself any more.*

As new days kept dawning and still none of the three fell sick, Mariah's nagging certainty that they would still succumb turned to doubt and finally fell away altogether. They worked in the garden, both Deborah's and others nearby. It was a constant battle with the flies. Even though they were more interested in the dead, they still visited the crops more than anyone liked. When they finished work one of them often stomped around the garden waving branches until the swarm went away again.

At the five-week point they noticed a marked drop-off in both flies and wafted smells. Peter estimated that the corpses would dry up completely before too much longer, and they would be free of the constant stink. Summer had long turned to autumn; now, the first real cold of winter came on. They gathered wood to burn in the stove, and stored plenty of potatoes and onions in the basement, along with whatever vegetables would keep well. Some other plants might grow through winter with the help of the fertiliser if there weren't too many frosts.

<hr>

Bastian and Zhu had driven a long way since their meeting. They had stopped for the night between quiet fields and slept a few fitful hours in their seats. The morning brought more miles, and yet more, the contour of the land changing as they passed out of Bourgogne, crossed the Massif Central, and dipped into the valley of the Loire saturated with chateaux. Bastian wondered if Zhu was aware that they would soon run out of land, and what they would do then if all the Continent was dead.

The flatlands approached and swallowed the truck whole. Ahead loomed a misty apparition, a fairytale castle in black and grey. "What is that?" asked Zhu, pointing.

Bastian shrugged. "Let us find out."

It was much farther than it looked. The truck rumbled on, the fortress growing larger and larger until finally all the land fell away.

Bastian drove out onto the causeway and they trundled along for several more minutes, water on both sides of the road. Finally, water blocked their way and he pulled up short of the tide. The road led straight into the water; he thought he could make out a similar ribbon of road climbing out of the sea at the foot of the castle.

"It's going out," he said. They sat there in the truck, watching the water recede and reveal more of the road with each minute.

The sun dipped below the swampland that extended to the horizon on their left; the full moon rose on the right, dim and blood-red although the sky was clear. An eclipse. Bastian and Zhu stared transfixed as Earth's shadow crawled away from the lunar face. When the moon shone white again, Bastian roused from a pleasant half-doze to discover the entire stretch of road was dry but for a few puddles, though the retreating waves lapped not far distant. He started the engine.

Zhu woke then, too, and watched wide-eyed as they traversed the man-made bridge of earth and stone. They arrived in the shadow of the castle and entered through a series of gates just wide enough for the truck to pass. Bastian stopped and made as if to turn. "Seen enough?"

"Please, can we go on? It's so pretty." Zhu was enthralled, staring at the quaint medieval buildings that surrounded them. Bastian sighed once and steered on an inwards route, though he didn't know why. They had reached the end and there was nowhere else to go, perhaps.

The road narrowed in and became more bumpy as it ascended, ancient houses leaning in on both sides. Finally the truck had to come to a stop at the foot of a long, long flight of stairs leading up into the belly of the enormous church that sat on the pinnacle of the rock.

The last of the engine's rattle faded away into silence. Zhu, too, was silent, and Bastian didn't know what to say or to suggest. They were high up now, high above the tidal flats and far from the low shoreline that disappeared in the black of night. He was about to turn to his young companion and suggest leaving, when moving shadows forced their attention forwards.

Two figures ran down the steps towards them. Bastian's first reaction was horror, and Zhu clutched at his arm; yet when the men reached the vehicle, they slowed, as if uncertain. Bastian decided their faces were more curious than dangerous, so he clicked open his door. Zhu gripped his elbow harder, and he returned her intense gaze for a moment. "It's okay." He hoped he was right.

Gently he loosened her fingers and ever so slowly, he got out of the truck. "So," he said to the men. "Here we all are."

131

The fish was split four ways that night. Conversation was subdued but Zhu was amazed she could even be a part of it, amazed that there were four people still living. No woman and no young person, for which she was particularly sad. She mostly sat silent and listened to the three men discussing what to do next.

Candlelight flickered on their faces in the high fortress chamber. The burning sticks in the stone hearth did little to heat the room, so Zhu poked around in the scattered trunks and found several layers of clothes to warm herself.

Eventually she grew sleepy and found a dusty velvet couch to rest on; in her slumber she heard what the men decided. They wanted to take Noah's boat and head for England—perhaps the island would be spared.

An image of this venture took shape in Zhu's subconscious as her dream made it into fact: herself and three men in Noah's ark, fighting their way through enormous waves of blood.

She found herself awake, then, as the discussion continued.

There would have to be a search made in nearby towns for more *essence*, enough to carry them across La Manche. An extra tankful would be preferable in case of bad weather, but they would have to make do with whatever they could get.

The Frenchman muttered. "We should leave the kid behind. She'll only slow us down, another mouth to feed."

"*Non!* Why would you say that?" The African's fist pounded the table.

Bastian stared at the Frenchman. "I will not leave her alone."

"Got your eye on her, have you?" There was a sneer in the voice.

Chairs scraped back. Zhu, tense, squinted through closed eyes. Bastian stood over the others, fists and forearms clenched, angrier than she'd ever seen him.

Noah was deep in thought. "What if she's the last woman in the world? What then?"

"We'll have no talk of that," said Bastian, clearly uncomfortable.

"But we will need to, someday." The as-yet nameless Frenchman cast a glance at Zhu that made her shudder.

On one of his scouting trips around town, Peter found a glasshouse. They made a project of dismantling it and carried it piece by piece to a vacant yard nearby. This required yet more trips walking across town and back again; somehow always on the lookout for other people like in the days of old. Mariah often found herself pausing when she crossed Bangor's main street with a section of metal or glass on her back, peering up and down the once-busy thoroughfare. But despite the occasional rattle of neglected windows in the gently soughing wind, she was the only one there.

She finally brought the last piece on its journey and approached the place where Peter and Aileen were reassembling the structure. Laughter reached her ears and she smiled herself as she leaned the glass pane on the ground. "What's the joke then, eh?"

"Oh, the usual." Peter reddened.

Aileen held up a piece of metal and turned it to discover which way around it should be attached. Her dark eyes glittered. "If we want to repopulate, he'll have to be a polygamist."

Mariah gulped and exchanged a quick glance with Peter, who was concentrating very hard on fitting the framework together.

He sighed from his seat on the ground. "Is it not bad enough to be the only man left in the land?"

"Aye," said Mariah, "to marry both of us would be too much to ask."

Aileen spluttered into another peal of giggles. Peter studiously tightened another nut. "But say we were to have children. Would they be immune like us?"

"Maybe the virus died out," said Aileen.

Mariah nodded, hands on hips. "Possibly. Like the scum doesn't last beyond a week or so—we have to grow new batches all the time and reapply it."

The three of them slid Mariah's last pane into the frame and shimmied it until it fit. Peter slotted in the last bolt and motioned to Aileen to tighten the nut.

"I guess we won't know unless we try," said Aileen, biting her lip.

Mariah's gaze shot up to the woman who had already lost three babes. "I don't want to try."

"Then," said Peter, "I guess we'll be the last."

133

The Welshwoman stomped the windswept clifftop path above Marloes Sands. She was alone, the last of the Cymry, and angry about it. Why couldn't someone else have been left behind? But no, she was the one sentenced to a life of unbearable solitude without so much as a dog to talk to.

The setting sun turned the sea to gold and the small islands of Gateholm and the more distant Skokholm to stark black silhouettes. Delicate strands of rutilant cloud flared in turn and progressed to darker reds and greys. The scruffy green of the cliffs took on a glow it never had at any other time of day. The woman smiled just a little. This was still just as beautiful as ever—and she could have her fill of it every day instead of working insane hours at the fish processing plant in exchange for just a few morsels of piscine innards. Now she had plenty of fish in her hovel. The thought of it made her stomach rumble, and she laughed at herself before turning to make her way back home, where she would light a fire and cook her meal.

Her face towards the south, she squinted at a pillar of dark haze that rose from beyond the cliff's edge. Perhaps she was seeing things, but she didn't think so. She hurried her steps along the curved and trampled track until the contortion of the land allowed her a view of the beach.

A fire! The red flame flickered against the sunset-tinted sand, dark driftwood forming its structure and fuel. One of the shadows moved.

People, she muttered, and sought the next safe descent from the cliff. It was one of the steeper ones, requiring care if she wanted to stay uninjured, so she forced herself to move as slowly as was needed. Eventually, two or three storeys from the bottom, her patience failed and she slid painfully on the dust and grit until she landed in the cool sand.

She took only a moment to gather her wits and dust off her rear, then she launched herself at a sprint across the beach. The strange fire was dying down and the moving shadows were gone. She ran faster.

There were only embers left when she reached the place. Human footprints both large and small dotted the circumference; she followed the four rows towards the breakers, and dashed after, only seeing the big tin dinghy against the silvery water when she was almost upon it.

"Hey!" she called, waving as she jogged into the cold, shallow sea.

The four occupants of the boat stared blankly at first. Then the youngest one, an Asian child, let out a wail of something the Welshwoman hoped was joy. She waded in far enough to grip the pitching gunwale and stood there sizing up the three men—she didn't like the look one of them was giving her. She ignored him for the moment and asked the others, "Where are you going?"

The black man smiled. "Wherever there's life."

Mariah pushed open the peeling door to yet another abandoned house, Aileen and Peter at her side. All the houses were abandoned now, of course, but it still felt like they were impinging on people's privacy. The people whose dry bones now lay in their homes where they had fallen. Peter closed the door, blocking out the winter wind although it was not a great deal warmer inside.

The method was familiar now: the three spread out to the different rooms to check if any usable items could be found. Aileen headed for the kitchen, Peter for the backyard, and Mariah crept up the stairs although there was no one to disturb.

In the upper hallway lay a pile of cloth and dust. Mariah averted her eyes. Poor soul. They all were. The bedroom revealed more remains, but a tallboy was partially stocked with sheets and clothes, and the wardrobe held two old woollen blankets. Clouds of dust arose as Mariah drew them out, but they could be shaken clean and used to keep warm. She carried her booty downstairs and placed it on a clean section of floor.

"Is that you, Mariah?" It was Aileen. "Come take a look at this."

Mariah followed her voice into the sunny kitchen. Aileen stood before an open pantry, regarding its contents, then shifted a little. The daylight fell squarely onto rows of glass jars. The two dropped to their knees.

"Is that..." Mariah touched a finger to a jar lid.

"Preserves. Don't know what, but there's likely sugar in it."

Peter clattered in, bearing a wooden bucket. He set it down. "Got something?"

Aileen's eyes gleamed. "Dessert."

"They must've had a Senate guard in the family, to get food like that. An' I doubt very much if it was part of their actual rations, if you know what I mean." Peter hefted a jar, popped the seal and twisted off the lid. He sniffed. "Blackberries!"

Aileen leapt to a drawer and yanked it open. "Spoons for everyone. Dig in!"

The preserves melted on Mariah's tongue, bringing back memories of the times when she was a little girl and fruit was common. Of course it was common enough now, after a fashion, but the fertilised fruit was dry and tasteless no matter how they watered. It simply grew too fast. But this... *This* was real.

A giggle bubbled up and she swallowed hurriedly before letting out a deep belly-laugh. Aileen shoved the jar in her face. "Here, keep eating. There's plenty."

Peter laughed too, then the three of them joined in a sustained burst of hilarity and pure enjoyment as the wind whistled around the house.

❧❧❧❧❧

Talking filled most of their hours—there was little else to do when the fierce rains kept them from going out. There were unusual storms from time to time, too, with extreme forces of lightning, wind or hail—reminding them that they were alone with the vagaries of a planet largely abandoned.

They told stories from childhood, their growing-up, incidents recalled both fondly and not so fondly. They told of their lives under Senate control, how they kept themselves going in those oppressive early days in the workforce.

Rain was now an almost constant companion. So it was that when one brumous day the rain never came, by mutual consent they all headed for the beach. It was the first sight Mariah longed for when the confinement drove her mad, and she wasn't about to let this opportunity pass by.

When they came to the shore, she set off alone along the expanse of sand. The sea was steel-grey and wild, while the wind whipped her face. The beach was bleak and winter winds made mountainous waves. Gulls sat upon the wind above her. Beyond them the sun shone eerily pale through faceless white clouds. Spray rising from the crashing ocean formed a mist that blanketed the outline of the land, transforming it to an ethereal cloud-world. Blinking, she trudged on. She remembered again the day she had spent with

Naomi in this very place just a few months ago. How everything had changed! There had been the very real possibility of losing her, but no one expected that the whole world would be lost in her aftermath.

She passed several dozing black Angus cows and calves. Such a shame they had become too wild to approach—the milk would be a welcome addition to their vegetable diet. She continued on to climb the small knobby hill at the end of the beach. Puffing slightly, she scrambled to the top and surveyed the vista. The city was still vast in its expanse; from this distance, across a curve in the coast, it looked as it always had, but the accustomed sounds of habitation were now stilled. All the thousands of homes and towers were completely abandoned, as if some eerie evacuation had emptied them of life. A lone freighter ship hung slightly askew at anchor near the narrow end of the Lough by the city proper, and on the opposite coast, giant chimneys stood as monuments of industry looming through the mist. Towards the east, the ocean stretched to an endless horizon, but Britain lay just out of sight, where Mariah's mother had once visited in the time before the last Troubles. Britain had been a hard taskmaster to her beloved Ireland in bygone centuries, but the relationship had improved with the modern age. Mariah did not hate her as some had done. She turned and made out Peter and Aileen—tiny figures back along the beach in the haze made by the pounding surf—then stared once more out to sea.

A dark speck in the waves. It was much nearer than the vague horizon, yet so small that it disappeared when she focused on it directly. She blinked and squinted hard; the object moved. She watched it grow larger and nearer, then, to her surprise, heard the whirring of a motor and voices.

Mariah slithered down the wildly spreading damp grass to sea level and puffed out little clouds of steam. She ran to Peter and Aileen but no explanation was needed: they heard it too.

They called and shouted. Soon the large tin dinghy was just beyond the breakers. Its occupants waved and yelled, but the ocean drowned out their words. They revved the motor and cut through the waves. Soon Mariah and Peter were wading through the shallows to greet them, now ignoring the coldness of the water. Seizing the sides of the boat, they pulled, and the new arrivals jumped out. Together they lifted the boat far up the stony beach.

There were three men and two women. One man was dark-skinned, and a girl with raven-black hair must be from much farther east. The others were more like the local pale kind.

"We come in peace," offered one man by way of greeting. "My name is Bastian." His voice was warm and cheerful, and he spoke with a strong accent. Mariah wasn't sure, but she didn't think he was a Briton. He laughed nervously then, but his joy was visible. The ice was broken.

"Where have you come from?" Mariah ventured. "And what is your story?"

He strode forward and offered his hand, which she grasped. "I am glad to find a healthy land where the plague has not struck. But first we need food and water—we have been upon the waves for longer than I like."

"Of course!" Mariah unclasped his fingers and shoved her hands into warm pockets. Then she could no longer face them and turned away abruptly. She would have to disappoint the strangers completely.

The locals guided them along the quiet streets to home. They took in the rows of little houses, and appeared to be listening. There was no sound at all except the wind and the footsteps of this small group. Mariah glanced at Peter: smiling, and Aileen: detached but curious.

At the house, they ate a meal of boiled potatoes with spinach, which the visitors devoured as if they hadn't eaten in a month. As they finished, Bastian broke the silence.

"We have come from a land once enslaved, where we were forced to work for nothing. But a foul plague wiped out the overseers, together with our families and indeed the whole population. We found one another eventually as the only survivors and decided to journey together to a new land where there was neither slavery nor bloody blight. This tiny boat has carried us these seven days in wind and weather." He frowned. "But why is your city so silent?"

"Our city is empty!" Mariah's tears flowed as hope vanished from their faces. "Do you not know? The sickness came also to us on the winds of heaven. We have lost all our kin. All society lies in decay. We are all that remain." She took a breath and continued. "Friends, you have come to a good place. We have everything we need, the land is pleasant. Be welcome—we will share our lives with you."

It was not the better world they hoped for, but Mariah was still glad they had come. The new arrivals would occupy one of the nearby houses. Peter and Mariah insisted on checking it out first, and as they suspected, there were corpses turned to dust and bones. Carefully, they filled several sacks with the remains and tore up the carpets while Aileen kept the others occupied.

On finishing, Mariah and Peter stepped out into the cold, starless cloudy night. The darkness was almost utterly complete; but something bright caught Mariah's eye in the distance, over towards the industrial zone inland from Ballyholme beach. When she looked, it had gone. She frowned. Must have been seeing things.

"You okay?" asked Peter.

"Oh…yeah. It'll be nice to have a bit more company, won't it?"

It was Peter's turn to frown, but now they were back at Deborah's door. Mariah stepped into the front room where the small gathering sat subdued.

"Your new home is ready! Want to see?" She smiled as best she could.

For some days they left them to recover from the rigours of the journey, feeding them well and finding more clothes for them to wear. As time passed, Mariah learned their names and stories.

Bastian was from the deep interior of the continent, a high and landlocked place of alps and rivers. At first he had travelled alone in an abandoned overseer-vehicle for as long as the fuel held out, always with the hope of finding a land that was clean. He travelled through vast desolation in industrial zones that had once been highly populated, yet in all of Germany he found no survivor. The stench was everywhere and he avoided cities when he could, until he ran out of petrol completely. He had walked to the next city, chosen a truck from outside a decaying factory, and had been driving many hours in the wilderness that, in the absence of signage on the winding back road, he suspected now traversed the old territory of France. Then he came upon a figure running along the road. He was finally able to coax her to join him in the truck. In this way they went on to the coast.

Zhu, who came with Bastian, was only just a teenager. Her family home was some distance to the south of where Bastian found her, and there lay all her kith in their blood. Her clan had migrated to this remote part of France before Zhu's birth; she considered herself a native. No one in the small town had survived, so she ran into the wilds of nature to drown herself in grief. The shock was still upon her now, but she had survived the dampness of the journey in better health than the others: she was the only one without a persistent sniffle.

Dark-skinned Noah immigrated to France shortly before the travel restrictions clamped down. Originally he came from North Africa, even farther distant again. There, slavery had once been common, and indeed the people had long ago sold their brothers to other lands for work. The abolishment of this practice caused great rejoicing, and so the recent slavery of the worldwide Troubles were particularly odious to this people whose great-great-great-grandparents knew what it was to fight for freedom and gain victory. He had survived on the northwest coast of France, where Bastian and Zhu found him, then they cast off in the boat in search of better shores.

Rowena was an average kind of Welshwoman, if averages still existed in the world. Below her light-brown cropped hair, her eyes told of suffering and loss. She was unnaturally quiet at first; like all the survivors, the grief was still embedded in her soul. Yet Mariah observed her face when Rowena thought no one was watching and discovered a compassionate person she wanted for a friend. She was the only Briton—had found the others when they landed on a beach in Wales. Her withdrawn behaviour was strange to Mariah until she considered that she herself would not be any different if she had been the only Irish survivor, suddenly thrown in with complete strangers.

The fifth new arrival was a mystery. Scowling darkly, his face spoke only umbrage and bitterness. Mariah could not think ill of this natural reaction, yet it dampened the general mood. He spoke little and it took a long time to find out that his name was Lucas, a Frenchman.

Whooping in the street summoned Mariah from her bedroom soon after dark on the first day of January. Lucas twirled there with a bottle in his hand and some sort of bag in the other; Noah carried a wooden crate not far behind him.

"Good finds, then?" Mariah tried not to yawn. Looting was so last year.

Noah approached and set down the crate. "Look at this."

Squinting in the dimness, Mariah made out a series of glass bottlenecks. "Wine?"

"Happy new year," hollered Lucas to the world. He tripped and spilled the contents of his bottle and his bag—glinting bling scattered across the road and he dropped to a crawl, gathering up the jewellery again. For all the good it'd do him.

Noah set down his backpack and fished out a can. "Wine and caviar. Time to celebrate."

"Thanks. You didn't have to share."

He shrugged. "What fun would it be all on my own?"

What fun, indeed.

Winter closed in even more. They huddled in their houses, sleeping many days away in weariness of living. The French practised their rusty English, and Bastian helped, since he spoke it quite well. They often laughed at the guttural sounds he produced when explaining German.

In the chill, they grew cranky and irritable. Arguments broke out frequently—Mariah was sure she'd fought with everyone at one time or another. Even so, the loud voices and slamming doors were echoes of other times with other people now lost, and for a few moments she almost fooled herself into believing that none of the horror had ever happened.

They occupied themselves as they could. Noah continued to search among the empty houses and find objects to keep himself amused—a guitar, a cookbook, several bicycles and an outdoor barbecue found their way home over time and did indeed increase the quality of life somewhat.

Bastian read books, as many as he got his hands on—whether novels or how-to books, encyclopedias or comics. Rowena set about sewing a huge patchwork quilt made up of tiny pieces cut from clothing she found on forays into the neighbourhood. Mariah often sat with her and watched as her needle poked up and down, up and down, and they talked much and discovered a deep sort of kinship that went beyond common experiences.

It was on one of these occasions that Rowena revealed she was a geneticist. Mariah's jaw fell open. A corner of Rowena's mouth twisted upwards. "Don't you know what that is?"

"Well, of course I've heard of it before. I just wouldn't have expected you to be one. You don't seem the type."

Rowena's laughter filled the room. "Yes, believe it or not, I've spent years of my life in a white lab coat, examining virus samples in test tubes…"

"So you understand how the plague worked?"

141

"Generally, yes."

"I've always wondered what made us immune—why we didn't die when everyone else did…"

"I suppose I could try and find out why. But I'd need a proper laboratory, like at a hospital—probably a DNA sequencer."

Mariah gazed unseeing at the apple tree outside the window, the same one where Liam had kissed her beneath its boughs. Now, its large, strangely bulbous fruit swung heavily from the branches. "The Royal in Belfast is a pretty big hospital. Do you think they might have what you need?"

Rowena shrugged and reached for another square of cloth. "Maybe. But that would mean we'd have to get samples of infected blood." Mariah screwed up her nose, and they laughed.

"Want to try sewing a square? There's another needle here somewhere…" Rowena showed Mariah the technique she was using to stitch the pieces together. They changed the subject by silent and mutual agreement. They were the immune. Surely now they were safe. No need to go poking around in dead bodies. And as they found more things to pass the time, peace returned in some measure.

It was during this winter that I struck on the idea of writing this history. I suppose some of the others may have descendants eventually, so there will be someone to read this someday. Strange to think that I am probably the only writer in the world. The irony of this does not escape me. And so I labour on to finish what I have begun. Panoramic empty years stretch out in front of me. So alone. Life is only made up of what we can see with our eyes and hold in our hands, and there is little enough of that. I must make something of it.

12

faith

NOVEMBER 2013—JANUARY 2014

Jet engines roared and Faith gripped her journal and pen. Too late to back out now and say she wanted to stay home. She couldn't explain where the months had gone since she decided to go to Germany; now she was strapped to the seat that would carry her there. Other members of the group sat around her, but she didn't know them yet and was not currently inclined to strike up conversation. Faith flipped open the book and began to write.

28 November.

Here we go. John said I should do this, to improve myself. Well, we'll see about that. I've just decided I hate heights. And—takeoff! Eek. I fear for my life, not really, but the terror of flying is about the same thing.

One hour later: Have gotten used to being in the air, more or less. It's still freaking me out. We'll be there soon.

Wow, just wow. Yesterday was the most intense thing I've ever experienced. We landed in Frankfurt, transferred to an ultrafast train, and rode it through stark winter landscapes of snowy meadows and black pines, punctuated by long tunnels and quaint villages perched in valleys. The group, six of us, got off the train in Regensburg where local students met us and whisked us to a bus which took us several miles out of town. As we left the city centre proper by way of a narrow but very solid cobblestone bridge, I looked back and spied a jumble of red roofs and church spires extending in both directions along the riverbank. It was as thoroughly medieval a skyline as one could imagine, except for the incongruous inclusion of hundreds of satellite dishes pointed at the sky. When we got off the bus after a half hour, we had to walk up a bit of a hill to get to the home of our hostess—Elsie, a lovely motherly type from what I've observed so far.

3 December.

This is not at all what I expected. My writing's all wonky because I have to do this in the bus—there's no time otherwise, they keep us so busy. I'm supposed to cook dinner at home tonight. Anyway, after one day to recover from the long journey, we headed into the old city to the homeless shelter where we are to assist for these two months. The work includes cooking, of course, and there's an attic full of secondhand clothing to sort for handouts to the needy. But I didn't know they were going to send us out into the streets as well. For part of the day, we are to talk to the beggars and tell them to come to the shelter for food. I don't really like talking with so many strangers. I mean, I really don't like it. It exhausts me. I asked if I could just do the in-house work, but the locals looked at me weird. This is how they operate and apparently having foreign visitors on the job helps attract people who need to come. Well, I'll try my best to handle it, but I'm NOT a happy camper. Whoops! Here's our bus stop—

8 December.

I am dying inside. Day after day we bus into town at an ungodly hour, work hard in the kitchen and clothesroom, and spend afternoons chatting up bums. That's really what this is about. Yes, they need food and whatever help we can give them, but mostly they are reluctant to accept it. They're a rude and antisocial bunch, they don't want what we're offering, yet I'm forced to offer it again and again. The worse problem is my teammates who came with me. They seem to think this is normal. Some of them have done this before, true enough. Today, Helen asked me if I struggled with depression. I said no, of course not, then she said, "Please don't be so morose then." Morose? I think I just don't talk as much as her. Also, she doesn't like my dress sense.

17 December.

I just learned that the shelter is closing for a couple of days before Christmas. I'm pushing to be able to get out of this place. Amy and Joe are keen to come with me to Paris.

23 December.

We did it—the three of us in France for two days. We went on the train and it took all day each way. I remembered a few of the main sights from my school lessons and the others had no idea, so I was our guide and we rushed around viewing things and climbing things and acting like tourists. Ascending the Eiffel Tower at night was like a dream, with the sparkling city laid out below. It was all a bit stressful, to be sure, but a weight lifted off my mind—only to crash down again when we arrived back here in Regensburg. It's oppressive, this place, somehow…

4 January.

So Helen dragged us to Rome for a "break". I didn't want to go, asked to stay behind and just hang out with Elsie—who didn't mind—but no, this was not permitted. I thought the Germans were rude, but they have nothing on the Italians. Shouting in the streets and overinsistent street hawkers and a cheap, tight hotel suite that we all had to share. Now we're back in Regensburg yet again and I can't wait for all this to be over. Still, I enjoy the culture and history around here and how it seeps into me. It's all so…old, so colourful in its antiquity, even if that contributes to the dark cloud that seems to hang over it.

15 January.

Interesting day. I finally had it out with Helen, but not like I imagined. I mentioned to Amy that the methods we had to use were really, really bad for

145

introverts. Amy went to Helen and insisted that we get the girls together to hash it out. Amy proceeded to explain how hard I was finding things, and Brenda very passionately agreed. Lizzy didn't understand at all, and Helen was having trouble with the concept, so we backed up and talked about different personality types and how not everyone could thrive under identical circumstances. We ended the evening on a better tone than we had begun, even if I wasn't entirely satisfied.

27 January.

I'm done for. Stayed up a bit late last night talking to Elsie, then woke up early this morning and decided to doze off for a just a few more minutes. When I came to myself again, it was to a circle of concerned faces looking down at me. I felt around my mental space and discovered a very great gap—everything was gone, and my head hurt so bad. Slowly over the next hours I recalled where I was and reread my journal, such as it is. Eventually I must realise that not everything comes back, especially if I'm not at home and if people make a fuss and don't know how to handle the situation of returning memory.

We go home tomorrow. I can't wait to get away and start fresh. This has all been a total loss.

13

MARIAH

APRIL 2080

Belfast grumbled no more. Her people were gone, slowly disintegrating in her atrophy of houses and streets. It rained again, gently, one of those bright wet days when water amplified the light and turned it to effulgent silver. The dog had returned to his old haunt at Shankill Road, the lean-to that provided the best shelter from precipitation.

The rain fell on the chaotic muddle of fertilised flora, grown into grotesque shapes before expiring as its newfound life ran out. It fell on the hardy weeds that still remained, uncaring, stronger than ever, in their scattered corners. It fell on back gardens choked with enormous vegetables in advanced stages of decay, their trees in a worse state than they had been before the fertiliser came, the earth turned again to lifeless sludge between the walls. It fell on the drooping verdigris cupolas of once-ostentatious public buildings, the copper rooves now endowed with a pale green patina. It fell heavily, dislodging loose rooftiles and pouring into the houses below, where there was no one to suffer or care. There were more potholes now, more red bricks that fell from the old edifices and crumbled slowly into the ground.

No mellifluous singsong of brogue yet filled the workplaces, although it was the hour. No wild wains roamed the streets in play. No grandparents kept an eye on them. There was no muttering about the Senate or the evils of politicians; no cyborgs supervised the byways of the city.

The River Lagan flowed on, unceasing, into the Lough just as it always had, sending currents past Carrickfergus and Bangor. The hills still stood guard on either side, though no one was there to see them—to look and anchor their lives and say, that is Antrim and that is Down, and this is where we are.

The dog grew nervous as night fell, although no more rocks would fly over the Peace Wall; no more packs of ravenous dogs threatened his life. He was the only one, and he was lonely. He could sleep without disturbance but he did not. The wrongness of the empty city pulsed in his every heartbeat, keeping him awake, wondering in his doggy way what had happened.

Even the Peace Wall was crumbling, without the residents on either side to take care of it. Such a stubborn, long-standing bastion, a symbol of both safety and war in a locality that had seen many deaths over many years.

The Protestants, most descended from Scottish immigrants, had wanted Northern Ireland to remain with Britain not least because they long enjoyed various privileges. The Catholic minority wanted the island to unite as a republic together with the Catholic South and its equal rights for all. Later the fighting developed into a focus on religious identity, then finally it existed just because it had always been that way.

Animosity died hard when there were murders unresolved—murders by and of the local police, murders of widows and children who were caught in the crossfire. Peace was not easy when every child in certain generations had grown up with such psychological trauma that it was compared to that of the London Blitz.

The dog eventually fell asleep and, with nothing to wake him, remained slumbering until daybreak. His head shot up—he'd heard something. Like a rock falling. He stood carefully and poked his nose outside, then, smelling nothing particularly amiss, ventured into the day.

A quick scan of the area showed where the sound had come from: a section of the Peace Wall that had disintegrated all at once, dropping several bricks beside the lean-to. The dog approached, sniffed the edges of the hole, then slipped through without touching the precarious structure.

He had not been on this side of the wall in this particular place before. The houses were a little smarter, a little better-kept, though the difference was fading faster every day. Nosing into a garden, he found a large pumpkin that was partly putrid, and used the rotted hole to get his lower jaw inside and gnaw it open.

When he had eaten his fill of the dubious vegetable, he went and sat by the gate in the forlorn hope that someone—anyone—would come home.

The cold winter slowly drew to a close and the warming breezes brought life to the chill ground. The changing season and new growth springing up was a balm to Mariah's heart. The survivors shed their heavy woollens and ventured into the sunshine. They laughed and cavorted in the cool waves and colour returned to the world. Everything was grand, all things considered, and given the situation, she should have been content.

"I'm going rock climbing," Zhu said at breakfast. "I used to do it all the time." She reached for another mandarin from the precarious mound piled up on the back patio. The little citrus tree had flourished in the glasshouse.

"Isn't that dangerous?" objected Lucas. "You might fall and hurt yourself. Or you might die. I can't allow that. We need all the women we've got." He laughed. "But at least there'd be more food for the rest of us then."

Zhu glanced pointedly at the abundance of mandarins, then threw him a dirty look. Mariah threw one of her own. It was like Lucas was doing his utmost to make everyone hate him. Later, Zhu set off for the boulders at the far end of the beach, and Peter went back to reading from the books Bastian had gathered.

Winter's deadness was gone, but in its place restlessness gnawed at Mariah. Humanity was all but gone from the silent land and purposeless existence—waiting for the end. After them, no more would live. They were surely the last gasp of the aged world. Empty years unrolled ahead in Mariah's imagination; there had been a time when she would have wanted children, but not now, when the same vile plague might befall them—and so even though it pained her, she decided she could never consider a real relationship with any of the survivors. In that sense, nothing had changed. She was alone before the disaster, and alone now, too. Perhaps the others were coping better, so she kept her despair to herself, not wanting to drag them down.

They planted crops again and soon were eating of them, thanks to Naomi. Mariah still missed her.

One morning in the early part of summer's heat, she brooded more than usual and decided to go for a long walk. No one wanted to go with her, so she set off alone for the land beyond city limits. After an interminable row of houses—terraces, duplexes and singles—she soon passed through an area that had once been termed industrial. The large square buildings were made for practicality and not style, so she was glad to get past them and out towards the open places.

She walked at first on a broad expressway, then a country highway that cut straight through the bucolic landscape towards the south, a fine road that allowed her to walk without thinking much about it. It was the Newtownards road, a place that had only recently had a reputation for being dangerous to be in alone. Now it was as safe as anywhere in the land. It dipped and rose with the landscape, giving the impression of an undulating ribbon when she looked into the distance—a cracked grey ribbon overhung with tree branches, some dead, some alive.

The road led past fields where long-haired sheep were still fending for themselves. One or two of them looked up placidly as she passed by, then went back to grazing. After leaving them behind, she came across a dead sheep. Flies buzzed around the body. She wrinkled her nose and increased her pace to pass it, but not before she noticed it lay in a pool of congealing blood. *Can sheep get Ebola?* Dogs could, but she'd not seen livestock affected before. Mariah decided to ask Rowena about it later.

Time slipped by, and the sun rose higher towards noonday as she tramped on. After what must have been several hours she found her way to another once-busy byway that led up to Scrabo hilltop, where she left the road and struck through the bush on the steep slopes. Coming to the foot of the tower, she squatted down with the long arm of the sea in the curve of Strangford Lough spreading out below. The view was clear to the east coast of Ireland from here, and…yes…she imagined that might be the Dublin shore ghosting through the haze to the south, past the hulking mountain of

Slieve Donard. Quickly she checked the tower's door—still locked. Someday she'd bring tools and force her way in, to survey the land from the very top. She stepped back, hands on hips, and tilted her head back to inspect the pointy tower with the round appendage on one corner, perhaps a spiral staircase.

Even in the old days it had always been quiet up here—so it nearly felt normal and she almost imagined none of the dying had ever happened. She was well familiar with the spot from long-ago outings with family or friends, when they had travelled in cars and arrived fresh and lively to chase about and splash one another on the beach far below. But now she was alone and miles away from all humanity—not that all humanity was very much these days. She let her mind drift to memories of better times: Naomi, Deborah, Da and Darian, school friends from the time when freedom still reigned, and the days spent in Guild gardens near here much later.

Mariah leaned back on the grassy bank, linked her hands behind her head, and allowed herself to doze off with pleasant recollections passing before her mind's eye. It wasn't without pain, but time had healed the grief somewhat. The sun was warm, the spot comfortable. As she lay half-awake she found herself wishing she could fall asleep and never have to rise again. To escape from this wretched existence and snooze in blissful peace forever, dreaming of better days.

She woke disoriented and found the sun was well past its zenith, though still high. Was there movement behind her, or was it just a dream? She sat up, stiff from sleeping on the hard ground, and stretched.

"Hey there," came Peter's voice from the bushes, from where he presently emerged. Mariah frowned, then smiled.

"Don't sneak up on a girl like that."

"I thought you might be up here, and it's not good for you to be alone. Not good for any of us. So I gave you a few hours' start, then came after you."

Wait. "How'd you know I like to come here?"

"Liam told me." He cast his gaze down. "He had it bad for you, you know."

Mariah wasn't sure what to say to that. "I—I know."

Peter settled on the grass beside her. "So how are you...really?" He studied her face and something in his eyes unnerved her.

She told him of the gnawing unrest that had come upon her since winter's passing. "We have no purpose any more. We are tormented with grief, we're the last of our kind, we live comfortably and all we can do is wait for the end, " she finished lamely. With no more words to add, she pleaded silently for him to understand.

He nodded slowly. "I don't think any of us is without frustration." The smile in his eyes betrayed a greater happiness than the serious words he spoke.

Mariah ignored the contradicting signals, but wondered if he understood as well as he said he did.

"Quit staring at me, willya?" Mariah got up to go. Peter was too attentive and it made her restless.

She charged down through the foliage, picking a steeply inclined path so that Peter couldn't hover so much. She grabbed at the slim trees, one after another, and swung herself down the bank towards the highway.

There was a vaguely familiar buzzing, to which she failed to pay attention. She forced her feet onwards.

Peter shouted. "Look out!"

It was too late. She blundered into the source of the sound.

"Bees!" They swarmed in a hollow within a group of trees, and now she was in the middle of them. She flailed her arms and tried to back away—but running uphill backwards in a forest is not the easiest thing to do. Sharp pain bit across her hands, arms, and even her face. Then someone grabbed her shoulder and pulled her back.

"I think we'll go round thataway," said Peter as he guided her away from the angry bees. She sank down on the leafy forest floor and tried to examine the damage to her skin. It had hurt worse than it really was; she pulled out three stingers from one arm and two from the other, then reached for her face. There was only the one stinger, but she couldn't get a grip on it.

"Where's a mirror when a girl needs it…" she muttered to herself.

Peter pushed away from the tree he was leaning on and squatted down to inspect her. "You don't need a mirror. Let me get that out for you."

"Gerroff!" She pushed his hands away. "Don't touch me."

"Fine."

Mariah groped her face with her two index fingers, wincing as she brushed the stinger. "There it is." She poked at it from both sides at once, but it wouldn't shift.

Peter stood a little back, arms crossed, smirking.

"Wipe that look off yer face." She returned to the task at hand but only succeeded in releasing more of the venom into her cheek. It burned more than the other five stings together.

Finally, Peter tut-tutted and uncrossed his arms. He moved closer and laid his thumbs on her cheekbone. She flinched at the contact. *The nerve of him!* But he was concentrated on gently pushing his short thumbnails towards each other to release the venom sac. Finally it slid out and he shook it to the ground. She surveyed the bees' trees: old-fashioned beehive boxes stood between the trunks. Turning back, she caught Peter's eye. Both spoke at once, the coolness between them notwithstanding.

"Honey!"

Slowly they approached the scene again, and Peter reached for one of the slotted frames. He pulled it carefully out of the case, causing a fresh swarm of disturbed insects. He sucked in his breath sharply and let the frame fall back, but not before they'd both glimpsed the golden treasure layered thickly within. Without thinking, Mariah grabbed his hand and pulled out the two stingers he'd collected.

"We just need to find a way to calm the bees, then we can harvest the honey!" Peter's gaze strayed up the gully and his eyes grew wide. Mariah followed his gaze. Beehives were lined up in the forest as far as the eye could see.

"This must have been someone's bee farm," she said. They took in the sight of rows and rows of flaking white-painted boxes. Eventually, they turned away and continued bushwhacking until they arrived on the highway some distance farther down than where she had entered the woods on the way up.

The road was overgrown at the edges, since no one took care of its upkeep any more. But it was still a good wide path, and they headed back down the hill. It was a long way home and they were silent for most of it. As they entered the city limits, brighter reflections filled Mariah's mind. They reminisced about the old days before the dying, and then even farther back, when there were no Troubles—at least, not the kind that had come later. This kept them happily occupied until they turned into Cliff Road, laughing at some memory of a funny incident. It was a golden moment: though life had changed drastically, all of the Troubles were truly over and would never come again. Mariah could smile and mean it—it was possible to remember days gone by without fighting off tears.

Peter stopped in the road before the house and reached for Mariah's hand. "I need to tell you something."

She snatched it away, turned from those shining eyes, certain she knew what he was thinking. "Don't. Please."

"Is there no chance for us, then?"

"You know I don't want to place a child at such terrible risk of death." She shushed his stammering objections with a wave of her hand. "I know a relationship doesn't have to lead to children, but really—how long is that going to last between passionate lovers without the, uh, tools of better times?"

He touched her arm, gently, as if she would break. "You do feel it too."

"That's of no consequence." She huffed and pulled away again. "It would be different if we knew we were safe."

She turned and pushed her way inside, but nobody was home. Must all be next door. They wandered over to the neighbouring house, where they were met by total silence.

Mariah caught a whiff of fear in the air and a shiver went through her. Peter's face betrayed the same. She was about to speak, but was interrupted by a groan from beyond the doorway on the right. Her heart pounded. The door was slightly ajar, and Peter laid just one finger on it. It swung open with a gentle creak. Fearful faces looked out.

Bastian lay on the bed panting. Mariah and Peter joined the others around him. There was a pile of bloodied sheets in the corner.

"It began this morning," murmured Aileen. She was pale and trembling.

"I'm so sorry!" Bastian's face creased in pain and there were tears in his eyes. Terror was on every face. No one needed to say a word; it was all too clear that the plague they despised had struck again.

Mariah hid her fear to ease Bastian's last days. The sickroom remained peaceful in face of his agony. In truth, the unanswered questions tortured her. Was it possible for the immune to get sick? Was the immunity perhaps only temporary, or had the virus mutated somehow? Would any of them live another day? Nobody knew.

In the end it was indeed all they could do to show Bastian a calm front, and it was precious little. He held on bravely for some days and then died in terrible pain, exactly as they had all seen it so many times in those tortuous weeks last summer.

That afternoon, after burying Bastian, they sat together silently. Fear welled up as it had not done for many months, the fear Mariah had believed was forever behind her. She did not know what to think—but surely if death came now, she would welcome it.

"It will soon be over, thank goodness," she remarked to the room, and her words clattered like weapons to the ground.

Peter raised his head and glared at Mariah with fire in his eyes. "How can you think so? Surely life is a gift, and we should rejoice that we still breathe!"

Aileen, beside her, stared with big round eyes. Mariah barely heard her as she whispered, "I want to live."

Mariah stared back. Gaped. Her breath caught in her throat. It was too much. She leapt up and rushed from the house.

Blind with tears and without thinking, she entered the once-secret portal next door and stumbled down to the old basement room. It was of course pitch-black and she groped till she found a candle in the niche by the door. Matches took a wee bit longer, but eventually her shaking fingers lit a tiny flame in the underground chamber. Familiar walls met her gaze; it had been a very long time since she had been in this room. She remembered the many meetings, the friends, the plans and strategies born here, and she remembered the first time she ventured down those stairs. She remembered the hope that welled up within her in those days as she finally seized the opportunity to step into life. Life! Surely the greatest of all gifts.

Mariah sat there until the candle burned low. Her breathing calmed, her pain eased, and peace was again hers. She did not know why she of all people was spared, but she was, and that was enough for now.

She stood, and with renewed vigour she blew out the candle and returned to the world above. Finding Peter sitting cross-legged in the hall, suddenly she knew what to say.

"Peter, I'm sorry. Life is a treasure, and we should seek to make the very most of it." Something made her unsure of herself in his presence. "That is, uh, I really don't want to die. I want to live."

"And we will," answered Peter with determination. "We will find a way." He pushed himself to his feet.

"What do you mean?" She smiled at him, but he remained serious.

"Just after you ran out, Rowena suggested taking a ride to Belfast to look for a laboratory setup in a hospital. Noah went with her. It's a long shot, but if there's any functional machinery, maybe we can find out what killed everyone."

"All the way to Belfast and back by bike before dark? That's crazy!" She strode towards the front door.

Peter followed slowly. "I guess they want to survive."

She paused at the threshold. *Me, too.*

14

faıth

⊱ ⋯⋯⋯⋯⋯⋯⋯⋯⋯⋯⋯⋯⋯⋯⋯⋯⋯⋯⋯⋯⋯⋯⋯⋯⋯⋯⋯ ⊰

FEBRUARY 2014

Upon her return from Germany, Faith spent an awkward few days fielding questions from her parents and acquaintances about the trip. When she persisted in monosyllabic answers, they got the hint and drifted away, leaving her alone, as she best liked it. The memory of Germany made her gag even now. All those people—and being forced to talk to them. So she had seen more of the world. But it had almost cost her her soul. Sure, maybe she was being overdramatic, but to her it was logical.

One rainy day, the clouds had lifted shortly before sundown, just like always, and Faith watched the comfortingly familiar play of colours across the evening sky. Whatever else might change, she could depend on a grand old sunset from her room.

The phone rang; the ID panel lit up with the Mercy Shelter's number, where John had told her to fly free. He'd meant well and he was a good friend, but that whole scene repelled her now. She narrowed her eyes at the glowing display of digits and bit her lip until the phone stopped ringing.

No, she didn't blame John. It was herself she was mad at. The last of the sunset faded from the sky, and without even turning on the light, she curled on her bed and fell into sleep, a sanctuary for her ragged soul.

Morning came with the songs of birds. Faith blinked a few times at the bright light from outside—she hadn't closed her curtains—before getting up to investigate the day.

Even though her window faced west, the glow of morning sun reflected back at her from every cranny of the outside world. She opened it and leaned out, breathing the sweet, damp air. An involuntary laugh bubbled up inside. It was a day for wandering the wilds.

She dressed quickly, snagged a banana on her way through the kitchen, and strode away towards the rising sun. The unseasonally springlike weather soon had her shedding her coat, which she knotted around her waist, making sure the banana was secure in its pocket.

At Ballyholme she descended to the sand and danced back and forth with the waves. Not in them—the water was surely far too cold for that—but the day would come soon. *Then I'll catch you.*

Finally, at the end of the beach, she noticed a little dirt trail that led up between the lush hilly pastures and the coastal blackrock. She stepped up onto it and felt like she'd started an epic quest.

The slope was easy, though the path was narrow and twisted around the outcroppings. Each turn opened up new vistas of moss-filled inlets, waves crashing to the harsh shore, and inviting patches of grass that had grown among the rocks.

As the coast started to curve back around to the right, she found one such patch and rested there to eat. Her back against a standing stone, she squinted at the sky and its puffy little clouds that played tag with the sun, sending shining rays chasing across the bay while the gulls wheeled overhead.

Funny. She could almost discern her home from here, on the other side. So close, and she'd never ventured here before. It might yet become one of her favourite places in the whole wide world.

Tucking the banana peel back into a pocket, she stood and considered her next move. It was early yet, there was plenty of day left, but she had no more food.

Well, she'd have to make do. There was more to be discovered.

She wandered on at her easy pace, stopping often to marvel at a flower or a particular angle of rocks and sea. Above her in the fields, an occasional cow made an appearance, until, passing a lone house, she came upon a small village nestled in a bay. She racked her brain for its name...she'd once known what lay out this way, had perhaps visited by car.

Groomsport. That was it.

The tiny town slept still. It was Sunday, after all. Faith crept by its shuttered shops and to her delight, found a continuation of the coastal path. She embarked upon the next leg and wandered another hour through winding shorelines, past little rocky coves, a rusting pile of metal that might once have been a fishing boat, and a caravan park, until she regretfully decided she should turn back.

On the return journey, everything went by faster. It wasn't new or unknown any more; now that the scenery was familiar, time flew apace until she found herself in Groomsport again.

The village had come to life in the meantime. Delicious smells wafted from the bakery and Faith contented herself with standing nearby to inhale them, not having thought to bring her purse.

Her rapturous sniffing was interrupted by the sound of bells. She glanced up at the steeple. It couldn't hurt to wander by the church on this bright, sunny spring day. The bells faded away as she came level with the steps. Curious, she hesitated and was about to move on when the door opened, and a tall, angular man about her father's age stepped out.

"Hello," he said, "I haven't seen you around here before."

It was a strange thing to say, but his enthusiasm was disarming. "Uh—I'm Faith Diamond. From over Bangor way."

"I'm Taylor Wallace. Pleased to meet you." He fiddled with his collar and Faith noticed it was one of those funny church ones. So he was a priest. She was about to sidle away when he called out her name. "Faith Diamond! I've heard that name before. Wasn't it you that went to Germany with the Mercy Shelter mission?"

Chills coursed up Faith's legs. The new lightness of this bright day threatened to crash down around her. She could only nod, mute.

"Aye, I read about it in the local news. It must have been grand." There was a wistful tone to his voice.

"Um, no, I hated it."

"Why's that then?"

"I only want to feed people. They made us go out and drag people in who didn't want to be fed."

"Aha, that old trick."

"I'm good at growing food and cooking it," said Faith. "Not making people eat it."

Mr. Wallace laughed. "Fair enough." He regarded her pensively for a moment with a glow of concern in his face. He drew breath, paused, and finally spoke again. "Did you know we have a sort of food kitchen here in the church? And community gardens."

"Is that so."

"In fact, I was hoping to infuse some new life into all of that. My daughter will help…and this other young chap. Would you like to join in?"

Faith glanced sideways at the trickle of people now entering the building. Several smiled at her and she had a sudden desire to work with a team again, one where she could do what she did best and not be pushed around. "Uh…sure, I guess so."

He gave an incredibly wide smile and shook her hand. "Welcome, then."

Faith ducked inside and sat herself in the last pew. After three hymns, Mr. Wallace got up to make the announcements. He peered at the scraps of paper he clutched, and drew breath to speak.

"I am pleased to tell you that we have secured the services of three wonderful young persons to oversee our community food service."

This guy is moving fast! She shifted and fidgeted in her seat as he went on.

"Keira Wallace, Davin McRae and Faith Diamond have agreed to assist us in this vitally important work."

Faith stared at him, then shut her mouth when she realised it was hanging open. Certainly couldn't accuse him of being slow on the uptake. She practically felt his excitement and just plain joy at the new development, radiating all the way to the back of the room.

During the remainder of the service, Faith failed to pay attention to Mr. Wallace's sermon, but she did notice how he preached with extended hands and an uncanny light in his face, as if he were a direct channel for love. Perhaps she was distracted from the sense of his words, but his simple happiness spoke volumes.

The service came painlessly to an end, and the people filed out of the pews. Faith followed them, not sure what to do next, but once outside they all went into a hall just across Main Street. Coffee was served by comfortable ladies as little children chased about among the milling throng. She accepted a steaming cup and sat down in a sagging chair against the wall.

"Hey, Faith!" She looked up. "It's Keira." The seats on either side of Faith were taken, so she stood before her, hands on hips. "Girl, it looks like we've got some organising to do!"

Reassured by her warm grin, Faith smiled too. "Which one is Davin again?" she asked, glancing around.

"Oh, I just saw him over that way." Keira waved her hand in that direction. "Come on, let's grab him."

What would he think about being grabbed, Faith wondered as they navigated their way across the room between clusters of chatting coffee drinkers. But she liked the way Keira talked.

They came upon two young men deep in conversation who almost resembled identical twins, but not quite. Keira pointed. "Davin is the older brother, and Donnell is the other." She interrupted them without hesitating.

"Donnell, you'll have to let me steal Davin. We need him." Donnell's eyebrows went up, but there was a smile on his face. Keira proceeded to grab the older brother's arm—she wasn't kidding about that—and steered him away. "You can talk to him at home!" she flung over her shoulder.

Faith glanced at Donnell, who shrugged, unconcerned, when he caught her eye. Following the other two, she fished a piece of shortbread from a bowl on a low table and bit into it. *Mmmm.* It had been a long time since that banana.

They headed for the kids' corner of the room and dropped down into the big beanbags. A moment of silence followed, but Keira's mirthful gaze banished any awkwardness.

"So from what I understand, there's this handful of folks, all ages from kids to retired, that want to help with this. Our job will be to show them what to do in the gardens, for one thing, and then organise community events where everyone is invited." A natural-born leader, then, this one. "Got any good ideas?"

"We should see about having a regular group meeting," said Davin staunchly.

Faith nodded. "I'll have to check out these famous gardens of yours.

Figure out what needs doing." Another idea came to her. "How about we meet at some other time, the three of us, to sort ourselves out?"

They settled on Tuesday night to meet in one of the church offices and discuss further plans. Then Keira invited them to eat with her family, in the church house on the other side of the parking lot. Faith was a little embarrassed to accept, but she was hungry and it was a long walk home, so she did just that and to her surprise found herself enjoying the small talk as they got to know each other—telling of the past. Keira had spent some years picking cabbages on a farm before beginning to study nursing, and Davin worked as a painter, although he was a qualified chef.

It was late that afternoon by the time Faith walked around the coast again on her solitary way home. Her footsteps scrunched on the stony path and she enjoyed the sunshine on her shoulders. In one morning everything had changed: a new project to be excited about. She had no regrets, although it had all happened so surprisingly fast. Some things were just meant to be.

The Tuesday night gathering in Mr. Wallace's office became a regular affair where they planned out the meals. Laughter was never far distant, and they teased each other mercilessly, knowing it was all in fun. Friday nights were the community meals where a dozen volunteers joined them to prepare the food. At her first one, Faith got up nervously and requested the sea of faces to think about volunteering for garden work.

The very next day, several people showed up while Faith was up to her elbows in the wet muck of the garden patch. She wiped rain from her eyes with the top of her forearm and reflected that she was, in that moment, perfectly happy.

Weeks and months went on, and Faith came to know Keira and Davin very closely, as well as becoming acquainted with the group of volunteers. They were an interesting bunch, if something of an amoebic mass. All had in common the desire to help feed the hungry in their local community and they learned gladly from anyone who had knowledge to share.

Faith had that knowledge and gave it to all who came with questions. At times it was exhilarating—and she wondered if her Mercy Shelter teammates had felt like this in Germany. But this was completely different. Now she was where she was meant to be...now there was no overwhelming sense of despair, no being forced to act as live advertising for a service the hungry never wanted.

It was quite the opposite now, with Keira as a dynamic motivator, Faith giving instruction on high-yield gardening, and Davin running the kitchen, the setup couldn't be more perfect. Faith longed to accomplish more, now that she was full of motivation, and entered the summer intake at Queens University in Belfast. She chose to study agriculture, of course, to fill out what she had deduced by herself, and a side topic of German, strangely enough, because she had learned a little of it from her trip.

As the weather cooled off in earnest, Keira put forward the idea of doing a people-skills seminar to help with the positions of leadership they found themselves in. They found a suitable course that was running in Londonderry, and the idea of getting away for a weekend appealed to all three, so they drove up in Keira's old green Chevette and booked into a youth hostel there for a few days.

On the first morning, Faith awoke with a start in the strange bunkbed. A face—there had been a face in her dream. A man, but not Davin, and not anyone else she knew, although she could swear he was almost as familiar as her own mug in the mirror. She shook her head and the shreds of his appearance vanished from her mind; she hauled herself upright and teetered down the ladder on tender toes to begin the new day.

It was cold and rainy, but they enjoyed the small-town feel in Derry. They cooked simple meals in the hostel's kitchen and spent the daylight hours at the local business institute. They walked along the riverbanks in the evenings, discussing what they had learned and skipping pebbles into the water.

On the way back home they detoured to Ballycastle, where Keira's grandmother lived in a cottage by the sea. Although they couldn't stay long, she gave them tea and cake and made them promise to come back soon.

Most times she would use her scooter to get over to Groomsport these days, but when she had the time to spare, she loved to walk the coastal path that had first led her there in the spring. Its ever-changing miniature vistas of sea and stone never ceased to bring her joy.

Working with Keira and Davin for the common good of Groomsport had an electrifying effect on Faith's inner life. Rather than being withdrawn and alone, she shared her life with them and found herself happy. She still suffered from memory losses; some mornings she would wake up with that stabbing headache and vague emptiness and slowly realise what had happened. She would be tired and quiet on those days, but otherwise, she reflected, she had an almost storybook-perfect life—she would hardly have written it differently herself.

15

mariah

april—may 2080

Having become too spooked by the utter emptiness of his old haunts—even the lack of rocks hitting his roof held an inherent wrongness that sat badly with his soul—the dog fled the city to the east, crossing the Lagan one final time, passing the shipyards and the City Airport, and continuing on around the coast.

He followed a forgotten trail between ancient trees and ocean cliffs. The misty rain floated and pelted him from all sides, sylvan shelter notwithstanding, until he was soaked through and shivering—never mind that it was nearly summer. He hurried on, hankering for a dry place, descending a steep curve, finally bursting out onto the wide beach at Helen's Bay. The white sand glistened in the rain; beyond, the remains of a green, an enormous house loomed half-ruined. The dog jittered. There was no life here.

A ray of sunshine split the cloud long enough to form a rainbow over the next promontory. The dog was eager to pass by this creepy house with its sharded windows, and trotted quickly to the end of the beach. There he found another steep path that soon led him high above the sea once more and into a large stand of surprisingly surviving pine.

His nose told him something was foul but he did not want to go back. Cautiously he continued, one silent step after another, until a crumbling concrete doorway came into view, cut into the side of the hill. He paused at the threshold long enough to ascertain that all within were dead, then turned his face away and trotted on, ever eastward, in search of he knew not what.

Only moments had passed on his continued trajectory when something leapt out of the undergrowth and bit his leg. He howled, shock and pain mingling with the fear that he would have to fight for his life. Then all was still and he realised this was no living attacker.

A crude trap made of mismatched blades and rusty springs had hold of his left rear ankle. The more he shook it, the tighter it clamped him, despite its rickety appearance. Dizzy with the ache, he collapsed to the ground and worried at the metal contraption with his teeth.

Hours passed. His lips and gums grew raw from gnawing at the rusted metal. But he was making progress; there was nothing else he could do. At great length, as it was getting dark, the spring broke under his ministrations and the clamp came loose. Instantly the paw throbbed as blood coursed through it fully again, then leaked out and seeped into the ground. The dog shivered uncontrollably. He was only just able to drag himself the few feet back to the bunker of death, where he would at least have protection from the rain and wind. He licked his deeply torn ankle until it stopped bleeding, lay down on a disintegrating carpet that was far too close to diseased human bones for his liking, and swallowed as he peered into the utter blackness.

He did not sleep a wink that night.

Peter and Mariah busied themselves with the jungle of fruit trees in the front yard, throwing expired greenery onto the road, scattering new seed and applying fertiliser, and finally collecting the ripe fruit to stow in baskets, which they then carried into the house. It was dark when they finished, and they leaned on the front fence in silence while they watched for Rowena to return with news.

After an eternity of its own, there came the whish of rubber meeting the road, and soon Noah coasted into view, one hand hanging by his side. Rowena was right behind him.

Figures materialised from the houses: Zhu, Lucas, Aileen, silent as the night. Rowena dismounted and gave a little smile as she came near the group waiting together.

"Hey, we took it easy on the way back. It's a long trip!"

Noah nodded his agreement and stared round at expectant faces. "Uh…can we go inside?" The awkward circle broke up and they moved towards the front steps.

Rowena let out a sharp puff of air. "Steady on! There's no way I could have any results so quickly!" The tension in the air lessened slightly, and no one else spoke until all were seated in the living room with lighted candles and some rubbery sun-dried vegetables, although no one was hungry right then except for the two cyclists. They each consumed several chunks of tomatoes and capsicums while the others watched.

"Well, Noah knew where to find the Royal Hospital. Across the river and just past the city centre. It's a big place, though—like several hospitals at once. All full of skeletons now, of course." She wrinkled her nose. "We trekked through a bunch of buildings for ages, and at the farthest end of the third floor we found a laboratory containing some machinery we can use. Of course there's no power to run them on, but I'd expect a hospital that size to have some kind of backup power supply."

"That's all you can tell us?" Lucas got up and made to leave the room.

"This is going to take a lot more work than you think. But I don't think anyone's too busy to help, right?"

"What's actually involved in finding out if we're still safe?" Peter asked.

"Okay. First we have to get power to the lab. Then I have to see if I can run the machine at all. After that, I have to get samples from all of us, from Bastian's infected blood, and if possible, also from someone who died in the first outbreak last year."

Aileen leaned forward. "I get it. Then you run a test for each sample, and bingo! We know why we're immune."

"Not so easy," Rowena said. "I have to prepare the samples—I used to do that all the time, but I hope I haven't forgotten how. That involves

167

fluorescent labelling, which will take some time to do properly. Then I can run it through the sequencer—that's the easy part. The machine will spit out a sequence of letters, then I'll have to go through them all, looking for similarities, perhaps a sequence we all have in common for some reason, and how it's different to the sequences of those who have died…"

Mariah had no idea it was so complex. The work ahead was not particularly enticing, but she spoke in spite of herself. "Let's do it. Rowena, we have to know."

Lucas, still standing by the door, cleared his throat loudly. The others gave him their attention.

"Eh, I might be able to activate that backup power for you. Or at least rig up a car battery so you can run the damn machine."

"Thank you." Rowena's voice broke the silence once more. "Come with me tomorrow and we'll see what we can do. Right now, I just want to sleep."

Peter nodded and left, clapping Lucas gently on the shoulder in approval as he passed. Mariah got up and took hold of a candlestick to carry to her room. It was a start.

Late the next afternoon, Mariah and those who had remained behind gathered once again in the front yard, talking in subdued voices. Finally, Rowena and Lucas came into view. They were deadly serious, but hope shone in their eyes.

Rowena leapt off the bicycle and threw it to the ground.

"Lucas is a genius! You should have seen it!" Still atop his cycle seat, he looked at the ground and protested, but Rowena went on. "We couldn't find any backup system. But he went round gathering batteries from all the ambulances on the grounds, wired them all together, and figured out a way to convert the voltage to what we needed."

"All I did was isolate the room from the power grid and attach it to the batteries. The sequencer has its own adapter to plug into, so it doesn't matter what strength you feed it." He grinned sheepishly. "Easy enough, really."

Producing a cloth bag, Rowena reached into it. "I brought enough swabs for all of us. I'll take the samples right now, if you don't mind." She took a scrape from inside each person's cheek, packing and labelling each sample.

The next morning, she braved the back room where Bastian had died, and scraped some dried blood from the floor.

"That's all I need," she said, holding up the sample in its plastic bag.

"Are we going to clean up in here one day?"

Mariah wrinkled her nose. "Yeah, sure. I'll do it right now. What about the other sample, from someone who died earlier?"

"Plenty of examples down at the hospital. I'll use a piece of a dry bone or whatever."

"Okay, okay!" Mariah waved her away.

Rowena laughed and headed towards the street to seize a bike. Mariah gathered buckets and scrubbers and some kind of soap in a half-squashed plastic bottle and went to work.

Days passed, each much like the others, except that Mariah swore the tension rose with each hour. Soon they might know why they were immune, and perhaps they'd find out if it'd stay that way. Rowena returned each evening, tired from the long ride.

"Why don't you just sleep over there?" Aileen asked her. "Surely a hospital has plenty of beds?"

"That's true," said Rowena, "but most of them are full of stiffs. I'd rather be with the living than the dead…"

After a week of testing, Rowena appeared at the front gate just after dark with a heavy satchel slung over her shoulder. Inside the house, she opened it and spread a sheaf of papers over the low table.

"These are the printouts with the results. Now I have to read them and find matching sequences, if there are any."

ACTG. AAGC. TGTT. Made up of only four different letters, the code filled page after page. Mariah's head swam just looking at it. "You're serious, aren't you, Rowena? You have to read all this stuff?"

Rowena nodded, still perusing the printouts. "Can you guys maybe find me some coloured pens? So I can mark the patterns I find."

Noah grinned and left the room.

"Expert salvager on the job," Mariah said. "I bet he has a good idea where to find some."

And so they passed the days with the usual harvesting, cooking, beach walking and scavenging. Sometimes Mariah stitched bits of Rowena's quilt to keep her company as she analysed the papers.

One evening Mariah was loading giant apples into baskets yet again when the front door burst open.

"Mariah! Are you there?"

"I'm coming, hang on!"

She set down the basket and stepped between the twisted branches of the orchard. Rowena ran down the front steps, waving two sheets of paper.

"Mariah, do you know your blood type?"

"Uh—not exactly. I do remember that it's a negative one, but that's all."

Rowena nodded. "Yes. O negative, from what I've seen in your sample. Same as me." Mariah shot her a puzzled look, but Rowena wasn't finished. "Do you know if you suffered from Regent's disease when you were very young?"

"Is that a blood disease? Mum once told me I had a blood disease as a kid, but I don't know if that was the name."

"Near enough. Want to know something else?"

"Go on."

Rowena looked up at the fading light of day. "Mariah, I have O negative blood too. And I suffered a severe case of Regent's at the age of eleven months. I nearly died, you know."

Mariah's mouth fell open. "Are you saying that's where the immunity came from?"

"I can't say for sure. I've only compared your results to my own so far. I still have to check all the others, and Bastian's, and the other samples from the hospital. But I'll look out for these patterns."

Mariah sat down on the front step, reached for an apple from a nearby basket and bit into it, then talked around the chunk of fruit. This was no time to worry about manners. "Sure. You and I both have this blood type, and we had this blood disease. Why would that make us immune?"

Rowena leaned on the railing and stared at evening's first star in the deep blueness above. "I don't know. All I know is that Regent's adds something to your DNA. It's a real weird disease and no one has ever really understood it. We can ask the others if they know their medical history that far back, and I'll look for the pattern it left behind in your blood and in mine."

A short time later, as the others returned from their day's occupation, Rowena and Mariah peppered them with questions about Regent's disease and blood types. Aileen was sure she'd had it, Noah said his parents told of nearly losing him, Zhu and Lucas didn't know, and Peter remembered being sick when he was three, without knowing what the illness was called. Only Lucas was sure that he had O negative blood.

"Well, from this information, it seems likely enough. But give me a chance to go through all the sequences properly," Rowena said. "This might be the answer."

They went about their insignificant little lives a few days longer, growing impatient to know the truth. As the silent hours passed, Mariah wondered if the childhood disease had saved all who remained. If that were true, then there must be more survivors elsewhere.

Finally the day came when Rowena made her last trip to the Royal Hospital. She carried one more sheaf of papers in her bag, riding home again in the evening light as the others sat waiting on Deborah's front steps.

"These are the printouts for some O negative victims in the hospital. I hope I'll find the difference between their DNA and ours."

"How do you know they're O negative?" Lucas asked.

"It was written in their patient charts. You know, those papers the doctors always write on at the foot of the bed?"

"All right, all right. Give the girl a chance to look over the stuff!" Noah's playful voice had a serious hint in it now. Rowena's blink lasted so long she nodded off for a moment.

Peter must have caught it too. "But not tonight. Let her rest. She's been working so hard—the last thing she needs is a burnout." He stood to go into the house. Mariah yawned and followed. Perhaps they did have all the time in the world.

The next day drew to a close as Mariah pedalled home from the beach with a basket full of kelp. The seaweed looked unappetising, but served to add flavour to many meals. She carried it up the front steps, through the house to the kitchen, and searched for a bucket to store it in until a sunny day came, for spreading it to dry. Then they would shred it and use it as seasoning, like salt but less salty. She set the filled bucket down by the back step and did a double take at the figures moving in the shadows of the next-door garden.

"Hey, what's up? Are you guys dancing?" Mariah marched to the unruly hedge and pushed herself through the gap they had cut in it. Aileen and Zhu stopped their twirling and rushed to assail her. Rowena gave her a tired grin from an old wooden seat, while the other two both spoke at once.

"It's true! We're immune!"

"Not conclusive, but more than likely—"

"It can never get us!"

They leapt around her, whooping like little tomboys. Mariah manoeuvred her way over to where Rowena sat and lowered herself to the ground by her chair. Rowena watched the others' joyful exuberance a little longer.

"I can't find out how the immunity works. This is just a guess..." She sighed. "We all had Regent's disease years ago. I found parallel patterns in everyone's DNA except Bastian's. He only had a part of the code added by Regent's—enough to keep him immune for the first version of the plague."

"You mean there are other versions?"

"One other at least. The one he caught and couldn't fight off."

Just then, male conversation rumbled from the road, with the creak of wooden wheels. The menfolk had been up in the forest cutting wood for the fires, and now dragged it home on a ramshackle old cart. Aileen and Zhu rushed around the side of the house, squealing the happy news. Then they all came around back to insist the scientist herself tell it again. Mariah scanned their hopeful faces slowly: Noah, Lucas, Peter.

Rowena began again. "My guess is that Bastian did catch Regent's as a child, but it didn't run its full course. Somehow he was exposed to a new mutation of the virus—maybe from those sheep Mariah mentioned, because the host has to be alive for the virus to mutate in—and his immunity, well, it just ran out."

Noah squatted to the grass. "And the rest of us? Are we safe?"

"Well, from what I've found out, we all had Regent's disease to its fullest extent. That means this version of the virus can't attack us."

Lucas let out a gentle whoop of joy. Rowena was quick to explain further. "Now look, I don't know how Regent's makes us immune. But the fact is, we all had it, and we're still alive. I'm just adding two and two here, so we get four. Get it?"

Nods of assent went round the huddled heads, and silence fell.

Then Zhu spoke. "I remember, before the Senate years, in school we learned about smallpox—that outbreak a couple of centuries ago or whatever. Some guy found out that getting cowpox made you immune to smallpox. It was the first vaccination."

"Just like Regent's disease made us immune to this mega-virus." Peter smiled.

They were still again. Rowena leaned back in the chair, more exhausted than Mariah had ever seen her. The other girls bounced off each other a little longer, then went inside with Noah and Lucas to find some food.

Mariah turned back to Rowena. "You rest now, girl. You've done far too much work. Lie on the beach for a few days and get your strength back."

"I might just do that. But you know, it was worth it…now we know we're safe!"

After she tottered inside to find her bed, Peter and Mariah walked the few steps to their own back door. She breathed deeply of the fresh night air and realised the tension was gone. Peter was happy, too—she felt his smile, even if she couldn't see it in the dark.

"We really are safe, aren't we?" The words bubbled out of her.

"Seems like it…" Peter pushed open the door and held it for her. "I never forgot what you said, you know, about needing to be safe before…making future plans. Now that our minds are at ease…"

Mariah's throat constricted. She held up a hand. "Whoa. Easy, soldier. I'm not ready for that." She only wanted to fly away on the wings of hope somewhere inside her dreamworld.

Safe. We're safe. Really safe.

Pains came upon her in the darkest hour of the night. At first it was hardly noticeable and she rolled over and slept again. The next thing she knew, she awoke screaming. Sweat poured from her as she tried to ignore a thousand daggers deep within. She cried out again and was vaguely aware of sounds in the house as others heeded her call. The door opened and two candles entered, carried by Peter and Aileen. In the light of the flame they wavered slightly, fear on their faces. *But we're safe!* Another pain stabbed her in the very centre, then she realised for the first time she was dying. It didn't take long to discover the bed was already full of blood. Aileen bent over her and wiped sweat from her eyes. Pain seized her again and she wished for it to take her quickly.

No! cried a voice within her: she had chosen life, and she wanted to live. So she shouted it to the four walls and the four winds of heaven: "I will not die! I will live!"

Peter seized her clenched fist. "Aye! That's the spirit! Hold on!"

Aileen looked at him as if he was mad. Mariah well understood why. This sickness could only end in death. But she had only recently rediscovered the will to live; she was determined not to let it go. Through the haze of agony she held to that one thought.

After that, time lost its meaning as days and nights merged into a cacophony of endurance. Peter was often at her side, and the others came now and then. She saw Rowena's sad face groaning, "Why? We thought we had this figured out..."—but Mariah had no answer for her.

Rowena returned and took a swab of Mariah's blood that leaked out everywhere. "Let's see if we can find out what happened." She squeezed Mariah's limp hand and went away for what seemed like forever.

In the end Mariah had no idea how long she held on, but from the inside it was an eternity. The time came when everyone realised the final crisis was close—a battle no one had ever won before. Rowena appeared, bag-eyed and weary yet determined, and sat once more at the bedside. "Mariah, this is a different strain. I never saw it before, not anywhere in last year's plague, not in Bastian. You've got something worse, but maybe your immunity can beat it. Can you hang in there just a little longer?"

Mariah had no strength to speak and the pain threatened to steal her consciousness again. Even so, in her delirium she became aware of Peter kneeling beside her bed. He clasped her hand in both of his and bowed his head so low as to touch it, weeping and mumbling. Mariah could not identify the words, yet his whole heart was in them. She resisted her final sleep and in doing so, caught what he was saying; it sent a tingle through her dying bones:

"Don't leave me now, my treasure, my last and only joy...please, live!" He repeated himself, the words tripping over each other. "Live, and be my love." It was a litany pouring out of his deepest soul.

Drawing a deep, rattly breath, Mariah whispered, "Peter!"

His head jerked up and he grasped her hand tighter—she continued with difficulty, "Help me hold on." She forced another inhalation and finally managed to say, "I can win if you help me."

Mariah blinked as a fire descended on them both. Somewhere in the back of her tormented mind she realised she was probably hallucinating, or so close to death that these were the heavenly lights if such a thing existed, but in that moment she took it as the gift of life. Peter leapt to his feet and gently took her face in both his hands. He bent over and slowly, gently kissed her forehead, while she watched the play of ethereal light. Within her failing body she felt something shift. The light faded and she gasped, one or two long, cleansing breaths, not laboured—clear like she hadn't been able to in days. The crisis was over.

She spat more blood and stared up at Peter. "It's—it's turned…"

He let loose with a roaring whoop as he straightened, his echoes fading quickly from the room. Aileen peered in, woken by Peter's shouts.

Mariah continued to void her lungs of the foulness. She choked less now. She reached five clear breaths before she had to cough up again, then ten. She relaxed into the filthy sheets. *Alive*…just immune enough after all. She heaved an enormous sigh.

Peter knelt down, coming face to face with her, and he enfolded her in his arms, sweat, blood and all. The door softly clicked as Aileen left the room. Peter whispered, "You've come back to us."

It was then that Mariah knew beyond all doubt that he loved her, and she buried her face in his shoulder and cried hot tears of joy.

There followed several more weeks of further recovery for Mariah after the news of her improvement flashed around the few members of the tiny community. Astonishment was on every face and shocked whispers echoed through the silent world as she slowly regained her strength. Eventually, Mariah emerged from the sickroom with a pile of soiled laundry and discovered it was a beautiful summer morning. Hurriedly she threw the sheets down by the steps outside and sprang into the street. Throwing her head back and her hands to the sky, she laughed aloud for joy. It was so good to be alive and breathe the fresh clean air and reach for the little white filaments of clouds hanging in the sky. How could she ever have wanted to give up on living? Then she stood still and listened to the wind in the trees and the song of the birds. They had survived the killer virus, but her own kind was now an endangered species. Aloneness panged her; she dropped her gaze to her dirty and bloodstained feet. Never mind the rest of her. *Yuck.* Time for a wash!

Rushing back into the house, she stuffed a towel and some clothes into a duffle bag. Then she ventured into the back yard, where Noah had piled up a few of the better-functioning bicycles he had collected. Choosing one, she checked the tyres and the brakes. It was a bit rusty from long exposure to the elements, but still in working order. A pump lay among the weeds that grew in the cracks in the concrete, so she stuck that in the bag too, and leapt aboard. It had sure been a long time since she'd ridden. The first tracks she left were wobbly and zigzagged, but then it all came back to her. As her mother always said, you never forget how to ride a bike.

And so with great joy she pedalled down the hill towards the ocean, smelling the fresh, sweet air, and opening her mouth to gulp it down.

Gravity let Mariah's wheels skim almost clear to the far end of Ballyholme. Past the empty houses on the wide, cracking streets. Past the hopelessly overgrown gardens and those full of dead, malformed plants because the fertiliser had run its course and they hadn't applied more. Past the promenade with its fading multicoloured housefronts all in a row. Past the seawall and the stony part of the bay. After letting the bike fall at the very end of the road, she made for the curve of soft sand. Sparkles glittered on the water and a soft breeze blew in her face. She plunged into the chilly sea, splashed around till she was clean, then wandered dripping along the beach, enjoying the salt and sand on her skin. Soon she came to a place where fruit trees grew in a garden that had now gone fully wild and hung over the crumbling wall here and there. Finding an early apple—a natural one, for the fertilised fruit grew all year round—she bit into it and rejoiced in the juicy tartness and for the new strength in her bones, for sea and sunshine, for life and all good things. For the others sharing the journey with her—and for Peter. Her heart beat faster and she tossed the apple core over the garden wall. *He said he loved me.* She only had a vague recollection of it, but she was fairly certain it had been real and no dream. His face betrayed it every time he looked at her.

She settled in the sand and lay there a while, enjoying the warm wind and the sun on her face. Something within her was more alive than she had ever known it before—the dark brooding was gone, and in its place there bubbled a love more glorious than she had believed possible. Her spirit roamed far and wide. *He loves me.*

And he would be worrying about her! Her first time out of the house in weeks, and here she was rushing off by herself for hours at a time…She got to her feet and noticed that the world glowed brighter. *So it should be,* she thought, *so it should be.*

She wandered the short distance across the beach to where she'd left the bike, and gave the bloodstained seat a quick wipe with the towel, which she then discarded. Not paying any particular attention to the roads, she set off in the general direction of home. Her mind flew free and she pondered Peter's love in her heart. How long had he loved her? As for herself, she had been far too grief–stricken from all the Troubles to notice anything.

She brought herself back to the present and noticed she was in the wrong street. Here were no houses with gardens. It was more of an industrial area, with cheaply-built, faceless blocks that once contained work centres and the like. She stopped and sought the sun to get her bearings; it had gone down already, but it had left a red-streaked sky to the west. She had gone too far inland. Swinging the bike in a circle, she put a foot to the pedal again and was about to head off in what was hopefully the right direction, when she caught a glaring light out of the corner of her eye. *Light?* But the power supply had been down for months, even in official workplaces. This needed closer investigation.

Out of habit she pulled the bike to the roadside and left it there—although no one was about to run it over if she left it in the street—and slipped between the concrete bunkers to the back building where she'd spied the glow. Indeed, there was a light visible through the high factory windows. On the roof, solar panels. A power source! Perhaps they could move it to Deborah's house and use it for themselves. Curiosity drove her on.

The big front door was locked, but round the side she found a small door that let her pass. Inside, to her great surprise, were rows of computers—and all of them running. *I guess if the power source is functional, and no one turned them off…*She approached a computer. It was not much different to the ones she had once used at work, before everything changed—a very distant past now, distant in mind if not so very far in months. She had done things with computers every day, the boring data entry and programming and tasks with networks and software and printers, but what use was all that now?

She recognised a familiar operating system on one of the computers. The screen's background graphic bore the words "NON-PUBLIC SURVIVAL RESEARCH".

A non-public unit. Like the one they had wanted to transfer her to just before the deadly virus came to Ireland. History and fate were quicker in the end—she had gone into hiding for other reasons. This was the big secret, then, and there was no one to make her disappear if she learned it now.

She sat down on the dusty seat in front of the desk and watched her hand reach for the grimy mouse as if it was her second nature. The glow of the sunset was fading and the glimmer from the screen lit her face as she opened the program entitled "Survival System". She called up the help file to look for a description.

There appeared on the screen the elements of a wiring diagram. In the centre was an outline of the human body. Machines and wires were drawn in, attached to wrists, eyes, and other various parts of the body. Then it dawned on her that the whole body was "dressed" in a fitting suit with tubes for air, nutrition and waste, and a concentration of gadgets around the head, especially covering eyes, ears, nose and mouth. She had heard tell of similar survival suits used for patients in comas, but this headgear was unlike anything she had ever known.

Why provide stimulation for the senses—sight, sound, smell and taste—if the patient is unconscious? She moved the selector to the head area. The view zoomed in and showed various elements with labels like "Video Output" for the eyepiece and "Audio Signal" for the ears. One thick cable appeared to be wired into the head under a label reading "Data Input".

This was a virtual reality prototype! Much debated, these systems included hygienically-isolated, reduced-temperature life support, but also allowed the subject to continue living in a constructed, conscious world where all five senses would be stimulated. Many people had scoffed at the idea and claimed no such thing was possible, hence the arguments that rose from its rumours. Mariah squinted up at the cables that wired the terminal into a network. *What if it was true?*

She clicked around the program a little more and discovered that it was able to create artificial environments with a bewildering range of options to simulate an entire lifetime from childhood to old age. Living spaces could be planned and the characters of family members defined. Events like travel, marriage and childbirth could be set in a timeline, albeit with an option on free choice so that the person on life support would still control his own virtual "life". The database also contained highly detailed information on countries and cities, facilitating virtual travel, and from the pictures she browsed through, it might be nearly as good as the real thing. Mariah imagined "visiting" Paris or Rome in the days before the Senate-caused Troubles—not much was impossible with this machinery. Maybe she had found something to occupy the empty days, if anyone could be bothered learning all the ins and outs of this very complex software and machinery.

Raising her head, she realised she had sat here quite a while, since it was now completely dark outside. She remembered the hardness that had come into the world, and with a last glance over the incredible system, she stood up and retraced her steps. There in the dimness loomed a row of white cabins. Running her hand over the surface, she discovered many wires, tubes and cables built into the wall. So these were the "rooms" where a person could be kept alive indefinitely—both physically and in the mind, with programmable experiences. It was just too crazy to be true, and it gave her a strange ache in the pit of her stomach.

She found the door, and went back to the bike. It was dark now but she squinted at the sky and thought she found the North Star peeping through the clouds. So home lay *that* way. The pedals spun under her pumping legs. She would tell the others of the find, she decided, and maybe someone would figure out how to move the solar panels and reconnect them at home so they would at least have light. *If we really need it!* They were in the habit of rising with the sun and slept soon after it set. Coasting along Cliff Road, she laughed at herself and pushed open the gate in the glow of the rising gibbous moon, just before it went behind a cloud.

16

faith

december 2014

Notebooks and papers covered the low table at Keira's parents' house, along with three refilled teacups, a large teapot and a carton of milk. Davin leaned over to copy another ingredient from one list to another. "Sixteen pound o' carrots the Donaghadee grocer donated. How are we supposed to use that?"

"Soup," Faith said, "soup's always good."

"Wi' just carrots in it? We're short on onions, we need those in the stew."

"Put some cinnamon in it and call it carrot cake," said Keira, sagged on the beat-up pleather couch, staring blankly out the window at the wintry garden.

Faith and Davin glanced at her sideways. It wasn't such a bad idea, though.

Keira focused on Faith. "Say, don't you reckon we met somewhere before?"

"Well, of course that's true." Faith giggled. This was awkward. Keira must be making an elaborate joke. "We met earlier this year, so we did."

"No, no, I mean before that."

Now it was Faith's turn to stare blankly. "Somewhere around town, yeah, maybe?"

Keira tut-tutted and went back to the list of donations. The cold day drew in around the house and the silence mouthed ice patterns onto the windows. Faith wondered if Keira maybe hadn't been under too much stress lately. She'd have to see what she could do about that.

Almost the entire community turned out to share the Christmas meal they put together with help from all the team. The hall was decorated with crepe-paper twirls that ran from end to end, and someone had laid pine branches on each table, with beribboned gingerbread men clustering around as gifts. The carrot cake soup went down a treat as the first course. Faith was kept on her toes ferrying dishes and serving up; by the din and clatter in the hall, everyone was having a great time.

Keira passed her on one of her forays and caught her by the elbow. "Listen, are you sure you're really from here?"

If Faith hadn't been carrying an empty tureen, she would have tapped Keira's forehead gently with her knuckles. Instead, she spoke. "Are ye right in the head, girly? Maybe we should give you some time off."

Keira only shook her head, looked at the tip of her shoe fidgeting on the scuffed wooden floor, and moved away. Faith frowned. She didn't like this, but they had to get through tonight. Later they would talk and get to the bottom of it, she promised herself.

Hours later, when the kitchen was finally clean and the leftovers stored or given away to departing guests, Faith collapsed onto one of the wood and metal stacker chairs in the hall. Laughter reverberated out of the kitchen—Davin and Keira. Faith smiled faintly. If those two didn't end up together, she'd be very surprised.

Keira emerged and took in the sight of Faith. "You look hammered. Come on, I'll drive you home."

She'd have to return for her scooter, but right now she didn't care, and only nodded, letting Keira lead her to her slightly beat-up Chevette. When they both were settled in their seats, Keira started up and backed out of the parking slot.

Faith tried to get a handle on what she had been thinking earlier, that thing she wanted to talk to Keira about—Keira doing too much, being too tired, going funny in the head. Faith blinked. She was too tired herself to articulate it, and laughed aloud.

"What?" asked Keira, shooting a concerned look.

"Oh…just…we both need to stop working so hard."

"Really? What makes you say that?"

"You. You've been talking odd stuff lately, have you noticed? And me—look at me, I can hardly stay awake."

Keira's face turned serious. "Our biggest party of the year. Of course it's going to take more work than usual. But we can take it easy now for a while, yeah."

"There's more, isn't there?" Faith probed. "You think there's something strange going on with me."

It was a statement, not a question, and Keira didn't deny it.

"I guess I might as well just say it and see what happens." Keira sighed. "Now pay attention, because I'm only going to say this once, and if you don't get it, I'll never ever mention it again."

A chill ran down Faith's back. "You're weirding me out."

"Never mind that," said Keira, and continued.

Faith felt a familiar darkness creeping up on her, blacker than the country night outside the car. Keira drove on towards Bangor and spoke, but Faith couldn't make sense of the words. *No!* She really needed to hear this, to understand what was bothering Keira. She pressed a hand to her forehead as if that would force the pain and blankness to retreat.

It was no use.

The rising tides of nothingness swamped Faith's mind and she was gone from her body, floating in another place. Lights shot across the insides of her eyelids, as they often did when this happened. Suddenly the brightness flooded her and she yelped, swiping at her eyes. The blaze faded slightly and she saw that she lay in her own bed, though the room was lit with jumbles of colour.

She squinted and thought that was the old painting of Bangor's Main Street back on the wall, but it couldn't be—she'd destroyed it with her own bare hands, years ago, for being too ominous a view of her hometown.

"You're dreaming."

Faith jerked upright in bed. "Who's there?"

"Oh, no one of consequence." A tall, pale figure stepped into one of the pools of light. "Like I said, this is a dream, and you're perfectly safe."

"Why wouldn't I be safe in my own room?" Again Faith glimpsed the dark clouds of the hated picture and wondered if she was really where she thought she was. As if to further confuse her, for a millisecond she felt herself transposed onto a rocky, forested mountainside high above a fjord. The wind was icy, but before she even had time to shiver, the vision was gone.

The woman moved closer to Faith's bed, her long hair glimmering in strands of blue and gold illumination. "Just relax and you'll be fine."

Heart racing. Of course such an instruction would have the opposite effect. Faith gulped and focused on the face before her. She could honestly say she'd never seen this person in her life before. "Who *are* you?"

"Nope, not yet." Her visitor raised a hand and appeared to be looking at someone behind Faith's shoulder. "Yep, it's me. I didn't die—would I lie to you?" She returned her attention to Faith. "Me? Little bit Cherokee, little bit German."

Faith widened her eyes and turned to see who she had been talking to, but there was nothing there. Only her window, and the black night beyond.

She turned back. The room was empty, and the peculiar lights were gone, as was the "ghost painting". Faith shook her head. Weirdest dream she ever had.

Scrambling out of bed, she noticed she was still fully clothed. Huh. How had she gotten here in the first place? She padded to the window and looked down.

Wait—was that Keira's car on the street? That's right, Keira had brought her home, but Faith's brain had failed her somewhere along the way. Keira must have led her to the bedroom.

There was the sound of the car door opening. Faith stood for a long time, observing the dark shadow of her friend who appeared to be staring up at her window from beside the vehicle, though Faith was sure she herself couldn't be seen. Finally, Keira got in the car and drove away.

Faith reached back in her mind to remember the extraordinary dream, but to her horror almost all of it had vanished. All that remained was a vague impression of the woman's face and the last words she had spoken: "Little bit German."

17

mariah

june 2080

Pursuing his slow, limping way clockwise around the coast of Ireland, the dog passed a multitude of bays and hamlets and stony black shorelines. At length he rounded a final curve and beheld the central part of Bangor. Signs of abandoned habitation were everywhere—once-white housefronts now shifting to a dirty grey, houseboats sunken at their moorings, untended gardens first gone extravagantly wild and then dead from lack of fertiliser.

The dog approached the place where Main Street met Queen's Parade near the water. He breathed deeply—and tasted a scent he'd almost forgotten: humans. Alive!

Ears perked and nose in top gear as he pressed it to the ground, he followed the odour of living people through the byways of Bangor. He had to favour his wounded leg so much that at times he simply tried to gallop on three legs to gain speed. But the injured leg would drag on the ground, making him yelp and slow again.

The scent was strong. In good time, it led him up to 45 Cliff Road. He sat in the street listening unseen to voices in the garden. There was no anger or malice in their tone, not even stress, but he settled on his elbows to make triply sure of that fact before he would present himself.

For a while he licked his throbbing ankle; it had started to bleed again. The humans continued to talk and laugh. They sounded so happy, and the dog's yearning grew so potent that he could wait no longer. He neared the twiggy hedge. A man and woman sat on a bench against the house, and the garden was tidy and loaded with food.

The dog spotted a gap in the hedge. He wriggled his way into it, sat still a while, then moved a few inches closer until he emerged on the inside, hidden from the humans' sight by bushes that grew close to the perimeter.

Desperate with the conflict of loneliness and hope, he pushed in between the bushes to get a better view. The woman looked briefly in his direction, but the two continued their conversation without interruption. The dog watched a little longer and tasted the pheromones of human attraction on his tongue. Not like the two cyborgs and their doomed love—never like that. This was natural.

He inched forward again, now in plain view. The woman turned. "Look," she said.

***

Mariah and Peter sat in the garden that summer's evening after the others had gone inside, leaving the "lovebirds" to their dreamy looks. It was dark already, and after a stifling hot day, lightning flashed across the sky again and again. Soon the rain would come, but until it did, they would enjoy the lively cool breeze that preceded the storm. A slight buzz emanated from the back corner of the yard, where Peter had set up a few beehives transported out of the forest on the handcart. There was a rustle in the blueberry bushes, too big for bees to make, but Mariah paid it no mind.

"Just think, this storm is just for us tonight," remarked Peter, sliding ever so slightly nearer to Mariah on the garden bench. His arms and hands were dotted with red spots from bee stings.

"Oh, right," she countered, "and what about the birds and the trees and the vegetables and the bugs...?"

Peter grinned. "But none of them can enjoy it like we do. So much power in these bolts of lightning. If only we could harness it somehow—just a little—imagine that! We could have electric light again, and heating for winter, and even cook properly on a stove instead of over a fire…"

Mariah let her gaze drift to the smoking remains of the burned wood they had used to make their meal. Just then, the wind picked up sharply and scattered a few embers over the paving. The bushes rustled again, more insistently, slowly.

"Hmm…power," she mused, as another flash lit up the sky, accompanied by a gust of wind. "Yesterday I went the wrong way coming back from the beach and I found some solar panels in an industrial area…"

"But not functional?" inquired Peter.

"Well, yes, because I had a look on the computer and there was this weird program I never saw anywhere before."

The astonishment on his face was caught by the next lightning strike, and she went on. "Yeah, it was like cryogenics and virtual reality all rolled into one. If we figure out how to work it, we could travel the world even though we have to stay right here! But it looked totally crazy. Everything was there to make it work. Still, maybe the solar power is more interesting for us…"

The bush moved. This time Mariah was sure of it. "Look." She pointed, and just as Peter turned his head, a dark shape emerged. A dog. Limping towards them, tail cautiously awag. The humans exchanged a glance and Mariah held out a hand in the near-dark. The creature snuffled it, whining.

"Where did you come from? I thought all the doggies died." Peter let the animal sniff his hand in turn.

The thought of her brother's Jemima sent an unexpected pang through Mariah. "He must be immune like us."

Peter fondled the dog's soft ears and it rested its chin on his knee. "Been on his own a long while, then."

First droplets of rain were falling, and they came faster and faster. They got up to go inside before the downpour. The dog was reluctant to follow—he'd surely had reasons to mistrust people—but he entered in the end. Mariah lit a candle and squatted to inspect him. Patchy brown, soulful eyes, and…what was this? "Look here, he's hurt." She rose, fetched a wetted cloth, and, since the animal refused to enter the bathroom, knelt right there in the hall and carefully cleaned the muck and dried blood from the wound on his leg. The dog drew back at first, but let her help him, flinching only occasionally.

While she worked, Peter continued to pet him, then squinted at the result. "Doesn't seem too bad. Should be fine now that it's clean."

"Aye, but look how thin he is. Do we have some stew left?" Mariah bustled off to the kitchen to answer her own question, and set down a bowl of sloppy cooked vegetables. The dog slurped it up and licked his lips.

He capered around a little, then ran to the front door and whined. Peter sighed and went to open it; the dog exited slowly and settled down in the recessed entryway. Mariah hoped with all her heart he would still be there in the morning.

Yawning, she said good night and let Peter kiss her cheek. It sent a shiver down her back to think where this might someday lead.

As she slipped upstairs for the night, she glanced back at Peter, who was still standing by the open door. Now rain was pouring and thunder rumbled overhead, and yet another lightning flash framed him and the dog in the doorway for a fraction of a second just before he yanked it shut to keep out the damp. He looked sunken in his thoughts.

That night as the summer storm raged, her mind wandered back to the idea of virtual reality. *Wouldn't it be fun to visit all those famous places we've only ever heard about in stories?* Her drowsy fancies were wild—strangely populated with patchy brown mutts.

At morning's light she bolted upright, anxious to find if their new furred friend was still with them. She clomped down the stairs and tore the door open.

The dog jerked his head up towards her. His tail beat on the concrete step. He shivered—the nights were still cold—and got to his feet. Mariah ran a hand down his back, damp with dew. "You poor thing. Come in here." She moved to the hall press and found a towel, then turned. The dog had come half inside, sniffing the air. "Come on," said Mariah again, and he came. He let her rub him down. "No more sleeping outside, d'ya hear, Rufus?" She fluffed his ears with the towel and he pressed his muzzle to her face, giving a quick lick.

Steps sounded on the stairs as Aileen appeared. She blinked. "Where did that come from?" The dog cowered back from her approach. She muttered something, scratched her head, and kept her distance.

"He found us." Mariah smiled as she played with a fold of skin at his neck. "Eh, Rufus."

"Is that his name?"

"It is now."

Peter emerged from the back room, sleep-dazed, and grinned. "Mornin', all." He approached Rufus. "Hullo, fella."

The dog skipped around from one person to another, loosing little yips of pleasure. Peter laughed, then blinked, and his gaze narrowed on Mariah. "Tell me more about those computers you found."

***

"This is Rufus," said Mariah when they crossed the hedge and joined the occupants of the other house. Zhu squealed, so that the dog's ears pulled back, but she made such a fuss of him that he soon relaxed. Rowena smiled and joined in. Lucas and Noah hung back, frowning; Lucas was his usual uninterested self, but with Noah there was something different this time, something wrong. Mariah addressed him. "What's the matter?"

"I hate dogs. Got bit when I was a kid and never got over it. Nasty creatures."

"Well, you don't have to come near him. He probably knows you'd prefer that, too." Mariah was a little hurt for Rufus, but she supposed the reason for Noah's fear was legitimate.

In the next few days Mariah was occupied with the dog—cleaning his wound each day, enjoying his company on her walks at the beach and around town, and coaxing him to come in at sundown. Soon he was sleeping on her bed each night.

Peter, on the other hand, was preoccupied with the system she had discovered. He asked Mariah again and again to describe it—the equipment, the cables and cabins, and most particularly the computer program with its vast possibilities for creating personally tailored worlds. It fascinated him, although she wasn't sure why—in the light of day, the idea was quite silly, simply too ideal to be true. So she kept changing the subject.

Then one morning she awoke to a cry of dismay. Rushing out of her room two steps behind Rufus, she followed the sound out to the street, which was now distinctly overgrown. Aileen curled there in the fetal position, sobbing.

Mariah rushed to her side and laid a hand on her shoulder. "What is it?" she shouted over the wails. Peter was running out of the house. Aileen turned her face to Mariah, full of an immense fear.

"We're all going to *die!*" she yelled, grabbing Mariah and pulling her close. Rufus growled a warning.

"What—why?" Mariah raised her head and looked towards the house where the others lived, just next door. Zhu and Noah were dragging something out of the door. Their faces betrayed their fright.

It was Lucas. They shoved him into the street, and Zhu raised a trembling finger to point at him. "He's sick!"

That was all she said, but dread rose up to fog Mariah's vision. There was blood on his clothes, a little welling from his nose, not yet very much. It certainly resembled the killer virus they all knew much better than they liked.

Rowena had come out of the house now too. Lucas picked himself up from his hands and knees and wiped a little blood from his nose. Apparently the sickness was in an early stage. The rest stood around him on the road, each too stunned to speak. Rufus sat close by Mariah's leg.

"What is to be done?" asked Peter finally in a gentle voice.

"Send him away before he infects all of us!" cried Zhu. Noah agreed.

"No!" screamed Aileen, still beside herself. Clearly they were provoking each other to more panic than Mariah had seen since the main wave of the plague.

Rowena stepped in. Her words tumbled out. "It's possible that we could catch this from him, unless we're very lucky and it's mutated back to a non-airborne, contact-only virus—but we still can't stay near him because we aren't more immune than him. Most of us have a stronger immunity than Mariah, which is why we weren't at risk from her."

Peter opened his mouth to speak, but hesitated when Zhu muttered again about sending Lucas away. Peter held up his hand. "Wait, hear me out! Some days ago, Mariah discovered a functional life-support system!"

There was a great murmuring. Noah turned on Mariah. "Why didn't you tell us?"

"It didn't seem important at the time…" Indeed, she was only now beginning to decipher the significance of the find. Rufus dug his nose into her palm and she let her hand rest on his head.

Peter went on. "This kind of system was invented to create a partial coma while keeping the body alive. One other function is to isolate the body completely from the outside world."

Finally Mariah understood. The sealed, cooled body suits in the airtight cabins would also protect from infection.

"But that's not what it was made for!" Mariah objected. "How can we be sure it will work?"

"Uh, er…I don't know," Peter said.

Rowena nodded. "Sure. Cryogenic cooling would most likely protect us from viruses. They only attack living things, warm organisms. Reduced temperature makes a highly effective disguise."

"What kind of life is that, though?" Noah griped. "A partial coma, and getting freeze-dried, just to stay alive? What good will that do us? Everyone has to die sometime anyway!"

Mariah agreed silently. Surely it would be better to die than to live on artificially in a world that had so little to offer.

"That's the question," Rowena said. "It's possible that the virus itself will die out in time, when it has no more hosts to mutate in…"

"So we can programme the system to wake us, say in fifty years, or a hundred, and we'd be safe?" asked Peter.

"I do think we could most likely live on after that without fear of the virus. And we wouldn't age in that state, at least not like we do out here." Rowena flapped a hand at the dilapidated street to indicate the entirety of the real world, and silence fell again as the little band of survivors pondered this.

Then Mariah remembered something. "Hey! It's not like it would be boring." How she had dreamed of Paris and Rome… "The whole thing is fitted with this complicated virtual reality system. So while we sleep…"

"We could be doing anything we wanted!" exclaimed Zhu with shining eyes. She gave Noah a whack on the shoulder. "Did you ever want to climb Mount Everest?"

Noah grinned. "Or go to Las Vegas?"

"Or live in a world without the World Senate," Rowena said.

"That first and foremost," answered Peter. "I believe this could be our key to surviving."

It was then that Lucas spoke up for the first time. "I want no part of it!" he growled. "I would rather stay in the real world where I can believe my eyes."

Mariah gaped at him. Horror at Lucas' fate mingled with hope for herself and the others. Zhu and Noah were almost dancing with joy, Rowena glowed with new confidence, and Peter too was radiant. It was clear that Lucas would not live much longer, unless a miracle of his own should happen.

Noah turned to him. "No one can help you now anyway."

It was the truth. Lucas stood slumped and extended his hand to Aileen. "Come, madame, let's rid ourselves of this insane bunch!"

To Mariah's horror, Aileen stepped to his side and gripped his fingers. Lovers…that explained a few things.

"I'm yours, Lucas, you know that. Let's get out of here. You'll get better, just like Mariah did!" She wiped tears from her cheeks with her free hand. He laid his arm around her shoulder—the virus was attacking him more slowly than Mariah had ever seen—and the two of them walked away without looking back. Rufus whined but did not move from his spot beside Mariah. True enough, there was land and wealth in the city's surrounds to sustain many people. But Mariah ached to see Aileen go, who, although she hated the Guild so, had been a friend to her. Couldn't Aileen admit that there was little hope for Lucas? Although, if she loved him fiercely, maybe—just maybe—she could help him pull through as Peter had helped Mariah.

Peter, Rowena, Zhu and Noah stared after the two long after they disappeared from view, but then switched to chattering about the possibilities of the life support system.

"There's no time to lose," proclaimed Peter. "We have no way of knowing how long we are spared."

18

faith

Faith longed for the strange dream to recur so that she could discover more about the woman and the valley she'd glimpsed. But it never did return in the months and years that followed; nor did Keira have any insight on the matter, insisting she had only helped Faith upstairs that night and nothing more. When Faith pressed her to tell the "important thing" she'd been about to say in the car, Keira would only shrug and look away. Maybe Faith had imagined that part along with her nocturnal visitor.

There were plentiful helpers in the community kitchen, so that when finally Faith approached the last of her classes at the university, she decided to leave the garden work in other hands. This left her free to pursue…something else.

For many years she'd imagined someday spending time in New Zealand. She'd watched the movies, investigated options as a volunteer farm worker, and even decided where she wanted to go: an organic vineyard situated on a moderately-sized island that was truly isolated and yet almost within sight of a large metropolis. Now the time had come, and her savings had amassed sufficiently to pay for the fifty hours of flight she would require to get there and back again. She began setting the preparations in motion.

From that moment of decision, time whizzed by as it often did for Faith. In her own experience she simply skipped over those months and arrived at the thing she had chosen to do, with merely a summarised memory of what she had done in between—in this case, her final exams and much time spent with her friends Keira and Davin. Memories of the latter grew more awkward as time passed and it became obvious that the two were more than friends. Faith had acknowledged herself to be the proverbial third wheel, and was glad that she could remove herself for a while. Maybe even meet that special someone for herself, although she barely let herself hope to be anything but alone. It was just the way things were.

And so she found herself once more on a plane. Three flights later, she awoke over ocean near Auckland to a hot airline breakfast. It wasn't even half bad.

Faith had written down all her instructions for finding her way to the island of Waiheke. Once there, her host would pick her up at the wharf. But first she had to take a bus—it picked its way laboriously through sprawling suburbs as the sun rose, where palms and pines jostled for space among cute bungalows and little old-worldy shops. Urbanity increased over the next half hour, the buildings becoming larger, sleeker and more commercial, coming to a head as the bus rumbled across a flyover that encompassed several different flows of motorway traffic. Finally, it drove down a clogged main street where almost every building was fitted with a solid awning—to protect pedestrians from weather, Faith presumed. It must rain a lot here. When the street came to an end at the water's edge, the bus did not stop yet but continued out onto a wharf. Faith alighted and went to find her ferry, which berthed just opposite.

A rain squall hit her in the face as she scurried towards the ferry terminal; June was winter in the southern hemisphere, after all, but it wasn't too much colder than the Irish summer she'd left. Faith lined up to buy a ticket, then lined up to follow the other passengers onto the gangway carpeted with blue non-slip rubber.

The little ship's horn sounded and it moved off into the harbour. Waves tossed the wide catamaran from side to side once it emerged into more open waters a few minutes later, but it was a stable craft and Faith felt safe on board.

The crossing was quick, the ferry not too busy around noon on a weekday, so Faith was able to wander about the three different levels including the open air deck on top. With the wind buffeting her face, she watched the islands as they passed—several innocuous farmland islets, and one darkly looming volcanic cone that barely changed its silhouette as they angled around almost half of its circumference. A large freighter moved in from the gulf and other, mostly smaller ferries zipped around in the immediate vicinity.

The ferry slowed as it entered a bay at the head of the largest island she'd seen yet. Due to the scant commuters at this time, she disembarked without delay. She pulled her suitcase behind her down the long jetty, its wheels clacking on the salt-worn planks.

The farmer—or more properly *vintner*, she thought with amusement—waited on land, wearing khaki shorts and a heavy woollen bush shirt, checked in blue and black. He acknowledged her with a single-finger tap to the brim of his shapeless hat. "Another scrawny one," he said. "We'll soon fix that."

Faith frowned, then took in his raised eyebrow and the smirk he wore. She laughed. "Nice to meet you too."

He heaved the suitcase into the back of a vehicle he called his ute—"Short for utility," he said, and invited her to climb into the passenger seat. She did so with only a little difficulty because it was so high off the ground, and the floorspace inside the vehicle was encrusted with dried mud, just as the outside was well-splattered. She was going to a farm, after all. It would hardly be an authentic experience if there wasn't a good deal of dirt. She had worked a lot with theories and plans for farming, but aside from her own personal front-garden vegetable plot, she was ashamed to admit to herself that she had not spent much time working the soil.

They drove up through a valley that was so picturesque, Faith could imagine herself inside a fantasy movie. But nature very soon gave way to a civilised little town centre, with a movie theatre that advertised "Couch Seating", a row of quirky-looking restaurants, and a miniature supermarket, all overlooking the golden sands and dark teal waters of the beach to the north side of the island. Yachts bobbed there at anchor, and quaint little houses peeked out between the trees on the headlands to either side.

All this vanished in just a minute or two of driving. Now they passed a fire station and a church, and Waiheke's south coast came into view with its own set of promontories and beaches. In the distance, the Auckland suburbs lined the horizon; she had tootled through there on her bus this morning, but this—this was a different world altogether.

Rather than experiencing time all in a rush, Faith now felt she had come to a place where time moved slower, where no one hurried, a community without so much as a traffic light to its name. The road curved around between more houses and beaches, crossed an estuary where several intriguing-looking houseboats sat on the low-tide mud. Then it climbed a hill and slunk past a cliff before the farmer turned onto a rutted gravel road. Not far after the turn-off, they passed a fancy entranceway of hewn stone bearing enamelled lettering. "That's the neighbour's place," said the farmer with a jerk of his thumb, and winked. "But our grapes are better." They pushed higher into the green hills, but thickets of spindly trees blocked the views until the forest ended abruptly at the edge of a sloping vineyard. A piece of scrap wood tacked onto a fencepost proclaimed "Arairoa Vineyard" in fading black brushstrokes.

"Here we are. Welcome home!" The farmer grinned and gunned the engine up the two narrow concrete strips that passed for a driveway. He pulled to a stop in front of a modest wooden house whose near end almost rested on the ground, but the far end stood on poles where the slope fell away. Faith jumped down from the vehicle and swayed a little, clutching at its doorframe for support. She stepped onto the veranda that surrounded the house, staring out at the vista of tangled ocean inlets, bush-clad coastlines and peeks of sandy beaches. And then there was the sea, that stretched to the misty grey lands delineating the horizon. Faith gripped the railing and inched towards the wondrous sight.

Her gape-mouthed awe was interrupted by the farmer's wife appearing round the corner of the house immediately in front of her. "It's about time! Lunch is getting cold. You must be starving."

The farmer passed Faith her luggage and smirked again, as if to say "what did I tell you?" Faith had to consider the possibility that he hadn't been kidding after all.

Lunch was a very satisfying quiche sort of affair, and then they showed Faith to her room in the basement and left her to recover from her travels. Tucked under the veranda, she could see a little bit of the gulf from her window if she leaned over the bed just so. She flopped down on her back and traced the cracks in the ceiling with her eyes. *This* was just what she needed, even if the mattress sagged and the blankets were threadbare, even if she had to live here under the house instead of properly in it, and even if she was going to have to work harder than she ever had before.

From the next day she was fully immersed in the rhythm of the work. Weeding, pruning, checking for bugs, training the vines over their frames, and finally at dusk, the watering accomplished by an irrigation system that she turned on and then watched to make sure there were no blockages in the hoses and sprinklers. Of course this was only needed if it hadn't already rained that day, and this being winter, it was like as not to be pouring. The vines were not quite dormant, as the temperatures rarely dropped below freezing, but it was a quieter phase in their life cycle. Faith kept records about the numbers of buds, and learned where to clip the vine so as to keep it balanced. The task was far more precise than she had imagined.

Once, she tried to explain to the farmer and his wife about her LandCare app and what it could accomplish. But he stopped her a short way into her presentation. "I can see the use of it for fields, now. But for vines? These plants have been established for years. You can't seriously be advising me to rip them out just to install those ridges of yours or to 'give the land a rest'—that would destroy everything we've built here."

Faith had to agree. Her system was not made for any operation with long-lived plants such as vines or trees. In a way it made her sad that she could not help more, but on the other hand, it was liberating. The best she could do was care for the vines, and that she would do.

At night she tossed and turned, frequently re-imagining her encounter with the woman in her bedroom the night of Keira's strange behaviour. There were other figures in her dreams too, prominent among them a sweet dark-haired Irish boy who smiled knowingly at her, but never said a word. *Dreaming is healthy*, she told herself, but she couldn't escape the sensation that these dream people were somehow real.

On her days off, sometimes she walked down to where the gravel road met the asphalt, and caught a bus to one or other of the villages on the island: Onetangi to the north-east, with its towering sandstone cliffs and miles of beach, or Oneroa near the wharf, with its cafés. Once she even took the ferry to the city and wandered around the concrete jungle in a daze. It was almost too much for her after the weeks of isolation, and she thought she felt the first twinges of a headache that might lead to memory loss. But she managed to get back on a ferry in time, and her mind cleared as it sped away from the clustered skyscrapers. From now on she would stick to her island life.

Twelve weeks went by, mostly very slowly, and Faith learned to savour every moment. She enjoyed the feel of dirt in her hands, the wind on her face, even the rain enlivened her. Most days when her work was done, she walked a narrow trail down through the bush to the nearest coastline, a tiny rock-strewn bay overhung by gnarled trees. She sat there on a large piece of basalt and watched the sun sink behind the headland, while exotic birdcalls resonated from the branches all around.

Finally, though she did not want it to, the final sunset came and went. The day after, both the farmer and his wife accompanied her to the wharf, and waved at her until she couldn't see them any more from her spot on the top deck of the ferry. She turned away and sat down, hunched inside her coat, the thrum of the ship's engine like the purr of a giant cat reverberating through her bones. It nosed out through the bay's opening and increased its speed, heading for town.

Once on the mainland, Faith spied a souvenir shop across the road and decided to pick up some small gifts for her friends. There were still a couple of fivers in her pocket; she pulled one out and traced the outline of Ed Hillary's profile. She pressed the silver button for the pedestrian crossing and watched the red man light up on the other side. People gathered behind her and in clusters opposite, so that quite a crowd grew at all four corners of the intersection. Faith idly scanned the features of the masses lined up facing her. But then her attention snagged on one person. She could swear she knew that woman. Well, she was about to get her chance.

At last all the traffic stopped and the red man changed to green with a high-pitched chirping. The crowds stepped out from both sides and lunged at each other almost like a medieval battle scene. Faith gripped the handle of her suitcase and tried to locate the woman. There—no, that wasn't her. Faith dodged the first barrage of walkers and kept going.

She blinked. How could someone disappear like that?

Then, right in front of her, blocking her way. The woman from her dream. The one who had appeared in her bedroom all those months ago, speaking so cryptically. Details of the dream swam back into Faith's consciousness even as she stared up at the face before her.

The taller woman stared back at her, not speaking, the two of them toe to toe amidst the maelstrom of pedestrians. The green man vanished and the red began to flash. For a moment more, neither woman moved. Then her counterpart sidestepped neatly and headed for the side of the road that Faith had started on.

Faith dragged her suitcase in a half-circle and followed after. She had to talk to her. Find out who she was, and why she knew her from a dream. Reaching the original curbside again, she searched the bobbing heads for the one she wanted. This proved difficult from the back view. Faith dashed back and forth in the moving crowd, squinting at faces, trying to recall what the woman had been wearing, but it was no use. She was gone.

Then Faith looked down at the wharves where she had so recently left her ferry. Vessels of various sizes bobbed there, most loading up with commuters. There was a jetty for water taxis, too—wait. Faith narrowed her eyes. That was her!

The woman climbed into the small yellow boat and disappeared from view under its canopy. Faith rushed for the jetty, only just remembering to drag her belongings behind her.

A burst from the floating taxi's diesel engine shattered her hopes. She pounded onto the jetty, which bounced on its pontoons at her arrival, but the taxi was already pulling away. Panting, Faith stared after it, longing for a glimpse of her mysterious ghost. The little boat left the ferry basin and put on speed as it turned towards the open sea, gone from sight in the next moment. The jetty was empty; she couldn't hire anyone and order "follow that boat!"

Faith watched a while, useless as it was. That taxi could be headed anywhere. She recalled the person from her dream with unusual clarity, for all it had been more than a year and a half ago, but couldn't grasp what her visitor had said—except that it mostly hadn't made any sense.

Eventually, Faith turned away from the water and resumed her long journey home. But the woman's face haunted her every bit of the way to the airport, every waking moment of the flights, and even more so after she greeted her parents and entered her own bedroom. She sat on the bed and reached out a hand to the place where she'd first seen the apparition. "Who might you be?" she whispered. "And why did you come back to me?"

19

mariah

---

june 2080

The dog abandoned his ceaseless roaming about the wasted city of bones. He'd found living humans and had no desire to leave them ever again.

He made a habit of resting on the front doorstep during the day, so as to know exactly all the comings and goings. Mariah and Peter were mostly together in their movements and the dog followed them where they went, watching nearby as they tended to gardens or sought useful items in houses where only skeletons resided, contorted in their final spasms.

But most of the time the dog lay on the step, sometimes sleeping but always happy in the knowledge that his people were inside. He reposed, comfortable on his side, the wide and ever-changing Irish sky spread out before him with its layers of fast and slow-moving clouds both light and dark, substantial and ethereal, solid or with gaps of clean blue. When it rained, he retreated inside Deborah's grandmotherly salon and watched the cascade of bright water from the giving heavens.

The sun eventually came out and the humans went to stroll on the beach; the dog tagged along, some distance behind but always keeping them in view. He sniffed at fences and lampposts as was his wont, but all the messages were old and fading except for his own that he left there in the frail hope that he might yet meet another of canine kind in the vast empty world.

Upon reaching the shore, he followed at a measured distance along the water's edge, nosing into piles of seaweed and the occasional terrified crab.

The sea changed its face from day to day or even from minute to minute. A giant, glittering reflector for the sky, it was at times a deep metallic grey or an intense teal green. When the sun shone in just the right way, it caused a thousand scintillations, making it hard to stare for too long. Sometimes it was flat like a mirror under skies so clear the humans talked about seeing all the way to Scotland; sometimes in wind the whitecaps rose, only to drop in thundering breakers on the sand. When the clouds descended in a nearly tangible haze, it was like a soft bubble of limited visibility around the little troupe of wanderers, where nothing existed except the water and the damp brown beach they stood on. They would pause to stare through the murk anyway, and the silence was eerie and complete but for the rise and fall of the waves.

Most often they walked farther than the end of the beach, entering the delicate landscape of strangely-shaped standing stones, long rocky promontories, and hardy shore grass that grew in sandy layers of sediment filling the cracks and crevices. Mariah called it Naomi's favourite place, and gripped Peter's hand tighter.

Eventually, wistfully, they would make their slow way home again, to cook large and tasteless vegetables somewhat improved by the addition of kelp, which they and the dog gulped gratefully.

Later, he would settle for the night on the inside of the safely closed front door or on the foot of Mariah's bed, content to know exactly where everyone was. That is, everyone who hadn't died or left.

❧❧❧❧❧

The small community in Bangor reeled at the departure of Lucas and Aileen. Yet Peter kept saying time was of an essence now, and Mariah thought he might be right. If the virus was still out there, growing and mutating, they would not be safe for ever, even though they had been immune. Of course, no one knew whether Mariah could become sick a second time, or whether Lucas could survive. She secretly attributed her own recovery to the motivatory power of Peter's love that got her through the crisis, not to a quirk of her immunity, but there was no way of knowing. There was no other case to compare her with.

Peter had Mariah lead him to the abandoned factory with the solar panels. They walked the wide streets of the industrial zone with its bare concrete buildings, Rufus loping alongside in his off-balance trot. As they went, Peter slipped his hand into Mariah's. She resisted the urge to pull away. He was all tense with the excitement, but his stiff fingers loosened up as he gave a sigh.

"Do you think I'm crazy?" he asked.

She pondered. Had no deep words, knew nothing. "Well, I would never have come up with this idea. But it makes sense now that you've explained it."

"If it works, we can make any old dream come true." He grinned and wove his fingers through hers.

This was a very big advantage. Mariah, too, was looking forward to enjoying herself for years in virtual reality, if all this was to be believed. "The question is, how real does it feel?"

"Maybe we could do a short test to find out," Peter said. "Aren't we there yet?"

It wasn't so easy to find. All the factories and work centres looked the same, and in the broad sunshine they would not notice the light that had first led Mariah there.

Finally she recognised the layout of a cluster of buildings. Yes, this was familiar. Now through to the bunker at the back, and round to the side door. Signs proclaimed "Limited Access", but nobody would enforce that now. She pushed it open, pulling Peter by the hand behind her.

They were met by the whirring of computers and the glare of neon lights. Mariah pointed out the sterile white cabins with their mass of wiring and tubes, then they pulled up chairs to a machine and peered into it. At first, Rufus ran around sniffing the perimeter of the room and all the strange objects in it, after which he settled down to doze near the desk where they sat.

For an hour or two she clicked around the programs, with Peter watching. Far beyond the variables she remembered from her first brief visit here, the possibilities were immense. For example, after creating a basic environment, the rest could be left to the subject's own decision-making while superficially unconscious. And if these decisions involved travel, the database was able to furnish a range of foreign environments also. Besides all this, there was an option to include "real" people, who were also attached to the system, in one's own virtual life. This was indeed an unexpected bonus; it meant that Mariah and Peter could be together, even as they slept an artificial sleep. With this, some of her initial scepticism faded away. This option would bring something real into an otherwise simulated life.

She clicked further, exploring the settings of the program.

"Look, we can even choose our own names." She turned to Peter, and to her utter shock he had gone down on his knees, gazing intently at her. He still held her left hand.

"Mariah, I—" He was stuttering.

Her chest thudded and the blood rushed to her cheeks. He went on. "I know you said you had to be certain we were safe, but I have learned to love you more than life itself. Will you be mine?"

She cast a glance back to the computer screen, at Rufus watching with interest, then dropped her gaze to the floor. Safe or not safe, who could be certain any more? Her guts still twisted at the thought that immunity might not be hereditary. *My children.* If the survivors were going to freeze themselves in these boxes, it wouldn't necessarily be a concern.

Another inner voice said *how unromantic can you get*—a marriage proposal in a dusty computer laboratory—but the strongest, most confident voice cried out its *yes* inside. Tears pricked her eyes, and all she could do was nod and fall into his open arms. Then she straightened up.

"Oh, Peter, but we'll have to get married before we activate this system. I don't want to wait twenty years to meet you in virtual reality!"

A slight expression of consternation crossed his features. She went on hurriedly. "But look, that won't be so soon as all that." Pointing again to the computer, she showed him all the things that had to be entered, from the colour of your house to the appearance and personality of your family members. Sure, they could work from memory a lot, using profiles of real people they had once known, but just entering all the information would take up a great deal of time. "I'd say it'll take at least two months' work to get our environments set up properly. Would it be acceptable to get married when we get it all finished, and before we get in those rubber suits over there?" She pointed with her thumb over her shoulder at the cabins.

Peter's mouth fell open. "That's okay—but what about our food? We'll have to pile up enough for years and years!"

Now it was Mariah's turn to be surprised; this had not occurred to her. Naomi's fertiliser would make it possible in a shorter time, but there was still a lot to do.

"Well, we have a ton of work ahead of us. Let's go report back to the others, and get started as soon as we can." She took a step towards the door, then looked again at Peter. "But I give you this promise: I will marry you before we enter our virtual lives."

He smiled, leapt up, and they walked out into the daylight. "We'll be apart for a time, but it will be worth it," he said.

"And when we wake up, we'll be the same as we are now."

Peter looked puzzled, so Mariah explained. "People in cryo don't age."

They both grinned. With Rufus tailing behind, hand in hand they walked home again, talking about the grain they would have to grow and the world they would have to build anew for themselves.

Back at the house, they first announced their engagement to the others. Rowena squealed and hugged them both and the others initiated a round of back-whacking.

After the evening meal, as it was growing dark, a cool breeze came up. They sat around the campfire discussing what had to be done. Mariah described the program in detail and explained that everyone was free to create a world, an environment to live in. Peter then brought out a sheet of calculations regarding the food supplies they would need. Each person would require a pound of wheat or oat grain a day. "For five of us that means a total of 1825 pounds or a little short of one ton per year, times fifty is around forty-five point six tons..." An incredibly large amount.

"But that's only for fifty years!" he pointed out. "If we want to sleep a hundred years, we'll need twice as much."

Hell. Even with the miracle fertiliser, this would be a huge job. Although a hundred years would most probably ensure complete safety from the virus, they would need far too much time now to grow supplies. And now was the time when the danger was at its greatest. So they agreed to rise from sleep after fifty years, hoping it would be enough.

"How will it even keep so long?" Zhu grumbled. "I don't want to eat mouldy food."

Rowena spoke up. "Airtight vats will go a long way towards preventing that. I'd like to volunteer to care for the crops while you're all working on the computer program."

Noah grew perplexed. "But what about your life?" He explained, "I mean, what about your virtual life? You'll need one too…"

"Well, yes, I will," answered Rowena. "But I don't want to spend months making it. One day of my time should be enough—all I want is a simple life, and you can plan me into your own stories if you want to. Surviving is more important than having a good time. And besides," she added somewhat pointedly, "I'll be in charge of my own destiny anyway. I'm sure I can direct a virtual life just the same as a real one."

After some discussion, they agreed to put Rowena in charge of the gardens and glasshouse and that she would call on the others when she needed help with harvesting. She would also make use of the nearest grain farmland and they would loot all of the food processing and storage locations across the city—starting with Mariah's Da's old workplace near their old home in Castlereagh. The supplies could thus be grown faster, and the rest would work on their virtual lives, taking care to include Rowena in their plans.

And so it came to pass that they made their way to the factory the next morning. Mariah gave a short explanation of how computers worked and what the mouse was for, then how to use the program, after which they set out to explore the unknown and make it their own.

Especially in those early days, the others came often to Mariah with questions. The system was not hard to learn, but in the days of Senate control most jobs had been manual labour and private machines were nonexistent. Only Mariah had worked with computers up until fairly recently—the others hadn't laid eyes on one for many years, if at all.

Late on the second day, Noah called out from his desk. "Hey, Mariah! What happens when I'm getting it on?"

Her face fell. She had expected this question sooner or later, after investigating the suit and discovering certain locations had plumbing instead of the tactile knobbles that otherwise stimulated the skin.

"Noah, I'm sorry. You can program it in, or make your own decisions once you're in stasis, but it can never really resemble the real thing. It's up to your brain's own activity to fill in the details."

Her glance caught Peter's then, and she knew he was disappointed. *All the more reason to get started before we activate this thing...*Mariah gulped and tried to dismiss this line of thinking before it threatened to carry her away.

Noah had stopped working, deep in thought. The poor guy. He'd probably made himself a Vegas full of girls, and he couldn't sleep with any of them properly.

"Don't worry, Noah!" Mariah called out. "You can kiss them as much as you want!" He grinned sheepishly and went back to typing, though this loss was perhaps a heavy one for him. *Well, it's not like he'll be lacking something he had here...right?* He would have to be strong.

Peter, too, was pensive. Mariah stood and moved behind his chair, laying her hands on his shoulders.

"I don't think we'll know the difference..." She bent her head to whisper in his ear. "But the computer is well able to simulate pregnancy and birth—and create a child's new character by combining our own."

He frowned. "Such a child wouldn't be real. I'll not father a non-existent being!"

She stepped around to face him and startled at his pain-filled face. "All right. We shall have no children inside."

He nodded, but still was gravely serious as Mariah returned to her workstation and entered the setting in the program. No children. She sighed. *There will be time enough for that after we awaken, when it is safe.*

She turned her attention to her own life that she was constructing. For her childhood, she programmed in a few pleasant but fairly basic activities that would repeat over and over. She immersed herself in this new world and barely noticed the passing of time. Her journal stayed close beside her and she made extensive notes about the life she was building for herself, so that it would all make sense in the end, much like writing a story—except she was writing her own future memories.

After a week or so she had programmed in characters for her parents and a few childhood friends. In fact, it was quite similar to the childhood she had known herself, except that the Senate didn't come and Ma didn't die.

She would still be the same person, although she did want to change her name. The name Mariah connected her irrevocably to her old life, the misery of the final Troubles and the great grief of the dying world. *And to the Guild.*

Having dealt with her childhood, she turned to the adolescent years. She programmed in various activities and a colourful social group, leaving plenty of options open so that she could make decisions herself while living the life.

There was one thing still wrong. She reached to fondle the dog slumbering at her feet. "Guys, do you think we can put Rufus in a cryo chamber too?"

Noah snorted. "You'd waste resources on a stray?"

"We could let him fend for himself. Like he must have done before he found us," said Zhu doubtfully.

"I could never. He'd die of loneliness, if not of plague." Despair rose up for her new friend. It might just be possible to get him into a human-shaped cryo-suit, but the virtual reality part almost certainly wouldn't work on an animal brain, and the entire ordeal might be more likely to kill him. Perhaps she had to try anyway. She blinked back tears. Had to change the subject.

"Hey, Peter!" she called across the room. "Tell me about your childhood!"

He smiled. "Well, I decided to grow up in another country. You know, getting to know other cultures and such."

Mariah was surprised at this, as she had supposed everyone would just describe their own actual childhood, as it was what they knew best. But he had a point. It would certainly be interesting. So she promptly saved her work, then scrolled the timeline back to her early childhood. She had left plenty of gaps here anyway, so she inserted an overseas trip with her parents. It even lasted a couple of years. She chose London—a location that had been famous in the old days as a cultural centre, where the Irish, too, had thronged to get a taste of the world beyond their island shores. She had never seen it, but she would now.

There, that ought to do it. She scrolled back to the point she was working on. Almost too simple, but the fact was that the program did a great deal automatically according to location.

It was time to build Rowena into her sequence. Mariah settled on fifteen as the age they would meet. For a few years they would do everything together, then after that, Mariah left the options wide open for both friends to choose their own way in life.

One by one she was ticking off the things she wanted to add into her experience. What else was there? A higher education, visiting Paris and Rome, and a fulfilled life. Never lacking food, of course, but not only that—Mariah would always be a Guildswoman, would always want to be involved with growing food. So she entered this requirement into the system, not specifying exactly how it should happen. The system combined with her own personality would provide the fertile soil for ideas to sprout…literally.

20

fΛιth

2016—2020

28 September 2016.

I've been having a grand old time hanging around home, doing all the things I've done all my life—digging in the garden, walking the coasts, the odd bit of cooking. There isn't much work to do, and I've got a reasonably self-sustaining income from the software sales. Theoretically I could do anything I want.

I have been thinking about that woman in my dream again. The one thing I remember her saying is that she was part German, and she said it in a weird sort of accent too. My only clue. I wonder—no...I hated being in Germany. Such a dark, oppressive place. But if that's where this woman is, maybe I should look for her there. It's a silly idea. Really, who goes hunting for people from dreams? But I have this odd sensation deep in my gut that it's really important. I need to find her. It feels like kismet. Somehow she is tied up with my destiny. I don't understand my incredible urge to meet her, but there it is. Can't tell anyone, they'd think I'm crazy.

19 October 2016.

I spent today with Keira, mucking around in the old community garden. They don't really need us there since they have so many volunteers now, and it's good to see the new managers doing so well with it. So the two of us grubbed in the dirt and chattered away. Keira let slip some pretty weird things with regard to Davin while we were weeding. She's got a total crush on him. I don't think she even realises. He certainly doesn't.

I mentioned to Keira that I have this peculiar desire to go back to Germany. She shrugged. Doesn't seem to find it strange, though of course I didn't tell her where the desire came from. "If you want to go, then go," she said. "Nothing wrong with that." Gah. It's just so…random.

Still, what else am I going to do with myself? Life here is nice and all, but it's kind of repetitive, and getting a bit dull. Maybe I do need another adventure. A longer one. What if I go live somewhere else? Now that's scary, but also exciting. Germany's as good a place as any, I guess, because I know the language, and I'll know some people if I go where I went before.

You know, I think I really might do this.

4 November 2016.

I raved about my plans to Keira for weeks now. Yesterday, finally, she set down her teacup in its saucer and eyeballed me. "Look, if you're going, then go. Just do it. Don't send yourself batty by waiting any longer." Then she went and drove me to the travel agency to see what they could do about flights. We discovered a last-minute bargain: if I left the next day it would cost almost nothing. I didn't buy a return ticket.

I went home to my parents and said "I'm leaving tomorrow." They were a little surprised, but they've always left me my freedom while remaining an ever-present support. Threw some things in a bag. What does one pack when one does not intend to return? Maybe it doesn't matter. I can shop when I've settled in.

Keira was quiet on the drive to the airport. "I'll miss you!" she blurted at last, and swiped at damp eyes. "Come visit," I said, and shut the car door firmly. I waved as she drove away, then turned to enter the building.

It was weird. The terminal was almost empty, though it's been busy every other time I've seen it. Just one check-in desk was open. Thank goodness it was the one I needed. I rushed over, dumped my suitcase on the carrier band, and shoved my ticket across the counter. "Passport, please," said a voice and I scrambled to find it.

"Going to live in Germany, then, are we?" The airline agent's soft speech brought me back to myself. My heart hammered. The girl went on. "I hope you like it there."

"Mmh," I managed, and finally looked her in the face. She droned on—something about the Irish being part of Europe which lets us do things like this, but I wasn't listening any more…because this was HER. The one from my dream. And here she was, right in front of me, talking to me. I blinked hard and fought for words. "Who are you? I know you."

She frowned slightly, then gave a compassionate smile. "Your flight's boarding in ten minutes. Better get along to security, no time to dally."

I was too shocked to do otherwise. So here I am up over the clouds on my way to Germany, more confused than ever. Why didn't I just stay there and make her tell me who she is? I could have gotten another ticket.

I came on this journey to find her. Now I've gone and left her behind.

30 November 2016.

Well. Obviously I didn't go running home at the first opportunity—I'm still here, in Regensburg, and intend to stay a while. It's strange how I was so fixated on the dream-woman that I took the step to come here, but seeing that face at the airport just maybe knocked some sense back into me. I mean, really. Who meets people in dreams and then in real life? She probably just looked a bit like her, same as the stranger in the water taxi.

Besides, if I went home I'd have to explain the whole dream thing to Keira and to be honest, I'm embarrassed by it. Although…I do still sometimes dream of that boy. He never speaks. It's like he's waiting for something from me. Not sure why, but I just know he's Irish. Maybe if I write down his story, he'd leave me in peace.

It's interesting enough here. I found a place to live, sharing a flat with a girl who works in a fashion shop. Also found a job. The circumstances of that were serendipitous, to say the least. I was sitting on the bank of the Danube, which is not blue at all, thinking about dreams and how utterly silly they are.

215

Then this couple came and sat beside me. The old chap started going on about how his son needed help in his grocery until I finally gave in and asked if he thought I'd be any use. They led me straight there and I was given an apron and put to work. I clean the shop floor, bring out the crates of fruit and vegetables in the morning for the street display and put them back in the cooler at night, and "freshen" the stock in the cobblestoned courtyard—whether by recutting the dried tips of zucchini stems, peeling a ragged top layer from onions to make them shine, or removing squashy cherries from a batch.

I like it; it's a life, isn't it?

16 February 2017.

Goodness, has it really been that long? Wow. Shows how busy I'm keeping. Work is tough, especially in these winter months when so much of what we do is in the open air. I bundle up and continue on. But that's not all—I've been having ideas. When we sort out the bruised fruit, the blemished vegetables, they are getting thrown away. I can see it pains the boss, but what can he do? So I asked him if he'd consider donating it to a community kitchen sort of group. He agreed immediately.

At the same time, I was meeting up with some of the students I remembered from my first trip, and more besides. Asked if they wanted to help me cook up some free food for whoever wants it. I have a few volunteers for that. Elliot is the one I knew already. There's a girl who looks the spitting image of Sarah. Yes, that Sarah, the friend from my teens who vanished so abruptly from my life. But this girl is German of course, and doesn't know anything about Sarah. Still, it's slightly creepy to see.

21 April 2017.

Quick note. We've got things up and running! We cook at my house almost every night, usually some sort of vegetable stew or soup, and then go round the streets handing it out in paper cups. Lots of people are happy to get it. Others just look at us suspiciously and pass. I'm excited about the potential to make a difference here. There are just as many homeless as ever, and now we're doing something different in taking the food to them rather than expecting them to come somewhere to get it. This is great! Now if only we had a couple more regular volunteers…

6 March 2018.

How time flies…Already we have been cooking for the city almost a year. I've spoken so much German that my English is starting to suffer for it, haha. We just got another new volunteer, Esther, who is totally passionate about the "mission" of saving what would otherwise be wasted. There are about nine of us now and we have become good friends by working together every night. I'm pretty tired, because I do this after a full day of work, but that's okay when I think of the good we're doing.

Long may it last.

1 September 2018.

Glorious day. Keira and Davin are married!

The ceremony was lovely, presided over by her father in the old Groomsport church, though he also contrived to walk her up the aisle as he should. The reception was a reasonably casual buffet in the church hall, calling up many memories of the times we spent there cooking and serving, except of course the wedding food was fancier. There was dancing, and lots of laughs.

Now I'm at my parents' house, in my own room that I haven't seen for nearly two years.

It's strange, knowing that it's not mine any more. Being here brings back the image of that woman's face from my dream. But I'm beyond all that now. I've found my place in the world and I'll be headed back to Regensburg real soon.

20 December 2018.

Exciting times! I've moved to a new flat, now sharing with Esther. This is so much better, because honestly it wasn't fair on my flatmate that we occupied the kitchen every night like that. But Esther is one of us. No chance of irritating her.

So, new apartment! The main living area is much bigger. Elliot thinks we should stop carrying the food out to the streets, and instead ask them to come in here and get it. At first I wasn't sure, but he can be very convincing. I guess it would be nice if we didn't have to go traipsing about in rain or snow.

Not many people come in to get the hot food, so Elliot said we should send someone out with printed invitations. He quickly made a roster so that one of us would go each day. After that, a few more people came. Some are addicts and they don't eat much at all. I learned that some drugs actually curb hunger. It breaks my heart. They're so skinny and they don't even want to eat.

We are wasting a lot of food now. Not only that, but we are wasting the effort and electricity to cook it. This isn't ideal, but I had to do something—slowly, slowly I'm reducing the quantities of "waste" produce I bring home from work. If there's less of it, then we cook less. Eventually I'll get it down to where it's just enough for the nine of us each night and we can stop begging street people to come in.

9 May 2019.

My plan was partly successful. The amount of food is about right for our regular group and any strays who wander in. But Elliot insists we should still go out on the street every night and invite people. So we do, reluctantly, and occasionally someone will come. At least I only have to do it once in two weeks or so.

Oddly enough, Elliot himself has been skipping his street duties, often saying he just didn't feel like it, or he forgot. On those nights he also "forgets" to show up at all, but woe betide if he hears that any of the others was absent. He is very talented at giving folks a dressing-down. I admit, oftentimes it's a relief when he doesn't arrive. And some of our number went away, never to return, after he had his little rant at them.

I'm growing tired of this. Physically, mentally—there is no time to breathe. I work all day and cook all evening, then clean up, and I can't escape because it's all in my own home. Is this burnout?

Mentioned to Elliot that I am exhausted. That I need a break, might even go back to Ireland for a while. That no one comes anyway, and that I'm not vital to the continuation of our project.

Well. I could see his mouth was getting ready for a tirade. Had no idea how bad it was going to be. He blasted me from here to the moon and back for even considering that I might skip out for a while or even just once. Reminded me sternly that all this was my idea and it would fall apart without me. I didn't believe it, but he left no room to object. He described my despicable laziness and how it was surely a sign of something lacking in my personal strength, which I should certainly work on. On and on he went until I was quite shattered.

At last he left, followed by the others who mutely let him shred me. I barely noticed when I was alone, so shell-shocked was I. It's been hours and I'm still sitting here, still quaking, still asking myself what just happened. It's a miracle I've been able to write it down. It seems like I'm staying. These are my friends and I don't want to let them down—and they seem to agree with Elliot. I wish I could escape. This thing I built, it's become a cage and trapped me.

Since when is he the boss? Come to think of it—who says this venture even needs a boss? But I can't even think about trying to change things. He'll be harsher the second time. I've seen it before.

That's why there are only six of us now.

21

MARIAH

AUGUST 2080

Mariah hunched over her computer and bethought Naomi. It had been over a year since she departed, but the gap she left was just as huge as ever. Now, though, there was a chance at solace. Mariah pulled up a blank character template and filled in everything she knew about her friend. Her humour, her drive, her view on life. Naomi had to have died, but she would live on through these memories now shaping a virtual person in Mariah's new world. Mariah would have a friend for life, after all—not a real person, but she hoped she wouldn't be able to tell the difference. She still gave the virtual one a different name, so as not to get completely confused, and built a dream husband for her.

Mariah didn't like thinking up names for people. She had one or two favourites, but nowhere near enough for the host of characters she had created. Well, the rest would have to go without names—would have to be defined by their personalities. Mariah preferred it that way. How she wished it could all be real…keeping the memories alive was all she could do.

They took time off from the programming when they needed it, so as not to be driven crazy by the constant computer work. The creation of her own new world engrossed Mariah to the exclusion of almost everything else. In the evenings they helped Rowena water the fields and harvest what had already ripened. They built vats at the factory and stored ton after ton of grain, to which they added wild honey from the beehives so it would be more nutritious and also to fight off bacteria. This food would be carried by tubes to their mouths at the times they ate in virtual reality. All this would be controlled by way of the decision-carrying cable whose end would have to be implanted in the brain through the upper forehead. The brain probe would create the taste of whatever food they believed themselves to be eating, while the tube delivered the sticky goo straight to the back of the throat for swallowing. Mariah wasn't sure how they would do when inserting the probe, since it had to be in precisely the right place to function correctly.

It was a fine summer day and the humans were not spending it in the factory for once. While they enjoyed a sleep-in, the dog exited the house via Peter's wide-open bedroom window and stood out the back, sniffing the morning air. Something was slightly off; something approached from the east. The dog decided to investigate. With a desultory glance back at the house, he set off down the road that would lead him to Ballyholme.

He passed down the wide suburban street, its brightly-coloured two-storey houses falling into disrepair, the nearest gardens cultivated by the humans, then after that the died-out overgrowth slowly sinking back into the earth.

Reaching the shore, he passed the old yacht club, descended the concrete ramp to the sand, and trotted along—the scent ever stronger in his nostrils although it would be far too faint for any human to detect. The dog now believed he knew who was moving closer, still very far off. He sat and watched the eastern headland.

Some time later, after the sun was high in the sky and the delicate dawn colours had leached away into blue and grey, he noticed Mariah, Peter and Rowena approaching along the beach.

"Rufus! What're ye doing, chum?" called Peter as he came close. Mariah greeted the dog in a wordless head-tussle, after which he resumed his eastward position. The humans settled in the warm sand and promptly went to sleep again, while the dog remained on vigil.

A sharp bark woke Mariah with a jolt. How much time had passed? Maybe the computer work was tiring her out more than she'd imagined. Well, today they had all the time in the world to sleep. Through half-closed eyes she observed Peter standing in the surf to cool his feet. The sea was blue-green and calm, like a knitted blanket. Peter shaded his eyes, looking down to the rocks at the point. He didn't move for a long time and she wondered what had caught his attention. The beach was wide, the tide low, and through the light haze of crystalline sea spray, the knobbly black promontory was still some distance away. The dog still sat motionless beyond Peter, still stared along the water's edge in the same direction.

Mariah squinted. Was that a person walking with slow, heavy steps along the rocky shore towards them? She sat up straighter to get a better view. Then she leapt to her feet and ran with Peter along the beach. Bare feet pounded on the sand, sending it flying at every stride. They met at the place the rocks ended.

"Aileen!" Mariah gathered her in her arms. She was frail, broken even, and her eyes were haunted. Wisps of hair fell around her face, thinner than Mariah had ever seen her before. Rufus frolicked around them.

"I know you know already, but I have to say it anyway." Her voice wavered. She moistened her dry lips and went on. "I made a big mistake. I was in love, you know. I should never have slept with Lucas. I mean, it could have killed me." She glanced at Peter, then at the sandy ground. He said nothing. "Then I went with him, because I belonged to him."

Rowena came up then, and they all sat down on a grassy ridge at the edge of the sand. Aileen went on to tell how she and Lucas had forgotten everything except each other after leaving: the classic starstruck lovers, for a few days and nights at least. Then the sickness had begun to take hold of him more and more—much slower than usual, but in the end this only prolonged his pain. Aileen had watched him decline just as she had her husband and family in the first instance.

Finally, Lucas had gone so very still that morning, and she had abandoned him in death to return to the rest—whether friends or foes, they were the only people left. She and Lucas had been in the old caravan park that came after Groomsport, so it was a long way back.

"I've walked all day," she concluded, "and I've decided there's no point being mad at the Guild any more." She glanced at Mariah and gained confidence. "We all bring our torment down upon our own heads."

Mariah managed a smile and leaned over to hug her. "Thanks. I know how hard this is for you."

Peter and Rowena stood by grinning at the reconciliation, then they made their way home. Aileen walked beside Mariah, and great was their rejoicing at the loss of the old bitterness.

Back at the house, they prepared a celebratory meal and called Zhu and Noah over to hear the news that Aileen was back. As they ate, they told her all about the lives they were building on the computers. She would need one too, of course; she could not be left behind alone now. But she could do as Rowena had done and create an adequate sort of environment in a fairly short time. Mariah vowed to herself to build her into her own life story and make her a special friend. The best thing about it was that they could still be friends after they woke up, but with many more shared experiences than before. Of course, the same was true of Peter.

Peter interrupted this dreamy train of thought. "Hey, Mariah! When are we getting married?"

Everyone looked at Mariah and the heat rose to her face, although that was the last thing she wanted. She laughed and smiled over at him. "You're right. We're almost finished with the system build. How about next Saturday?" As all eyes swivelled to him, it was his turn to go red. A murmur of laughter rolled around the circle.

Then he grinned. "Well, all right. Let's do it!"

So it was settled, and Mariah went to sleep that night in her room a good deal happier than she had been in the morning. She had regained a sister and friend in Aileen, and this time next week she would be a married woman, and bed a man at last. She shuddered slightly where she lay, but her heart was glad, so glad—and she hoped the best was yet to come.

That week they returned to their computer work with enthusiasm, since the goal was now in sight. Aileen began building her environment, after a crash course on the basics of the program. She, too, wanted to choose another name for herself, and Mariah built her into her own life at the point she was working on.

By this stage Mariah would be in another country, having followed the notion she had refused years before the Senate takeover. She well apprehended the nature of this privilege, to be able to begin again and do things right this time—even if it was only a virtual reality. Even now the hope was clear: in her artificial life, she would be more confident from the outset. She would lack for nothing, Without any Troubles to hinder, she would not run into a dead-end job as she had in real life.

There was something else they had wanted to do.

"Hey, guys!" She called to the others working at their screens. "We have to test this thing before we give our lives into its control."

All she got was blank stares, then Zhu ventured an answer. "That means we need a guinea pig. Who's going to volunteer?"

Silence. Mariah sighed loudly. Of course it had to be her. No one was as thoroughly acquainted with these systems as she, so they couldn't be expected to trust them without proof.

"All right, I'll do it." Her words dissolved the tension that had built up in the room. *Why not try it right now?*

Mariah set the program to begin at a point in her virtual storyline just after she had gone to London as a small child. Then she checked the exterior wiring, and used a mirror to make a pen-mark on her forehead where the sensor should go. She took a step towards the cabin door, then another. She was almost inside. She laid a hand on the rim of the door and heard a whine at her feet. The dog sat, tail still, looking up at her with those big, sad eyes.

"Oh, Rufus, I know, it's scary. But you can't come with me in here." She gulped once, entered the cabin, discarded her clothes and climbed into the suit. When she had zipped it closed, she called for Peter, who appeared at the door.

"Here, you'll have to insert this sensor at the top of my forehead," she said, holding out the decision-making cable with her rubber-clad arm. "I can't see up there to do it myself, but I marked the spot. See?"

The suit's lining was strange on her bare skin, with its myriad sensors on the entire inner surface. Goosebumps crawled across her arm and belly. When she moved, many wires swung with her, but she wouldn't be moving much more now. She lay back on the bench.

Peter came up, took the cable in his hand, and searched at her hairline for the right spot. They had studied the diagrams carefully, but now it was for real. The sensor was a thick, sharp, needle-like insert that had to be placed in contact with a particular nerve. It had to puncture the skull, but was short enough so as to not do any permanent damage if it missed its target. A wind-up piston on a moveable arm would serve to drive the probe through the skull-bone and into the brain.

"Okay, I think I've found the position." Peter kept one finger on it, holding the sensor in his other hand. "This is gonna hurt. Are you ready?"

Mariah took a deep breath. Despite her knowledge of the machines, her heart beat faster. Adrenaline pumped from her core out to fingers and toes. "Get me out in about two hours, all right?"

Peter nodded in reply, his face gravely serious. "Don't worry. If it's no good, we can still use these suits and cabins to put ourselves in cryo-sleep." He smiled suddenly. "Whatever happens, don't be scared. We'll survive."

Mariah now inserted the mouthpiece, then pulled the rubber suit over her head. Its hood reached only to the crown, leaving free access to insert the sensor. As she placed the facial output devices over ears, eyes and nose, Peter disappeared from view. The eye screens were blank now, of course, because the system wasn't turned on yet. She took one last conscious breath, but now the air was coming through the tubes and filters.

Peter's hands wandered her face, and the probe's tip rested against her prickling skin. A sharp pain entered her at the very centre of her skull. Her body jerked. The stinging in her head stunned her and she was frozen into place, although she wanted to scream at him to get her out, that she didn't want to go through with it after all—it had been a silly idea in the first place! He squeezed her hand through the rubber. There was a muffled click as he switched on the activation control.

Instantly the suit became much colder, and with the chill she imagined the fingers of death grasped hold of her. There was some mistake! It wasn't supposed to kill her!

As the cold increased, the pain from the needle vanished. Her awareness slipped away fast, and she was terrified, but her body was immobilised already and it was too late to go back.

Then she was gone.

There is a face in front of me. Who is that? I reach out a hand and encounter something hard.

"That's a mirror," says a voice behind me. Turn my head. Here is my mother. "That's you in there."

I want to ask her why, but the words that come out sound like "Intsie anga urka!"

Frustrated, I look back at my mirrored image and stare blankly. I remove my hand from the glass and the child in the mirror does the same. I open my mouth to say something, but my reflection moves with me. Mama was right! It really is me in there. I screw up my eyes in concentration. But this is really me out here too. Are there two of me?

This idea is too confusing, so I reach for the dolly lying beside me on the floor. She has a blue dress on just like mine, which I think is grand. Another me, but not like the one in the mirror. I can make the doll do whatever I want her to, not just the same as I do.

Mama holds a little box out towards me and it makes a click while I play with my dolly. Later there will be pictures to look at, but I don't know about cameras yet.

It is good to be here, although I don't know where I came from. If I squint hard at something, there is a soft glow around it, and if I squeeze my eyes shut, straight rays of light cross my vision. I try to grasp them, but soon learn there's nothing there.

More pictures cross my mind, an indication of time passing. As I become more aware of my environment, I walk around and learn that I live with my parents in a little house that is one of many identical buildings lined up along a narrow street among many other streets. In time I learn to speak—soon I talk incessantly. I also grow taller, and I'm proud that Dada calls me his "little lady". While he is at work, Mama and I go for long walks in the big city. Sometimes it is warm; more often we have to wear thick coats.

Occasionally it snows and the whole world turns white. In this way, a whole year soon passes—agonisingly slowly, in my opinion, as long nights, days, weeks, months and seasons unroll before my curious eyes. As I grow, I learn to love London with its big red buses and colourful population.

Then one day as we eat together at our little kitchen table, my parents explain to me that we can't stay here forever. I frown; I like it here. We come from somewhere else, they go on, an island far across the ocean, and we will go back there one day soon, all together. We will live near the sea, they said; that is good for swimming in when the hot summers come.

That night as I lie sleepily in my cot, I wonder what it will be like in that faraway land. Are there buses there too, and parks, and lots of people like there are here? My parents said it is a good place, so of course I believe them. I doze off peacefully.

Then, in the night, a dream! It is freezing cold. Hands pull on my arms and legs, which are suddenly far too long. Voices murmur above me. I can't make them out. Someone shakes me by the shoulders, then there is a sharp slap in my face and a stabbing pain in my head.

⁂

"Come on, wake up!" The words forced their way into her sluggish mind. This was beyond strange. What was happening? Hadn't she just fallen asleep in her cot? She moaned, and was shocked because her voice was so unfamiliar. Yes, it was her voice, but different somehow. Finally she got her eyes open and blinked hard. Against a bright white ceiling, three strange faces leaned in close. Confusion and fear filled her soul. Where were Mama and Dada? She tried to sit up, but she was attached to lots of black wires. She let out a whimper. She stared about her, blinded by fright. One of the three put his hand on her shoulder. She shivered with a chill that went deep into her bones.

"Mariah! It's all right—we got you out! How do you feel?"

She gaped stupidly at him. What was he talking about? She had a wonderful life and didn't need to be rescued.

"We need to get you out of that suit," he said, making for the door. "Uh, can you girls see to that?" He turned red and left the room quickly. The two women pulled at her arms and legs again as they peeled off her rubber skin and pulled a nasty sharp thing out of her head. They pressed something on the wound to stop it bleeding. A name echoed in her mind, and she spoke it.

"Peter!" But who was Peter?

The women brought other clothes to dress her. One of them laughed softly. "Don't worry, he'll be right back after you're decent! Are you okay, Mariah? What was it like?"

"My name's not Mariah!" she said suddenly, as the man called Peter came back into view. But what was her name? She realised she didn't know.

Then, with a rush, she remembered. She remembered that she was Mariah, she remembered the Troubles and the great plague, she remembered she was to marry Peter. Still her mind reached back into that numinous dream of a carefree life in another place, and she wept bitterly as the others held her tight.

Mariah went straight to bed and slept like a log. She awoke once in the pre-dawn hours believing she was a child in London and fought a strange disappointment over this, and later was still too exhausted to go back to the factory. Home alone with Rufus to watch over her, she slept several more hours, the dog by her side, and by the time evening came she had recovered enough to speak of her experience. When the others returned from the factory at nightfall, she had already made dinner. Peter gave her a quick squeeze around the shoulders by way of greeting, and when Rowena came in from the fields, they sat down to eat.

Afterwards, she looked around at her friends. Their questions almost burst visibly out of them, so she spoke without preamble. "It was beautiful. So beautiful." Thinking about it brought tears to her eyes. "When it was switched on, I was scared. And waking up was really dreadful. But the life itself—wow!"

She searched for words to tell of the freedom and innocence she had lived in. She described the teeming city of London, the house, the seasons. "In fact, it was more detailed than I remember programming it. The system is much more sophisticated than I ever dreamed."

Noah spoke up. "But does it feel real?"

Mariah dug her fingers into the fur of Rufus's head as he sat beside her. "When I was there, I forgot all about this life. You saw that when I woke up, I'd forgotten who I was—believed I was someone else. I didn't have a name there, because I haven't entered one in the program yet!" She reviewed the virtual life again and realised something else. "And you know what? Even though I was only in there for a few hours, in that time I lived about a year and a half."

Astonished cries ascended—everyone wanted to know more. "Sometimes the days went faster. Life was always made up of the same parts. At the beginning, I was just learning to talk. By the end I'm guessing I was three." She recalled intricate detail, more than she would usually remember from a dream, but it had a similar kind of vivid intensity. She spoke of the strange glow each object had, and the rays of light. She told them everything she remembered and it amazed even herself. Her fingers ceased their massage of the dog's head. He peered around at her, tongue lolling out, as if to ask why.

When she finally stopped talking, an awestruck silence enveloped them, until Peter spoke. "I guess the test was a success."

"There is one other thing." All eyes turned to Mariah again. "I mean—I know I was a child and all, but looking at it now, it was almost a bit…boring. I might have to program in some enemies so that I am challenged sometimes as well."

The assembled survivors fell to chattering about the lives they were building, wondering aloud what it would really be like to grow up "inside".

Later that evening, Mariah went for a short walk with Peter.

"It was so vibrant and alive," she told him. "It even seemed more real than all this here." She waved a hand to indicate the empty street. "And I felt so safe! Until I had to wake up, that is. But it was worth it." She stared into the dark sky, and he took her hand.

"Hey, don't forget we've got a wedding to organise!"

She sighed, then smiled. *Of course. We will be back in our virtual world soon enough.* Determined to make the most of now, she turned to face him and shimmied up close. He smiled and dipped his head so their noses touched, then she raised herself on tiptoes and tasted his lips. His arms encircled her shoulders; Mariah grabbed him around the neck and pulled him close, relishing his flavours of earth and sweat and sweetness of heart.

As for the wedding, there was not much to arrange. The girls had already searched the houses in the area and found a suit and a long white dress. It was more an evening dress than a wedding dress, obviously once the property of a woman somewhat broader than Mariah, but it would do.

"I'd like to get married on the beach," she said suddenly. "What do you think of that?"

Peter agreed readily, for he too loved the sea. They walked home, and found Aileen and Noah talking excitedly in front of the houses.

"We've decided we want to have the wedding at the beach," Mariah called out to them as they came nearer. Rufus bounded up, a little too fast for Noah's liking, who aimed a kick at the dog. There was a yelp as he skittered out of the way. Noah backed off. "Keep it away from me."

"Don't you dare kick my dog! He's not going to hurt you." Mariah stepped close to Noah and glowered in his sullen face, fists tight at her side. Silently, he pivoted on his heel and left them.

Aileen continued as if nothing had happened. "Fine, then we'll have the banquet down at the beach too. How about one of the parks at the shore?" They talked over a few details together, then turned in for the night.

Mariah dreamed of London.

In the week running up to the wedding, Peter and Mariah were careful to adjust their virtual lives to make sure they would meet and marry there also. However, they did not define a time for their "first" meeting, so that this would come upon them unexpectedly, much like in real life. They did wonder whether it would make any difference, since Mariah had forgotten every bit of the real world as soon as her suit had been activated. Still, as Peter said, they could not be sure it would be the same for everyone, or even for Mariah the second time. And they certainly didn't want to spend their lives knowing they would meet on a particular day.

Not forgetting Rowena, Mariah planned for her to come back into her life a second time, years after the first. Rereading her overall plan, she would often find gaps in it and enter something new at that point in time, including the challenges she believed she needed to keep her soul from stagnating.

So they all put the finishing touches on the artificial worlds they would be spending many years inside.

"Junko Tabei!" said Zhu suddenly one afternoon. Mariah glanced up at the huge grin on her face. Zhu leapt from her chair and paced up and down. "Junko Tabei was the first woman to climb Mount Everest."

Mariah had no idea. How did people learn this stuff? Mariah had heard that the first man at the top was called Hillary—which, to her, sounded like a girl's name—and that he came from somewhere far, far away. Ocean crossers, mountain climbers. It made sense. But Junko Whatsit?

Zhu went on. "I'm going to design part of my life to be like hers. I want to climb." Her eyes had an excited glow about them.

To each their own. Mariah smiled and went back to work.

As she was pretty much finished with her own constructions, Mariah helped Aileen set up a simple environment for herself. Like Peter, she wanted to grow up in a foreign country, so they entered the parameters for that and used standard settings to fill in the gaps. Mariah ensured once again that they would meet as young people, from Aileen's side this time, and that they would spend a good part of their lives together. As with many other things, they did not pin down how this would happen, preferring to leave it to destiny, which surely had an influence on the virtual world as it did on the real one.

Taking a quick break from the glow of the screens, Aileen and Mariah stepped outside into the paling afternoon light to stretch their legs.

"I'm going to be a pianist!" Aileen said after a while. "I've always wanted to be a musician—and now I can be!"

Mariah smiled. "Even such a short set-up gives you time to make sure you live your dreams. But let's hope there's much more for you than just a piano."

Rufus trotted up beside them and Mariah let out an almost-sob as he nuzzled her hand.

"What is it?"

"Aileen, I have to put him in cryo. I have to try. But I might end up killing him instead."

"Is it better to kill him now than leave him all alone?"

Indeed, that was the question. Mariah didn't think she could handle the choice, and yet, if the cryo worked for him, that was the most optimistic route to take.

They made full circle, reached the door they had left by and returned to their desks. There was so much to do that it distracted Mariah throughout those final days. It kept her from being overwhelmed by the strangeness of it all. There was so little time left, but they had prepared everything carefully and they were ready. Sometimes at night she would lie awake, pondering the new life she had seen so fleetingly—yet even in that glimpse it had been real. It had captured her, changed her with its freedom and simplicity, and she could hardly wait to enter it again. Indeed, she ached for it in the depths of her soul.

22

ꜰᴀɪᴛʜ

2021

"No, you can't go to London," said Elliot to Faith. "The things we are doing here are far more important than a visit to your little friend, and there's no one to take your place. Besides, all this was your vision and now you want to give it up and disappoint those who rely on it and anyone who might come in need of help."

If anyone ever came, ran through Faith's mind. She did admit there was sense in his words, the same words that came at her like a wall every time she suggested something he didn't like or didn't fit in with his narrow view of the world. So she said nothing more for the time being, but continued with her plans. He wasn't about to prevent her sojourn at Keira's. A few days surely wouldn't hurt.

Faith packed a small bag and left bright and early one morning, not expecting any trouble until she got back. On the way to the station she was horrified to espy Elliot striding towards her—but he hadn't spotted her yet.

She ducked into a side street and flattened herself against the wall until he walked past. Not quite trusting that he wouldn't turn around, she watched from the corner until he disappeared out of sight at a bend in the strangely deserted road, then scooted to catch her train.

She dropped into a seat as it pulled away, her brow creasing. Elliot was usually a late sleeper and never showed himself this early. Maybe he'd gotten a tip-off. Well, he hadn't caught her, and now it was too late. She grinned.

Keira met her at Heathrow and they took the Tube into Wembley.

"So, you're enjoying London?" Faith looked out the window but kept forgetting they were underground with only concrete walls passing by outside.

"Yep, it's grand. We both got jobs almost as soon as we arrived, and that's what we're here for, so we're happy." Keira peered at Faith. "You look a bit knackered though. Are you all right?"

Faith sighed. "Sure. I'm doing exactly what I wanted to do."

"But?"

"But…it's not doing any good and I can't get out. Keira, I'm trapped."

"Can't you just walk away?"

"Um. Maybe. But where would I go?" Faith tried to think of doing something else but there was just a big blank hole in her future whenever she tried to imagine anything different. It was like it was all blocked off. "I only have these five friends. We do stuff together most days. We do a lot of cooking and eating, but I don't enjoy it any more. It's not like Groomsport."

"We'll give you a good time here. Get your mind off it at least."

Keira was true to her word and showed Faith around famous bits of London. They lived on junk food and didn't speak of cooking, let alone of cooking for the poor. Davin joined them when he could, since his work hours were a bit peculiar. Faith laughed when he chewed through fast food with gusto, and he grinned. "Chefs don't like to bring work home."

The time passed too quickly and soon the friends were saying goodbye again. Releasing Faith from a long hug, Keira held her by the shoulders a moment longer. "You take care of yourself. I'm worried about you, hon."

Faith's words stuck in her throat. "I know," she squeaked out past an enormous lump, then turned and ran into the passenger-only area.

She returned to Regensburg several hours later and walked the quiet, dark streets to home. Esther was still up and greeted her enthusiastically. Yet she fell back into a subdued silence.

"What's the matter?" Faith growled. "It's Elliot, isn't it? What has he done?"

Esther shrugged. "Nothing much. And that's the point. I haven't seen him since you left."

That soon changed. In the evening there was a ring at the door. With dread all the way down to her boots, Faith buzzed the street door open and rested her head on the doorpost as she listened to the determined footsteps climbing the old building's central stairs. She was surely in for it now.

Elliot climbed the last few steps and stood before her. Wordlessly he motioned for her to move out of the way and let him enter. Slowly, she did so, gaze on the floor. She shut the door and turned to face him. Elliot's mouth opened and the flood burst out. "What were you *thinking?* You can't just leave. Especially not after I told you not to. I said you couldn't and you have to do what I say because I have your best interests at heart and also the best interests of the city, which you clearly do not have. Think of those hungry people we were unable to help because we didn't have you. Think of that food that went to waste. I even had another big fight with Teresa when she accused me of drinking too much. And it's all your fault. Bleh blah blah, blerm blabber blegh…"

A curious thing happened as Faith tried to listen to him. His words melted into meaningless babble even as his face grew ever more animated and contorted. Only occasionally could she catch a word, "responsibility," "disrespectful," and maybe even "foolhardy." Still, she got his point well enough—a point so sharp that it entered like sharp blades into her soul. The torrent of words went on and on and on until finally she could take it no more; she clutched her head and screamed, a long and tortured wail that encompassed all her frustration, all her torment, all the hurt done to her in the name of the city. She did not stop. She screamed until her breath was gone and even longer, until she lost her senses.

When she came to herself, she was extended on her blue couch, Esther dabbing at her face with a damp cloth. She tried to speak, but Esther shushed her. "Shh…don't worry. He's gone now."

The next day, reluctant, she threw herself into the schedule and soon was just as stressed as ever. Still no one came more than once to eat with the six of them. Still they kept on collecting throwaway groceries and cooking them every night. Day after day and night after night, this was how their time was spent. Elliot himself showed up only rarely, an unexpected relief.

As the months progressed, Faith found herself eating less and less of what they made. There was no point. She hated the gathering and processing of it; hated that it had turned her into a numb automaton with no option but to continue. She weakened and developed a persistent cough that annoyed some of the others. "You shouldn't handle food if you are sick," they would say. Faith had to agree.

She went, trembling, to Elliot. "Look, I'm all burned out. For real this time. It's making me shrivel up. I think I should throttle back on the cooking until I feel better."

"What?" Elliot's eyes and mouth formed O's. "You want to stop this vitally important work because you don't *feel* like doing it? What if everyone thought like that? We would do nothing!"

She held up a hand to stop him. This speech—he'd laid it on her a hundred times before. Maybe a thousand.

But he droned on. "Our work is more important than how any of us *feels*. Who would do it if you didn't? No one, that's who. It was your idea, and you want to drop it just like that."

In her mind Faith had an answer for every one of his barbs. Yes, it was her idea, but when had he grabbed control? Memory was foggy and she couldn't put a finger on it...he had just sort of snuck in and taken over.

Esther did not like the harrowing schedule any more than Faith did, especially since she was a student and her final exams were approaching. She told Faith she was going to go and talk to Elliot about reducing her time commitment. Faith didn't think he would sympathise, though she agreed with Esther. Again she failed to understand why he was calling the shots on a project that had been hers from the start. It was this fact that left her trapped, unable to step away from the situation, and with no control over her own dreams or the people who invaded her kitchen every evening. How did something that started so well turn into such a monster?

Elliot refused Esther's request, as predicted, but no one expected Esther's reaction. If she couldn't do less, then she would do nothing at all.

"Quitting altogether was my only choice," she told Faith at home later that night. "I didn't really want to go as far as that, but he wouldn't budge on the hours."

Faith was sorry Esther wouldn't be working alongside her, but admired her courage nonetheless. This was a life she wouldn't wish on anyone. They said goodnight and went to bed tucked up in their own rooms, and Faith reflected that at least she still had Esther as a friend to share her home with.

The next day, the phone rang. This was a fairly rare occurrence, since the friends met each other every day, so Faith answered it with some trepidation. "Hello?"

"Faith! I'm glad I caught you." Elliot's voice was distraught. "You know what you have to do now, right?"

Faith creased her brow. "No, sorry, I don't. What are you talking about?"

"Esther."

"What about her?" Faith tried to sound innocent.

Elliot's pitch increased to a whine. "She doesn't share our vision any more. Do you honestly not see what this means?"

"What do you mean?"

"You have to throw her out!" He was shouting now.

Faith's head buzzed. "*What* did you say?"

"Put her out on the street. With all her stuff. Right now."

Faith gaped and gulped for a few long moments. *He's lost his mind. No, actually he lost it a long time ago.* A wave of anger roiled up from her toes to her head and out to the tips of her fingers. "Well," she said carefully and clearly. "No. No, you can just *forget* that."

She slammed the phone down and seethed. *Wow, that felt good.*

Esther emerged from her room at the noise. Their gazes met.

"It's over," said Faith.

Both breathed deep and long.

Faith expected he would call back and beg and wheedle, but he didn't, and she was glad. No one came to their place that night to cook. No one came near them, no one called. It was really over.

A day passed, then another. Faith and Esther reeled with the sudden gift of time. Almost giddy, Faith enjoyed odd little miracles, like buying fast food and even throwing her leftovers away, something she would never have dreamed of doing before.

Esther had her studies to fill her time, of course, spending long hours researching at the university. When she came home, she would play the piano to relax, and Faith would sit reading a book nearby.

Faith filled her days at first with fresh air. She walked the banks of the Danube and Regen as far in either direction as she could go and come back in one day. She got on her bike, stiff with disuse, and ventured even greater distances, visiting great ruined castles on hilltops and gilded chapels in quiet valleys. She was careful around town, because she didn't want to run into Elliot; but luck was on her side: she always spotted him before he saw her, so she was able to get out of his way. Now she could pay attention to the picturesque buildings and landscapes like never before. She had always known it was pretty here, but now she knew it as a friend: a medieval city like no other, with its crooked walls and narrow alleys, brightly-painted ancient houses and grey carved churches, vineyard-swathed hills and broad tree-lined paths that twisted alongside the steady-moving river.

Time passed, and Faith grew bored with only walking. She'd read all her books over and over again by now, so she ordered in a fresh stack of English novels. She tore through them in days when they arrived, and soon ordered more. It was a drug—literature, carrying her into other worlds like she hadn't experienced since she was a child.

With the falling of dusk upon the ancient housetops one day, she closed a book and sighed. If only these worlds were real…if only there was a way to inhabit them more fully. She picked up the book and scrutinised the back cover again. There was a picture of the author, a woman not entirely unlike herself. Perhaps she, too, could write a book.

Over the days that followed, she scribbled down ideas and bits of plot that eventually gave enough of a basis to start writing. She wrote a title in the front of her blank notebook and set to work. Chapter after chapter poured forth; there was a strange kind of solace in letting the words flow out of her soul.

The university semester ended and Esther decided to spend her summer holidays in Greece, because she now had the freedom to do so. The apartment echoed empty around Faith. She threw herself all the more into her writing. In searching online for the answer to a question, she discovered a vibrant world of writers' forums where she promptly signed up, introduced herself, and asked a few questions. Soon she found some people who helped her with her writing in exchange for her opinion on theirs.

One day she awoke curled in a corner of the kitchen and as the pain in her head subsided, very slowly came to understand that her memory had been stolen once more. With no one to talk her through it, she had to wait it out. At the end of the day she surveyed her scattered thoughts and pronounced herself mostly present, even if things would never be restored like they were before. Great was the weeping that night as she bemoaned the gap where friends and a sound mind should be, and mourned the great silence of her life.

23

mariah

The last few days passed quickly in a whirl of excitement and activity as Mariah and her friends prepared for the wedding and their entry into the new world. On Saturday morning she awoke with a pleasant tingling in her fingers and toes. She pulled on some clothes and went outside. Aileen sat on the doorstep, enjoying the morning sun.

"I'm going down to the beach to wash," Mariah told her, then grabbed a bike that leaned on the wobbling fence. There was plenty of rainwater in the tank—this was Ireland, after all—but she preferred a natural bath and the taste of salt on her skin.

Aileen smiled. "Take your time, we've got all day!"

Mariah pedalled off into the morning freshness. Rufus loped beside her, his limp now only slight, his joy at the day much greater than the remaining pain. It was still early, and the air was crisp and alive with birdsong. Mariah rode past the empty houses, trying not to think of the bones each contained.

Yes, it was a tragedy. But now she was about to pledge her life to a man who loved her. She couldn't find it in herself to be sad today, except to wish that Da and Darian—even Ma—could be here to share the occasion.

After reaching the sandy end of the bay, she laid the bike on the grass and stepped onto the sand. She ran to the water and plunged into its refreshing coolness, making sure to wash her hair too. The salt would clean it well and give extra volume. When she was done scrubbing it, she lay back in the waves and floated. She closed her eyes and imagined she was flying—and soon, she could if she wanted.

⬥⬥⬥

The dog got out of the water quickly, leaving Mariah to splash around some more. Slowly he made his way up to the promenade and sniffed around, following this scent and that—mostly where small birds had been. Then a faint odour of something far more interesting rose to his nostrils. He wasn't certain—he had to find out—he glanced guiltily back at Mariah in the sea, and took off inland.

He snuffled at everything that might possibly bear an aroma. Nose to the ground, several blocks from the shore he almost ran into a hulking white vehicle with its rear hatch open. Five wooden chairs lay inside but there was still more room, so he hopped in to discover whether this was the source of the mysterious smell. Musty rubber and engine oil dominated the space. He was about to turn around and move on when two more chairs landed in the load bed. The dog leapt around, teeth bared in a snarl.

"Hey!" roared Noah. "Freakin' monster! Get out of there." He gripped a chair and pointed its legs at the dog, continuing to shout and curse and shove. The dog finally found a gap and made a run for it. His paws landed hard on the gritty road—his wound might have torn open again—but he ran full-tilt to the corner of the street, confused and sad. He stopped, one paw in the air, looked back.

Then a terrible noise cut through the air—Noah was in the driver's seat and had started the old van. He turned it and drove towards the dog, who, crazed with terror, fled in a direction he'd never been before. Noah laughed as he took a different turn and headed back towards home.

The dog came to an area of small, shabby houses and began to regain his

244

calm. He slowed his headlong flight. Finally stopped and licked at his bleeding leg. Nosed around the brick house walls that fronted right onto the street.

At the fourth house down, he smelled the message he'd thought he would never read again: a calling card from a female dog. And fresh! She had to have passed by here just today.

With one wistful glance back in the direction of Cliff Road—and a quiver at how much Noah hated him—the dog set out in pursuit of the enigmatic bitch.

Mariah enjoyed the sea for a good long while, after which she stood waist-deep in the current and retrieved a small comb from her pocket to untangle her hair, grown long in the time since the Troubles. Rufus was nowhere in sight—he must have headed off home already, perhaps in search of something to eat, bottomless pit that he was. She squeezed out her hair so it would dry better, and, stepping out of the sea, she walked back to the bike and set it upright before swinging aboard. Then she headed for home, taking it slowly so as not to work up a sweat and get dirty again. Soon she arrived and joined the others, who were breakfasting on fruit in Deborah's garden.

"There'll be a big enough feast later, so we don't want to eat too much now," called Aileen to Rowena, who was just coming out of the house. Then she caught sight of Mariah. "And here's the salty bride herself!"

This brought laughter from Zhu. Mariah looked about. "Where's Peter?"

"That's always the first question, right?" Zhu smiled at her. "Noah's getting him ready—you'll see him later," she said, winking.

"Come and eat something," called Rowena from the table in the garden, where there was a small pile of mandarins and sour green apples. Mariah wasn't really hungry, but hey—some vitamins would do her good, so she reached for some fruit. "And hey, has anybody seen Rufus?"

Just then, a sound came to her ears that was utterly strange, yet somehow familiar. They ran out onto the street and found a rusty van spitting ugly black smoke from its exhaust.

Noah leapt out with a flourish. "I found this not long ago on one of my walks," he explained, "and look, it still goes. I saved it for a special occasion—like today, Your Highness." Here he made a mock bow. A frown flitted across his face but disappeared as quickly as it had come.

"Hey, I'm just a bride, not a queen!" Mariah laughed, but was touched at his gesture. Apparently the others had known about the vehicle, for Aileen had already opened its back door and, with Noah's help, was loading the garden table into it.

While she and Noah piled the van full of food for the beach party, Zhu and Rowena took Mariah inside and set to work to pin her hair up in what they all hoped was an elegant design. It took longer than they planned, but maybe they hadn't expected to laugh so much. A short time later, the motor approached again. Then Aileen burst into the room.

"We're ready to go," she proclaimed, "everything's set up at the beach!" The girls helped Mariah get into the dress, and they trooped out to the van. There was no sign of Peter and Noah, nor Rufus for that matter. As Mariah looked around questioningly, Aileen read her thoughts.

"I left the two guys down at the beach to wait for us," she said as they all climbed into the vehicle. "It would have been a bit tight in here otherwise."

The van jerked as Aileen stepped on the gas and they were off to the beach. Strange to be riding in a bus—indeed, hardly anyone had used such a thing since shortly after the worldwide Troubles had first begun. They had learned to live without them, but Mariah was glad of it today. She looked out of the window beside her. The van glided past Bangor's silent centre and turned right, hugging the coast.

"Aileen! Stop here just a second!" cried Rowena, leaning into the front cab. She stared at an overgrown fence. "Flowers! You can't get married without *flowers!*" So they all got out and watched as Zhu and Aileen pointed here and there, and Rowena gathered a handful of what had once been someone's garden. Mariah had no idea what sort of flowers these were—they resembled overgrown daisies, in several colours.

"Here, grab this!" said Rowena, pushing the unruly bouquet into Mariah's hands. With some difficulty they got back into the van and were off again.

The beach was not far from where they lived, but with the van they were much faster. As they approached, Mariah realised her heart was beating fit to burst. She clutched the flowers tighter. Somewhere in the back of her mind she hardly believed it—she was going to get married! She shook her head slightly in disbelief, but it was true, and this was meant to be the happiest day of her life—*of this life, at least*. She refused to let herself dwell on her artificial life to come, or on the strange absconsion of her faithful companion Rufus—it would distract her too much from the matter at hand.

Aileen took the last turnoff and now brought the old van to a shuddering halt at the edge of a green park that lay before a small cove. High cliffs sheltered it on both sides while the calm sea sparkled in the sunlight. Noah waited to open the door for the girls.

They piled out of the van. Mariah straightened her dress while clasping the daisies to her with the other hand. Her companions stood close around so that Peter was hidden at first; then they opened the circle. The sight thrilled her romantic side through and through.

Peter stood some distance away on a grassy knoll just before the sand encroached. His grin went all over his face. Then Mariah noticed: someone had cut his hair! It had become long and wild, and like everyone else in the last years both before and after the disaster, he had left it mostly alone. Up till now, that is. Mariah's mouth fell open. She had to admit, his new haircut fitted better with the dark blue suit and white shirt he was wearing. He even had a tie on.

She took a step, and the others moved with her—Rowena and Aileen to her left and right, and Noah with Zhu in the rear. They came to Peter on the mounded earth. After a pause that was ever so slightly awkward, they began the simple ceremony.

Rowena said a blessing to start:

I wish you not a path devoid of clouds,
nor a life on a bed of roses.
Nor that you might never need regret,
nor that you should never feel pain.
No, this is not my wish for you. My wish for you is:
That you might be brave in times of trial,
that you might always have a friend who is worth that name,
whom you can trust. And who helps you in times of sadness,
who will defy the storms of life by your side.

Then it was time to speak. Mariah passed her flowers to Aileen and held Peter's hands in both of hers. She took a deep breath. "I vow you the first cut of my meat, the first sip of my wine, from this day it shall only your name I cry out in the night and into your eyes that I smile each morning."

Then Peter answered. "I shall be a shield for your back as you are for mine, never shall a grievous word be spoken about us, for our marriage is sacred between us."

They gripped fingers even harder and spoke the final lines together. "Above and beyond this, I will cherish and honour you through this life and into the next."

Still holding on, they turned to the others now standing in a semicircle around them. "Do you witness these vows?"

Each one said "Aye," then together, "We swear by peace and love to stand, heart to heart and hand to hand. Hark, O Spirit, and hear us now, confirming this sacred vow for this life and every other."

The meaning of this did not escape them—they spoke not of the afterlife as tradition might dictate, but of that other elysian world they had made for themselves. And so, with the sound of the breeze in the bushes on the hill and gentle waves on the warm sand, the promises were complete.

It was done—they were married, and so allowed themselves a quick kiss while the others looked on and crowed with delight.

Then time lost its meaning for a while, as they lost themselves in celebrating and feasting. Noah proceeded to play the old guitar with a modest skill, to their surprise.

Their friends had prepared the best meal the available resources could offer, and even though this was still a fairly vegan affair, they had done wonders with the little they had. There were stuffed red capsicums, fire-grilled eggplant slices on toasted barley bread, large quantities of roasted kebabs made of onion and sweet potato, and afterwards honey nut cakes topped with chopped strawberries from the glasshouse.

Yet Mariah's mind was not on the music or the food, as fine as it was—she wondered where Rufus had got to, and was continually distracted by having to think of herself as a wife. And every time she looked at Peter, she realised anew that this man was now her husband—and every time, it sent a thrill rushing through her.

Later that afternoon, their friends drove them in the van to a fine house overlooking the same sandy bay. They had obviously been hard at work in secret, cleaning it up and stocking it with food.

"We've lived this long in our old world, another two nights won't make any difference," insisted Zhu when they protested the delay in starting the system. "Besides, you have to take the chance while you can, right?" With a wink and a nod from some of the others, they all climbed back into the bus and drove off, Noah waving dangerously out of the driver's seat.

As the motor's rattle faded into silence, the two were left there alone. They climbed to the porch and sat there looking over the vast ocean.

Hours passed, and the endless water grew even bigger in the gently fading light of day. They sat side by side at first. Mariah leaned into Peter's warmth, enjoying him and the heady aroma of love.

They sat like that for a long time. Eventually she climbed onto his lap, encircled his shoulders in her arms, and laid her face against his. Electricity charged through her at his nearness, and at the knowledge that they would now take the gift they so desired and give of themselves in this night.

Indeed, she would have given herself to him there and then on the porch if they hadn't been disturbed by the now-familiar rumble of a motor. They disentangled themselves, suddenly cold with fear.

Feet ran up the steps to where they whiled away the evening. They recognised Noah, his face filled with horror. He stuttered so badly they barely understood him.

"Lu-luc-Lucas—he came back!"

Peter and Mariah glanced at each other. "He didn't die?"

"He did! He died just now!" He breathed, but it was more like a sob. "Aileen thought he died weeks ago, that day she came back to us, right?"

Mariah nodded. "She was wrong?"

"Lucas was taking a helluva long time to die anyway. I think she freaked when he passed out that morning."

Peter's breaths came faster, the frustration coiled within him. A pang of regret enclosed Mariah's own heart. *Our wedding night. It ends like this.*

"Nobody went near him." Noah's gasps grew shorter. "And when he went in his old room, we locked him in. But the virus may be in the air now. Rowena says Lucas had exactly the same immunity as all of us. If he died, we can all die."

Mariah leapt to her feet, nearly tripping over the long dress. "But we can

249

still survive! Noah, remember the system! It's completely isolated—we'll be safe if we can get in there!" She strode to the stairway to run down to the bus, then looked back.

Peter still sat on the bench next to the discarded daisies, a burning hunger in his eyes and his shirt rumpled and open where she had undone the buttons and slipped her hands inside. *This close.*

But if we want to live on at all, we must go now. Oh, Peter, I'm so sorry.

She burned for him as well. It was the hardest thing she ever did in her whole life to turn her back on him, hoist up her skirt, and clatter down the steps. After a moment's stupefied hesitation, he followed after with Noah close behind. They got in the van and slammed the doors.

"Get us home, pick up the others, and we'll head for the factory just as quick as this rustbucket'll take us," Mariah told Noah as he started the engine. They shot off down the hill. In minutes Noah drew up in the familiar street. Mariah wondered if she would ever see it again after tonight. She climbed out of the van, averting her eyes from a fresh trail of blood that led through the gate and around the side of the house Lucas once inhabited. Rowena, Zhu and Aileen waited on the front steps of the other home. Quickly they gathered there and looked to Rowena for an explanation.

"I'm just guessing, because there's no time to get DNA readouts. But if the host doesn't die, the virus can mutate indefinitely. Looks like it's been developing in Lucas' body for weeks on end, and now it's accumulated so many mutations that even the immune can't survive it." The tears in her eyes betrayed her fear. "I'm sorry. I just had to tell you we can't live much longer. We catch it, we're history!" She slumped into Zhu's arms, shoulders shaking.

Mariah muttered under her breath without realising it until afterwards. Then she shouted. "So what!"

Zhu and Rowena jumped back a little.

Mariah searched in their shocked eyes and found only terror. "So what if we can't survive this version of the plague! We have our isolated booths at the factory and enough virtual experiences to last a lifetime. This is not the end! But we have to hurry."

Understanding dawned on the faces around her. She couldn't believe they had forgotten the system they'd been working on for so many weeks. *Yet fear may do strange things to the mind,* she reasoned. Mariah was plenty scared herself, although she was convinced the system would keep them safe if they could just get to it in time.

Then Peter roused himself from the stunned silence he had yet to break, and herded the others towards the van. Now they understood, and ran for their lives. *Time's up.*

The terror of death weighed heavy. They rushed to the van, still parked in the street. Climbing aboard, Noah gunned the engine and it roared. Peter pushed everyone inside and only just got in when it took off, careening wildly down the road. Noah pressed his foot to the floor and although they were all rattled within an inch of their lives, Mariah preferred this to the alternative. About three subjective seconds later, they had pulled up to the factory building. They piled out and dashed to the open side door. With the coming of evening, a rich red streaked the clouds with glory. But Mariah had no eyes for beauty. They had to get into isolation immediately. Mariah entered the hall first and stood by the door as the others followed her in.

"Come on, come on!" she muttered while they raced by. They gathered quickly in a small circle before the white cabins, and she let her gaze drift over each person. Every one had shared her survival up until this day. Her eyes caught Peter's and even in the midst of fear, her heart belonged to this man. She spoke tersely. "All right. I've already shown you how to get into the suits. Go on and get them on—I'll come round in a minute to insert your cables."

"What about you?" asked Peter. "Who will attach your insert?"

Mariah grimaced. "Well, I'm gonna have to do that myself. I don't know how, but there's no other way. Someone has to be the last one in."

"Don't give me that," Peter growled. "You know I'm just as capable as you are. I put you under for the test run, remember?"

"Look. No matter who takes care of whom, there will always be one left at the end, and I'm the obvious choice since I know what I'm doing."

"Yeah? Well, I know what I'm doing too, at least as much as you." Peter leaned over her, ever so slightly menacing even though he just wanted to make sure she was safe.

Mariah refused to let herself cave to her husband. "Listen, and listen good." There was a moment's silence. "No."

They stared at each other. Finally, Peter's shoulders sagged and he turned away. "Fine. No use arguing with you."

She reached for him, spun him back to face her, and planted a kiss on his lips. Didn't want to let go of him, but pulled away at long last against the protestations of her heart and body. "See you on the inside! Now get going—it's now or never!" The others hesitated, and she shooed them with her hands. "Get a move on! No dallying!" Her voice was sharper than she meant. Rushed footsteps echoed as her companions entered their sanitised boxes.

They retreated into the cabins, while the deep vermilion sunset blazed through the high windows. *Red sky at night, shepherd's delight.* She tore her eyes away. It didn't matter; they wouldn't be around tomorrow. A thrill coursed through her, mixed with loss. *This is it.*

She entered her own cabin and blinked away the impressions of the painful neon lighting in the factory hall. Everything was in readiness, so she checked on the others and helped one or two into the tactile suits.

When everyone was dressed, she stepped back into the hall and took a deep breath to centre herself. Now she would have to attach the head cables and activate the systems for everyone. She was almost shaking with the adrenaline, but extreme care was required to insert the brain probes, or else the subject might sleep but never dream, and their efforts in world-building would be for naught.

Zhu was first. Her mouth twitched into a smile, and Mariah patted her shoulder, then pulled the headgear over her face, positioned the sensor at the hairline, and drew the piston arm into place above it. "Climb that mountain, girl!" Zhu flinched as the machinery forced the sensor into her skull, then Mariah flicked the switch, shut the door and moved on.

Rowena already had her facial sensors on and couldn't speak. But she might still hear something through the rubber suit with its inbuilt speakers. Mariah bent down and whispered, "Your destiny is in your hands now." Rowena nodded, lay back and waited for the needle-sharp probe. A cry of pain, muffled by the sensors in her mouth, unsettled Mariah. She activated the cabin. *She won't feel any more pain now.*

Mariah steeled herself and continued. Noah had his suit on, but was fumbling with the zip, so Mariah helped him get it all the way up, then adjusted his headgear. She guided him to lie down on the bench, then in one fluid movement she positioned the insert and activated the piston. The probe shot into his brain. She pressed the switch, ignoring his surprised gasp.

Okay, maybe that was a bit *too* heartless. "Three down, three to go," Mariah muttered, exiting his cabin. A dream-state had come upon her…but no, she must get on top of her inner tumult to finish this. *Do not drown in the strangeness.*

Aileen sat on the bench in the next cabin, hope and fear fighting across her features. Mariah took her in her arms, pressing a cheek to hers for a moment. A sob escaped Aileen.

Mariah grabbed her shoulders to look her in the face. "Don't be afraid!" She hugged her one last time and pulled the facial gadgets into place, hiding her friend's scared expression. "We'll meet on the inside. Now lie down here." Mariah held the sensor at the right position, then the piston's short but violent movement inserted it through the layer of bone. Aileen's body went rigid and she moaned. Quickly Mariah switched on the system, stepped out, and shut the cabin door with quaking hands.

Passing the empty booth that would be her own place of rest, she came to the second-last one. Peter already lay prepared on the bench, headgear and all—her heartbeat hammered even harder. *I love him…*but they had already said goodbye, and they would surely meet again somewhere in another life. He jerked a little when she inserted the probe, but he made no sound. She laid a hand on his rubber-encased shoulder before reaching over to the switch on the wall. He gasped as the coolants reduced his body temperature. Soon he would be gone, and Mariah had better get a move on as well. She lurched out and shut his cabin door.

Her gaze fell on the final booth, the one she had prepared for Rufus, and her heart broke. *Sorry, fella, we have to go.* She waited just a moment more, in case Rufus might come bounding in the door, tail high and tongue lolling. But there was no sound from any living creature.

Now came the hardest part: activating her own booth. She turned towards it, then with a rush she remembered: she had not yet specified her name in the computer programme. Danger or no, she strode across the concrete floor to a terminal and retrieved her data. It just would not do to go through her virtual life without a name, or worse, with the same one she'd hated all her life. But what name to choose? She still did not know. She took a breath and shut her eyes, searching her spirit for the right word. Then it came.

Faith. My name is Faith.

For an instant time stood still around her while she typed in that one word at the terminal. Her life flashed before her eyes, but not the life she had lived—no, what she glimpsed in that instant was the life of Faith that she had written, and that she would now live.

Faith.

The moment passed. She jabbed at the "Save" key and shoved herself away from the desk, the chair's wheels spinning madly.

She regained her balance, stood slowly, and glanced upwards a last time at the glorious redness of the sky outside the window. She entered the cabin and shut the door, making sure it was sealed properly. Peeling off the too-large white dress with a pang of hope deferred, she stepped into the tactile suit, zipped it up, and lay down on the narrow bench.

The wiring and tubing was in order, so she reached for the headpiece, placing it over eyes, ears, nose and mouth. She breathed once through the tube and took up the brain probe in rubber-clad fingers.

Her heart knocked wildly, faster and faster. This was not going to be easy—inserting the needle by touch when her hands were inside the thick rubber suit. She tried to calm herself for the tricky job of getting the head wire in.

But hesitation might kill her.

The wound from her experimental foray of last week was healing, but still painful to the touch, and she breathed a prayer of thanks for this unlikely assistance to find the place without anyone to help. Her fingers found the spot where the hole from the test run had not closed over yet. Guided by the old pain, with one hand she held the sensor insert between her head and the piston. The other gripped the piston. Unlike the others, she knew what came next. She clamped her teeth together and released the trigger.

Pain exploded through her and threatened to rob her consciousness, but she reached out her hand and groped until she found the switch on the wall. Soon she would be gone, too—she would escape this dark world to live in her own Paradise.

She flicked the activator to "on" and gasped as the familiar chill swept over her. The temperature dropped then and she remembered the fear that accompanied a departure from real life. Colder—colder—she was about to black out, but something didn't feel right.

The probe! It sat awkward, and her skull throbbed. *Is it in straight? Is the scar tissue getting in the way?*

This was wrong.

But now there was no time left.

Before she took another breath, gentle birdsong came to her ears. The probe functioned after all.

The jabbing pain in her head disappeared as the cold swept over her body, and she floated away contentedly in a sea of blackness to a better world. The world of Faith.

24

faith and mariah

All at once, it was as if her thoughts and perceptions were packaged and fed to her brain bit by bit. Each impulse was dealt with as it came, and each made a turn in some giant cyber-labyrinth. Soon the consequences of the first decisions she made were replacing the brain processes and sensations she had known in the real world. Its memory slipped away, but it was no loss at all. She was getting too much input to care.

Sound. Birdsong. *Decode.* Summer morning. *Action.* Open eyes. *Visual.* A bedroom. *Detail.* Books. Toys. Pictures on the wall. *Information.* It's your bedroom. *Memory.* Cold, dark place. *Assess.* Dream or nightmare. *Sensation.* Shiver. Warmth. *Thought.* This is real, that other place was a dream. *Result.* Forget it. *Movement.* Get out of bed. *Information.* Be careful, the bed is high up. *Change environment.* Enter kitchen. *Consume.* Cornflakes and milk. *Visual.* Cat. *Emotion.* Joy. *Sensation.* Cat fur. *Activity.* Television, then books.

At the end of the day, these parcels of command and input were coming so thick and fast that they created a constant flow. Somehow Faith was aware that she had come from another place, but she no longer grasped it, and her brain hurt when she tried. However, this did not overly concern her, since this life she had been given appeared to be a grand one and very enjoyable. After a few days she was able to ignore the commands that accompanied everything she did—*Decode. Activity. Sensation.* They were not truly necessary, and once she learned to recognise them for what they were, it was easy to push past them, as it were, and concentrate on the content of the input, which was the stuff of life.

So she played in the park, read books, went with Nana to the hairdresser and to church on Sundays, and ate good food including much from her own garden until the bullies destroyed it. She did rebuild, though it never was quite the same again. Her days varied little, so that her life was repetitive, but this did not prevent her enjoyment of it.

She often suffered from bad dreams in the night. Sometimes she would again wake up convinced that she came from somewhere else—a strange, otherworldly sensation. But she had learned about dreams and nightmares now, and that they were not to be taken seriously, so she shook off the ominous chills and went on with living her carefree existence.

After a very long time, her thinking patterns changed and expanded as her life broke out of the restful but repetitive patterns of childhood. It was around this time that she first suffered strange bouts of memory loss. Sometimes there would be a flash of light, or a glimpse of a white room, and always there came this pain in the centre of her mind. In any case, afterwards she did not remember who she was, and it took several hours for memory and full consciousness to come back. More often than not, there were gaps in it as it returned, but at least she knew that she was Faith and that this life was worth living. And it was enough.

Often something dark and unknown brooded over her, haunting her, but she could not explain it. On the other hand, if she closed her eyes, coloured lights danced inside her eyelids and formed all manner of fantastical creatures. Eventually she found out that science called these phosphenes, but it didn't make them any less wondrous.

Sometimes years went by in the blink of an eyelid, and she grew up in beautiful Bangor by the sea. Memory losses returned again and again, most often after she had made a decision to do something different with her life—a trip overseas or a change in direction. It was almost as if her mind was unable to cope with the breadth of new sights and experiences it was offered in each different place or after serious changes.

In her teens she achieved a regular income from selling her LandCare apps, so her life was a little boring, she often admitted to herself. But she did her best to liven it up with research and trips, and later the kitchen work at Groomsport, although the new things did cause her memory to glitch.

Then came the day she decided to move to Regensburg, without fully understanding why. It was as if the decision had been made for her; it had simply entered her heart and refused to leave, so that she never had any peace in any other place, no matter how beautiful. And she did try to ignore it, to be sure—but even long daily walks in the countryside did nothing against her itchy feet. She had to be gone. There was nothing else to it. So she moved one day in a hurry, leaving everything behind, and found a job and a nice flat in her city of dreams. She got in with a bunch of people who liked to feed the hungry and proceeded to build her whole life around them. Some years went by in a flurry of effort and downwards-spiralling circumstance, and then one day it all crashed down. Alone again.

Another day came, heavy with portent from the moment she opened her eyes. She was unable to concentrate on anything and barely managed to make a cup of tea. After striding up and down the living room countless times, her restless feet took her through the doorways and stairwells, down to the bottom of the street, and across the road to the riverbank.

It was a sunny summer morning. Tendrils of cool night air still swirled in and out of the light mist. The Danube wore a mysterious mood, refusing to remain one colour long enough to determine it—inky black, then palest blue reflecting the sky, then green-grey where the haze hung over the river weed dancing in the current. Faith's thoughts danced also. *I can live without suffering inner torments day by day. I can move on.*

She walked along, keeping her eyes on the uneven cobblestones so as not to trip and fall. The ancient path was deserted, unusual for the time of day. *Where are the dog walkers, the joggers, the drunks that sit here all the time?* She stopped and gazed around, enjoying the solitude. No matter. Perhaps this morning was meant for her alone.

Raising her eyes, she let them meander along the sharp edge of the river path to where it vanished behind the most venerable of bridges in the middle distance. Then she returned her gaze to the rough stone beneath her feet. Years of life in Regensburg scrolled across her memory, scene after scene of Germans expressing their astonishment at her decision to leave her home country and come here. *But I don't want to be admired for what I've done. I want to be loved for who I am.*

Unbidden, this new idea shot into her heart. A shadow caught her eye beneath the bridge, and a man stepped slowly out of the murk. He watched his feet carefully as he walked. His shirt was the exact same shade of blue as a dress Faith hadn't been able to resist buying recently. Dark hair swung over his ears, and he appeared unshaven, at least for today.

Faith realised her gaze was consumed by him, and in that moment, he looked up. Bewilderment and surprise registered on his face as he stared at her. She dropped her gaze, suddenly self-conscious. *What am I wearing?* Oh, the blue dress.

They continued to walk towards each other, stopping when they reached a distance of a few metres. His jaw moved and silent words formed on his lips. Then he spoke. "This is going to sound really strange…" His apologetic tone didn't hide the earnest voice, the unmistakable Irish lilt. He looked at the stone path, then out over the river and back to Faith.

She only returned his gaze. *What is this? What's going on here?* She waited for him to continue.

"I dreamed of you last night. I saw you! And I heard a voice…it said to me, *Have faith*."

She stepped closer. A curl of mist rose up from the rushing water below. This man was a stranger to her, yet it was like she'd known him all her life. Had she seen him in her dreams too? *I cannot account for this, but I must speak these words.*

She opened her mouth. "Haven't I seen you somewhere before?"
Bad pick-up line, girl. But he didn't notice.

"Would you like to go for a coffee? Maybe we can figure it out," he said.
That was just as bad. But she didn't care.

He offered his arm, and they turned to enter the city. From that day, she never looked back. It was meant to be: he won her heart and swept her away just as she'd always imagined it happening. She could not shake off the sense that she had spent all her life waiting for him.

Faith married Irish-born, German-raised James Petersen a few years later and they stayed on for some time in Regensburg, making the most of the beautiful city to take long romantic walks along the Danube river. Then Faith tired of the place, deep in her bones, as if they cried out to her, "Enough!"

She spoke with James of what they would do, and she told him of her desire to go home to Ireland one day. To her surprise, he was enthusiastic about this idea and prepared to quit his job and move. So after nearly a decade in Bavaria, Faith said goodbye to the city where she had suffered so much and so inexplicably, but also won many battles and gained the strength to start all over again. Esther had met the love of her life by now, so Faith was at ease about leaving her behind in his capable hands.

So it was that she returned home to Bangor with her husband trailing behind. He found Ireland new and different, and a challenge at times to his perfect sense of order, but he learned to love it for Faith's sake. She loved him all the more for it.

She dragged him along to the old church at Groomsport, where many people still remembered her from the work she did there before. They secured a house overlooking the beach at Ballyholme, and Faith spent many happy years there with James, spending much of her time writing in the upstairs lounge with its big picture window, its comfy couch, and her favourite tea-set. If ever she lacked inspiration, all she had to do was raise her eyes to the ever-changing panorama of ocean and shore, and the hills across the water to the northwest; and the sunset was always the same. James was everything she ever wished for: attentive and deeper than anyone she'd ever met before, so that she often joked that he might be the only real man in the world. Yes, this was a good life. Finally, she need not be alone. She had encountered much in the world, experienced other sunsets in other places, but now she had James, and she had come home. For a while, at least.

In the course of time Faith decided to study English literature at Queen's University in Belfast. If she was going to be a writer, it was wise to deepen her knowledge of books and their history. She took the train into town each day and played well the part of a student. Her classmates were astounded to discover she was ten years older than them, with a number of published books under her belt—they insisted she looked like she wasn't a day out of high school. Faith found this hilarious.

One day, in perusing the departmental noticeboard, Faith spotted a brochure about international literary exchanges. Participants would be assigned to a random location somewhere in the world, billeted with a local student, and attend special classes for three weeks. The mystery of it appealed to her; she'd travelled a fair bit in her corner of the world, but to have someone else decide her destination had a certain charm to it. *Yes*, she decided, *I'll do that, if James doesn't mind me taking off.*

He didn't, so she sent away the forms and paid her deposit. Then waited on tenterhooks to find out where she would be sent—she hoped it was somewhere exotic. The fateful envelope arrived and with shaking hands, she opened it and read the brief missive. Gulp.

America. Some place in the middle of corn country.

Not what she had been expecting. The surprise of it sparkled in her lungs and she grinned as she read on. Her host's name was given along with a phone number and an email address.

"Well, well, Riley Bourne, we shall see what comes of this."

Riley's face rose out of the crowd in the airport lobby. The unknowns fell away and there she was, she whose likeness Faith had become familiar with over the past several weeks since they had learned the exchange had paired them up.

As usual, Faith spotted her quarry long before being seen herself, and paused ostensibly to blow her nose. In fact she hung back to get a better look, observing unseen from beyond the last divide between the security area and the public part of the airport.

They had chatted online, but with the reserve of strangers newly introduced. Yet there was a spark of kinship and Faith hoped they would both loosen up in the presence of an actual human. In all the hours of three interminable plane trips, Faith's travel-dazed mind had doubted again and again whether Riley would like her, whether the trip would bring fulfilment like she hoped, or would they be cold and distant...?

She'd dozed in her sardine-class seat, jolted awake by turbulence two or three times, shreds of dreams wafting around her head. Was that—*Riley* she saw, floating out of the blackness of her old room at her parents' house? Surely not, but...the resemblance was eerie. The encounter in New Zealand returned to her sleepy mind, and again, it seemed she was thinking about Riley; as also with the airline agent that time in Belfast. Faith shook her head to clear it.

Her eyes fixed again on Riley's face and Faith wondered if she felt herself watched. A look of concern flitted across her features, then was gone.

Finally Faith gathered up her gumption and moved along, knuckles white on the handle of her trundle bag. She stepped out past the barrier and turned to the right, where she'd seen Riley. Riley stepped closer. Now she would see her.

Their gazes met, eye to eye, though Faith had to crane her head back a bit. A tall one. "Um, howya?" she offered, falling back into her mother's brogue.

"Well, hey there," said Riley, exactly like she always had on the phone, in an accent so American it could have been fake. There was that frown again, but only for a moment.

Faith guessed her thoughts were much like her own. She remembered how quickly Riley always ended her calls, and hesitated. Should she hug her? Possibly not yet. She dropped the bag in her right hand and stuck it out.

Riley shook her head. "Probably shouldn't."

The question reached Faith's face before she could stop it. Riley's expression hardened and she pointed at herself. "Static."

Faith laughed nervously. "Oh. Is that all?"

"I kid you not. It's pretty bad." Riley sighed. "It's like this. I build up a static charge, and it zaps when I touch most anything—including people. Dang strange body."

Mine is too, but not like that. "Wow. That would make it interesting to use a cellphone."

"A cell? I wish," said Riley, and fell silent.

Faith smiled. "So how bad would you zap me?" She shuffled closer and held out her index finger.

Riley's eyebrows went up. "Well, it's not like getting electrocuted. For the most part."

"Go on then, I'm curious."

Slowly Riley withdrew a hand from her jeans pocket and lifted her finger to meet Faith's.

Pop. The shock that began in Faith's hand worked its way through her core and out to her other extremities. It was not altogether unpleasant.

Lost in the memory of other embraces, Faith leaned forward and hugged Riley without fully realising it. Riley stiffened, then relaxed some, and Faith stumbled back, a rich scent of clean hay and horses in her nose.

"Well, girl," Riley said, surprise shaping her grin, "here you be."

Riley served Reuben sandwiches for supper, which Faith had never had before. As they polished off the last of the sizeable stack, Faith licked a strand of sauerkraut from her finger. "Those were amazing."

Riley sighed. "Glad you think so. I hate cooking."

"Yeah, right."

"No, really. Never liked it, then add the static crap and WHAM! Instant hatred. It helps if the pan and utensils have insulated handles."

Faith turned her head towards the kitchen nook, decorated with a row of bear and elk stencils near the ceiling which she found highly foreign, and spied the thick wrapping that had been added to the skillet's grip. "Are you static right now?"

Riley shrugged. She reached over and tapped her finger on a metal rod attached to a wire that disappeared into the wall. There was a tiny sizzling sound, then she poked Faith in the shoulder. "Earthed. All gone. For a while. So…now it's your turn to tell me something weird about *you.*"

Faith shuddered involuntarily. "You won't freak out?"

"Babe, I gotta repay the favour."

"Okay." *Well, I met you in a dream fifteen years ago.* She couldn't tell her that. Unless…Riley's look was strangely knowing. Had she seen Faith in dreams too—and was she just as nervous of revealing it? *Nah.* Couldn't be. Faith moistened her lips. "I go blank sometimes. Lose my memory."

"Really? Tell me more."

"For up to an hour. Most of it comes back, but in pieces. It's like no one knows how to deal with it properly. I've been whisked off to hospital and treated like a maniac. Some people avoid me when they know. I've lost friends over it."

"So…how does one deal with it, theoretically?"

Faith smiled. "With calmness, for one thing. No doctors, no hospitals, no funny looks, no change of environment. I guess it would be nice if someone was with me and just kept telling me where I am, who I'm with, and who I am."

"You forget who you are?" Riley blinked.

"Not permanently, thank goodness." Faith bit her lip and turned her face away. Perhaps it was too soon to reveal her greatest weakness.

Riley reached over and laid a hand on hers, the static ping now so tiny it scarcely registered. "Quirks maketh the woman."

Relief flooded into Faith. Perhaps she wouldn't lose this friend before she even fathomed her. She tucked up her feet and turned to inspect the bookshelves. A set near the top caught her eye. "Anne of Green Gables! Special edition? I want to get that someday."

"That's my favouritest series ever."

"Serious! Mine too." Faith scanned more titles. Lewis, Austen, Tolkien. A good array of classics.

"At least we can agree about good talent."

They laughed and talked until deep in the night, not realising how the hours were passing. Faith was tired from travelling, but she didn't care. She'd found someone who understood her: enough of a rarity in this world that she wanted to drink of friendship and never stop.

Then a shadow crept up on her gaiety. Something wasn't right; she had been here before, had experienced exactly this evening but in another time and place. *The dream? Riley had been there.* Even that assertion felt wrong. Everything was wrong. She opened her mouth to tell Riley, to beg for help…

The great nothingness swept in upon her. She floated a while in a freezing black sea under a starless sky—it might just as easily have been white that surrounded her—seeing nothing, hearing nothing. After a very long time, a voice came to her ears, speaking continuously with a slow and measured cadence and foreign drawl, but at first she made no sense out of the words.

"I know I just said this, and this feels kinda silly, but it's what you told me to do, so I'm Riley and I'm pleased to meet you, Faith, and to have you at my house for a little while. You and I are going to be great writers and great friends, I can feel it in my bones. I probably wouldn't say this if you were fully lucid, but you're not going to remember this, are you, so it doesn't matter what I say, as long as I don't stop and leave you in a big blank hole. I can't imagine what it must feel like. You're Faith, I'm Riley, and welcome to my house. My horses are just out there in the barn, and tomorrow I'll teach you to ride. It's strange how much we're alike—we like the same books, we both have pretty major quirks, and you truly don't care that I'm static. I don't mind that you've forgotten me now, but you'll come back around, or so you said. Come on, Faith, it's been thirty minutes…I'm Riley, in case you're in there."

Slowly, Faith opened her eyes. Riley prattled on, so gently, as if she were carrying on a completely normal conversation. Faith checked her mental state: a bit scattered, but intact as she hadn't believed possible. "Only half an hour? That's almost a miracle."

Riley jerked her head around and scrutinised Faith. "Are you really back—do you know where you are?"

"I think so. I've never come back this fast before."

"Has anyone ever just talked to you before?"

Faith shook her head. "You're the first."

"Are you really okay?"

Faith stretched and peered around the cosy room. "I'm in America for the literary exchange programme. You're doing it too, as a host. And I'm so glad to know you."

"Not bad. Not bad at all."

"Riley, are you real?"

"The real deal right here in front of you, 3D, live colour. How's that?"

"You're almost too good to be true. Your soul is so like mine—we could be the same brain in two bodies."

"Eww!" Riley poked her tongue out.

Faith seized a cushion and whacked her. "Oh, you know what I mean."

"Yes, I do," said Riley, suddenly serious. "And that's the freaky thing."

They finally turned in for the night. Faith lay in her small room missing James, somewhat absurdly she thought. There was plenty to look forward to before she went home.

The laughter of the children playing on the beach wafted up on the warm breeze. Tall coconut palms shaded Faith's chair on the terrace. She took a deep breath of clear air and drank in the endless vista of sea and lucent sky.

Keira stepped out of the house and Faith grinned. The two had been friends since Groomsport and had many other adventures in London, in Timbuktu and in other places together all those years ago. Now she waddled over, wrapped from neck to knee in a neon green lavalava, and wearing white fluffy slippers that matched her hair, although it wasn't at all cold. Faith clutched a tall teacup and smiled up at her..

"Been dreaming again, Faith?" She was older now, but the life force within was the same as ever.

"Yeah, chicky. Remember Timbuktu?"

"Remember Geneva? How everyone thought I'd have the baby then and there?" she retorted with blazing eyes.

"Remember Munich? Those endless train trips!"

"Remember the kids from Bangor?"

"Remember Tuvalu?"

"Remember London?"

They laughed together at the old memories. Faith did remember, although it was all so distant now, she might as well have read them in a book. Keira let herself down into the wicker chair next to Faith's. They surveyed the beach where Keira's grandchildren cavorted in the gentle waves. An angular figure stumped along the sand beyond them. It was Davin, wearing a striped shirt and a floppy hat. He gesticulated at an unseen person. Age had drastically reduced his reservedness—either that, or somewhere along the way he lost the ability to be embarrassed.

Faith reached for the book always at her side, opened it and wrote. Her hand shook a little, but that didn't stop her. The years of peace and companionship in this beautiful place had given her a deep joy, and more than once she had cried for joy. Now she wrote again, fancies taking flight, escaping from an old and weary body on the wings of the tinkling piano Esther was playing in the house. She, too, sometimes complained of rusty fingers, but all agreed that they had come to a good part of life. Faith was particularly thankful that Keira shared her grandchildren so generously, since Faith and James had been unable to have a family.

Yes—it had been a good decision for them all to come together and spend their so-called twilight years in this blessed place. The Tongans were a kind and quietly effervescent people who welcomed the newcomers to their island home. Faith sometimes wondered if Esther missed Germany, but if so, she never let it show.

This week, though—this week had its own charm. Tomorrow—

A decrepit island taxi rattled up the driveway and Faith bolted to her feet, wincing at the pinging in her hips. She strode around the corner of the building and came face to face with Riley, who had just gotten out of the car. Faith flung her arms wide as Riley hurtled to a stop and grabbed her in a hug. She was too distracted to notice the slight static zap. "Riley! What are you doing here? I wasn't expecting you until tomorrow."

"Blasted dateline. Did I get the day wrong?" Riley looked all innocent.

Too innocent, thought Faith, and whacked her in the arm. "You turd. You set it up just like this."

Riley couldn't contain a giggle. The two collapsed in peals of laughter. "You—shouldn't—hit old ladies like that!"

"Just when did you gals last see each other?"

Faith finally let go and turned to Keira. "Oh, about a month ago. But it's always a big deal to reunite with a kindred spirit."

"Indeed it is." Riley smiled. "So this is where you live now, huh? I might stay a while, if that's okay with you."

Soon she was playing borrowed grandma to the children, telling them stories and breaking up fights over her lap space.

Later in the day Faith and Riley walked along the beach. The sinking sun now set the ocean ablaze with ethereal shimmerings. They walked slowly in the red-gold light, following their shadows back to the terraced houses where the children already slept, their little bodies exhausted from ocean-swimming, sand-running, tree-climbing island life.

After the evening meal of sweet potatoes and Davin's specially concocted sauce, the others vanished into their bedroom and shut the door. Faith and Riley sat in companionable silence a while longer. Riley smiled at Faith. "You're really happy here, aren't you?"

"Yes. Yes, I am. I often feel guilty about it because…you know, James isn't here to enjoy it. But he had seventy good years before the downhill ones came, and for them I'm grateful."

"I was hoping to convince you to move to America, maybe nearby, maybe share the same house…"

Faith shot upright. She had come to love the corn country after all. "I thought you'd never ask. Well, the winters up there are a bit harsh for these old bones. But you could come down here during the worst of it."

"Nice. I'll take you up on that one." Riley stretched out a hand and the two shook hard, up and down, while electricity zinged at the touch. "Goodnight, friend o' mine."

"Goodnight, m'dear."

Faith lay before the open window and surveyed the canopy of stars, amazed at what had become of her once-ruined life. The terrifying dreams and the memory losses had long haunted her at every step. For years she had longed to die before morning came because of being trapped in her own dream, and even after she got away from Elliot's shadow, it took years again to come out of her shell. The former things were never restored—dreams of feeding millions left her well alone after that. Yet in the course of life's path, she had become a writer instead—and who knows? Maybe that was the greater calling after all.

It was pleasant to lie there and bathe in this astonishment while falling asleep. The night passed slower than usual…then she slept, and the dream lasted forever. She revisited scenes from her long life: childhood, her wedding, her writing. She was happy to be in Tonga, happy that Riley had come. She had no more need of waking now. It was not morning yet.

Then a door opened and a bright light shone around her. She must be still dreaming. Her head hurt, but she looked up and boggled. "James?" Her best beloved, gone these seven years. He came to her side.

Someone else came too. Riley's face floated before her, unclear in a mist. "Hey, are you okay?"

Faith couldn't answer, too awestruck by the sight of her dead husband.

He spoke. "Faith, it's time to shed that skin. Will you come with me?" A big grin split his face. How young he was! *But that's natural. We are leaving our old lives behind.* James held out his hand to her, waiting.

"Faith!" It was Riley, the sound of her dear voice fading even though she shouted, her hands clutching at an immaterial shell. "Faith, breathe, dammit!

Don't you dare leave me."

Riley was real—Faith's heart broke knowing what was about to happen. But it was James who gripped Faith's hand. She hesitated just a single moment longer, sensing the warm tropical night and Riley's touch on her skin one last time as her friend faded to the substance of a dream.

Of course. *I am ready*. It was time to go home.

25

Belfast

2179

Faith reached for James' hand. The cosy hut vanished around her—the whole world was gone. Suddenly, she gasped for air, and he knelt by her, holding her tightly. Her head was tight, her body chilled and trembling.

This doesn't feel like heaven, she puzzled for a moment, *but James is here, so it must be.* James fussed at her head, and there came a dull pain above. *He's just taking out the sensor.*

Then all of her sleepy mind focused itself on that one fact. *The sensor! I'm waking up!* A shiver ran through her body and she fumbled for the zip at her neck.

Sitting up, she wriggled out of the rubber and swung her legs over the side of the bench. James stared at her, and she searched the depths of his eyes.

"Oh, James, how I've missed you!" she whispered, and fell into his arms. Then, like a huge explosion begun by a tiny spark, she remembered all the world outside and that her life as Faith was only a dream. Oh, but it felt real still. Real enough to touch and hold and live by.

An overwhelming sense of grief swept over her as her heart held fast to Paradise. *I've lost Riley. And Keira.* Some comfort soon followed as she realised she had James back. She gazed at him hungrily.

"What is it, Faith? Wasn't it just this morning that we talked about your new book over breakfast?"

Aghast, she lifted her head and stared at him, her gaze catching on the bandage stuck to his forehead. "How can this be? My love, you died seven years ago."

His jaw dropped. "They woke me first. I came out of stasis half an hour ago—I was in a pretty bad way, and they gave me regeneration shots. As soon as I could stand, I came to you."

Faith shook her head. Seven years in half an hour. Who would have believed it? But who were "they"?

Her eye fell on the discarded white gown that lay on the floor, and she lost her train of thought. It was dirty around the hem, where she had draggled it in the muck so, so long ago—a whole lifetime.

James followed her gaze, then stooped to retrieve the garment. He helped her get it over her head and she pulled it down to cover herself. *My wedding dress.*

"Take it slowly, my love." James supported her, and little by little she was able to put weight on her feet and stagger towards the door. What would she find outside?

"James, how much time has gone by?"

He did not answer, but gave the cabin door a push to open it. At first she was blinded by the glare from the familiar neon tubes of the factory. She raised a shaky hand to shield her eyes. The other clung tight to James as her vision cleared.

The room was full of people. A silent awe lay upon the men, women and children as they stared at the couple. Faith glanced at James and noticed then for the first time that he had his wedding suit on.

Of course…they had entered the cabins on their wedding night.

And her husband wasn't called James at all.

Here they were, the bride and groom, awakened from their sleep. Faith's wide-eyed gaze took in a straggly bunch who stood near. With a shock she recognised her companions of the immunity: Zhu, Rowena, Noah and Aileen. So everyone had made it.

Faith clung to the man she loved and remembered. His name was Peter and she should call him that in this world. But who was she, really?

A white-haired woman from the newcomers stepped forward. Faith would recognise her anywhere. "Keira!"

The woman frowned. "Naomi. It's Naomi, remember? I found my own cryo chamber. But I was Keira...inside. I figured out that you were Faith...*Mariah*."

Faith peered at her as she approached and couldn't help noticing the faded scar high on her brow, and the smooth-worn Guild pendant that hung from her neck.

Naomi wrapped her in a hug and there were tears in her eyes when she stepped back. "I knew it was really you. I had to come find you—it took far too long. I hated to think you thought all this time that I died. We'll have to sit down for a long cuppa very soon. Let our doctors check you over, okay?"

Two women and a man rushed to greet Faith—she still couldn't properly think of herself as Mariah. The man entered the cabin she had recently vacated while she let the women measure pulse and blood pressure and temperature with the equipment they carried, and she noticed that they, too, carried the mark on their foreheads.

Hope flickered in Faith's soul. Perhaps she would yet find Riley among those who had been attached to the system. She fingered her own wound, slick with blood, before someone slapped a dressing on it.

"State of exhaustion. You need to rest up before anything else, but vitals are fine," announced one of the lady doctors, pulling out an injection needle. "This will help you regenerate after your stasis." Faith winced at the prick, but it was over in a moment.

The man emerged from Faith's cubicle holding the blood-smeared brain insert. "Look, it's warped," he said. "Did you use it more than once?"

Peter nodded. "Yes. She did a test run before we all went in."

The doctors gathered around to inspect it.

"It's a wonder it even worked, they're not reusable."

"You didn't have glitches in your virtual reality?"

Faith stared around at them. "It was as real as this here and now. More so, in fact." But the word *glitches* gave her pause. What about those memory

273

losses, those weird dreams? She'd been lucky to get away with so few problems.

The whole assemblage of visitors followed the newly awakened towards the open front of the building, which they had never used before. Faith blinked suddenly in the bright natural light that poured from the cloud cover. *Ireland the Cloudy,* she thought with a grin.

Then she beheld a wonder: hanging in the air some fifty metres above them was a huge bubble-like monstrosity bearing a windowed cabin below it. *An airship!* And there in the cracked old road was a smaller craft, tethered now by both ends to nearby posts. Faith had heard of such things, but the technology was so ancient that it had gone out of use long before her days, in either life.

Beyond it, quietly watching from a safe distance, was a pack of dogs. Faith squinted at them where they sat half in and half out of a narrow gap between two ugly industrial buildings.

They were brown and black with varying patches of brindled grey; each one was somehow familiar, as if each one was a part of... *Rufus.* Sudden tears stung her eyes.

Though... these dogs weren't tame. Couldn't be, after so long without humans. They had to be curious. Faith stepped closer and the animals shrank back; she halted, dropped to a squat and held out a hand. "Hullo, fellas." Her own speech was strange to her, so long unused except inside her head. "I had a dog like you once."

Between the barrel chests of the canine clan, a gap opened up and a small nose poked out. The young dog, not much more than a puppy and coloured almost exactly like her ancestor Rufus, trotted unafraid up to Faith and sniffed at her hand before giving it the tiniest of licks. One of the older dogs wuffed a warning, and the pup skittered back to the group.

Faith straightened, smiled. Someday these dogs would be loyal companions again.

She found her voice again. "Will you take us to our home to rest?" Faces pressed around, smiling and nodding, and James—*Peter*—explained the location of their houses overlooking the bay. They were conducted to the small craft, where they entered the room slung beneath the air balloon.

The six Bangor sleepers were joined by a few newcomers. Outside, others released the ties. Without a sound, the graceful ship rose into the sky.

274

Peering out of the small glass pane nearby, she recognised the sprawl and smudge of the City, then as they rose higher, the coast and the mountains across the water.

A gentle chug began as the engines started up and the craft swung around. The distance was really too short for flying to be necessary; but Faith—*Mariah*—drank in the view of land and ocean as they drifted along. Peter stood by the pilot, watching how he flew the machine.

"And if I pull this lever, flaps on top of the balloon open up, we lose a little gas, and we come down."

Peter pointed, and soon the wee man had brought the craft to a gentle stop on the severely cracked tarseal in front of Deborah's old house. They stepped out onto the road.

These houses had been strongly built, but the evidence of time now scratched their faces. Colours and whites had all faded to dim greys, fences hung askew or had disintegrated altogether. Gardens showed a healthy wilderness, not the rampant growth of the fertiliser days, and not the dead muck of the times before that, but a green that hinted at actual recovery of the soil. At Deborah's house, the gate had fallen from rusted hinges and lay rotting in its gap, now encroached upon by the regrowing laurel hedge from both sides.

Noah, Zhu and Rowena headed to the next house. James, Esther and Faith climbed the steps to their home and pushed open the door with a terrible creak. Inside they found piles of dust in every corner. They ascended the narrow stairs, which groaned under their weight. Esther—*Aileen*—vanished into her old bedroom, and Faith had a hand on the doorknob of hers. Then a thought came to her, and as she thought it, a sudden hunger overcame her fully. *Now is the time.* She looked up at her husband and a grin split her face.

"James—uh, Peter—whatever!"

He only stood there in the middle of the hallway, gazing at her.

She let go of the doorknob and stepped towards him, conscious only of the growing conflagration within. "We never did finish our wedding night properly, did we?"

Peter blushed then and she seized him by the hand, pulling him with her into the room. Ignoring the billows of dust they stirred up, he took her head in both his hands and stared at her for the longest time. The dust settled slowly. With every passing second she became more certain that she would burst into flame. It was time. At last.

Finally he spoke, and there was a fire in his eyes.

"Not in this world, that's for sure!"

about the author

Grace Bridges is a dreamer whose muse blows best when it's fresh from the sea. A graduate of the University of Auckland, she edits novels and translates German for a living, and writes from her hilltop in New Zealand although faraway places call to her just as often. Her writings appear in various international anthologies and magazines, and she is working on further novels and short stories in *The Vortex of Éire* series. She is inordinately happy that her hair has started going silver.

www.gracebridges.kiwi

If you enjoyed this book, please consider writing a review on a book website. It really does make a difference!

acknowledgements

To Chila Woychik, who set me on this journey, disassembled my brain to get at the heart of the story, unleashed the power of description, inspired many specific aspects, urged me to make it what it is today—from attic inception to near completion—and wouldn't settle for less than my best. Thank you!
To Katherine Coble for the back cover description with a truly expert touch.
To Kat Heckenbach for design advice with a keen sense of style.
To Heather Young for graphics assistance in the final stretch.
To all who aided with time and space to write, and all who have supported and encouraged me over the years to create my own worlds with words.

Splashdown Books

Ground-breaking science fiction, fantasy and paranormal. Since 2009.

For authors: Innovative hybrid imprint system.
If approved, use the Splashdown brand
while retaining all control of the publishing
process. See our submissions page for details.

SplashdownBooks.com

Dear Author,

Do you need help
publishing your book?

I am an experienced
independent publisher and offer
the following services:

Editing and Proofreading
Cover Design
Print Typesetting
Ebook Formatting

www.gracebridges.kiwi/hire-me

Fast responses.
Thorough work.
Satisfied customers.

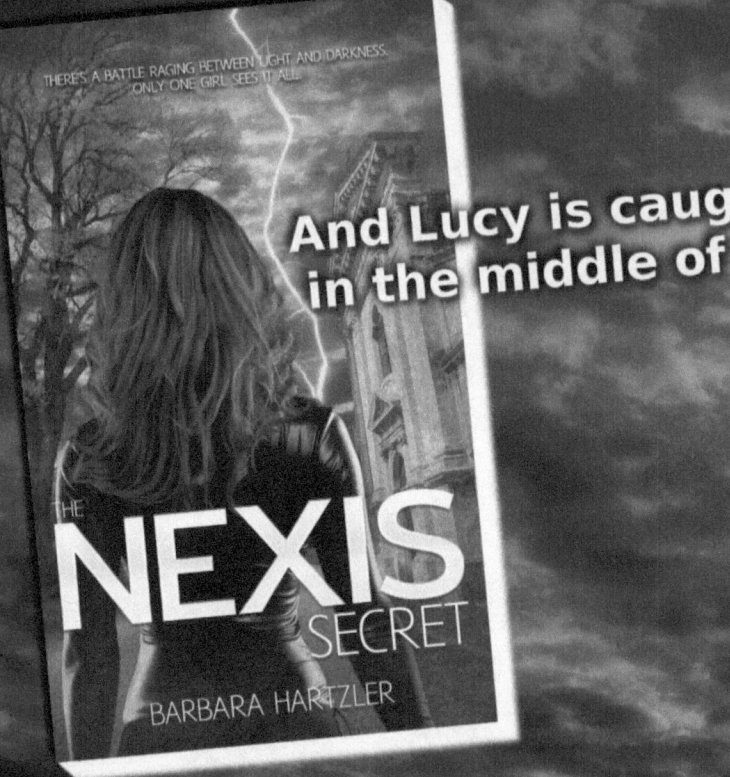

MONTROSE ACADEMY HAS A SECRET.

THERE'S A BATTLE RAGING BETWEEN LIGHT AND DARKNESS. ONLY ONE GIRL SEES IT ALL.

And Lucy is caught in the middle of it.

THE NEXIS SECRET

BARBARA HARTZLER

It seems like any other snooty prep school, until Lucy finds herself seeing strange visions of wraiths, prophets, and angels. Now two rival Romeos are vying for her allegiance, including the Nexis Society president. When Nexis can't reel her in they resort to cyber-bullying, vicious threats, even rogue priests. With the help of her new-found guardians, she must find a way to stop the twisted Nexis plan to rule the world.

THE NEXIS SECRET
BY BARBARA HARTZLER

WWW.BARBARAHARTZLER.COM

THE VORTEX OF ÉIRE

SCIENCE FICTION BY GRACE BRIDGES

MARIAH'S PROLOGUES
A FREE SHORT STORY EVERY MONTH

Subscribe at
www.gracebridges.kiwi

www.ingramcontent.com/pod-product-compliance
Lightning Source LLC
Chambersburg PA
CBHW050712180626
46814CB00002B/395